ALSO BY ELÍSABET BENAVENT

A Perfect Story

Everything I'll Say to You Tomorrow

All the Truth in My Lies

ELÍSABET BENAVENT

sourcebooks casablanca

Originally published as *Toda la verdad de mis mentiras*, © Elísabet Benavent, 2017. Translated from Spanish by Rosemary Peele.

Published by Sourcebooks Casablanca, an imprint of Sourcebooks
1935 Brookdale RD, Naperville, IL 60563-2773
(630) 961-3900
sourcebooks.com

Originally published as *Toda la verdad de mis mentiras* in 2017 in Spain by Suma de Letras, an imprint of Penguin Random House Grupo Editorial. This edition issued based on the paperback edition published in 2017 in Spain by Suma de Letras, an imprint of Penguin Random House Grupo Editorial.

Cataloging-in-Publication Data is on file with the Library of Congress.

Printed and bound in the United States of America.
VP 10 9 8 7 6 5 4 3 2 1

1

I'M A LIAR

COCO

The first problem on my list of "things that keep me up at night" is that I'm a fucking liar. I'm not sugarcoating it, dear Coco. You're a bullshit artist.

I have one of those names that were so popular when I was a kid that we always had to label all our stuff with our last names. Mine was so common, I ended up sticking with the nickname my brothers gave me. And...here I am at twenty-eight, still introducing myself as "Coco."

About the lying thing, I swear it's not pathological, and I only let those fibs slip out in an attempt to survive the jungle that is being twenty-eight, being in love, and being a total idiot. And making bad choices. I'm good at that too. But let's take it one step at a time.

Any story can be told three ways: the short way, the one that's somewhere in the middle, and the long way. Like life itself, which version you choose says a lot about all the things you want to keep quiet. And the biggest lies are always the ones you hide from yourself.

I could take the simple path and give you the no-frills version: I'm head over heels in love with my best friend, who's also my roommate and the ex of one of my other best friends. My last name should be "Complications" instead of Martinez because it really fits me way better. To make a short story a little longer, I could confess that sometimes I say stuff to my friend

Aroa like "Hey, Aroa, he's such a weirdo... Do you really wanna get back together with him?" And it's probably best if I don't mention all the bullshit I spew about how frustrating he is to live with. These are just little white lies, right?

Love makes us cruel.

If I go with the mid-length explanation of how I ended up here, I'd have to add that life is complicated. I mean... I fell in love with Marín by accident, and even though that should make me feel less guilty... Forget it. I fell in love with my friend's boyfriend (while they were still dating), I destroyed my peaceful roommate situation, and now I've become some kind of pathological liar. But...what did the universe expect me to do? I only lie because I'm trying not to create an apocalypse in our friend group.

Still, even if that version is closer to the clusterfuck that is my life, the most honest and real way to tell the whole story would start with a simple: I met Marín in a bar.

I didn't fall in love with him at first sight. Marín is one of *those* men—a needle in a haystack, the kind you can't believe is real. You think I'm exaggerating? Fine, judge for yourself: Marín is persistent. He's honest. He's so polite he's practically British. He's chaotic but brilliant. He's obsessed with music and has the perfect song for every moment. He has that thing you can't fake, being born with the gift of elegance. When he smiles, it must get dark somewhere else in the world. He's fun, a good brother, a good roommate. A triple threat: He's hot.

He's good in bed (judging by all the "God, Marín, don't stop. There, right there, keep doing that... Fuck! That was amazing!" floating out of his room when Aroa was still his girlfriend), a good friend, a good conversationalist. A natural at getting over himself. He could have felt sorry for himself his whole life for the bad luck of having an alcoholic mother who never took care of him or his sister and coming from a family with very limited economic resources. But no. Because he's Marín, of course, and he pulled on his ripped jeans and his white shirt and proved to everyone that you can't always get what you want, but your attitude and hard work help a lot.

So, yeah, I met him at a bar, and a week later my lease was up on my hovel and I was moving all my earthly possessions into his house because I was sick of living alone. He had rented a beautiful apartment on my favorite street in Malasaña (close enough to the center but still quiet), and an exchange student from Belgium was moving out, leaving a room free. From the day he invited me to have a beer in his kitchen, I felt like it was my home. My refuge.

His friends became my friends. My friends, his. The years flew by. The apartment filled up with cacti—which miraculously survived our complete neglect—and with framed artwork. We dubbed one side of the hallway "the wall of fame," where we hung caricatures we'd drawn of all our friends, acquaintances, and random people who passed through the house. We were growing. That was the most beautiful part of all. Growing alongside him as a person and in our careers too, through support, hugs, and unconditional trust in each other. When I moved into his place, I wasn't earning a bad salary, but I was still a little grossed out by the auction house where I worked and spent pretty much every waking hour. He was just finishing up his degree and working as a waiter. Our fridge usually looked like a desolate tundra littered with a few cheap beers, half a lemon, and at most four yogurts, until we forgot we were thousand-aires and went back to wasting our pennies on alcohol (me) and slices of pizza (him). Now that I think about it, I miss when Marín would eat microwaved pizza at five in the morning. But he got his dream job at a major label as a "product" manager for a few emerging bands and artists. And I've come to terms with the luxury of selling paintings for outrageous amounts. So the apartment is still stunning but now has a fridge full of special Alhambra bottles, face masks for tired skin

(I don't get much sleep), and food that makes him happy. A few years back, Marín started treating his body like a temple: He doesn't smoke or drink, he doesn't eat processed crap, and, get this, for his last birthday he asked me to get him a bread machine. It's not like he's a star in the kitchen, but he tries so hard...like everything in life because, babe, Marín doesn't know how to do anything in halves. And ever since then I eat homemade multigrain bread for breakfast.

Come on, aren't you falling in love with him a little? Wait, you don't have all the information yet. You'll see: We have a little chalkboard in the kitchen where we leave each other messages. Once he wrote that he had realized happiness was just spending a little time looking around at home, watching the curtain in the living room sway in the breeze coming in off the street. "That's the image that comes to mind when I think about being happy. Our house."

No. He's not in love with me. After that beautiful soliloquy, he added, "Living with my best friend: just to be clear." Just my luck...

When he gets mad, he furrows his brow and won't look you in the eye, but that only makes him look even hotter. He has beautiful hands. He's affectionate like a cat: only when it comes naturally because he doesn't know how to fake it. He has beautiful feet, for fuck's sake. The way he irons shirts kills me (sometimes in his underwear, for the love of God). And he loves me so much, so very much, that on the days when I can't find myself, all I have to do is look at his face to remember that I can, that I'm worth it, that I'm good for something, that I deserve it. Not for him, but for me. But there are days when I just see it in his eyes. But he loves me as a friend, you know. A best friend.

Welcome to the friend zone, a circle of hell reserved for idiots like me. It's been more than a year since I realized I was in love with him, wondering why we never hooked up on some lonely night, why I introduced him to Aroa hoping they would hit it off, why it took me so long to realize that

Marín is my *him*. I can't stop thinking about how our destinies could have changed if I just hadn't made a few stupid decisions.

Pretty fucking messy, huh? Well, wait until we get into the fact that I was so scared of being found out that I've spent a year pretending (like the fucking liar I already told you I am) to be madly in love with my ex, another member of the friend group, one of those "It's not you, it's me, the ladies like me too much for me to stay with just one for the rest of my life" guys and… Hold on, it gets worse… My ex is a poet.

Let me give you some advice: Every woman should have a list of men who aren't good for them, and despite all the temptations, they should get tattooed on their forehead that if they meet someone with any of those characteristics, they have to run in the opposite direction. The top of the list, contrary to popular belief, isn't a singer or a guitar player or a hell's angel… It's a poet. The poet as a figure, as a symbol, as a legend. Like the dude who will whisper to you, write to you, recite to you…always completely aware that he's in love with the muse and he'll never be faithful to you. Look, I'm not saying all poets are unfaithful. What I'm trying to say is that they have the words for love embedded in their brains, and they weep from their fingers when they write… That makes it complicated to stay with a woman who doesn't suffer, who doesn't make you suffer, who doesn't get bored. Because, babe, the poet needs to feel at any cost—their creation depends on their feelings. A relationship with a poet is like a roller coaster, blindfolded, where you never get used to ratcheting up or plummeting down because the change of direction can be a matter of seconds. There are people who love this, but I'm not one of them. For me, the unbridled passion of kisses that were almost more teeth than tongue, the arguments that were as ridiculous as they were impassioned under the blinking neon of a pharmacy in Chueca, the nights of fucking and poetry and the completely empty mornings…didn't make me happy. And I didn't make him happy either. Sometimes, I felt like I was trying to domesticate a rhino and keep it as a pet.

Plus, in this specific case, for Gus, the Instagram star, the it boy of the new poetry scene, the wunderkind, my ex, my friend… It turned out to be very difficult for him to say no when temptation knocked on his door. He never cheated on me, fine, but that's just because I'm not the type who considers jerking off over dirty Instagram DMs to be infidelity.

So here I am, pretending I'm tormented by his poems and his stories. Sometimes I even use them to cry out my frustration about loving Marín, faking like I'm devastated by the same old poem that, if I'm being honest, I have no clue whom he's writing about now. Because he's writing about someone, I'll tell you that, because I know him and he's definitely in love.

I know this isn't good, that I'm a liar and that this trip we have coming up, spending a week with three of my best friends twenty-four seven, isn't good, but no use crying over spilled milk, Coco.

It's Blanca's bachelorette party, and that is the only important thing.

2

THE WAY WE ARE

COCO

Marín gets to the party when I'm ready to leave, so I stay. That's just what you do when you see the guy you like out of the corner of your eye: pretend to act natural and try to look like a Parisian who couldn't care less and doesn't even know how chic she is. Kind of a challenge when you happen to be nowhere near Paris, by the way.

I would've known he'd arrived even if I hadn't spotted him in the crowd, because the vibe always shifts subtly when he's around. He's the kind of guy who people are just drawn to. He's...magnetic.

I'm watching the stage where Aroa's DJing when I notice a little commotion in the garden. When I turn to look... There he is. He just got here, and someone is already fetching him a mojito as he greets everyone he crosses paths with. As always, he's brushing away that unruly lock of hair swooping across his forehead. Up until last year, his hair was a lot longer, but one Saturday he got out of bed with the sudden urge for a change and cut it himself. I found him in the bathroom, armed with scissors and a YouTube tutorial. He just needed my help to touch up the back. That's Marín...renaissance man: He knows how to do everything.

Loren, my fabulous and sparkling best friend since high school, casts a glance in his direction. “He just got here and as always, he’s the center of attention the second he shows up, the bastard.”

“You’re just mad because he doesn’t even have to try.” I smile at him.

“Do this.” Loren points at my mouth and waggles his fingers like he’s wiping something. “You’re drooling, babe.”

I snort and roll my eyes, turning back to the stage where Aroa is remixing a campy song with a great track we love. I think it’s for Marín. She spotted him in the crowd too.

I look at the time and sigh. It’s not even late enough to gracefully call it a night. It’s not like I’m not a party person. It’s just that…those parties, the ones that are so “bougie,” so “cool,” so “Instagrammable,” they’re just not my thing. Honestly…they drain me; this one is packed with people who would look down their noses at you even if you were dressed by a Coachella-coded stylist. They seem even more salty than I am that I had to come straight from work and didn’t even have the chance to change. A couple of hipsters looked me up and down when I got here, I guess for wearing such a formal dress and heels, but I don’t care… If I want to sell expensive things to people with money, I have to embody their image of the model daughter.

A couple drops of sweat slide down my back, and I bet I’ll be sloshing around in my shoes in no time. Instead of wearing platform sandals or distressed ankle boots like the rest of the regulars, I’m wearing Salvatore Ferragamo heels, passed down from my mother, which I usually pair with a dress for work. Right now, I would write an ode to my grimy Converse. If I’d known when I left home this morning that Aroa was going to invite us to a big party, maybe I would’ve put on something more like the sequin top (which is so loose there’s the constant threat of a nip slip) she’s wearing. No, I wouldn’t have. When we met Aroa, Loren, Blanca, and I were all so immediately intoxicated by that je ne sais quoi that makes her so unique, so stunning, so smiley, so optimistic…

so perfect. She's one of those people you immediately want to be friends with. I think that's why I rallied and came to this party tonight even when I didn't feel like it. I want to rebuild the relationship we had before she started dating Marín. I'm not the only one who feels like she ended up drifting away from us.

I turn around and ask Loren if he wants something to drink. If I can't leave yet, the next best thing would be another drink to cool me off. He shakes his head and lifts his glass to show it's still full, singing what he thinks are the lyrics, even though he's getting them all wrong.

I slide up to the crowded bar. Still, I have to wait a long time, listening to some guy with super long hair and a beard bloviate about music. If Marín heard him, he'd punch him. I almost want to punch him myself.

Finally, clutching my drink, I move to the side, looking for a cool breeze, pull out my phone, and see a message from Blanca. She's saying she had to work late because it's the last day before our trip and she has to get all her ducks in a row (well, what a surprise, the little workaholic) and that she's going to have to flake on this one. I imagine her putting on her martyr face as I read:

BLANCA:

I know it'll be one of those parties Aroa will say I'm the worst for missing, but the only thing that sounds good right now is taking off all my clothes and lying on the hallway floor, with my bare ass on the cool tiles, dramatically feigning my own death.

I answer completely honestly that she's not missing anything.

Her response pops up right away.

BLANCA:

Nothing to report? Is the whole gang there?

I write back:

COCO:

Nothing to report. Gus has been radio silent all day. Marín just made his appearance, and Loren and I looked like proud parents, standing here beaming over our friend. Aroa is DJing again. People are buzzing and half-wasted. And I want to leave already. As usual.

BLANCA:

Send me a photo.

I pull up the camera app and point my phone, flash and all, at Aroa raising her arms in that "DJ getting fired up" pose. I send it without a filter or a caption.

Blanca pings back immediately.

BLANCA:

Jesus, how gorgeous is our little vixen. Give her a big kiss from me and say congratulations for somehow doing yet another thing so well.

That's the thing—as soon as Aroa told us she wanted to learn to DJ, we all knew she'd end up having a knack for it, just like everything else. Aroa is one of those people who dabble in everything and yet somehow master all of it, and on top of all that, she's super beautiful. The female equivalent of Marín. Their thing, I guess, was a matter of fate.

"Put your phone down, woman. You're at a party," someone next to me whispers.

I jump and stifle a scream. He's much closer than I thought.

"Jesus, Marín, you scared the shit out of me." I clutch my chest and take a breath before turning and giving him a single kiss on the cheek. "I was just about to come find you."

"Wild party?"

"It always is when Aroa DJs. She turns everything she touches to gold. So...are you gonna reward her with some cock?"

"Wanna see it?" He offers with a mocking glance.

"Nah. I don't like seeing sad stuff."

He lets out a chuckle and gives me a soft punch in the ribs, like you would to your bestie. What a cross to bear...

"What are you drinking?" he asks, looking at my glass.

"A virgin mojito."

"Ah, like you."

Now it's my turn to laugh.

"You're pretty late...with that joke and to the party."

"You should never be the first one to get to a party."

"Or the last. I've been ready to leave for ages."

He grimaces and checks the time discreetly on his phone.

"I got off work super late. You look like a snob and a half in this dress," he teases. "Did you borrow your mother's best dress for VIP funerals?"

"Nope. It's for your grandmother's wedding."

Marín laughs even though I can tell he's trying to keep a straight face.

"We opened an exhibition today," I explain. "So I had to pretend to be classy."

"You are classy. It's just your own brand of classy."

That's what my mother says, but she's obliged to love her youngest daughter.

I glance back at Aroa. The rest of us are shining with sweat, but she's glowing from a few strategic strokes of subtle powder highlighter she will have just dashed on, completely confident, not even looking in the mirror. She's so blond, so sun-kissed golden, with those intensely blue eyes and pert little nose…

"She's so beautiful, that fucker," I murmur.

"Yep."

I catch Marín's eyes on Aroa and feel a pang of jealousy. Jealousy like the one Gus described a few days ago in one of his Instagram poems: "Jealousy like hot, smoking tar, oozing into a puddle in my chest." But I swallow all of it: the jealousy, the tar, the idea that I'm projecting my ex's poems onto someone else, not even giving a second thought to who actually wrote them. I swallow it all down with a sip of my cocktail.

When I look back at Marín, he seems different.

"You good?" I ask.

"Yeah." Marín peels his eyes off Aroa and looks at me again. "I'm just tired."

There's something dark in his eyes, which are usually so clear…

Sex? Desire? Longing? Lust? That pretty girl, the one bouncing and grinning behind the turntables, is no longer his. Not even a little. And nobody knows why.

He swipes the alcohol-free mojito from my hand and takes a swig.

"I thought you already had a drink," I say slyly.

"It was going to be too strong."

No other explanation necessary. Marín rarely drinks. Just a couple of beers if the occasion warrants it… But it has to really warrant it. I'm very well aware of his reasons for this, and I completely get his disdain for drunkenness, especially when it goes too far.

While I casually sway to the rhythm of the music, I see one of Marín's friends making his way over.

"Angelito," I say, announcing his arrival and nudging Marín.

"Great. He'll worm his way into any event worth going to," he says bitterly.

I raise an eyebrow, but it's too late to ask. Angel is already in front of us.

"Man, it's Anchovy and Sardine. How are you?"

"We're here and very salty," I retort cheekily.

At least two years ago, we earned the nickname "Anchovy and Sardine," the ingredients of a snack that they call "A Marriage" in Madrid. And since we always show up everywhere together…

"Dude, we missed you at practice yesterday," he tells Marín.

"I know. I had a ton of work. I'm going with Noa on part of her summer tour, and there are a thousand loose ends to tie up," he apologizes as he sweeps the hair off his forehead.

They haven't made eye contact once, which hasn't gone over my head, but I'm too busy making a mental note of the name of the singer he's touring with so I can stalk her online later and decide whether to be jealous. As if knowing how much he loved Aroa, the most beautiful girl in the world, weren't bad enough.

"I'm gonna grab a drink. Anyone want one?" Marín asks both of us, but he's only looking at me.

"I'm all set."

"A beer would be great, man."

Marín slides away with a smile and says hi to at least five people whose faces I don't even recognize on his way to the bar six feet away.

"So what's up, Coco?"

"Not much," I reply, shrugging.

"You still work in that art gallery for crusty old people with too much dough?"

This is one of the things that bug me most about Angel; a few years ago, he started feeling like his "cool" factor was sharply declining, and his way of trying get it back is by being cynical and mocking what other people do. I know that my work isn't what young people are dying to do... I mean, if I just say I work in an art gallery and whomever I'm talking to imagines one of those hipster Malasaña spots where they sell pieces by emerging artists, I guess it's cool enough. But then I'd be lying by omission. It's not that kind of place.

Last week I sold a Miró. *A Miró*. I spent months working on the deal. It was a piece from a private collection, but the two parties finally came to an agreement and the gallery and I each took our cut. These days, after the financial crisis, it's hard for a gallery to survive on selling just the paintings on the walls. We act as dealers too.

So I decide to counterattack his comment snidely. "Are you still drinking the chocolate milk your mother brings to your bedside every morning?"

"Hey, man, don't get all aggy. You know how much I love you." Angel slings his arm around me and tries to kiss my temple, but I wriggle out of it as fast as I can.

"Quit it... You're so damn touchy-feely."

Angelito and I have a cordial relationship, as long as we don't spend too much time together. I resent how hard he tries to seem cool and constantly invades people's personal space, especially women's.

"I hear Blanca's send-off is gonna be amazing."

I turn to face him again. "Loren and I planned it. Would you expect anything less?"

"What's the plan?"

"The key to keeping a secret under wraps, Angelito, is not blabbing about it."

My fanny pack buzzes with a message, and I tap my phone on again. I'm surprised to see it's from Marín.

MARÍN:

Make up an excuse and say goodbye. I ordered a cab.

A smile spreads across my face. Now I have an excuse to escape and to leave with the person I really want to.

"Angel, excuse me for a sec, I have to tell Loren something."

I pat him on the forearm a couple of times as a goodbye and wend my way through the crowd to Loren. I spot him by his hair. It's unmistakable.

"I'm outta here," I say into his ear.

"Already?" he shouts indignantly.

"Marín called a cab."

"Fucking lame-os," he grumbles. "I mean, hopefully today you at least get to touch his cock."

"Loren, for the love of God, one of these days someone's going to hear you say that."

"Coco, the way you moon over him, it'd be a shocker if no one noticed you're butt-crazy in love with your 'best friend.'"

His air quotes piss me off, so I give him a slap.

"We have an intense week coming up. Don't use it all up today, firecracker."

He pouts but leans forward so I can kiss his forehead as usual. Then he kisses mine. Once I've been "blessed" by his goodbye kiss, I turn to the stage and wave my arms like crazy, and when Aroa looks up, I blow her a kiss.

~

Marín is leaning on the wall around this mansion's garden. I have no idea who owns it, but that's how it always is when Aroa says, "Hey, I got an invite to a party. Why don't you come along?" You never know who the host is, but you're never left wanting for a pool or a cocktail bar. And, of course, this has only gotten worse since she started DJing soirees on top of doing a little sporadic modeling work, babysitting children two afternoons a week, and having an amalgam of other confusing jobs that somehow meld together seamlessly alongside casting calls for her budding career as an actress.

Marín's face is glowing in the light of his screen. He's wearing an indecipherable expression. It's something to do with work, I'm sure. Marín is very focused when it comes to work. I take advantage of how absorbed he is to give him a long look. God, he's so handsome. His eyes are light, lively, and always so shiny; his thick eyelashes, his perfect, slightly long nose. His jawline… His jawline drives me crazy. I'd have a church wedding just to his chin. And have we discussed his dimples?

He's wearing his "uniform" of jeans with a white T-shirt, which could also be black jeans with a black T-shirt or those slim highwaters (which expose his ankles) with a white T-shirt or white dress shirt, if the occasion calls for it. In winter he has a warmer equivalent, but always along the same lines. He's a hipster to the extreme. His only extravagance is filling his wardrobe with exactly the same garments. Anyone who doesn't know him would think he never changes clothes, but I once counted six pairs of black jeans in his closet.

I take a deep breath and walk toward him with a kind of resignation. I don't know when I fell in love with Marín. Or maybe I do. Yes, I think it was that afternoon when he cracked open two bottles of Coke, passed me one, pushed his hair back from his forehead, and made a toast, leaning against the window frame in the living room of our apartment. The sun was shining, making a bright-orange halo around his hair, and I knew the tingling in the pit of my stomach had to be love. I'd been feeling things that didn't add up for a few months, but I always said it couldn't be. My secret. I fell in love with Marín. And I'm the one who introduced him to Aroa.

Their breakup, which came out of nowhere and they never explained, didn't make me feel any better. You don't mess with the ex your friend wants to get back together with.

"Marín." I get his attention.

He looks up from his phone and smiles. My stomach flips, as always. Does he suspect at all how much I love him, how much I want to be spooning him in bed and hearing him say we'll grow old together?

"Is staying at parties for five minutes your new technique for seeming cool?" I blurt out.

"Only if the party is terrible." He slips his phone into his pocket. "I shouldn't even have come at all."

"Tomorrow's Saturday. Do you have to work?"

"No." He shakes his head vigorously, glancing over at the street, in case the headlights belong to the car picking us up. "But my aunt is dropping Gema off early."

"Is Gema coming to spend the weekend?" I ask giddily.

"Yes. And tomorrow we're going shopping. She says she wants to find her own style. She doesn't want to go around dressed like everyone else in her class. Is she the best teenager in the world or what?"

"She is." I pat his arm. "She has a good role model."

He grimaces, I guess thinking about his mother…

"She has a brother who's the shit," I clarify.

"Well, that's true." He pretends to swell with pride.

The cab's headlights seem to snake through the shrubs on the path, and we both jump and hurry over to the cobblestone street. But at that exact second, a few musical notes make us stop dead.

"No!" we both shout, looking at each other.

Our song. One that Marín was excited to show me when it was a single before it even started playing on the radio. One that became a hymn in our house, where we almost installed fan belts in the living room so we could reproduce the music video, where the singers leap into flight with a hypnotic naturalness. "Lost in Your Light" by Dua Lipa with Miguel.

"It always plays when we're leaving," I groan.

"This is a better spot than the dance floor." He winks and strides over to the driver's window, where he knocks a few times. "Excuse me."

I hear the driver say his full name, and he nods.

"That's me, but... Can you do me a huge favor? They're playing our song. And you have no idea what a good dancer this little lady is. Can you wait until it's over but leave your headlights on?"

The driver smiles, and Marín reaches for my hand. "Come on."

"No fucking way!" I laugh.

"What do you mean, no fucking way? Do me a solid. This guy wants to go home, Coco. Don't waste time!"

"Look at that face! You're the one who's wasting time!"

"Don't do it for me," the driver says, sticking his head out of the window.

"We're going to miss the best part of our routine... When you do the 'honey' part," Marín grumbles, still holding out his hand insistently.

I give up. I never really had a chance. I take his outstretched hand, and he drags me in front of the car. We get there just in time for that "honey" that makes him laugh so much, and he twirls me around dramatically a few times.

We dance. Of course.

As always, we forget we have an audience. We're dancing on our own, like we do at home when everything's normal. We dance, and I fall in love with him a little more with every step, if that's possible. We spin, we laugh, I shimmy, he flips me around, I sing to him, he sings to me, we make fools of ourselves dancing like total idiots, but it's not actually that bad because Marín doesn't know how to dance badly. He has rhythm in that fucking devilish body of his, and as much as he tries to look stupid, he does it in such a sexy way. And that night, in that garden, he brings out the big guns.

~~~

When we clamber into the back of the cab, we're panting and even the driver is smiling.

"Traditions should never be broken, right?" Marín says to him.

"Of course."

He flops back into the seat, buckles his seat belt, and pulls his phone out of his pocket.

"Stop working already," I say, whacking the screen.

"It's not work. It's..." He furrows his brow.

"What's going on?"

"Aroa," he mutters.

"She texted you?"

"Yeah. She said she saw me in the crowd and she was in the mood for a kiss."

I raise my eyebrows as jealousy nibbles at my side.

"I didn't know you were in that phase." I look out the window. "I thought the whole thing was much more...cold."

"It is. Sometimes I get the feeling that she forgets we're not together anymore."

I raise one eyebrow. He always uses the phrase "We're not together anymore." Never "I broke up with her" or "She broke up with me." No reasons, no culprits. They seem to have decided it was better this way.

I'm not going to be the one to delve further into it.

Marín turns toward me, putting his phone back in his pocket. "What can you tell me about Blanca's bachelorette party? Or are your lips still sealed?"

"You said you couldn't come, and I'm not authorized to give information to 'third parties.' If I tell you, everyone'll end up knowing. We've kept the secret for months now. I'm not going to fuck it up days before the 'event.'"
~~~

"You think I can't keep a secret?" He thumbs his chest. "Plus, you're leaving in three days. I wouldn't even have time to put my foot in it."

I roll my eyes, and he pinches my side, making me jump. "Stop. I don't negotiate with torture."

"If you tell me, I'll let you sleep in my room."

"We rented an RV and we're going on a tour of the most ridiculous camping spots we've ever found."

Yes, I'm a pushover, but the thing is my room is like an oven.

"Fuck..." He flashes his teeth in a smile. "None of you has any self-control."

"None at all."

"You're all the fucking best." He gives me a sidelong glance and puts his hand over mine, which is resting on the empty seat between us.

The darkness in the car, which is hurtling down a practically empty highway, lets me blush undiscovered. The millions of stunning butterflies that just started fluttering around my stomach are just for me.

Marín doesn't move his hand until, a few minutes later, he sucks his teeth, reaches for his fucking phone again, and answers a call.

"Hi, Aroa."

I don't know if it's the three beers I practically chugged when I got to the party or the disappointment of realizing that there's always the enormous, deformed thing called friendship between Marín and me. It won't even let me fantasize, but my mind fills with predictions...and none of them are particularly good.

Because the truth is, for a long time I've had the sinking feeling that he's not done with Aroa, that she's been pretty squirrelly about her obsession with Marín, and...let's be real here...that the epic bullshit about still being in love with Gus is going to catch up with me, not to mention the fact that Loren is sick of being the only one I go to with all my shit. My only option is to confide in Blanca. You can always count on Blanca. She's chill. She doesn't have mood swings. She's been a little weird lately, but that's probably just because of nerves about the wedding. At the end of the day, we're all nervous about this wedding, right?

3

THE BUILDUP

COCO

I love Marín's room. That's why, when I wake up, I stay in bed luxuriating in it. I don't have many chances to do this. I don't like invading his privacy, and when he's in here, I can't deeply inhale his scent, grinning like an idiot riffling through all his shelves and calculating how many records, CDs, books, and tchotchkes in them were gifted by me. I like being part of his "den." I like that it's always so clean and organized inside the chaos of music in all forms and devices he listens on.

I hear noise in the kitchen. The sound of dishes clinking together and Marín padding around barefoot. I'm used to my days starting with his sounds. With him clearing his throat when he turns off his alarm clock and lingers there for a second. Most mornings, even though he gets up an hour earlier than me, I follow his every move from my bed, wide awake and staring at the ceiling, while I fantasize about him bringing me breakfast, giving me a kiss that tastes like toothpaste, and saying to me, "I love you. Have a good day." Other times I'm less innocent, and I think about getting in the shower with him and burying my nose in his back while I fumble around in front until I grab his cock and hear him moan. Watching him fog the shower door with his moans like the windows fogged in that scene in *Titanic*. You know the scene I'm talking about. I watched it at an impressionable age too. But…if I did that in real life, Marín would die of a heart attack and his last words would be "What the hell are you doing, Coco?" Well, I'm grabbing your cock, Marín. Babe, sometimes it feels like I have to explain everything to you.

I'm turning into a pig. I'm going to stop. I'm in Marín's bed, and I can't masturbate here, tangling myself up in his sheets and the smell of his cologne embedded in them. I can't? Right? I'm going to meditate on it for a second. No, I can't.

My right hand moves down without permission, but the left is faster and grabs my phone from the bedside table.

According to the experts, that simple, automatic gesture condemns the rest of your day: If our first contact with reality is through our phones, we're setting ourselves up for a shitty day. Stress, anxiety, bad moods, hypersensitivity… Sounds familiar.

I push that all aside and open Instagram. The first thing on my feed is Gus's latest post, which I look at before I can stop myself. Somehow, the poems, phrases, and photos Gus posts flavor the day with a poetic justice that surprises me. Sometimes he writes things that stun me because it's like he had access to everything I feel about Marín. I should probably tell him… He would understand. He's the most intense person I know, the kind who wants to know everything. No. I can't tell Gus, who has a mouth like a mailbox. But…why the hell haven't I told Blanca either? Because I feel ridiculous. That's why.

I turn my attention back to Gus's poem:

Sometimes I jerk off hoping that,
when I come
you'll disappear.
Maybe I think you'll leave the way you came in,

through fucking me,
swimming in my desire,
moaning in my mouth.
And I'll instantly forget
everything I unlearned
with you.

Come the fuck on. This is what I'm talking about. Now I'm going to spend the whole day thinking about nothing else but Marín mounting me like a stallion.

It's time to get out of bed. His bed. But before I get around to it, the door creaks open slowly. I'm tempted to pretend I'm asleep, but I smile when I see him come in.

"Did I wake you up?"

His expression is the same as always. Every day I hope that something in him will change when he looks at me: that his eyes will shine more, he'll bite his lips, nervously tousle his messy hair…any of those tics he had all the time when he was with Aroa. But they never come.

"What time is it?"

Marín sits on the bed and tugs my phone out of my hand before he answers.

"It's nine thirty, early for a Saturday, I know, but Gema's going to be here any minute, and if she sees you in my bed, she'll go off again about how we're hooking up and don't want to tell her."

I nod and make a move to get up, but he gently pushes my shoulder back onto the pillow. An invisible cloud of his scent wraps around me.

"Stop doing that," he says seriously.

"Doing what?"

"Stop running to see what he's posted the second you wake up. It's not healthy. It's hurting you."

I realize that my screen didn't lock and Gus's poem is still there, like a smoking gun. I groan and close my eyes.

"If you really think it's over, stop doing that. But if you actually want him, go balls to the wall for him. This in-between stuff doesn't make sense. It's been more than a year."

If he knew… If I followed his advice, I'd have to leave this house, find another apartment, and get out of his life. And I love Marín too much to do that.

The buzzer rings, and he stands up; he's wearing cotton shorts and messy hair. Nothing else. I should be used to it by now; I've lived with him for years, but starting a few months ago, the feelings it provokes in me have been getting worse. If Blanca knew what I felt, she would tell me to stop wallowing.

"That'll be my sister. Hop out of my bed."

"Did you sleep okay on the couch?" I ask as I climb out.

"Convincing the landlord to buy that couch was the best idea ever."

He drags a smile out of me as soon as he starts talking. I have to control myself to stop it spreading and splitting my face in half.

~

I make Marín's bed in the time it takes Gema to get up the elevator and scurry off to my own room. I come out to say hi in my pajamas and messy bun.

"Holy mother, look at those tits!" I yelp before I can stop myself.

She touches them proudly and nods. "I filled them out a little."

"Take those socks out of your sweater right now," her brother scolds her as he passes by.

"You take out the one in your crotch. You're not fooling anyone."

I laugh silently and subtly slap her hand.

"I'm gonna go down and talk to Auntie for a second," her brother says.

I stand there staring at Gema with my arms up and smile.

"It's pretty early, cutie. You're going shopping?"

"You're not coming?" She makes sad puppy eyes at me.

Of course I want to go. Gema cracks me up. I'm the youngest with five brothers, and I've always wanted to mentor someone on a shopping spree so they don't make the same mistakes I did… Not to mention how much I like spending time with her brother. But it's her day.

"I wish," I say. "I have a lot to do today. Next week is Blanca's bachelorette party."

"I wish you'd take me with you."

"There are things I'm not ready for you to learn about life, at least not yet," I tease. "You don't need to rush into knowing how depraved human beings can get. Bachelorette parties are an apocalypse."

"Will there be naked dudes there?"

"Does Loren count?"

Gema bursts out laughing, and from her expression I would say…no. Loren doesn't count as a naked man according to her. He babysat her too many times.

Marín still hasn't come back up, so I take Gema into my room so she can pick out a book. While her brother is off on tour with that Noa girl (mental note, I still need to find her on the internet in case she's a goddess and I'm not dying with jealousy yet), her aunt and uncle are taking her to see her grandparents and there aren't many people her age there, so at least she'll have something to keep her busy.

I'm trying to reorganize a few things when she asks me if she can take "this." When I turn around, I see her holding Gus's first book of poetry, the one he published with a tiny publishing house right when I met him. I smile remembering the inscription he wrote on the first page: "Stay by my side forever, Coco Puff. And forever will be as long as you decide."

"You want to read Gus? I thought you didn't really like him."

"No, I do like him, but... He's kind of a drag," she says, her lips pursed.

"You don't have a crush on him, do you?" I ask her.

She wouldn't be the first girl to fall prey to his disdainful attitude toward life, his sparkling eyes, and his dirty poems about love and sex. I did the same thing. I wouldn't blame her, but... She's staring at me totally freaked out.

"What? No! He's so old!" Blessed fifteen-year-old. "Plus, he's your ex-boyfriend. A girl never falls in love with her friend's ex."

Take note, Coco. Even teenagers can see how obvious that is.

I sigh and grab the copy she's holding. It's a good book; he says he's not especially proud of the poems that fill its pages, but I think they're littered with real stuff. They're like shotgun blasts of life... Now he shoots more accurately. In two years, I know he'll write an intimate, sensitive, and heartbreaking novel that will stun us all, but essentially, he'll never divert from the truth he defended inside here.

"This book is beautiful," I tell her. "It's full of swear words and expressions that your aunt won't want you repeating. I don't know if you're getting me, but he says real things."

"About love?"

"About love." I sit down on the bed and look up at her from there. "About sex. About yourself. About fear. About ego. About life in your twenties, I guess."

"So do you believe love exists and lasts forever?"

Oy. The little munchkin has gone and fallen in love on us. I don't know who it is, but it's obvious Gema is experiencing her first love.

"I think it exists and it's for forever because if we really love someone, even if it ends, we'll always keep loving them a little, right? For what we were." I clear my throat when I see her making a face like she doesn't understand me. "Love exists, munchkin, and you wanna know something? It's beautiful and all that, but above all, it's free."

A rustle alerts me to Marín leaning against the doorframe, listening to us. When our eyes meet, he smiles proudly. But no. His eyes aren't shining and he's not biting his lips or tousling his hair with his fingers, nervously.

"Look, here's your brother. Go on, get outta here. I have a life to get to."

Marín winks at me and whispers a "thanks" for entertaining her while he talked to his aunt. The truth is I love being with Gema. It keeps me young and reminds me of when life was all intensity and a constant passionate drama.

Before they leave the room, I catch Marín eyeing the book his sister is holding. He furrows his brow and then heads after her but quickly doubles back into my room.

"Do you have plans today? Don't you wanna come with us?"

"I'm going to see Blanca."

"To warn her about the bachelorette week?" He smiles.

"She's nervous. Someone showing up at her door with white wine and sushi will cheer her up."

"Sounds like a girls' afternoon,'" he jokes in a la-di-da voice.

"Later we'll watch a few tutorials on how to do our own French manicures and how to French kiss."

"Idiot." He rolls his eyes. "Listen, I can feel a disturbance in your force. All good?"

If we put my urge to kiss you at a ten in the "good" category and how impossible that ever happening is at a zero on the same scale, then no, Marín, nothing is good.

I blink slowly. Then I smile with my teeth, which, thanks to years at the orthodontist, are perfectly straight.

So it's pretty clear who wins first place in this tournament of lies. Now we just need to find out who's going to be runner-up.

4

MY SECRET

COCO

When I get to Blanca's house, my left arm is aching from holding my phone up to my ear. I used the walk over to call my mother and say goodbye before the bachelorette escapade, and that gave her the perfect opportunity to warn me about the danger of 200,000 everyday objects, recite a list of foods that can help us tan well, and remind me about the need to have safe sex.

"Mama," I groan affectionately. "I have to hang up on you. I just got to Blanca's house."

"Remember to send me a message when you get where you're going. Eat raw carrots. Be careful about leaving bug spray in the sun and, please… Take care of yourself. Take care with the boys. There are a lot of horrible diseases out there."

"Okay, Mama…"

"And stop by home on your way back! I'll make you a cocktail and you can tell me everything."

My mother… She's such a character.

Blanca seems kind of agitated when she opens the door. She's dressed, made-up; the house seems spotless; and she's clenching her phone. Her beautiful brown eyes are sparkling. I don't know if it's because she's excited to see me or because she's about to cry. I'm a little freaked out, but her wide smile brightens her expression.

"Hey! Coco!"

"Who were you expecting?" I ask with a furrowed brow, watching her run her fingers through her brunette bob.

Her expression changes, and she shoots me a panicked look.

"Tell me this isn't a prelude to my bachelorette week! For the love of God, swear to me it's not going to be one of those bachelorette parties where the girls all mercilessly laugh at the bride, dress her like a giant penis, and force her to beg for change while she sings on the subway."

"You're so twisted. If I ever get married, all I ask is that you don't organize mine."

I hand over the bottle of white wine I bought on the way and a bag with the name of a fast-food sushi chain I know she loves. She eyes me suspiciously.

"If you're worried I drugged the food like they did in *The Hangover*, I'm starting to think you're gonna be pretty disappointed by what we actually have planned."

"Ay, shut up, shut up."

She takes the bag and finally lets me in. Just as it seemed from the door, the apartment is clean and organized. There's not a trace of Ruben, her fiancé.

"Where's your future husband?"

"He had plans."

"So what were you doing?"

"I mean…nothing. Just sitting here. I don't trust any of you, so I woke up at the crack of dawn and plastered on makeup in case you came here to catch me off guard."

"We're people of our word, sweetie. If Loren said Monday, it'll be Monday. The little emperor has everything planned to the second. Or at least that's what he's led us to believe."

She seems anxious, and a pang of doubt over whether we've gone too far with this bachelorette trip twists in my stomach, right when her phone starts making a repetitive noise.

"Fuck," she groans when she looks at the screen. "I'm gonna grab some wine glasses and the corkscrew. You take the bottle to the living room," she orders me.

Whatever conversation she's involved in is agitating, judging by the way she's crashing around in the kitchen. I'm about to go see if she's okay when I hear Loren's name and I relax. It's just Loren…who could make the midday sun nervous.

"What does he want?" I call out.

"To fuck me up the ass!" Blanca answers without a trace of tact.

"Tell him if he hurries he can come eat sushi with us."

"I don't need you yelling at me." She's still talking to Loren when she brings over two glasses, although I notice she's studying my expression. "I need a glass of wine the size of the Copa del Rey. Of course I know what the Copa del Rey is, you jerk! And that's the size I need."

She rolls her eyes and agrees a few times before she hangs up and hurls her phone at the couch.

"What's going on?"

"Nothing." She clears her throat. "He was just scratching his need to overwhelm me with anxiety."

I raise one eyebrow. Her laptop is open on the coffee table, but intuition tells me there's something else. I want to tell her that I'm the queen of lies and this has made me infallible at spotting them, but that would expose me. My mother can't help but use Blanca as an example of every good thing in the world. It hasn't made me despise her, because I love her and because she makes up for her impeccable track record with all the stupid stuff I know she's capable of that my mother has no idea about. Like on her birthday one year, when Blanca stole a cart from the supermarket and forced us to roll her around in it all night long.

"Coco..." Blanca puts on one of those good little girl smiles and settles next to me on the couch, moving aside a few cushions. "Coquito..."

"Oh, God... What do you want?"

"Liposuction," she says with tender eyes. "Actually, some kind of liposculpture that can magically make me fit into a size eight. I'm not asking for much, just one size down."

"What?"

"It's a joke. Well, it's not a joke. I want that, but you can't help me there. You can do one better though. Give me a hint about the bachelorette party..."

"No fucking way!" I laugh.

"Just one thing!" she begs. "One tiny thing! What should I bring? Who's coming? Where are we going?"

I stand up, rummage through a kitchen drawer for the corkscrew, and come back. Seeing her is like finding an abandoned puppy on the sofa. Her expression, the bags under her eyes that makeup can't hide completely and are a result of her more-than-fifty-hour workweeks in her law office, where I'm sure she'll end up being the youngest partner in history. I can't help it: I melt.

"Fuck... You're the worst." I suck my teeth. "I'm not going to tell you where we're going, but you need comfy clothes, like vacation clothes, something to go out in, but not a lot, bikinis, a towel, flip-flops, and... makeup basics."

"That's it? I'm not going to risk my life if I show up without hiking boots or something like that?"

"Loren and I organized it," I say. "You know we're such big fans of physical exercise."

"What do I know! What if Aroa got involved in the planning?"

"That would mean us doing yoga at dawn, not scaling a vertical cliff face. Relax," I say, grabbing the bottle and concentrating on opening it. "It'll be fun."

"Who's going?" I have no intention of giving in more, but when I look at her, there's something pleading in her eyes. Blanca is really nervous. "I need to know at least who's going to be at my bachelorette trip, Coco. I swear I won't tell anyone."

I give in. "Just us."

"Us who?"

"Loren, Aroa, you, and me."

Her shoulders seem to slump, and she sighs and rubs her face. I can't tell if it's relief or disappointment. We tried to get her colleagues from the office and a few friends from university who she was still in touch with to come, but the dates didn't work.

"No one else could make it," I clarify.

"I know, I know. I understand."

"We wanted it to be a mixed group." I'm babbling on because something tells me she's disappointed at having such a small crowd and I feel obligated to apologize for everyone else. "But Marín couldn't make it because of work. You know he's going on tour with that girl, Noa. And Gus was too broke. We told him to just contribute whatever he could, but he didn't want to. He said he would feel bad."

Blanca grabs the glass of wine I hold out to her and clinks it against mine.

"Too bad Marín can't come. Not for Aroa though, obviously," she adds quickly. "It's just that…he's the apple of my eye. Don't tell Loren."

"Nothing he doesn't already know. Marín is the apple of everyone's eye." I sigh.

"Listen… Does the fact that Gus isn't coming have something to do with…you two?"

"Us? No, no. I think it's more about being totally strapped for cash, and he can't imagine spending a week with Loren, twenty-four hours a day without the calming presence of Marín. That was going to end up in the news."

"Better this way, right?" She looks at me doubtfully. "Because...you... and him? I mean... You're not still in a bad place, right?"

And there she is, my best friend, Blanca, the most trustworthy person I know.

"Blanca..." I sigh.

I hold my breath. She does too. Am I saying it? I'm saying it. I'm going to spend a week stuck in an RV with her. She's going to notice, even if he's not there.

Here goes. To hell with secrets. To hell with the belief that I'm actually protecting Blanca from an uncomfortable situation by not telling her.

"I..."

"Coco..." She grabs my hand and smiles. "Coco, it's fine. Don't spiral, okay? This is how love is. It'll pass. Give yourself time. Who gets to say how long it takes to forget someone?"

"Right." I make a face.

"The important thing is...do you want to forget him? Do you want to start again or do you want to try to make it work?"

Marín's face floats up in my mind after that question, but I push it away with a lie.

"I'm getting there," I promise.

Blanca smiles. I smile. The sushi's going to make me sick, I know it.

5

I WISH I COULD PACK HIM IN MY SUITCASE

COCO

White wine causes terrible hangovers, like really bad. I notice my eyelashes feel heavier than they should, and when Gema found me crashed out in the living room, all she could muster was "Oh God." I threw myself onto the couch as soon as I got home. Apparently I didn't even take my shoes off, and I still have my keys in my hand.

"Now I know why my brother doesn't drink."

She said that when I managed to drag myself over to the coffee maker and turn it on. Normally I'm pretty restrained when it comes to alcohol. It's been a million years since the last time I got so wasted I vomited in the doorway and fell asleep with my hand on the wall to make the room stop spinning, but yesterday I polished off all that wine. Maybe it was nerves, maybe the buzz of knowing that tomorrow, Monday, we're finally heading out.

Marín makes me look up from packing, standing in the doorframe. He brought me a coffee granita he made himself with cinnamon and lemon and no sugar and that, by the way, taste like licking the devil's ball sack. I love the guy, but there's no way I'm even thinking about drinking this thing, obviously. He's talking about that girl Noa's tour. Because I got so plastered at Blanca's house, it completely slipped my mind to google her, but this morning, Gema and I "stalked" her social media. Noa's sixteen. She travels with her mother. With her mother and Marín.

"Are you all packed?" I ask him.

"Yeah. I just need to add four more things. God." He rubs his face. "I can't believe I'm gonna miss a weeklong vacation just to ferry that girl from concert to concert."

"Hey, look for the silver lining. You'll probably have time to go to the beach."

"Yeah, to buy her lemon-lime Popsicles," he grumbles. "What are you gonna get up to?"

"Well, the plan is…" I sit on my heels and look at him. "Scoop up Blanca at her house in the RV covered in streamers and all that shit. Then we're heading to Torrevieja, but first we're making a few boring pit stops to throw her off. We're in Torrevieja for three nights, at a nutty campsite that has tons of waterslides and all that stuff."

"Sounds awesome."

"Then we have one night of boondocking, hippie style, and the last stop is Mojacar, but we haven't actually booked the campsite in case Blanca is more into the wild camping."

"Wait!" he yells. I spin around, scared, and see Marín smiling. "When will you be in Torrevieja until? Noa has a concert there! One of those 'Top 40 Summer Pop Hits.'" He grabs his phone from his pocket and fiddles with it. "On Wednesday!"

I blink. This can't be happening.

Lord. I haven't been to mass since I took communion, but please, please… Please let this be a sign.

"You couldn't have told me this earlier?" I slap on a carefree, funny tone.

"When I told you I was going to be on tour, you kicked me out of the WhatsApp group for the bachelorette party 'so I wouldn't leak any information to the opposing team.' That's a quote." He laughs.

"Yeah, well, according to the plan, we'll be in Torrevieja until Thursday morning."

"Well, we'll have Wednesday for you to join us. Better than nothing, right?"

Better than nothing? There's a fucking pagan festival in my stomach, bonfire and all. Dancing around it are all my illusive hopes, raising their voices above the trail of smoke curling into the sky from the fire, singing songs about how beautiful our love story will be when we finally star in it on this trip.

"It'll be cool," I say, turning back to my suitcase.

"And a good opportunity."

Excuse me. A what? I'm paralyzed and I don't even want to turn to him to ask, "An opportunity? To what?"

"To be your wingman so you can meet someone, Coco. Your thing with Gus was great, but it's over. I'm sorry to be so harsh, but you have to get back to building your life without him. I really like him, he's a good guy, but as your boyfriend… Admit it, he left a lot to desire. Plus, look at you… You're not exactly following him around trying to get close to him again."

"I do follow him around," I justify. "We're always together."

"Yeah, together, but never alone. You act like colleagues. It doesn't make sense for you to 'wait for him.' He… I mean, you're not stupid and you probably know this better than anyone, but he's out there living his life."

Gus sleeping with half of Madrid is something I've taken as a given since the day we broke up. And it didn't even bother me back then, but I have to pretend it affects me.

"I know that already," I add sulkily.

Marín perches on the edge of my bed and gestures for me to look up. I lift my eyes to meet his and swallow. His pupils are so dilated from the tenuous late-July evening light in my room, and it feels like he can see right through me and read every one of my fears and lies.

"Coco… You're an incredible girl. You're fun, intelligent, you never keep quiet, you're very pretty, you have a personality that people fall in love with"—*Mama, send help*—"and you're thoughtful, charming…and a thousand other things. If you want to be alone, that's fine, but if you actually want to share your life with someone and fall in love, don't cling to something that's dead. Either make it your mission to get him back or do something else. Live, Coco."

I nod before I turn back to my suitcase, which I'm filling unusually meticulously, stretching out the process. I avoid his gaze until he announces he's going to make dinner and leaves. I don't want him to look at me and know how scared I am by the idea of starting, living again. Especially considering that if Marín hasn't shown any symptoms of loving me up to this point, he's not going to, no matter how long I drag it on. And that only means one thing: I have to make a decision. Either I tell him and let Jesus take the wheel or I move out of the apartment with whatever excuse will cause him the least pain possible and…start again. For real. And without lies.

6

RIDING IN THE "IMPERIAL BOOZER CRUISER"

COCO

Loren and I look at the monster in front of us, and we're a little freaked. I don't even bother to hide it; he does. We put our hands on our hips at the same time, pretending like we know what we're doing. In front of us, the mammoth structure gleams in the summer morning sunshine. There's barely any breeze, and it feels muggy. A hellish day is coming. I hope the air-conditioning works. So far this summer has been the hottest of my entire life.

"And I think that's everything," says the guy from Campering K2 responsible for explaining how the RV works. "Any questions?"

Hundreds, but I don't say that. I slipped into a deep coma after he explained how the bathroom works and how to empty it. Loren looks at me under cover of his sunglasses as he says we understand. I flash him a smile right as he starts to laugh riotously. And beware of Loren's laugh—it's more contagious than the flu.

No, we don't think it's funny. It's just all we can do so we don't lose our shit. This is going to be more complicated than we thought.

"Are you stuck on the toilet part?" he asks us with a smile.

"A little," I admit.

"It's nothing. Really. It's much easier than it seems. So who's driving?"

"Both of us," Loren rushes to say.

"Him," I answer. There's no way I can control something that big without mowing down everything that crosses my path, like in an action movie chase.

He hands the keys to Loren.

"Well, that's everything. It's all yours. I'm sure you're going to have an amazing experience. You'll see. You're going to come back in love."

~

We both climb up into the camper and study it in silence. It's very pretty and incredibly well equipped. I never thought an RV could have this many amenities. Kitchen, living room, bunk bed, double bed… Everything the perfect size to make the most use out of the space. I open the fridge, the cupboards in the "kitchen." I sit at the little table and smile excitedly; if I ever get married, I want my bachelorette party to be exactly like this.

"Imagine us all sitting here, eating," I say and immediately get the feeling I sound like a little girl playing house.

"It'll be so cute. We'll eat on the patio, under the pop-out awning."

"We don't have a table or chairs for the patio, but sounds good."

"Minor details."

"We have to christen it."

"The Death Star," Loren says sadistically.

"Can't it be something a little gentler? Something that doesn't mention death, if possible. The…Millennium Falcon, if you want."

"The Millennium Alcohol, boom."

Loren settles in the driver's seat with a smile and focuses on connecting his phone to Bluetooth. He's made a bunch of themed Spotify playlists for the trip, and I'm pleasantly surprised when I glance at them. I figured Aroa would be in charge of that, but we didn't want to put that on her plate too. To tell the truth, since she and Marín announced their breakup, we've been scared to even sneeze around her, and I think she's used to it. I don't want to bring it up, but she hasn't lifted a finger to help us organize any of this. Since we haven't seen her shed a single tear, we're spoiling her, trying to avoid the day all that self-control explodes.

"Do you know how to drive this hunk of junk?" I ask, when I hear Karol G.'s latest track playing.

"Of course," he says tersely, which means he really doesn't have it down.

"The steering wheel is like a bus. How do you see to turn it? What's the highest speed it can get to? Do you know how to park it? Do you remember how everything works with the lights and the water? We can't let Blanca drive; she's gonna want to. We'll never get the deposit back. I don't wanna die."

Loren sighs and turns around to look at me. He smiles, and I do too.

"If you don't shut up, I'm sticking you in the fridge until you suffocate, and then I'll chuck you into the first ditch we come across."

~

Aroa is waiting for us outside Loren's parents' bar when we pull up yelling and honking the horn. The whole street is staring at us, plus everyone sitting on their balconies, but we roll down the window and put on a display that a discreet person or anyone over the age of fourteen wouldn't dream of. Loren's dad comes out of the bar armed with a frying pan, which I know from experience can shut us up. We immediately turn down the music.

"You morons!" Aroa cracks up. "You couldn't find a bigger one?"

"You know I like it with a little junk in the trunk!" I reply.

"Dad!" Loren yells as he climbs out. "Give me plastic chairs!"

"Where would I get those from?"

"From the goddamn terrace? And a table! The big foldout ones."

"Oh, of course! So when people come to have a beer I'll just have them sit on my lap, huh? You couldn't be more of an asshole if you tried."

Aroa and I flash each other a smile. We're used to the way Loren and his dad communicate.

"Is all your stuff in there?" I point at the backpack resting at her feet.

"Yeah. Except my sleeping bag." She turns halfway around to show me the roll strapped to her back.

I take her around to the luggage compartment and open it so she can put her stuff in. She's wearing her blond hair pulled back in a loose braid, hanging over one shoulder; an oversize black T-shirt; and jean shorts that show off her bronzed legs. On her feet, she's wearing old boots she must be boiling in.

I look down at my black V-neck cotton jumpsuit and my Converse that are still just as dirty as how I found them under my bed.

"I'm super excited about the bachelorette trip," I admit.

"Come on, girl. We're not exactly going to Tomorrowland."

"But it's Blanca's bachelorette trip."

"Um...right. Yeah."

But she doesn't sound very convinced. I don't know why, but something feels off here. Still, I keep my mouth shut and fake it.

"Hey, Coco... Did Marín leave yet?"

"Yes." I pretend not to care while I look for the streamers we're going to use to decorate the camper. "When I woke up, he was gone already. He left me a note on the kitchen counter saying he wouldn't be back again before I left."

Should I tell her he's coming to the campsite in Torrevieja on Wednesday? Or would that give her time to prepare, make herself even more stunning and make him fall in love with her forever?

"I think we're going to see him in Torrevieja. He has a gig there..."

Aroa doesn't let me finish. She grabs my waist, spins me around a few times, and picks me up, thrilled.

"Ah! It's destiny! This is a sign, Coco. This is the universe, bringing us together in Torrevieja. On the beach. The beach is our place. Any beach. Just the beach, in general. On our first trip together we made love on the beach, you know? And I came three times!"

I bite my tongue just before I say what I'm thinking: "Well, you know, it's kinda uncomfortable…with all that sand." It's not like I haven't had time to accept that Aroa and Marín were sleeping together. When they started doing it, it didn't bother me in the slightest. I still remember Loren and me stifling our laughter as they really went at it one Sunday in Marín's bedroom. I had to admit I was head over heels with Marín when the mere mention of him having sex gave me reflux.

"Coco!" Aroa exclaims, still thrilled. "You look like a guppy!"

"It must be love. It's in the air," I grumble. The fact that she only seems excited about this bachelorette party after Marín's name came up makes my morale fall a little. Aren't we supposed to be friends? I don't know if it's her or me—lately I've been so sensitive—but it makes me realize that, at some point, I must have become Marín's roommate to her and nothing more.

"Come on." She elbows me gently and smiles sweetly. "The Gus thing…"

I zone out as soon as I hear his name. What a nightmare.

"Did you see his poem today?" she interrupts herself. "Really intense. I mean… Blanca would kill me if she heard me say anything like this to you… But I think he's still hung up on you."

I furrow my brow. Too much information in one measly sentence.

"Look…"

Aroa pulls her phone out of the back pocket of her shorts and scrolls through Instagram until she finds the post of the day on Gus's profile and holds the device out to me. With all the excitement of going to pick up the RV, I hadn't even remembered to look.

The first thing I see is his face, and that's rare. He doesn't usually publish his poems with photos of himself, but there he is. With his neat beard, his round eyes, the shadow of chest hair peeking out from the neck of his shirt. I feel nothing when I see him, even though I know he looks good; I'm sure the 320 comments the post has already gotten are people who all think the same thing.

"The poem..." Aroa gestures at it, obviously thinking I'm so enraptured looking at him.

I'll get over it, I promise.
I just need a minute.
To breathe.
To close my eyes.
To swallow.
To stop yearning.
To stop smelling you when you're not here.
To banish your name, every version of it.
To tear your laughter from my head
and a winter from my skin.

Don't worry, you go ahead.
Let me feel like crap for a minute.
Let me cry for you,
feel pain,
miss what I missed before.
I just have to chew on my rage,
shame,
memory,
the lie,
that we made ourselves believe,
about what we were,

or were not.

I'm getting over it already.

I promise.

I gape at Aroa, and she nods smugly.

"Totally still sprung."

Okay, okay, okay. Calm down. Read it again. To stop yearning, smelling, your name, your laugh, a winter, having pain, memory, what we were.

"No way," I say nervously.

"Coco, why don't you message him and tell him to try to come on Wednesday? The Wednesday of love!"

"The Wednesday of what?"

Loren comes toward us, schlepping two plastic chairs that look like they came from the bar storage room.

"Wait, I'll help you."

"No, no." He drops them on the ground. "Tell me about this Wednesday of love."

"Marín's coming to see us in Torrevieja on Wednesday." Aroa claps excitedly. "And Gus is still in love with Coco. Look."

She snatches her phone out of my hand and gives it to Loren, who reads the poem.

"I hate poetry." He sighs, but he keeps flicking his gaze between the screen and my face, following what he's reading. "This…yeah. Well. Nothing new. Gus is a bummer."

"He's not a bummer!" Aroa exclaims. "He's in love!"

"He's a poet," I add, stealing the phone again to read it one more time.

"But Coco… You're not over him and…look. He's not either. Loren, get ready to spend the night under the Valencian moon because this"—she gives the "Millennium Alcohol" a few pats—"is going to become a love boat."

Aroa's hopping toward the bar like the light-filled being she is.

"Do you know anything about this?" I ask Loren, Aroa's phone still in my hand.

"No."

I stare at him. His mouth says no; his eyes say: *Don't ask me anything else.*

"Are you gonna make this a problem?"

"You're going to make this a problem yourself with all these lies. You should at least tell Blanca," he whispers seriously. "I've been telling you that for months. Faking being in love with Gus so no one suspects you're dying for Marín is not a good idea."

"Is Gus in love?"

"What do you care at this point?"

"Just so I know if he's gonna…"

"Now you're gonna play this movie? Coco, please, the four of us are going to be trapped in this RV together for a week."

~

I don't really get what his last comment is supposed to mean, but before I can ask him, his dad shows up with Aroa, who's happily toting two bottles of wine.

"Go on, sit down. I donated some red rations," Jose says.

"Dad, we have to go shopping!"

"Shopping, shopping, shopping…just take the wine and get out of here."

7

IN A RUSH

MARÍN

Noa is sitting in one of the chairs in the meeting room with a bored expression and her phone in her hand. If I could, I would make her eat it.

She's the snottiest teenager on the face of the planet. She wants everything, demands everything...and then she doesn't even appreciate any of it. My boss decided that I could get this girl "on the right track." Just because I don't scream, cry, kick doors, or throw things like some of my colleagues doesn't mean I don't have a limit. Although, to be honest, this girl crossed it a long time ago. And now I have to chaperone her on tour.

"And there won't be a makeup artist?" she asks sullenly, looking up from her brand-new phone for the first time.

"No," I say, flipping through the folder given to me by the poor intern whose job it is to take all the documents and organize them: tickets, the car rental, hotel information...

"Well, that sucks. Can't we demand one?"

I side-eye her mother, who's looking at her like she's afraid of a tantrum and only takes two seconds to beg me with her eyes to take charge.

"No. We can't demand one, Noa. The record company is the one who's eating the costs of all these gigs. It's promotion. Do you remember when we explained to you about promotion?"

"Fine then, you can eat the cost of the makeup artist too, right? I need to look pretty at the gigs."

She throws me a pseudo-seductive look, and I bite my upper lip, looking at her mother.

"Pilar, please," she says. "If Martin says it can't happen..."

A year working with them and she still doesn't remember that my name is Marín, not Martin. I sigh and run my fingers through my hair.

"Pilar..." I plead.

"My mother can call me Pilar, but you call me Noa, okay?"

I have a mental micro-orgasm imagining myself putting my hands around her neck and throttling her until dear little Pilar turns purple. I smile.

"There's no makeup," I give the final word. "Or hair. We've arranged the wardrobe with a brand you need to mention on social media."

"And who's gonna take the photos? You?"

I swallow. I've been tempted to talk to Coco hundreds of times about this girl and how much she pisses me off, but I never have because I think she would encourage me to kill her. Or she would do it herself. I don't want to spend the rest of my life in jail or have to take Tupperwares of tortilla to her in the women's prison.

~

When I leave the meeting room, the intern gives me a sympathetic look and I roll my eyes, taking advantage of the fact that they're behind me: a sixteen-year-old tyrant and a mother who doesn't know how to handle her. Any junior record label project manager's dream.

"I'll see you at four," I say to her mother. "At the station. Try to travel light. I'll bring the wardrobe. As soon as we get there, we'll pick up the rental car."

I walk them to the door and then slump into my chair. On my desk, besides the company-issued laptop and phone, I'm greeted by a mug smudged with coffee grounds and Coco's face smiling at me from the side. It's the worst photo in the world—she's cross-eyed, she has chocolate smeared on her teeth, and her hair looks like a bird's nest—but that's what makes it so funny. She has one with my face, with more or less the same expression, at her office. It was a secret Santa gift from Loren last year. Mine says "Sardine" and hers says "Anchovy." We're not exactly what you'd call normal in this group.

I see my boss come out of his office, and I jump up to try to intercept him.

"You're still here?" he says.

"The train doesn't leave until four thirty."

"Go on…" He stops and smiles. "Get out of here. Relax a little if you have time. You're going to need to muster a lot of patience."

"She can really sing, but…" I sigh.

"But she's a huge boob-buster."

I furrow my brow. "A…boob-buster?"

"Oh, yeah. My daughter says I have to make an example of eliminating micro-machismos from my language. At our house, we're smashing patriarchal language, and 'ballbuster' has negative connotations for women. So now they make me say 'boob-buster.'"

"Well, you won't believe it, but she's kinda right."

"This time she is. Not like when she told me I'd look good with a goatee."

"I don't know if I want kids." I smile at him.

"Gema turned out okay."

I can't help but laugh. Ever since I told him there are sixteen years between Gema and me, he's been convinced that she's actually my daughter. If he weren't so into music, he would've been great at writing soap operas.

I recover quickly. When I cross the threshold of the record label's imposing building, the temperature contrast makes me shiver. Or maybe it's an "itchy neck," an intuition. I won't be back for a month because I have time off after. Will I still be the same person?

I grab my phone and click on the first contact who shows up in my call log. She picks up on the third ring.

"Lemme guess, you're so bummed about missing the best bachelorette party in history that you just quit your job so you can join the camper crew?"

"I don't like the whole camper crew thing," I hear Loren say in the background.

"Coco..." I try to get her attention because she's cracking up. "Where are you?"

"On the patio of Loren's parents' bar."

"Are you all drunk already?"

"Aroa and I are a little. Loren's not. He's driving."

"Good." I check the time, ignoring Aroa's voice trying to tell me something through giggles in the background. "It's noon on a Monday. You're kicking things off right."

"Full throttle. What are you offering?"

"They gave me the morning off. I wanna give you all a hug before you leave. Will I make it in time?"

"Go to Blanca's house and keep her company. Something tells me we're gonna be late to pick her up."

"What time are you supposed to be there?"

"Eleven thirty."

"For fuck's sake..."

~

Blanca's wearing a black strapless dress and a denim shirt tied around her waist; she's ready for the adventure, and she smiles when she sees me at the door.

"I thought you weren't…?"

"I'm just here to say goodbye," I clarify before I give her a hug. "Where's Ruben?"

"He has stuff to do," she replies without missing a beat. "Do you want something to drink?"

"No. But you should probably take a shot or something to catch up."

"Do you know something?"

"I dragged it out of Coco yesterday." I shrug. "Don't worry. You'll like it."

She looks at the closed door, like she's expecting someone to burst through it at any moment.

"Did you come alone?"

"Yeah. I left the Huns' army stockpiling alcohol."

Blanca cackles and gives me a warm hug.

"Please tell me you imposed a little sanity on this bachelorette trip."

"I wish, Blanca, but they didn't let me have any say, honestly. I found out yesterday. The whole handcuffing-you-to-a-stripper thing seemed like a bad idea, but…"

She elbows me, and I let my laughter calm her down.

"Come on. I'm going to make you a lemonade while I drink straight from the bottle of Catalan cream liqueur I keep on hand for emergencies."

~~~

They screech around the corner on Blanca's narrow street like they're driving a Vespa instead of a fucking tank. A tank covered in streamers, to be specific. They're honking, waving their arms out of the windows, and blasting the music as loud as they can. The image looks like something out of a hellish music video directed by an insane monkey. Blanca covers her mouth with both hands and takes a deep, exaggerated breath.

Blanca's mouth is hanging wide open.
~~~

"You're too much, you bastards!!" she yells. I can't tell if she's horrified or charmed.

"I'm dying! I love youuuuu!"

Okay. Honestly, I'm seething with jealousy. Why the hell am I missing this? For a teenager named Pilar who makes everyone call her Noa. And to keep a job I love—that too.

I get the feeling they've forgotten I'm even there when they clamber out to hug the future bride, but Aroa wastes no time popping up in front of me.

"Thanks for coming," she says, biting her lip.

I know it's not exactly sordid, but the truth is…it's sexy. Everything about her is.

"No problem." I look away. "I wanted to give Blanca a hug."

"But we'll see you on Wednesday, right?"

"Yes." I nod. "But she doesn't know that."

"It's so great you're coming…" Her fingers caress the cotton of my T-shirt in a seemingly distracted way, but I take a step back.

She looks at me. I look at her. Fuck…

"Sardine!" I yell in Coco's direction.

"Talk to me, Anchovy."

She doesn't come over. I beckon to her, but she seems to resist coming closer.

"Come over here. You're so annoying," I tease.

She drags her feet over to us with a clear expression of disapproval: She must think we're flirting.

"What do you want?"

"You're not going to give me a kiss before you head off in the mobile club you're driving?"

She blinks kind of nervously, and I kiss her on the forehead.

"You grouch. You're like my sister when she goes on a trip…"

"Well, I'm fifteen in my head, so that tracks," she says self-deprecatingly.

"She's anxious because she just discovered Gus still loves her," Aroa pipes up.

I raise one eyebrow, and she looks at the ground automatically. "What's up with that?"

"Aroa's being paranoid. Come on, say goodbye. We have a lot of ground to cover."

I plant a kiss on Aroa's temple and immediately hurry over to the other two, not giving her a chance to respond. One more minute and she'd be on her tiptoes in front of me, looking deep into my eyes, biting her bottom lip, asking me for a kiss. And no.

"What's the deal with Gus still being in love with Coco?" I ask when I get close to Loren, who's tessellating Blanca's suitcase with the others in a kind of Tetris.

Both straighten up quickly without looking and smack their heads on the gleaming white frame of the camper.

"What?" They both say at the same time, rubbing their necks like it's choreographed.

"I don't know. Aroa just told me."

"Bah…" Loren waves it off. Aroa has always been kind of a romantic, it's true. "Anyway, what does it matter to you?" he asks, waggling his eyebrows.

"Dude, it smells like drama to me. I'm worried about Coco."

"Worry about yourself. Come on, honey."

I can't help furrowing my brow, but I don't say anything. I wouldn't know what to say if I wanted to.

I'm fine. I repeat it to myself every morning when I wake up. I'm fine. It hurts—of course, it hurts—but it's true what they say about time and breakups. Every day it hurts a little less. Although, I still have no idea how the hell we got to the point of no return, how the hell we spent so much time together and started to really get to know each other so late, how we didn't stop time to tackle what ended up happening. I don't know. I don't know anything. I don't even know if I still love her.

They almost leave without saying goodbye, in a cloud of giggles, cheers, and chants while I'm a mere bystander. I want to be climbing into the RV with them instead of standing there like a gawker, watching them take the music away with them. Besides my obvious predilection for Coco, who I would follow to the end of the earth, Blanca has always been special to me. So determined, so acerbic and intelligent. There's something magical about Blanca…and I'm missing her bachelorette trip.

"Be careful." I pat the gleaming bodywork a few times, like it's the flank of a huge but docile animal that they're riding off on.

"Have fun," Coco calls out with a wink, sticking her head out of the window.

"If you weren't my best friend, I'd pull your hair out," I joke.

"Jelly."

"And you know it."

Loren winks right before he starts up the engine. They leave a long black skid mark on the street, and I shove both hands in my pockets. What is this thing strangling my stomach? Am I worried about them? Am I jealous they're going to have fun for a few days and I'm not? Was it that look from Aroa? How weird Blanca has seemed for the last few months? Or…Coco? It's been really hard to hide everything that's been happening from her, and something tells me this trip is going to escalate a lot of things. Everything. Aroa's not going to be able to hide that there's not as much light in her as it seems for such a long period. Me either. My lies are starting to plague me.

I check the time, sigh, and start heading to the metro station.

8

ON THE ROAD

COCO

We have more than six hours on the road ahead of us, but Blanca doesn't know that. I turn my head and see her inspecting everything from her seat, blown away. About a year ago, getting tipsy on beer at El Viajero, we were both complaining about being clichéd adults who had never gone camping as kids.

"How can people expect me not to be basic when I don't even know what the inside of a tent looks like?" she said before she downed the rest of her glass.

Blanca is the daughter of an overprotective mother who was afraid her daughter would run off to join the circus and wouldn't survive the experience. Blanca now looks like unicorns are going to float out of her eyes on clouds of cotton candy every time she blinks. Every once in a while she just gives a little clap. She's so excited it's almost painful to let her believe our destination is some shitty campsite in the middle of nowhere.

"Loren, why don't we stop for lunch at a rest stop and then we can go straight there?" I whisper.

"Get the fuck outta here." He laughs. "I'd pay good money to see the face she's gonna make when she thinks we're going to sleep in the middle of nowhere."

"You did pay good money. This bachelorette trip cost an arm and a leg."

He waves his hand like it doesn't matter. None of us are loaded, but there are some things that, honestly, money can't buy.

"Hey," Loren says. "This whole Gus thing… You didn't believe it, right?"

"Believe what? That he's in love with me? No, not at all." I force out a giggle.

My ass is so tightly clenched I'm basically sitting on one butt cheek. A tiny part of me did believe it.

Gus has been writing some pretty intense poetry lately…the kind that would be impossible to write if you weren't in love with someone. When we were together, I didn't give a fuck, but that's because I knew our relationship was pretty superficial: wine and sex, going from one reading to the next, and not very much intimacy.

But now…he shows up with some excuse everywhere we go. He calls me much more often than usual (last week it was to tell me he had eaten an expired yogurt, for Christ's sake), and when we run into each other, sometimes he's smiling like a six-year-old who's been promised a piece of candy, and others, his brow is so furrowed you could hang curtains from it. I try to search through my memory… Those times he seemed so bitter… Was I with Marín?

God…I think I was.

I side-eye Loren, who shoots me a quick look.

The other day Gus told me I looked really beautiful. I caught him staring at my boobs when I bent down to pick up a coin. Didn't he wink at me when he said goodbye? Could he be jealous because he figured out I like Marín?

"Coco…" Loren whispers warningly. He must have been able to tell from my face that I was doing complicated mathematical calculations.

"What?"

"He's not in love with you. The last thing we need is for you to get obsessed with that now. We have enough going on."

"Like what?"

Loren looks in the rearview mirror to check that Blanca and Aroa are busy and not paying attention to us. "Marín. Marín and Aroa on Wednesday. And you. Great party."

"I'm not going to make a scene."

"I hope not." He sighs.

He runs his fingers through his hair. It's not the first trip we've gone on together. Something's bugging Loren.

~

The landscape gets drier as we get farther from Madrid. The sun is relentless, baking the yellowish weeds growing on the edge of the highway. The music is playing much more quietly now, but it seems like none of us have even noticed because there's still a festive vibe.

Aroa doesn't like silence because she says it feels very dry to her, so I've spent the last ten minutes waiting for her to break it with some inane question. I smile when I hear her say to Blanca, "When are you getting the dress back?"

"I'm not sure yet. They're going to call me, but...I guess I'll be able to pick it up the week before the wedding." Blanca inspects her nails, painted bright red. "One less thing."

"Everything else is all set already? Shoes, earrings, lingerie..." She raises her eyebrows suggestively.

"Lingerie? I'm planning on wearing the same underwear I do every other day."

"The seamless nude ones," I joke.

"Exactly."

"No!" But even though Aroa thinks this is a total deal-breaker, she still cracks up. "You can't do that! Nude?"

"What do you want me to wear? A red thong? Girl, the dress is nuclear white. You can see my veins through it!"

"Listen, lady… Find some pretty white-lace thong and a matching bra. I don't know. Something special. It's your wedding night."

Blanca snorts, making it clear she thinks it's bullshit, but Aroa doesn't back down.

"We'll get them for you."

"I think Blanca would like it better if we give her money to pay for the Roman bacchanal of a wedding dinner," Loren points out.

"Of course, but on top of that. We'll buy you the sexiest, most empowering set we can find."

"But why? Nobody fucks on their wedding night! The only thing I'm gonna want to do when we get home is take a shower and sleep until my leg hair grows."

"Yes, they do, dude!" The blondie cackles. "You should stay in a hotel that night and go at it, like newlyweds."

"Aroa, I have to confess something to you… Ruben and I are sinners and…we've already done it. You know… We've done stuff. Naked. We've done 'it.'"

Loren and I crack up.

"You idiot! I know you have a great sex life, but that night is special."

"What couple who've been together more than a year still have a great sex life?" Blanca asks, throwing her head back. "There are a lot of myths around the sex life of couples, but don't let that fool you. Your little cucumber itches, and you go in search of relief. No rose petals or fireworks."

"Well, Marín and I always had incredible sex, and we were together…"

Three years. You were together three years, I think bitterly.

"Like three years," she ends up saying. "And we still do." *Wait… Wait…*

Wait... Even now? When was the last time those two...? "Marín strokes me, and...I melt. Every time I look at his mouth, logic flies out the window, and all I want is for him to touch me, to kiss me"—*help*—"to lick me, fuck me up against a wall"—*seriously, kill me now*—"and for him to come, groaning, with his head thrown back..."

Loren takes his eyes off the road for a second and looks at me. There are probably patients in the middle of a rectal exam who are making cuter faces than me, but I turn back to them again and swallow.

"Isn't that how it was for you with Gus?" Aroa interrogates me.

"The thing is, the only thing Gus and I were good at was boning. And even so...there were issues."

"Issues?" Blanca raises her eyebrows. "You never said there were issues. Just that...that it was all explosive."

"It was." I look at the highway again as I nod. "We fucked like rabbits, sometimes for hours, but..."

"But? You're going to complain about a guy who can do it for hours?" Loren teases. "For hours, girl, what are you thinking? If I get to fifteen minutes I want a medal for the Spartan Race."

"I mean... It lasted hours because..." I look at Loren, who seems into the gossip even though he's concentrating on the road, and then at the girls, who are waiting with raised eyebrows for me to finish the sentence. "It's just that sometimes...he wouldn't come."

Aroa's chin drops, and she looks confused. "*He* wouldn't?"

I watch as we exit the highway and merge onto a smaller road that, a few meters later, turns into a kind of path. I guess Loren has decided this is an inhospitable enough place to play the prank on Blanca and make her believe this is the first stop on our trip. A decoy before we continue on to Torrevieja, where we've booked a site at a campsite that looks incredible. I look at Loren, who gives me a cute wink.

"Huh! He didn't come?" Aroa exclaims shrilly.

"Him. Like I always told all of you… I would come sometimes four times in a row. There were days I would go to work and even my eyelids hurt." I smiled to myself, remembering Gus pushing me onto my desk at my office and pulling my panties down while he whispered that I was filthy.

"And he didn't come?" Blanca is the one to insist this time.

"No. Not even a drop. Other times it would be so much I'd be glued to the headboard, to be fair."

"Come on, girl, you're so refined and elegant. By day you sell six-figure paintings to Madrid's high aristocracy, and by night you give soliloquies about semen," Loren says, side-eyeing me.

I cackle, and without thinking, I add, "Good times."

We all fall silent, and I repeat that phrase to myself. Good times. Yes, they were. Marín and I were best friends. Gus would grab my hand and lead me to great dive bars to drink wine and make out. They both made me laugh. Now I'm always weighing my words, in front of one or the other…

"You'll get back together. I know it."

Sometimes Aroa's optimism pisses me off, I have to admit it. I know her personal magic illuminates her every expression, always smiley, always so sweet…or her other favorite thing is to say what you want to hear, which kind of gives me the ick. But, no, Gus and I aren't getting back together, and it worries me that someone, even if that someone is Aroa, thinks it's so obvious.

"Are you going through a pre-wedding sexual crisis?" I ask Blanca to change the subject.

"No. I don't think that's it. It's just that…we're both so busy with work. We barely see each other."

"You work in the same office." I smile.

"Maybe that's the problem. We see each other too much without actually seeing each other."

Loren shifts uncomfortably in his seat, and I realize it's been more than two weeks since I've seen Ruben. I look at Blanca, whose gaze is lost on the road.

"Are you two okay?" I fire off point-blank, even though I should probably be asking her when we're alone because I know that deep down, Blanca is actually easiest to bully in smaller groups.

She looks at me too, and I know she's hesitating, even if it's just for a second, even if it's only internal, but she answers, "We're nervous about the wedding, and work doesn't help, but this bachelorette trip is going to be great. You have no idea how much I've been looking forward to this. The four of us alone, having fun… A whole week of vacation with my best friends in an RV. What more could I ask for?"

I can't really describe the roar that explodes outside, instantly infiltrating the passenger section of the vehicle. It's a bang, followed by a screeching noise from, I think, the brakes. We don't have time to think about it because Loren seems to lose control of the RV, which is making S's on the road for a few seconds that seem to last forever. The wheels are sliding around on the asphalt, causing a hell of a lot of smoke.

Aroa lets out a high-pitched cry, filled with anxiety.

When the RV finally brakes on the side of the road, I realize that Loren must have been holding his breath, because he sucks in a huge gulp of air before he looks at the three of us.

"Is everyone okay?"

"Fuck… That was terrifying! What was that?" Aroa cries out.

"Tell me we didn't hit anything! Please! Tell me we didn't hit anything!" Blanca prays in a howl.

"Fuck me and my spirit guide," I whisper.

All our voices mix into gibberish, and Loren unbuckles his seat belt and gets out without a word. For a moment, the only thing we can hear is the pebbles covering this rural road crunching under his sneakers.

When he pokes his head back in, he doesn't look like he has good news.

"First stop," he announces.

"Are you fucking kidding me?" Blanca complains. "If you're fucking with me to try to make me think you have nothing planned and that we're going to sleep in the middle of a field, the swerving wasn't necessary. You almost gave me a heart attack, you idiot."

"Fucking with you?" He laughs reluctantly. "Everyone out. We have a flat."

9

WHERE THE WIND TAKES US

COCO

We shouldn't have left Madrid so late. Even people in China could've told us that. It's five in the afternoon, it's already been an hour since our tire blew, and the roadside service from the insurance on the "Imperial Boozer Cruiser" can't find us. And it's not his fault, by the way. We're basically in the middle of a goat farm, and—guess what—there's enough service to make calls but no data, so we can't send him our location. Our attempts at giving directions don't seem to be helping, and we've already quelled three tantrums from the little emperor—that would be Loren.

This has set off Aroa's sometimes infuriating optimism.

"Come on, kids, we have chairs, a table, cold beers, and a bunch of left-overs from Loren's parents' bar... What else do we need? There's no rush."

The no rush part is relative. We don't know how long it will take to get hooked up to electricity and water at the campsite. But to do that...we'd have to get there first. We still have, if I had to guess, four hours of driving left, but we're stranded on a country road in the middle of nowhere, probably in Cuenca, but the harsh reality is that we don't know where we are. We obviously weren't paying very much attention to the signs on the highway.

"We're going to die here," Loren says, lifting a cold Coke to his lips.

"Have a beer, dude," Aroa says, trying to cheer him up. "One won't matter and it will help you lighten up a little."

"It won't matter? With my luck, the highway assistance will finally show up, they'll fix the tire. and two hundred meters later the Civil Guard will stop me and make me blow into something."

"It's one beer, dude, not a crack pipe," I say, giggling at how he blows everything out of proportion.

He shakes his head and hands over the Tupperware of Russian potato salad his mother made. It weighs as much as one of those newborns who make the news for being born the size of a toddler. And it's amazing.

Marín loves Russian potato salad. On Sundays, we often eat potato salad and Spanish tortilla, with our chairs in the living room and our feet propped up on the ledge of the almost nonexistent balcony. I make one dish; he makes the other.

I sigh.

"Why are you sighing?" Blanca asks me, putting her hand on my back. "Don't worry, Coco."

"I'm not worried," I lie.

"You are. I know you like I birthed you, but it's okay. This is just a little hiccup. One more story we can tell about the bachelorette party. It'll just add to the legend."

I see her smile and waggle her eyebrows as she sips her beer, and it makes me smile too.

"I wonder if Marín got there yet. Where was it he was going?" Aroa mutters dreamily.

God, she's so annoying about Marín. She can't talk about anything else lately. Or maybe she never did. Stop, Coco, you're being malicious. You just have a grudge against her because you think they're going to get back together.

She's taken off her socks and shoes and has her feet perched on Loren's chair to his abject horror. He doesn't like being touched by feet. Or getting too close to boobs.

"Do you dummies remember when we were planning this bachelorette trip and someone mentioned this could happen and we all cracked up?" he recalls.

We can hear cicadas chirping in the trees all around us, but nothing else. Not a single car has passed since we got the flat.

"It's like a typical Hollywood film where everyone's dead by the end," Loren moans. "And of course my character will be the first to die. Hollywood never liked homosexuals."

"Aroa will be the first to die, Loren. Beautiful blonds with big tits are always the first, usually when the murderer finds her taking a shower or having wild sex."

"Patriarchal language," Aroa points out with a smile. "That's how the movie industry indoctrinates us: The ones having a good time are the first to die."

"And the gays. The gays die first too."

"The virgin always survives… I still have a chance," I joke.

"Oh, yeah? Because I seem to remember that just a second ago you were howling during four-hour sex sessions with Gus," Aroa retorts.

"It's been so long since the last time I had sex, I think I've revirginized."

"Exaggerate much?" Loren laughs.

"Exaggerate? Of course…"

"How long has it been?" Blanca asks wickedly, with a sardonic smile.

"I'd have to try to remember."

"Well, go on, do it. As far as I know, the only entertainment we have right now is talking, and this is my bachelorette party… I was expecting a bunch of gruesome conversations about huge dicks and stuff like that."

"We do have a deck of cards," I quickly point out to my interrogators.

All three burst out laughing, but I was serious. I don't feel like trawling through my memory…or to inspire anyone else to. I don't want to find out that Aroa and Marín had sex yesterday morning or something.

"October of last year," I say, giving in to their stares.

They do mental calculations. I can almost hear them thinking November, December, January, February, March…up to August.

"Ten months? You really are a virgin! With who?"

The question, of course, is from Loren, who always wants to have all the tea on everything, including who we're banging, especially if it's the kind of guy who makes you do the walk of shame the next morning. He says we threaten his super-stable life (because he's been in a relationship for six years) and he lives vicariously through us, but I know it's because he loves giving us shit and our stories keep him up at night. They should take us to schools to talk about some of our experiences. We would be a really effective birth control method. Kids wouldn't even want to try it.

"With Gus."

Silence sits down at the table with us and serves itself a helping of potato salad. I shift uncomfortably.

"I didn't tell any of you because I was embarrassed," I add. "Too much of a cliché even for my boring ass."

Blanca smiles.

"So how? I mean," Aroa clarifies, "it's not like I want all the gory details, though that too. I mean how did it happen. And, considering you're so sprung on him, how?"

"I mean, the thing is"—I wriggle in my seat as I interrupt her—"it was so romantic and ethereal I didn't want to tell you so it wouldn't ruin the magic."

Loren laughs so hard he snorts Coca-Cola out of his nose. I think he might've clocked that I'm just fucking around.

"He sent me a message that said: 'I'm rereading that shitty poem I wrote to you about eating your cunt, and I got hard as a rock. Should we take a little stroll down memory lane?'"

"Please tell me he didn't say that." Aroa covers her eyes.

"That's what he said, sweetheart. Maybe he didn't use the word 'cunt'..."

"I'm sure he didn't. You just love adding that in whenever you can," points out Loren, who's always griping about how filthy-mouthed we are.

"But it was something like that."

"And it was good?" Aroa insists.

Was it good? I mean... Wouldn't the normal thing be gushing about the encounter and obsessing a little over the chance that it might mean something?

I fake a sad puppy face. "It was great, and it was exactly how it always was with us in bed."

"Smashing," Loren pipes up impishly.

"But now it's been more than, what was it? Nine months?"

"And she hasn't popped out a baby."

"Can you shut it already, funny guy?" I beg. "A long time has passed, and obviously any hope I had that it might mean something has gone to shit."

Plus, it was a disaster. We did it on my desk, and he hit his thigh on the corner and lost his erection and then eventually we came at the same time. Plus, we didn't have any condoms, and I made the terrible decision of letting him raw dog it. He had to stop twice so he wouldn't come inside me, and he ended up coming on my thigh. I took an early pregnancy test two weeks later because I was scared that my life would become three times weirder with an unwanted pregnancy.

"So how long has it been since you've had sex?" I ask Loren.

There's a silent exchange of looks between us. Mine is panic because I just realized that, in my attempt to change the subject, I started a round-robin that's going to lead to Aroa confessing when the last time she slept with Marín is and I don't think I can stomach it. Loren's look says he's going to rip me a new one as soon as he has the chance. He must be thinking I'm the biggest idiot.

"You're asking me at a good time… We had a little dry patch, but yesterday Damian came home from work all hot and heavy."

"And gave you yours," I point out wickedly.

"Yeah, and even yours too, which apparently you needed."

I crack up, and Blanca turns to Aroa.

"What about you? Drought or monsoon?"

"I guess somewhere in the middle." She shrugs and seems kind of mortified. "I slept with someone I was filming with a few weeks ago. It was a huge mistake."

"Marín and you haven't… You know… No relapses?"

I feel Loren's flip-flop connect with my shin, but I pretend I'm titanium and nothing can hurt me.

"Well…in the beginning we did a couple times, but not for months now. He says that if we've decided not to stay together, it doesn't make sense to keep sleeping together."

Dear God. Thank you. I'm going to start going to mass with my mother every Sunday. Well, not really, but maybe I'll go by a church and put a few euros in the altar to the patron saint of liars.

"Makes sense…if we knew why you broke up." Blanca makes a face. "Maybe this bachelorette party is the time to drag all the skeletons out of the closet and clear the air."

"Drop it," Loren murmurs, looking embarrassed. "Secrets are secrets."

"It's just that…" Aroa goes over to the table, picks up a fork, and plays with the potato salad. "You know, it's a couple thing, and we don't want it to tarnish the rest of the group. When we're all friends, it's hard to share this stuff. We decided at the time that there were 'irreconcilable differences' because, well, a couple doesn't always agree on the path they should take to keep growing and…"

"Okay, okay." Blanca nods at her. "We're not gonna peer pressure you. If it makes you uncomfortable, let's talk about something else."

"What about you?" Aroa returns the question.

"Well…it was…um…a month and a half ago."

"A month and a half?" Aroa and I yell at the same time.

"I told you we've been slacking off." She pushes her hair out of her eyes and makes a funny face.

"It's fine. It just means more passion for the honeymoon," Loren points out with a smile.

"Yeah, true," we all chorus.

Blanca springs up from her seat and looks into the distance. "What is that?"

"A car!"

"We're not going to die!"

"Come on, girls. Let's blow this popsicle stand. We have a lot of road to cover."

10

HELL

MARÍN

I figured in the mind of this sixteen-year-old girl, a fling with her manager from the label, who's fourteen years older, seemed viable, but I had no clue she would deploy all her "weapons of seduction" the second the tour started. Not with her sainted mother right there and definitely not so brazenly.

The fact that she's a spoiled child is obvious, and that I would never fall into that game is obvious too. I'm a thirty-year-old dude. But on top of all that, to her rabid frustration, the thing is I'm a pretty professional guy. I wouldn't get sucked into this mess even with the love of my life because I'd never get close enough to find out that's what she is.

Pilar touched my leg on the train while I was going over some stuff on the iPad. Her mother's head was lolling, and she was snoring softly across from us.

Get your hand off me or I'll rip it off. That's what I would've liked to say, but I restrained myself to politely moving it off and trying to talk to her about boundaries in professional relationships. And I say "try" because she cut me off to say, "Men and women can sometimes let themselves get carried away by their instincts and it's not that deep."

"Instincts?" I asked her. "But, Pilar…you're still practically a child."

I thought that brush-off would make her rethink whatever she was thinking, but all it did was encourage her. She inched closer to me and whispered, "Noa. I'm Noa to you. And, you know what, Marín? You smell so good I can't help but wonder what you taste like."

Welcome to hell, Marín.

Since that indecent proposal, I've counted twenty-six looks at my crotch, but the obvious kind, the kind a girl does when she wants you to know she's thinking about your equipment. Plus, she asked me if I can take photos of her outfits (after biting her lip in what she seems to think is a seductive way) and she made it clear that she doesn't wear a bra with some of them. I tried to beg her mother for help with my eyes, but Noa had sent her to find sparkling water. Sparkling water, of course, because the girl can't just drink a soda like any kid. No, she has to drink sparkling water and pretend it's a gin and tonic.

So…ever since the journey started, I've wished thirty times that she would fall off the stage. Nothing serious. A sprained ankle, a broken elbow…something that would prevent her from continuing the tour.

I thought about calling Coco and telling her all this, but I don't want to call her just to whine. Especially not when she didn't let slip the whole thing with Gus to me. Whose idea was it to tell Coco her ex was still in love with her? Gus is my buddy, but he's not the dude I want my best friend to be in love with, to be honest. He's not a bad guy, but he's all over the place, he has too many ass-kissers around him, and he's spent the last few months…

I don't want to tell Coco that I've seen him making out with women in practically every bar in Madrid since they broke up, that he even asked me explicitly not to tell anyone, I guess because he doesn't want to hurt her. Plus, I get the feeling he's hung up on someone else now. Gus is one of those guys who sleep with even more women when they start catching feelings for one.

~

I come out of my room and bump into Pilar in the hallway, apparently waiting for me.

"Hi," she says in a lazy way I guess she thinks is sexy.

I bite my tongue and don't say all the things I wish I could about what's actually sexy, like an adult woman who's secure in herself. But I sigh and reply, "Hi, Pilar."

I notice how much it bugs her that I won't call her by her stage name, but she recovers quickly because she's probably reading it as a game. Damn.

"Can you help me with my dress?"

"Isn't your mother around?"

"She doesn't know how."

"I find it hard to believe she doesn't know how to work a zipper," I snort. "You need to be ready in ten minutes."

I take two big strides and knock on her door. Her mother opens it, and the half-panicked look she always has in her eye makes me almost feel bad. Her daughter drives her crazy, and I get it, but she's her responsibility.

"Sorry...Pilar has to be ready in ten minutes"—*breathe, come on, this is the moment*—"and when I say ten, it has to be ten. A tour is not for amateurs, and I can guarantee the music industry has no time to waste on people who don't take their career seriously. We're investing resources in your daughter that could be dedicated to someone who is more committed and serious. Please don't waste my time."

I give Pilar a shameless, mischievous grin as I head toward my room. Her eyes are wide.

"Ten," I say slowly.

My boss is going to fire me.

~

When I close the door to my room, I have the urge to throw open the window and scream that I'm the king of the world or tear my shirt off while I howl, but instead I pick up the phone on my bedside table and dial Sardine.

"You're not gonna believe this," we say at the same time.

"You first," she says to me.

"I just went full domination with Pilar. You would've flipped. You're always saying I'm a pushover. Those flannel panties you wear would be on the floor!"

"First of all, they're not flannel."

"Whatever. They're ugly," I say, just to bug her, like I do every time I do the laundry and come across a pair.

"Second of all, I have my doubts that you were as tough as you think. You probably just seemed tough to yourself in a fit of macho pride."

I lean against the outdated dresser in my room in this hotel that's so… rural, and I smile. "Even I liked it. Tonight I'm going to fuck myself."

"Argh, God. This whole episode of phone masturbation is pretty weird. Plus, who the hell is Pilar?"

"The artist formerly known as Noa. Pilar is her real name."

"You shouldn't call her Pilar if you don't let her call you by your first name. Fair's fair, right?"

"Nobody calls me my name, honey, and…fair my ass."

"All this power is going to your head," she teases. "But…what's up? The little one is unbearable?"

"Unbearable is an understatement. You go. What's going on with you?"

"We blew a tire on the RV."

I almost burst out laughing, but I manage to contain myself and hope she keeps talking.

"In the middle of a country road. There was no 4G or 5G or even anyone who could find the G spot, considering how shook we all were.

We were stranded there for two hours, in the sun, waiting for highway assistance to find us."

"Did they find you or are you all going to get eaten by coyotes tonight?"

"I'd throw you to the coyotes, you jerk." I hear her laughing. "A car passed by, and they took Blanca, who we all know is the only responsible one in the group, to the nearest town, and from there she was able to give them directions on the phone, with the help of the man who picked her up, to our exact location. And they came to rescue us."

"Were they burly firefighters from a calendar?"

"They were the same age as my dad, and they looked like him too."

I picture their faces while two gentlemen with plumber cracks changed the tire… Fuck me, I have serious FOMO.

"Did you make it to Torrevieja in the end?"

"No way. We lost too much time, and then," she whispers, "Loren lost his shit." I hear him grumble in the background. "Yes, you did lose your shit, Loren."

They start arguing for a few seconds, and suddenly I hear her sigh. "He lost it, believe me."

"I believe you. How much longer do you have to go?"

"So far that we're considering stopping anywhere we find, even a service area, and spending the night there. We're tired, and we don't want any more accidents."

"Sounds good to me."

"Thanks, Dad."

"No worries, child."

"Argh. Gross," I hear her complain. "So what're you gonna do with this newfound gift of leadership?"

"Well, I'm going to get my stuff and take that girl to sound check, like I'm a pit bull."

"Like you're Pitbull the singer?"

I let out a chuckle, and it spreads to her.

"You have no idea how pissed I am to be missing this trip. I would've known how to change a tire," I point out, somewhere between sad and braggy.

"You don't even believe that yourself, dude. These wheels look like Optimus Prime's balls. But, I mean, I get it. You're dying to be with me. With us, I mean."

"With you all and with you." I emphasize the last word. "I'll let you go, Sardine."

"Stay salty, Anchovy. Over and out."

~

Noa is a little listless during sound check, but thinking back, I think it's the best one she's done to date. It's too bad she's such a pain in the ass, because she sings like she wants it. Someone must've given her bad advice and told her that if she wants to be treated like a star, to be respected as someone with the world at her feet, she has to be a tyrant, fickle and egotistical. It's kind of tragic.

Her dress is practically nonexistent but so eye-catching that even I have to admit it looks good on her. She looks less like a bratty teenager and more like an artist who we'll be trying to launch internationally within a year. I made my reservations about her shoes clear, but her mother says she's used to walking around in even higher heels and her feet never get tired.

We have dinner in a bar nearby, with the whole team involved, in one way or another, in this tour of summer concerts. Sound techs, project managers, road managers, artists, DJs, a few people from the radio station sponsoring this event…a lot of people. I'm watching Noa's act from the wings, checking out of the corner of my eye that everything's going smoothly. We did plenty of rehearsals, but it never hurts to be on the lookout. The bassist is playing when he's supposed to play, and she's singing when she's supposed to sing and dancing like she always does despite the heart-attack heels she's wearing.

I fix my gaze on the audience in the front rows. They're admiring this girl; they want to be like her; they think her life is everything they've always wanted: fame, money, youth, and beauty. They don't know the effort and the sacrifices Noa's career will entail if everything goes well; I don't even think she knows.

I have to stop thinking like this. It's the first day, and I'm already overwhelmed.

Cheers and applause alert me to the act ending. The event presenter goes over to Noa, mic in hand, and asks her a few short questions that consist of talking about how much is left to discover on her album, the rest of her tour dates, and, most importantly, the insane number of views her latest single is getting on YouTube. She answers; she's nice; she laughs; she almost makes me feel tender again. Maybe deep down my talks are having some effect and she'll turn into a person one of these days.

When she blows a kiss to the audience, I take that to mean she's ready to come backstage and I instinctively move toward her. I want to get her down from the stage safe and sound and get her back to the hotel with her mother. Then…

I see her wobble slightly and take another step forward. She stepped on a wire, but she only stumbles a little before she seems to recover her balance. I've been fantasizing all day about her falling off the stage, but I'm not really very clear on what would happen to me if that fantasy became a reality. I try to mime to her to be careful, pointing sternly at her heels, but I would've been better off shutting my big mouth because she's still mad at me for my attempt at a pep talk. She does one of her hair tosses, which gets most of her hair out of her face, but one strand of hair gets stuck on her glossy, shiny lips, and to top it all off, her false eyelashes don't help. Everything happens in slow motion: She steps on another cable, her ankle twists, she loses her balance, and her hair swoops like an arc across the sky, colored lights darting across it. Before the presenter can grab her arm and I start sprinting toward her, she vanishes into the pit between the stage and the audience.

Huh…now what?

11

THE CALL

COCO

Gema loves yapping with me. She likes lying next to me in my bed and telling me things that are nothing like the typical teenage worries. She's always given me old soul vibes. Marín spends a lot of time worrying about that. He's already told me a few times how worried he is that his sister might follow in his footsteps and end up not having an adolescence.

Gema's dream is to travel across Spain in a van. Not like us, of course. She wants one of those snub-nosed Volkswagens, decked out inside with a mattress and a kitchenette.

"I wanna go the summer after my first year in university. I'm already saving up."

I don't want to tell her that she won't be old enough by then to rent a car or that it's very unlikely she'll find someone to rent her a van with those specifications, but she's dreaming and next year she'll probably be all about, I don't know, imagining herself surfing in Hawaii. The important part of all this is that, thanks to her, I found a kind of forum where campers who are into this kind of travel have made a map of the places where you can wild camp with a motor home or a van, and thanks to Gema, that's where we are now.

It's the dead of night, and we've deviated from the route we were planning to follow, but we're all set up on our patio with plastic chairs and table. We can hear the sea and chattering from a few people who are camping about a hundred meters away. Until we stopped here, I had no idea how beautiful it would be to do this with my friends.

I call my mother once we've set up camp. She says she's drinking a cocktail with a very exotic-sounding name and that she's painted something beautiful. She tells me to have fun; she asks me if I miss Marín and then says she thinks she wants to adopt a dog. She barely gives any time to answer between one thing and the next. My mother is... scatterbrained. She's not your typical mother. She worries—of course, she does—but she tends to infuse her head scratchings with a hilarious, Dalí-esque tone: If she tells me to be careful, not to talk to anyone on the street and other things mothers say, she always adds something surreal to spruce it up, like "Do you believe in reptilians, Coco? I don't, but there's a woman in this neighborhood who sometimes makes me wonder." I want to be like her when I grow up. She's...simply lovely. When we say goodbye, she tells me to have fun and live a little on the wild side so I can tell her interesting things when I get back. That's who she is.

Blanca's making a Greek salad in the kitchen of the camper with Loren's help. It's very efficient, but it's a cramped space, and they told me that just standing there in the middle, frozen like a moron, wasn't actually a big help, so they threw me out. Well, actually they asked me to set the table and relax with a beer. And that's what I'm doing.

Next to me, Aroa is toying with her phone. I don't want to ask her if she's WhatsApping Marín. My phone is resting on a stack of paper napkins, stopping them from blowing away in the wind. I messaged Gema to tell her she would love this, and after I spoke to my mother, I have no other reason to keep it in my hand.

My eyes are adjusting to the pristine darkness, and the sea is beautiful, dappled with silver shards of the moon's reflection. Calm. It's been a long time since I've felt like everything was this peaceful.

"Poem."

Aroa doesn't add anything else. When I look at her, the light of her phone shows her mischievous expression.

"What?"

"Gus posted another poem. Don't you wanna read it?"

No. No, I don't want to, but I nod and reach over so she can give me her phone.

If you miss me,
say it.
Say it drips in your chest,
pools during the day
and overflows into someone else's mouth at night.
Say that I'm part of your symphony of silence,
say that it's not worth the pain,
but here we are.

Shit. This is the first time in more than a year that I've bothered wondering who the muse behind all this is.

"Fuck, Coco, that's so beautiful."

"I guess." I hand back her phone and glance at mine out of the corner of my eye.

"Why don't you write something to him?"

"What for? I'm sure this is for some other girl."

"But what if it's not? I don't think it is."

"Do you want to keep going with beer or should we open a bottle of wine?" Blanca is looking at us, her silhouette illuminated by the light from inside the camper.

"Probably better to stick with beers," says Aroa.

"What are you two talking about?"

"Gus posted another poem."

"Another one?" She seems surprised.

"Yes. Another one about missing someone. Wanna read it? It's really beautiful."

"I hope he makes you president of his fan club." She sighs and flops into an empty chair. "Hand it over, then."

I study her expression while she reads it, but Blanca never really liked poetry, so this outpouring of words doesn't seem to impress her much.

"Pretty, I guess."

"I was telling Coco she should message him."

"Stop putting shit in her head." She sighs. "Coco, you do you, but if you want to forget him, the best thing to do is put space between him, this stuff, and you. Think about it… It could be for anyone. Or twenty girls all at once. You know Gus…"

Yes, I know him, and that's why I know this isn't some poem he just randomly dashed off or wrote to try to sweet-talk the girls he's flirting with or seeing right now. No. This is for someone specific, for someone flesh and blood, with fingers that have caressed his skin and made him feel at home.

Before I can add anything else, my phone starts vibrating quietly, muffled by the napkins it's holding down. I swap it with the beer I'm holding, and I can't help feeling a jolt of trepidation when I see that it's Gus. Calling me now? What does he want?

"It's him!" Aroa claps giddily. "OMG, love is going to win this week!"

Blanca looks tormented as I stand up and move a few steps away to answer.

"What's up, gangster?" I try to sound like always, like before Aroa planted this seed in my head. Does Gus want to get back together?

"Coco Puff..."

His voice sounds younger than he'd like. He says it makes him lose credibility at his readings, but I always thought it was a surefire weapon for his target audience: women predestined to fall in love with him platonically through his words. People in love with love.

"What's going on?"

"What's up?" he answers with another question. "Did you make it?"

"A series of unfortunate catastrophes knocked us off our route. We're missing a night at the campsite, but we're at a beach where you can camp, and...it's pretty cool."

It's pretty cool? Since when am I fifteen again?

"I'm glad. You have to go with the flow, Coco Puff."

"Did you call to check up on our physical well-being, or do you need something?"

"I can't call a friend just to talk?"

"That's not usually how this goes. What are you doing?"

"I'm at home."

"Alone?"

"No, I have five Playboy bunnies doused in cum and sweat in my bed."

"God, you're an idiot." I laugh and rub my eyes. "Are you okay?"

"Why wouldn't I be?"

"I don't know. You sound sad."

"I'm a poet."

"Sorry, I forgot. Gustavo Adolfo Becquer."

"Great, dusting off all my favorite nicknames," he adds petulantly.

"What's going on with you?"

"I should have come with you."

"It was pretty spendy. Don't worry, we get it."

"Yeah, well, I should have saved up by buying fewer bottles of wine."

I raise my eyebrows. Gus isn't the type to open up, especially not so easily. So now he's admitting he could have done something better… That's weird. Very weird. He usually reserves that for fights and breakups. He's the king of admitting mistakes when it's too late, but I've got him pegged… He's doing this because he doesn't want to fix the situation.

"Are you okay?"

"I'm lonely."

"Are you drunk?" I suddenly blurt out.

"Yeah. I think so."

"You got drunk alone?"

"I met up with a beautiful brunette, tiny, one of those I can toss around in bed with one hand. She wanted it. I did too."

I take a deep breath. I'm worried about my friend.

"Are you sad because you couldn't get it up?"

"Not getting it up would imply that I dropped my pants, which I didn't. I walked her to a subway station and then headed to Atocha alone."

"You didn't even make out with her?"

"I said I didn't drop my pants, not that I've suddenly become a monk."

He makes me smile.

"Does me talking about this… Does it hurt you?" he asks.

Jeez…he really is drunk. He's being such a weirdo. "No," I confess. "It doesn't hurt. I like knowing that you're human," I say playfully.

"I mean it… I don't want to hurt you."

"You're not. We're friends."

There's a strange pause. God… I should have made it clear months ago that I'm in love with Marín.

"How's it all going out there?" he asks again. "Are you all having a good time?"

"Yeah. We're about to eat dinner. We decided to take it easy this week. It wouldn't be bad for Blanca to slow down her pace of life a little. She's going to be the youngest partner at the firm but also the first one to have a heart attack in the middle of a trial."

"You have to take care of her. She never takes care of herself. She spends two hundred bucks on a bottle of lotion, but then..."

"Good old Blanca." I laugh.

Another silence.

"If I had the chance to go, I would," he says out of nowhere. "If Marín were free, we'd both come. We'd book a motel next to wherever you are. We could all be together. This whole bachelorette trip is kind of just an excuse, right? A chance to all hang out together, to make the most of the summer. We're always saying we're going to go to all these places, but we never do."

"Yeah. I guess so." *Should I tell him Marín is coming on Wednesday?* Before I even get the chance to bring it up, he barrels on.

"And now Blanca's getting married, and well... Nothing's going to be the same ever again."

"It'll be the same," I assure him. Is he having some kind of identity crisis? A turning-thirty crisis? "Hey, Gus... That poem you posted a little while ago..."

"Yeah, what about it? Did you like it? Short but intense, right?"

"Yeah, yes, I really liked it. But, listen... Who's it for?"

For a second I think he's going to tell me and I'm scared. If he says, "Coco Puff, it's for you," the world will collapse in on me. If he tells me it's for someone else...that would almost be comforting, right? But none of that happens.

"Poetry isn't written for anyone, Coco Puff. It's just there and you get sparked by some random phrase. It isn't an exact science. It's not as precise as putting a price on a painting and selling it."

There's no judgment in his voice, but I can tell he's lying.

My phone vibrates on my ear. It's a WhatsApp; when I pull the phone away from my ear, I see it's from Marín, so I hurry to end the conversation.

"Go to bed, sleep it off, and stop being sad, Gus. Being a poet doesn't mean you have to feel like someone who threw himself into the sea in the middle of a storm because some woman didn't love him."

"I'm so fucking bored," he moans. "You all abandoned me."

"And your dick doesn't work."

"It does work! Do you want me to send you a video of it working in my hand?"

"No, thaaaaannnkkkk you…" I exaggerate the sound of the consonants. "Call me tomorrow and give me an update on your state of mind. You're kinda freaking me out."

"Bah, don't act like my mom. I'm more into your wild side. Have fun, but don't go too far. I know it won't be the same without me."

"Obvs" is all I can say.

"Good night, Coco Puff. Take care of each other. You know."

I hold the phone up to my ear for a few more seconds, still with surprise on my face. He threw me off my game, and I don't really get what's going on with Gus, but something is happening. I was going to tell him that we're meeting up with Marín on Wednesday, but he left me so shook. I'll put it to a vote before I say anything. Anyway, is he really gonna trek all the way across Spain just to spend one night with us?

Suddenly, I remember Marín's message and grab my phone again.

She fell off the stage. Coco…she fell off the stage. I went around all day wishing she would break her ankle and she fell off the stage. Five stitches in her chin, a dislocated shoulder and a sprained leg. She went down like a sack of potatoes.

I just left the emergency room pushing a wheelchair with Noa sitting in it, the star I'm meant to be taking care of and polishing up, all groggy from all the painkillers. The

> call from my boss was surreal. My boss's boss was yelling, which was disconcerting because he wasn't even yelling at me. But anyway...this is my destiny. I don't really know if I'll end up like the boy in the café, but whatever. Anyway, I suddenly have time off and a rental car. What are we doing?

I have to reread the message three times before I understand it all. When I do, the biggest and stupidest grin in the world takes over my face.

So...what are we doing?

12

DON'T TRY TO ESCAPE YOUR DESTINY

COCO

I have to confess that my more chill side took comfort knowing that Marín couldn't just sign on for this bachelorette trip. Even someone as crazy in love as me appreciates some time lying fallow, a space without the other to think clearly. Feelings colonize you. Everything turns into data to be analyzed. Anything that can ostensibly be broken down into a sliver of hope will just make your anxiety spike.

So these days were supposed to be a peaceful sanctuary, the camping equivalent of going to Tibet to meditate with a bunch of Buddhist monks who if asked the question "What should I do about my feelings for Marín?" would answer "Ommmmm."

But no. Of course not. Because Noa broke her neck and now Marín is on vacation. And Gus is acting like a high-key weirdo.

I answer Marín's message:

COCO:

Yay, Anchovy, you're on vacation! Now all you have to decide is…what to do with the time that is given to you. Gandalf said that, not me.

He didn't answer, but I can hear the cogs of the universe turning behind me. Even the sky has a weird sheen to it. Or maybe it's just me, riddled with anxiety, nerves, and chills.

The waves roll steadily onto the shore, rhythmically breaking on the sand and making a kind of music. There's a muggy but pleasant breeze for one of those summer nights that would be suffocating in Madrid. While everyone else is pulling on jackets, organizing the disaster of their suitcases strewn across every surface in the camper, and planning what to drink, I'm sitting on the sand. And thinking. Thinking about Gus. Thinking about Marín. And ultimately, I realize I'm not even considering myself. My feelings for my best friend have eaten my life and vomited up something that resembles me.

Someone sits down next to me, and I'm not surprised to see that it's Loren. He has a cigarette dangling from his lips, and he raises his eyebrows expectantly. He knows something's going on, even though I haven't said a word because I don't want Aroa to catch on and I need time to transform my goofy, loved-up smile into something that looks more like friendship.

"What's going on?" he asks. "Is it about Gus?"

"No. It's about Marín," I whisper back. "He sent me a message. The girl he's chaperoning ate shit and she must've broken all her teeth."

"What?" he laughs.

"She fell off the stage. Marín is off work."

"And he told you he's coming?" Loren doesn't even try to hide how worrying he finds that prospect. "Please tell me he didn't."

"He didn't say it, but I think he's expecting us to call him all excited and tell him he has to come."

"That's exactly what's gonna happen." Loren rubs his eyes. "Aroa'll be all over it. You know you're gonna have to see them…?"

"Yes." I cut him off. "That's why it made me really happy when he first said it, but now…"

"Now what?" Blanca's voice startles both of us.

We didn't hear her walking across the sand toward us. She's barefoot and smiling.

"Marín's girl is busted," Loren tells her.

If someone gave me that little information, I'd have no idea how to reconstruct it, but Blanca smiles like she understands.

"Don't tell Aroa," she says with an enigmatic smile.

For a minute I'm sure she knows, but I suddenly figure out she's saying that because she's so pragmatic. Aroa's enthusiasm about the reconciliation must've seemed a little extra to her. Actually, I think Blanca's been harboring a little grudge against her ever since we realized she only cares about our friendship if it involves Marín, but Blanca will never say anything because she doesn't want to make a scene.

Blanca is really into chewing things over by herself and being very discerning about situations. I'm guessing she doesn't get where all this hope for them getting back together comes from. Aroa seems pretty sure it's just a matter of time, and she keeps droning on about it. I hear her, and...I believe it.

When Aroa reaches us, she's doing that happy walk that makes her look like she's dancing. She's graceful, elegant... She deserves Marín. "Anyone thirsty?" she asks with a grin.

"Let's get drunk," I say.

"And tell embarrassing stories," Loren pipes up, holding up a plastic glass that makes the red wine look like a black hole.

"Yeah? Well, let me start." Blanca rubs her hands together. "Did I ever tell you how this one time, at the office, I sneezed so hard I farted?"

~

Blanca's phone lights up a few times in the night, when we're all in bed. I only notice because she's sleeping next to me, in the bed in the roof of the camper, right above the driver and passenger seats. I'm half-asleep, and I feel like that mixed with the cocktail of wine and the shots we took as we giggled over every fart story has left me in kind of a daze. In the end, I figure it must be Ruben, trying to say good night to her. All I know is she answers concisely, and she's wide awake because Blanca never sleeps much, and she puts the phone back on top of the cupboard…face down.

Loren snores like a freight train.

Aroa looks like a nymph floating in the water on the bottom bunk. A few strands of her hair have slipped over the edge and fall in a cascade, pale, soft… All she needs is a few lotuses floating around her.

We left all the RV's hinged windows open with the bug screens in, but there isn't enough air flow in the morning to prevent it from being hot despite us all sleeping uncovered on top of our sleeping bags. There isn't even a hint of last night's slightly humid, refreshing, almost chilly breeze. Blanca isn't next to me, and I find her outside. She's tidied up the stuff we left last night on the table, too drunk and tired to worry about a few scraps. She's sitting in a sliver of shade and smoking a cigarette peacefully; the smile she gives me when she sees me appear through the door is a gift.

"Coquito," she whispers. "Tell me you want a coffee."

"Just one? I want a tanker truck full of coffee. Should we wake them up?"

"Them? You mean 'him.' Aroa's on the beach doing yoga."

I peer into the distance and spot her figure contorting into impossible positions. If I tried to imitate her, I'd have to be transported to a hospital in a helicopter.

We get the coffee maker boiling, and we put everything back in its place to clear space before Loren wakes up.

"Tomato toast?" Aroa asks when she walks up, barely ruffled, her skin just tinged a little pink from the exercise. "I'm going to take a shower and then I'll help. Come on, Loren, out of your hibernation! I know beauty sleep is important, but you can make up for it by drinking water."

"Water is for mermaids," he mumbles, still not very coherent.

I sit in the tiny living room while the coffee bubbles away. Blanca is in the seat opposite, and we're both clutching our phones. I'm sure she's checking her email while I open Instagram.

Poem. Of course. The photograph above it is a table full of manuscripts. The only words one can make out on one of the papers, much larger than the rest and in much more striking handwriting, are "I fell first."

Will you think about me?
Will you miss me?
Will you wonder too if everything went wrong because we tugged too hard?
Maybe you'll think,
like I do,
about when was the moment it all turned.

I think about you,
sometimes more than I'd like.
I'd like to banish you,
but you anointed your forehead with my fluid
and now you are the mistress of this empty wasteland
that dreams of you.

I miss you too.
I yearn for the crumbs of time we scraped up
with excuses and fear.
I yearn for the mood swings,
the nerves (your nerves),
the faint scent of your perfume on my clothes,
lingering from our farewell embrace,

sometimes with a kiss,
mostly just wishing we could.

You wouldn't believe it, but
I ruminate on my mistakes all the time,
I question my certainties,
I make holes in my memories,
until I find that corner,
that one,
and curl up in it.
In the sound of your voice,
in the raspy notes,
and the thick words you would speak to me.
In the surprise of your mouth,
making me feel so young,
Frolicking in bed,
in the smell of spit,
sex
and drama.
In the end I always wind up believing
that the first place it went wrong was in my head.
I fell first.

I look at Blanca out of the corner of my eye, but she doesn't seem to have noticed that I'm freaking out. She's still absorbed in her screen until her phone starts vibrating in her hand and she jumps.

"Fuck, that scared me." She laughs. "It's Marín."

"Why do people have to call at the crack of dawn? Why do you all have to be awake? Why me?" Loren whimpers from his bunk before he dramatically swishes the curtain shut, trying to keep sleeping.

"Tell me she broke a tooth."

Blanca smiles and then cackles.

Is he coming? Of course he's coming. I can picture his clear eyes, his tousled hair, which is actually strategically designed to look natural, biting his bottom lip as he smiles. I'm sure the hand that isn't holding the phone is fidgeting with his messy hair and he's leaning on a table, in some random coffee shop, while his coffee cools down a little.

"Huh?" Blanca's tone catches my attention. She seems kind of alert, uncomfortable. "You think so? I mean…" She looks at me slyly as she stands up. "You know better than me, but…don't you think that could be a little…?"

Blanca is far enough away that the sound is fading.

"Is it Marín?"

Next to me, drenched and half-naked, is Aroa.

"If you keep looking at me like that, I'm going to think about having an affair with you," she jokes as she dries her hair in a towel even smaller than the one wrapped around her…so basically a napkin.

"Sorry. It's just you look amazing and I hate you with a burning passion."

She sucks her teeth with a smile and sits down across from me. "Is it Marín?"

"It's Marín," I confirm.

"He's coming sooner, I'm telling you."

She's excited when she says it, giddy, and I suddenly want to die because Gus's poem pops up in my mind. I stand up in time to hide the internal torture on my face, saved by the burbling of the coffee maker on the stovetop.

"The coffee smells so good!"

"Please shut your mouths for once in your lives, you gaggle of whores." Loren always likes to mix politeness with insults.

"Call your boyfriend and tell him you're alive, lazybones," I order him. "Poor Damian is left without a partner every time you go out with us. He's going to be so sick of us by the end of all this."

"Now?" he whines childishly.

"Now. Come on."

He mutters something, but I hear him rustling around in his sleeping bag and then whispering, "Memels…," which in their love language means "baby."

I take advantage of him being occupied to get Aroa's attention. "Listen, Aroa," I whisper, but not because I don't want to disturb Loren.

"Talk to me."

"Did you see Gus's poem?"

"No!" she exclaims. "Is that it? Show me!"

I lift my chin toward my phone and go over to the small but hardworking fridge to pull out a package of turkey slices and a small can of crushed tomato.

"Oh, God, Coco." She rests her chin on her elbow looking dreamy. "You must be on cloud nine right now."

"That's not for me," I assure her.

"How can it not be? What other girl could it possibly be about?"

"It could be about other girlssss," I emphasize the plural, still speaking softly.

"This is for you. Missing you, reconsidering his mistakes, sad that it ended… I think it's super obvious he wants to get back together with you."

"To me it sounds more like he fucked it up with someone and instead of saying, 'I love you' to her face-to-face he's spreading his pain around social media."

I get nervous and push my hair off my forehead.

"You're mad," she declares with her doll-like face. "And that's normal. Breakups make anger build up. Even the most microscopic detail in the world can turn into drama between two people who can't figure out how to function, but there's no reason to throw in the towel at the first chance."

I stare at her, and I know she's talking about herself and Marín.

"Write to him. Tell him it's a beautiful poem. Ask him if he's less of a sad poet than last night. I don't know… Start a conversation. Don't make him shoulder all the weight."

I swear I'm starting to consider it when Blanca comes back into the camper, and when she does, the air fills with tension.

"Aroa, can you open more of the blinds?"

"Of course."

She hops up half-naked, and Blanca rolls her eyes and sighs.

"Jesus, you're so hot. Sometimes I question whether you and I are from the same planet."

"You're a dumbass." Aroa gives a flattered laugh. "What did Marín say? Is he okay?"

"Yeah. Listen…" She pulls back the curtain of the bunk where Loren is clutching his phone in the fetal position. He's in a stupor, talking to his boyfriend. "Hey! Can you come back from the dead for a minute? Thanks."

"Of course, sweetie, of course. It's just that you're such a drag," he says into the phone. "I'll let you go. Blanca thinks she's Julie Andrews in *The Sound of Music*."

Aroa and I stifle our laughter.

"Are we having breakfast inside or out?" I ask.

"Outside, right? It's not that hot yet, and that way we'll get a little sun. We all need more vitamin D, my loves," Aroa points out.

"Ladies…and gentleman. Um, Marín called," Blanca says.

"He's coming, right?" I pipe up.

"Yes. He's on the way."

My heart pounds in my chest. Boom, boom, boom, boom…like a

Viking war drum. I feel like everyone can hear it, and the vein in my temple is throbbing like a neon sign on the fucking Vegas strip. I'm holding my breath.

"He's on the way to the station to pick up Gus. I don't know what you have planned, so I told them to ask you for the location of the campsite we're going to. I do know we're going to a campsite because he let it slip, but don't get mad at him, the poor thing."

I hear Loren snort. He's trying to be discreet, but he can't. And I get it. Marín here. With Gus. Good thing Marín is the only one who can get Gus to be less intense than normal, but…the two of them. Here.

The poems.

The melancholy.

Romantic ideas.

The possibility of being wrong, confused.

A round of applause breaks my confused, chaotic stream of consciousness. It's coming from Aroa, who's clapping euphorically and endlessly. She adds in a few little jumps, which makes her micro-towel slip to the floor and leaves her butt naked in front of us in all her glory.

Great. Gus and Marín here…

With Aroa.

Why does that bother me so much?

13

CHANGE OF PLANS

MARÍN

I have to admit that Gus was never one of my favorite people in the world. He embodies everything we're sold as what you have to do to be a successful dude, but nothing I would aspire to turning into. Don't get me wrong... I admire him. He took his passion and turned it into something that could reach the whole world. But...let's be honest: He's cocky, the classic fuckboy who never wants to compromise, the kind who always has the perfect line some girl won't be able to get out of her head the rest of the night (or the rest of her life, which I'm scared might be the case with Coco). He has a cock worthy of a porn star, and most of the time, he acts like one. He writes poems about love, but he doesn't want it. He avoids it, and sometimes, in my opinion, it even pisses him off. He's a character from a book, walking around in the street. A shameless peacock, a big drinker, and even though I don't think he's an alcoholic (I know that problem very intimately), he's on the way to developing an addiction to rough sex. And a systematic emotional block. One day he's going to end up on his ass.

But that's the CliffsNotes version. But knowing him... Really knowing him gives him other nuances, because the truth is he's fun, charming, a nutjob, and a good companion. As guys we can sometimes get all weird about being intense with other guys and talking about the lightness of being, but you can do that with Gus. Plus, he gives good advice…which I never take. And he has intense feelings. He feels things like a punch in the gut.

That's why, this morning, when I had tied up all the loose ends after Noa's accident and I was left alone in my hotel room, lying down, fully clothed and staring at the ceiling, he popped into my head. Yesterday, after I texted Coco, I sent him a message describing the whole mess with Noa. Two seconds later he was calling me to suggest we go join the bachelorette trip. I told him I'd let him know, that I had to think about it because…I don't know, I was scared of just showing up there and messing up the plan. I thought Coco would scream at the top of her lungs and be tripping over herself to invite me to join Blanca's bachelorette trip now that I'm off work, but she didn't. She pointed out that this was a good time to think about what I want to do. And that's a trap because let's be honest, I should go to my grandparents', pick up my sister, and take her somewhere, camping just the two of us or to do something fun. And I want to, but…I also want to be a thirty-year-old dude without family or money worries, at least for four days.

But first I called Gema.

"I'm free. The brat took a tumble yesterday, and she's with Jesus now."

"She died?"

"Fuck no."

"If an artist dies on you, you'll totally get fired, big bro."

"You're always so worried about my emotions. Hey…what should we do?"

"What should we do about what?"

"I'm free, cutie. I'm on vacation. Should we plan something?"

"Aren't you going to Blanca's bachelorette party?"

"Do you think I should?"

Gema cracked up.

"I'm the teenager here."

"Should I go or not? I'd have to play the supercool big brother."

"Supercool? OMG, you're super annoying. What are you gonna tell me next, that you invented the wheel?"

"Actually…we'll have more time for us to do something now that I'm not going to be with Noa on tour. I could… I could do both, you know? Go to Blanca's bachelorette trip for a few days and then come pick you up and…"

"You could also come pick me up and take me to the bachelorette party with you."

"You'd be bored stiff," I lied.

"No way. Coco texted me yesterday and told me I would love it. Take me."

"No, and that's my final answer. We're not going there under any circumstances, Gema."

"Okay. Then don't take me," she grumbled. "But you should go and get your ass wet at the beach. And do something fun… You're like one of those monks who do scary chants."

So I called Gus and said we should go. If we both go, the whole gang'll be there, which is how it should have been from the start. All of us together, putting any bullshit aside, like my breakup with Aroa and the strange tug-of-war between Gus and Coco. Our personal shit doesn't matter; all that matters is us as a group. Lately I've been tormented by the idea that we're drifting apart, and I feel responsible. That's what happens when you go out with someone from the gang for years; when everything ends it affects more than just the two of you.

Gus seemed to be waiting for my call. He didn't even ask many questions. Just where are we meeting, if I would pick him up at the station, and if I needed anything from Madrid. I was about to ask him to bring me a pair of balls for when Aroa's insistence breaks mine.

Aroa was the first one to send me a message when she found out we were coming.

AROA:

Dear Marín,

👯 🥳 Let the good times roll! I can't wait for you to get here... 🥳 🥳 👯

I see Gus get off the train with a duffel bag slung over his shoulder. He couldn't have a wheely suitcase like everyone else. No. He has to put his stuff in that bag that's so like a hipster New York writer's. He's wearing a worn, dark-gray T-shirt and a pair of skinny black jeans that are a little saggy at the waist. I think Coco will like it. Shit, Coco...you're going to get sucked back in by someone who one night you confessed to me was number one on the list of guys who aren't good for you and in some way I'm going to feel like I caused it.

We head toward each other at the same time, and when he's in front of me, he throws his bag to the ground and hugs me, slapping me on the back.

"Fuck, Gus, your hugs are like the Heimlich maneuver. One day I'm going to spit out my spleen."

"You're such a wimp, " he quips. "Guys should hug too."

"Interesting reflection coming from a guy who's never said, 'I love you.'"

"I have to my mom. I say it to my mom every day," he lies easily. He grabs the sunglasses hanging from the neck of his shirt and puts them on before he leans down and hoists his bag up. "So what? Are we going?"

"Yes, we're going. On the way you can tell me all about the poetry scene in Williamsburg, you hipster."

"This is style, not fashion."

He sweeps his hands up and down his outfit. A few girls are undressing him with their eyes as they pass. He'll never be an objectively handsome guy, but he'll never need to.

As I drive to the address Loren sent me, Gus updates me on his projects and tells me stuff about his work routines. "You have to read Kerouac, Marín. You really have to."

"If Lorenzo were here, he'd shut you up with a punch."

"I know." He flashes his imperfect teeth in a wolfish smile. "Remind me to talk about this stuff when I see him. I love getting him all riled up."

"And provoking Coco," I slip in there.

I regret it the second I say it because he glances over at me with one eyebrow raised, looking like he's hesitating, and I would bet he's a little freaked out by my statement.

"What are you talking about?"

"I don't know. The poems..."

I actually haven't read those poems; I don't know why, but I don't want to. But if Aroa is so sure he's writing them for Coco...

"Is this going to be the cliché speech the girl's older brother gives the delinquent who he thinks is trying to seduce her? Just so I can figure out the shortest answer to your question and be done with all this shit."

"Are they for Coco?"

"No."

He says it firmly, but if I've learned anything about Gus over the past few years, it's that he can say no now and believe it to the tips of his toes and then five minutes later his moon will be in Saturn and he'll cross his heart and swear the answer is yes. He's a weather vane.

"Sorry, dude. Coco is my best friend, and I'm scared of seeing her get hurt."

A slightly dry laugh escapes his lips, and I look at him out of the corner of my eye. His foot, sheathed in a grimy black Converse, is propped up on the seat of the rental car (it would be silly to return it early when the company already paid for it), and he's gazing out the window.

"What's so funny?" I ask.

"Did you really fall for that too? You believe Coco's still crazy about me?"

"What do you mean?"

"Come on, Marín, bro. You know her pretty well. You really think Coco acts like a girl in love around me? Think about it for a second."

"I don't know how Coco acts when she's in love."

"Me either. She never was with me, and she's still not." He lifts his sunglasses enough so I can see his eyes and raises his eyebrows meaningfully.

"Why would she lie about that?"

"I didn't know she confirmed the rumors herself."

"Well..." I'm afraid I just spilled the beans, so I hurry to fix it. "She didn't confirm it. She just didn't deny it, I guess."

"Distraction maneuver. Trust me. Coco might sleep with me today, tomorrow, yesterday, but she's hung up on another guy...or another girl."

Another...girl?

~

We stop to eat lunch halfway. Gus is always hungry, and he always wants fries and a beer. If he keeps going like this, he's going to become a cautionary tale: young poet dies of heart failure. That would sell a lot of books.

We talk about music, concerts, artists, box sets... Gus isn't a music lover, but he likes to know what he's talking about and he's really into a lot of bands, so he's been to more gigs than me, and that's literally my job.

We stretch lunch out as long as we can and take our time with the driving we have left; we want to give everyone else time to get to the campsite and get the RV set up. We should be calling motels, but we take our time with that too.

It's six in the evening by the time we park the car and traipse toward the entrance of La Marína campsite. We stop by the information hut and explain that some of our friends are on a site, that they must have arrived not too long ago, but they won't release any information. They mention privacy laws a few times and suggest that we call them.

"If they tell you what site they're at, whose name it's under, and how many days they're staying, we'll let you in."

"Site 297. Under the name Lorenzo Hernandez. They're staying two nights," I say, reading Loren's WhatsApp.

This place is like a city. Organized into numbered streets, there are tons of tents and campers, and not all of them look like a vacation spot; there are people here who, judging by how seriously they've taken it, must live here.

We find the RV easily. They've unfurled the side awning and set up a table and chairs right under it. But they're not here.

Gus tries to peer into the camper, but he can't see anything; they have the blackout blinds down.

"Where the hell are they?"

"Let's go see if they're in the pool."

The pool is decked out with three pretty high water slides, like as high as the third floor of a building. As soon as I see them and realize they're not just for little kids, I know they must be there, probably loaded on wine. One of those ideas that end with Coco getting hurt.

"Is that them?"

Gus points at four screaming hooligans who are laughing and pretending to push each other. They're lining up to go down the blue slide, which is not the steepest, but it has four lanes. They want to launch at the same time, and knowing them, they probably want to do it holding hands or with some kind of elaborate choreography. Tomorrow they'll act like it was super cringe when they recount it, but right now they think it's hilarious. They're acting like they're in a summer beer ad.

"Fuck me. Look at Aroa," I hear Gus murmur.

"Hey, take it easy," I reply.

"I can't look at Coco because she's like your sister or Aroa because she's your ex-girlfriend. Can I get permission to look at Loren or…?"

I laugh and give him a playful slap. "Look at her as much as you want. I'm not her boyfriend, and even if I were, there's nothing inappropriate about that."

"Someday I'll dedicate a poem about this to you."

I look up. Aroa has a body exactly like what the magazines say a female body should be. She's thin, athletic, bronzed, and very pretty and has a good pair of natural tits. So right now when she's in a bikini jumping around with excitement because it's finally their turn, it's a pretty nice view. Gus growls, and I elbow him in the ribs.

"Didn't you just say I could look?"

"Yeah, but don't objectify her."

I side-eye him, and I get the feeling that Gus isn't actually looking at Aroa. Next to her, Coco and Blanca are shoving each other and trying to tickle each other. Coco probably said she needs to piss… She always says pools make her need to pee.

Blanca is wearing a black-and-white polka-dot bathing suit, pretty low-cut but retro. She's voluptuous, with a tiny waist and all the right proportions. She's pretty just as she is, but she's always going on about needing to lose weight. Actually…she's beautiful, mostly because she gives off this kind of energy that just glows, but no, I could never think of her like that.

Next to her, Coco adjusts her strapless bikini covered in watermelons. When she bought it, she told me it was a paradox.

"It's watermelons, but it gives me two cantaloupes…"

At the time I laughed, but it's true. It really hoists her tits up. The bottoms have a kind of playful ruffle. I look over at Gus again to see if he's checking her out. I can't tell. Am I worried? I'm worried.

"Do you need a tissue? You're drooling."

"Don't be a dumbass."

Suddenly he sounds much more hostile than he did a minute ago. He must be having one of his mood swings: His moon is probably passing through Pluto or something like that.

"Who are you looking at, dude?"

"Nobody. I'm not looking at anyone."

It's their turn. We lean against a mosaicked wall, right in front of the lifeguards, and one of them is holding up a phone, ready to take a video.

"Do you think we'll get splashed from here?" Gus asks.

"The last splash didn't go this far."

"Yeah, but they're going to come down doing some crazy shit, and I'm sure they'll make a tsunami."

"And a cyclone in the Philippines. Come on, pretty boy. Relax."

They sit down at the top of the slide...and a second later we lose sight of them. A watery explosion greets them on their way down. They're holding hands and squealing, pulling each other out of their lanes. They're not right in the head. I love them.

As they come out, Loren is the first to see us. He yells, "Dude!" which makes it obvious the wine is really hitting him. The second to spot us is Aroa, who runs over. Next, Blanca. Coco hasn't seen us yet and...one nipple is sticking out of her bikini.

"Hey!" Blanca says kind of curtly as she fixes her bathing suit and swipes under her nose, which must have gotten filled with water when they got to the bottom. "You're here."

"You seem so happy to see us, girl," Gus says, pouting. "Do you wanna get out and give us some wine or should we take a picture of you?"

"They're already taking a video of us, thanks."

Loren points at the lifeguard behind us and thanks him. He clambers clumsily out of the pool, dries his hands on Gus's T-shirt, and takes his phone.

"I'm happy to see you too," the latter says, shaking off his shirt.

"Don't make it messy."

I know Loren didn't intend for anyone else to hear that, but…the alcohol must have diminished his capacity to control his decibels, and we all turn toward him. All except Coco, who's in her own world.

"Sardine!" I call to her.

She turns toward me with her hair in her face and one hard nipple still poking out of her cantaloupe bikini…I mean, watermelon.

"Are you doing erotic numbers now?" I ask her.

"Erotic-circus. What are you talking about, dummy?" She laughs.

"Your nipple." Gus points primly at her boob. "We can see your nipple, sweetheart."

"Bah…like it's the first time any of you have seen it."

But I can see her cheeks redden as she fixes her bikini.

I lean down a little farther, going closer and calling her over. "Sardine-y…you look like a fish in water."

"This'll wash a little of the salt off."

She leans her arms on the edge of the pool and beams up at me. Suddenly I swell with pride. That girl, the one who's always smiling, the one who organized this whole bachelorette trip for one of her best friends, who's trying to get over an unrequited love…is my best friend. And I'm so lucky that…

I feel two wet boobs press against my white shirt from behind and I know instantly that they belong to Aroa. My dick gives a little lurch that I can't control, so when she circles around me, wet, on tiptoes, with those drops running down her lips…it's too late to think about ugly things to get down the half-chub I'm getting.

She climbs up me, throwing her arms around my neck and kissing me on the cheek. I can't tell if she means to, but she's thrusting her crotch into my package and raises her eyebrows when she notices I'm hard.

"Wow," she whispers, looking at my lips.

"Wow..."

It's the only thing I can get out.

And suddenly it feels like you could cut the tension in the air with a knife. Are we welcome here or not?

14

THIS PARTY IS SO FANTASTIC

COCO

"Are you guys gonna sleep here?" Aroa asks.

We're walking back to our site wrapped in damp towels. Blanca seems awkward. She keeps sneaking glances at Aroa, who… Guess who she's walking with. I'd like to be clinging to Marín or riding on his back, joking and chatting about Noa's accident, but Aroa is like his shadow, and I don't feel like being a third wheel.

"No, no way. We wouldn't all fit in here. We're going to find a motel in town. And if we can't, we'll sleep in the car tonight."

"And what are you going to do now? What are your plans?" Loren asks, seeming to have lost his wine buzz in the past ten minutes.

I shift a little uncomfortably. Shouldn't it be a given that they're going to hang out with us? Our plans are their plans…

"Well, we're up for whatever. We'll go with the flow. Whatever you all feel like. We don't wanna just show up and…take over the plans."

That answer obviously comes from Marín. Gus just shrugs and says something through gritted teeth about drinking wine.

~

We take turns taking showers. Aroa asks to go last, I guess because she wants to keep talking to Marín, and I don't look back when I head to the campsite bathrooms, lugging my towel, my clothes, and my toiletry bag. I concentrate on the sound of my flip-flops slapping against the gravel of the (very few) empty sites I'm cutting across as a shortcut. I don't want to think about anything else and start spiraling about "How could he ever love me when she's his ex?" or "Get it into your head that you're about to destroy one of the best friendships you've ever had in your life." Fucking love; it stains everything.

Blanca runs to catch up with me and plasters on a fake smile. We go into the bathrooms in silence and choose cubicles opposite each other. We turn on the taps at the same time. My shower gel has a note in its aroma that reminds me too much of Gus's cologne.

"Blanqui...are you okay?" I raise my voice over the running water and the piped music so she can hear me.

"Yeah, why?"

"I don't know. You made a really weird face when they showed up."

"Right... Do you think it was really obvious?"

"Kind of."

"Well...it's just, you know how I am. I got used to the idea that it was going to be the four of us, and it shook up my mental plan a little. But the more the merrier."

"Marín seems really happy to be here."

"Yeah, I think so."

There's a playful touch to her tone that gives the impression that maybe Marín was moved more by the urge to be with Aroa than to spend a few days of vacation all together. This is the feeling I'm getting, but I admit I've been more paranoid than usual for the past few days. Really, I'm happy. Marín is addictive; when you spend a lot of time with him, it starts feeling weird not to. But I'm special only because I'm Sardine and he's Anchovy. We're a team. Besties.

I can't let this ruin Blanca's bachelorette trip.

~

We run into Aroa on our way back to the RV. We're fully dressed now, wet hair dripping onto our shoulders. We're joking about making Gus cook dinner. From now on, any plan is not just our thing; it's the whole group.

"Are the showers crowded?" Aroa smiles, still giddy over Marín being here.

"Not at all. Empty."

"Cool! I'll be quick, and then I'll help with dinner."

Loren must have gone ahead of Aroa to take a shower because when we get there, Marín and Gus are the only ones at the site. Gus is sitting in one of the plastic patio chairs with his legs crossed ankle over knee. I've always liked his ankles. They're slender but masculine, finishing off legs covered in dark-brown hair. Unlike Marín, Gus is very proud of his body hair. His chest has a thick layer of fur that I loved when we were together. Marín's not hiding it… He just has practically no chest hair.

Gus gazes at both of us with a pretty neutral expression, like when he's a little drunk; eyelids half drooping, lips between his teeth, hands fidgeting, tapping his thigh.

Marín pokes his head out the door when he sees us coming. He's holding a bottle of chilled wine and a stack of plastic cups.

"That was quick! Listen, for wine, do you use these or the bigger ones?"

"These." Blanca points with a smile. "Are you making an aperitif?"

"Of course. On top of everything else, we showed up empty-handed…"

"But with full mouths," Gus points out, apparently very satisfied with his turn of phrase, taking his phone out of his bag. I watch him open his Notes app and start writing.

"You." I give his chair a little kick. "Are you gonna pitch in at all, or are you planning on us serving you like a king?"

"You." He grabs my waist, spins me around, and then plops me down on his knees. He's still holding his phone. "You always treat me like a king. And I treat you like a queen. My queen."

"Ay, Gus." I go to stand up, but he grabs me.

"Coco Puff," he purrs close to my body.

I spring up when my eyes meet Marín's. No. I don't want him to think I'm about to get back together with Gus. I don't want whatever chance there is, however tiny it is, to disappear.

"You're acting like Angelito…so handsy. Hey!" I remember the party on Friday, and I turn back to Marín, who is pretending to be really focused on opening the bottle of wine. "The other day you seemed really cold with Angel. Did something happen?"

"She doesn't know?" Gus asks Marín with a kind of dopey grin on his face.

"No," Marín says crisply, right as he pulls the cork out and busies himself with that.

"What do I need to know?"

"Angel and Marín got in a fight, like in the playground at school."

"Did you throw down?" Blanca's suddenly interested, and she leans against the RV as she lights a cigarette.

"No. Blood didn't flow in the streets," Marín clarifies, seeming uncomfortable.

"Spill, spill." Blanca smiles at him, excited.

"It's nothing. It's just that…he made a comment that didn't sit well with me. I asked him politely to apologize, he didn't want to, I stuck to my guns, he did too, and we ended up…"

"Shoving each other," Gus teases, filling a plastic glass with wine and handing it over to me. "They were fighting over you."

He lifts his chin toward me and raises his eyebrows. My heart speeds up. It's sick how much princess stories, patriarchal language, and tradition have rotted our brains… As much as we're ashamed of it, we still like men to fight over us. I want to know everything, all the gory details, but I don't want to admit it. I sit on the steps of the RV and bite my tongue, putting space between Gus and me.

"Coco?" Blanca yelps. "You're not gonna ask?"

"I mean, I don't know if I wanna know," I confess. "It's kinda cringe picturing them like two gorillas, shoving each other."

"It wasn't like that." Marín leans on the table and crosses his legs at the ankle. "He got on my nerves, and he got up in my face like he wanted to scare me, so I moved away."

"He threw him through the air." Gus laughs.

"And how do you know?" I ask him.

"Because it was at soccer." He shrugs. "After the game."

"Is that why you didn't play soccer this weekend?" I ask Marín.

"Don't lecture me, please." Marín's looking at the ground. "It's not like I'm proud of it, but you weren't there to defend yourself. If you had been, you would've kicked him in the nuts yourself."

"I don't think so. I'm not violent."

Marín and Gus exchange a glance.

"What did he say?" I give in.

"That you probably meow like a cat when you take it up the ass," Gus declared easily.

I screw up my eyes and grimace. What the hell? "What the fuck were you talking about where a comment like that would come up?"

"That's the thing; it didn't come up," Marín pipes up.

"Men are so disgusting sometimes," Blanca says, looking mortified, before she turns to Gus to reprimand him. "Are you going to pour me some wine? Or do I have to do it myself?"

"We were just talking our exes and everyone else's exes whether we have good taste in women, that kinda shit." Gus seems to remember something, and he swivels in his chair. "But without objectifying you!"

"Wine, Gus!" Blanca exclaims.

Gus grabs the bottle and shoves it at Blanca absentmindedly, not pouring it for her or even giving her a glass.

"He took it way too far," Marín assures us. "It wasn't the first time he's said stuff like that, and...I'd had it."

I pat him on the cheek.

"What's for dinner?" Gus asks.

"If you keep being so rude, you'll be lucky if you can forage something to eat around here." Blanca flips him the bird to back up her answer, and he imitates her but adding his index finger and making a movement that looks suspiciously like something he knows how to do very well with his hands... He side-eyes me before he stands up.

"I'm going to make dinner."

"Leave it. I'll do it," I say.

"Well, I'll help you."

~

I don't miss the fact that the bottles of wine are flying especially fast tonight and that, for the most part, it's Blanca's fault. She keeps filling her glass over and over. And I get it because she's never had a great relationship with Gus and he's being a real asshole tonight. It's not like they're not friends; everyone in the group is, but...if she had to choose someone to save in a nuclear disaster, it wouldn't be Gus, and he knows it. Under normal circumstances, they have a pretty similar sense of humor, but they've never gotten very close. They're...acquaintances. Except when he gets stupid, like he is now. I think Blanca's drinking to make herself feel better about how Loren looks like he's about to jump up from the table, grab Gus by the collar, and choke him with his bare hands. If I really were still in love with him, I'd be miserable, to be honest.

"Blanca, put down the wine. No one's going to steal it from you," Gus says, putting his glass in reach of the bride. "You really do work hard, play harder."

"It's my bachelorette party. I'm supposed to have a good time."

"At this pace, you're going to have a good time vomiting into a bag."

"Hey, Marín, so was Noa a sight to behold?" Aroa changes the topic. She's leaning on the table, staring moony-eyed at him.

"She looked like a cuckoo clock, the poor thing. It's not like I'm happy, but…"

"You're happy," she says playfully. "We know each other, Marín…"

"I would've been fine if she'd had a month of diarrhea. Something not too painful. If she lost control of her sphincter, that would've been perfect."

Aroa makes a face. Before I can even consider whether they're looking at each other like two lovebirds, I let out a strident cackle that makes the whole table look at me.

"A whole stage full of poop!"

Great. Thanks, Coco. Your intervention made it more than clear that, far from being an adult woman worthy of the love of the most wonderful man you've ever met, you're five and you're stuck in the poop-jokes stage.

I push away my plastic plate littered with dinner scraps and rest my head on the table with my forehead on my hands, dying.

"Hey, Coco Puff, you seem a little nervous, huh?" Gus asks in a seductive tone.

"It's the wine."

"Coco loves stories about poop. They're our fave, right?"

I lift my head up from the table and see Marín leaning toward me, smiling. "They're the best."

"And farts," he adds.

"And that one where you were pissing in the Arenal Sound and…"

"Shh…" He puts his hand over my mouth, and I bite it.

We start playing slapsies over the table, and I'm dying of laughter, but in a natural way this time.

"Okay, kids, let's get it together. Hand me the tortilla. Come on," Blanca says.

"Blanquita, are you going to have seconds? Then you won't fit into your wedding dress and there will be crying and gnashing of teeth."

We all gape at Gus.

"What?" he says.

"Good thing that couldn't be further from being your business," Blanca says, thrusting a piece of tortilla onto her plate more violently than necessary.

"Such a shitty joke." I kick him under the table, trying to put out the fire.

"You girls say stuff like that to each other all the time and it's fine." He sounds indignant.

"It doesn't matter. Let it go," Blanca says.

"Of course it doesn't matter. It was just a stupid comment," Gus insists.

"A shitty one," Loren adds, glaring at him threateningly.

"But wait… What's happening here? Is it a gendered joke? I can't say it if I'm not a woman?"

Loren, Aroa, and I all start to answer, but Blanca cuts us off vehemently.

"No. It's not a gendered joke. It's a fat-fucker jokes. Do you know what fat-fuckers are, Gus?"

"You think I called you fat?" He points to his chest.

Blanca cuts a bite of her tortilla, stabs it with her fork, leans on the table with it in her hand, and smiles, "Gus…shut up."

Then she scarfs down the tortilla and asks for the bottle of wine.

Loren changes the subject, and everyone else follows his lead hoping it will defuse the atmosphere. I look at Marín and Aroa again; they seem like always. When they look at each other, isn't that the look I've seen in his eyes when he's with me? The gleam, the way he bites his bottom lip, the way he smiles when he makes a joke. Am I seeing ghosts? Insecurity, fear, yearning, all at once. When Aroa rests her hand on his over the table, I look away and find myself looking at Gus.

"Fucking hell," he whispers. "These people take everything too seriously. It was just an observation."

"It was gross and made you sound overbearing."

He scoffs, leans back from the table, and looks into the darkness that has started to hover around us and is only broken now by a streetlamp two sites away and the exterior light on our camper.

"What's going on with you?" I ask him because I know him and something's up.

He grabs his hair with both hands and sighs. "Can we take a walk?" he asks.

"Of course. Let me just clear some of this away." I grab a few plates and stack them up, and he snatches them from me and throws them into the trash can next to us as he stands up.

"Where are you two going?" Loren asks with a furrowed brow.

Gus is already a few steps away from the table and is looking both ways up and down the street that separates the sites, like he doesn't know they're asking me why we're leaving.

"I think he drank too fast," I lie. "A walk will do him good. I'm sure when we get back he'll be apologizing," I say to Blanca.

"Like I care."

We wander off aimlessly. I feel like I'm strolling through a cemetery. It's barely ten at night, but everyone seems to be sleeping already, except us and a few other campers who aren't following the European schedule and are still eating dinner.

Gus is walking fast. His legs aren't that long, but it has always been hard for me to keep up with his striding pace. I run a little to catch up. He looks at me. I look at him. There's something in his look that takes me on a trip that we took together: to the doors of clubs where we would make out, the plaza where we would always sit to eat something before we went home and fucked like animals. There's something here that reminds me how much I liked when his fingers would leave marks on my thighs—painful bruises but made from a lot of pleasure. The two faces of the same coin that were sex with him.

Gus? Do you feel it too?

I shouldn't have agreed to take a walk alone with him.

"I was getting overwhelmed sitting there," he says, a smile unfurling across his face.

"You're, like…weird, right?"

"I'm going to tell you something, okay? But you have to promise you're not going to tell anyone and you're not going to think it's a problem."

"Of course. What's going on?"

"It's just that…Loren's making me nervous, girl," he says with his particular brand of insolence. "It's like he's inspecting everything I say, everything I do…and he always acts like I owe him money."

I smile. Ay, Loren…the dad of the group. The protector. "No. It's just that Loren has always been very protective over us."

"So? Do I treat you badly? We're all friends here."

"Yeah, but you're my ex," I point out.

"And? Marín is Aroa's ex, and he doesn't look at him like that."

"Well, if Marín fucked half of Madrid since their breakup, he's been very discreet about it."

He stops and looks at me with a furrowed brow. "Coco Puff—"

"Don't get me wrong," I cut him off. "I don't… Like, I get it. I mean…"

"Calm down." He gives a half smile.

"I'm calm. It's just uncomfortable." I make a face. "It's awkward talking about your sex life, Gus."

"Jealous?" He raises his eyebrows.

"No. But I think…" Here we go; the wine is talking for me. "I've always thought sex drains you, Gus. It's your way of feeling like your own master, of feeling like you're in control, but after you fuck the very cute woman you met in a bar, instead of feeling good, you feel like shit."

"That's not true." He shakes his head.

"Maybe not. Or maybe you've never allowed yourself to accept that, surprise, you're human and you need affection that sometimes…"

"Try again…" He rubs his face and keeps walking.

I follow him. He doesn't say a word.

"Listen…"

I tug on his arm, and he stops. He looks at me. I look at him. Once again, I remember his fingers around my neck, with that look that changes his face completely. His mouth hanging open a little, his hips thrusting between my thighs, his cock pushing so deep inside me. Groaning. Reminding me how much I like feeling dominated in bed.

I come back to reality and let go of his arm, but not before I felt the tickle of his soft arm hair under my fingers.

"You and me," I say as firmly as I can. "We're friends, Gus. Good friends. Our past is…ours, but it's in the past. Forgotten affectionately and with love."

"What do you mean by that?"

"That I'm worried about you, that it seems like there's been something going on with you for the past few months, that I'm sick of you hiding stuff from me, you not opening up, maybe because of what we were…"

A smile sets fire to the corner of his mouth and spreads across his lips until it conquers it entirely.

"What?" I raise my eyebrows and his smile spreads to me. "Are you laughing?"

"A little."

"Why?"

"Because…we met years ago and you still don't get that it was never you. It was me. And this time, when I say, 'It's not you, it's me,' it was true."

He grabs my hand and kisses it. Then I stroke his stubbly cheek.

"We were idiots," he says with an expression floating somewhere between nostalgic and playful.

"For loving each other or stopping?"

He furrows his brow and smiles even deeper. "Girlie…you love me? No. That wasn't love. Love is what you feel for the one who's making your eyes shine like that. And I don't love you, not like that, but I admit that I'm jealous, Coco Puff. Because that"—he points with his eyes—"that I don't know how to do. With anyone. Even though I want to."

"You? Gus? The poet? Sweetie." I laugh. "You set Madrid on fire with the looks from all those girls who dream of you reciting poetry into their ears."

"Poetry doesn't always work," he adds.

"Yours does."

He interrogates me with his eyes, and I nod. Yes, Gus. Say it. Use the words. Bring your feelings to their knees, subjugate them in your way of containing them, in vowels, consonants. You've been driving this woman crazy with your suspension-filled ellipses…that end in her mouth. Now make her gasp for air.

And I swear I don't love him either, not like that, but even I'm, suddenly, a little jealous too.

15

TOGETHER AND TURBULENT

coco

When we get back, I get the impression Gus is feeling better. And in a way, I am too. Marín and Aroa could have been looking at each other like monogamous birds who could die from the pain of being apart, but they're not.

"Coco Puff," Gus says as we approach our RV. "Can I give you a piece of unsolicited advice?"

"Of course."

"Nobody's better than you."

Blanca's cackles are ricocheting brashly. Loren's trying to get her to quiet down. Everyone except Marín has that warm, blushing glow that wine leaves on the skin, but Blanca is practically on fire.

"Hi!" they greet us. "How was your little walk?"

"Fucking great," Gus responds, a little gruffly. "How's the wine? Good, right?"

"You want some?" They offer him the bottle.

I grab it and take a swig straight from the bottle.

"Should we play something?"

"Yes! What?" Aroa asks giddily.

"I'm going to get another bottle and a cigarette. Does anyone need anything from inside?" Loren asks.

Nobody answers, but Aroa holds out her phone.

"Plug it in. It's dying. It's been beeping for a while."

"Jeez…the video of the slide. I'll send it to you all now so you can see it."

Aroa flashes Marín an expansive smile. "I love that you were able to come."

"And I'm glad we could come too, right, dude?"

Gus looks up and nods.

"Hey." I elbow him.

He stands up and goes over to the window of the camper's kitchen. "Loren, dude, can you hand me a pen?"

"The muse is a demanding lover," Blanca chirps. "Write something, Gustavo Adolfo…"

I kick her and gesture for her to stop. "Okay…should we play something?"

"Cards!" Aroa suddenly yelps, jumping out of her seat and hurtling into the camper, where she crashes right into Loren.

"Did you watch the video?" I ask him.

"Yeah, but it's total dog shit." He looks at Marín and Gus. "And all you can hear is these two talking."

"Are we playing cards?" Aroa pops up smiling next to his chest.

"Let's do it."

Two more bottles of wine are polished off, but we stop serving Blanca pretty soon. She hasn't even gotten one single point in a game she usually trounces us all in. She's laughing like an idiot, knocking over glasses, trying to light a cigarette the wrong way round, and slurring more than she's talking. Two games of cards and her eyes start drooping shut at the table.

"We should get her to bed," Marín and I say at the same time.

"I'm tired," she mumbles.

Aroa watches Marín pick Blanca up like someone who's seen a ghost.

Aroa has been sitting next to him all night, all hyped up but, apart from that look, there's been nothing else. I know Marín. I know he loves her, but I think he's already made peace with the idea that their thing is not possible. I'm sure the reason for the breakup is something much more important than a simple exchange of opinions that didn't go the way he was hoping. Something big happened between them.

"Come on, Blanqui… Let's get you in bed."

"I have to take my makeup off."

"You're not wearing makeup, love," I say, standing up from the table and hurrying to help them.

She gets up, staggers, and kicks the table, threatening to topple a couple of glasses.

"I'm such a messy drunk…" She laughs at herself.

"You really are." Gus's comment is unnecessary, but it doesn't matter because nobody's paying attention to him and nothing's getting through to her.

Marín puts Blanca's arm around his shoulders and leads her toward the door, but when she tries to go up the stairs, she almost falls flat on her face. I take her other arm, and between the two of us we manage to shove her into the narrow camper where every inch has a purpose. She collapses onto a bed that's not hers, but no one gives a rat's ass. She curls up on the bottom bunk where Aroa slept last night. Marín crouches and brushes her hair off her face in a sweet gesture.

"Are you okay?"

"Mm-yes."

"Do you want a bag in case you need to throw up?"

"Rainbow. I'm going to vomit a rainbow." She turns back to us suddenly and laughs. "I'm going to vomit a rainbow, sneeze fucking hearts, and shit glitter because, love is so beautiful, the fucking whore!"

I kneel next to Marín and stroke her face. "Are you okay?" I repeat.

I get the feeling that Blanca is pulling away and hiding a sob, but it turns into a hiccup.

"Let me." Loren nudges his way in. "Wine makes you really cheesy, Blanca. Everything's okay. It's cheap wine. It gets you. You just sleep here and everything'll be fine."

Marín grabs a pillow and puts it next to her so she can hug it. "Keep an eye on her, okay?"

"What for?" I ask.

"If she vomits, make her do it on her side. We don't want the bride to choke on her own vomit at her bachelorette party." He stands up and changes his taciturn expression to a timid smile and eyebrow raise. "What? Why are you looking at me like that? I'm an expert. Taking care of drunks since nineteen-ninety..."

I give him a kiss on the cheek. I don't want him to think about that. Love is wanting to go back and undo everything that erased his childhood in one fell swoop.

~

We go back to the table, closing the door and leaving only the exterior light on. Gus lets out a protest. "Hey!"

In his hands he has a piece of the paper towel that we've been using as napkins, dish towels, paper towels...and he's writing on it. Poetry comes first. Then humans, starting with himself.

"Well, kids...I think at this point, since you haven't found a motel or anything, it's obvious you're going to stay here, right?" Aroa asks.

"I haven't had a single drink. We can leave now." Marín ducks his chin and looks at the time.

"There's an extra bed in the living room." Loren says. "The table comes apart."

"They won't both fit in there. They're too tall," Aroa snipes back.

"Well, you're the shortest. Maybe you should sleep there," Loren suggests.

"I'm sleeping in one of the bunks. Someone can fit in there with me. They're not very wide, but they're long. Maybe one of them will be more comfortable there."

"Blanca's sleeping in your bunk. You're the shortest of the group and you'll be the least cramped."

"Fine… Why don't we draw straws?"

She shoots Loren a look that could kill, and we both understand that she wants to sleep with Marín. What's she going to do? Manhandle his gearshift in a camper full of people? My lip curls as I realize I would do it too.

"Aroa, you're five five, Marín is six two, Gus is five eight, and Loren is a hunk of a man at more than six foot," I pipe up.

"Straws," she says through clenched teeth. I swear it's like when Bilbo Baggins sees the ring on Frodo's neck and wants to possess it—even her face looks different. Where did the wood nymph go, and who swapped her for Gollum? "Gus…give me five slips of paper."

"Huh?"

"Five little pieces of paper. Give them to me."

"Here." He tosses over the roll of paper towel, and with a patient sigh, she rips them up herself.

Things aren't going how she planned. Frustration. She's not used to having to deal with that emotion.

Loren helps Aroa and writes "bunk" on one of the scraps of paper, "loft bed" on two others, and "living room" on one. Then he scrunches them up into balls and cups them in his hands, shaking them like a maraca.

"Okay, the most innocent one should draw first."

"Me!" Aroa jumps up excitedly.

"You? No fucking way. Put your hand in, Coco. No one can beat you for innocence, my child."

I grab a scrap and read, “Bunk.”

“Amazing. Okay, my turn,” Loren says decidedly.

“Of course, go right ahead,” Aroa grumbles.

“Loft bed,” he says happily.

This guy is an idiot. I’m no fortune teller, but luck is the sluttiest of sluts. I can see what’s going to unfold—he’s going to end up sleeping with Gus…who’s the only one who has the power to make him lose his shit.

“Come on, Aroa…your turn.”

She studies the balls of paper, and her excitement vanishes immediately. “Living room,” she mutters grumpily.

That means…either I’m sleeping with Marín or with Gus. In a bunk bed. Long but narrow. A body and a half. Body to body…

“Come on, Gus, pick one.”

“I’ll sleep in the street or on my feet,” he grumbles.

“It’s not like I’m hoping you’ll sleep with me.” I sound touchy.

“Me either,” Loren adds, his hands making a hole with two crumpled paper balls between them. “Come on. Let’s go. Choose your fucking paper and stop talking like you’re Snoop Dogg, please.”

Marín and I stifle a laugh.

“What? Who does he sound like?” Aroa asks, wanting to get in on the joke.

Gus sighs, grabs a little ball, opens it, and shows it to everyone. It’s clear: “upper bed.” Loren grabs his forehead and sighs.

“Upstairs with me, Gus. But, for the love of God…if you recite poetry to me, I’ll flip you over like an egg.”

“Fuck, bro, so much hostility…”

“Anchovy and Sardine…top bunk.”

“Listen up.” Marín gives me a smile and holds up his index finger between us. “If you fart, it’ll push me out of the camper like a wave.”

"If you get cute and I can feel your penis, I'll make an iPhone case out of your foreskin."

We cackle a little and sit down again. It's still early. There are still bottles to empty. There are still anecdotes to remember. And since we're taking turns checking on Blanca to make sure she's sleeping soundly, we don't realize someone else is feeling bad—Aroa has her arms wrapped around her legs. Maybe it just got through to her that Marín isn't going to make an effort for her anymore, that he's never going to move the sky to fulfill her wishes again, that for him, she's lost whatever made her different from us. Now, the only special one for him is me. And that… That has to be a sign.

16

THE CLUSTERFUCK

COCO

I've never seen Aroa so subdued. Normally she just gives off this light that makes her irresistible. But tonight when she goes to bed, she looks beautiful but sad. It's like suddenly, the weight of the breakup is starting to make a dent on her. Something tells me there's not going to be sunrise yoga tomorrow.

I hear Loren and Gus griping in the darkness. One thinks the other is pretty close. The other is wriggling too much.

"Are you going to breathe that loud all night?" Gus kicks off.

"Yes. If you don't like it, you try not breathing and you can make up rhymes with my snores until you fall asleep…forever."

"Can we drop the poetry thing, jeez?"

"You are poetry."

"Come on, stupid. Come here."

"If you touch me, Gus, I swear I'll get the ick so hard I'll die and then I'll come back from the dead to trigger you for the rest of your life."

Marín, standing next to the bunk, is laughing as he takes off his pants and folds them. Oh, yeah, take it all off.

"Those two. Good night, blondie," he says to Aroa.

"Come here a sec," she replies.

He goes over, just like that, in his boxers, with his shirt still on, with his long legs… I can almost feel them brushing against mine in the narrow bed—I don't even care that he's so close to Aroa right now.

I hear them whispering. The light doesn't reach them, so all I can see is that he's crouching. I hear the scratch of a kiss, but I'd bet the hand I put eyeliner on with that it was on the forehead. Or at least that's what I want to believe.

He comes back to the bunk, but he doesn't use the ladder. He asks me to scooch over and propels himself up with his hands. I think I just came. Is that possible? I think I squirted.

"What's going on, Sardine?" he asks as he settles in.

All long legs, messy hair…

"Nothing." I shrug.

"Right…"

He finds a good position and stops moving. God. We're really close. Really, really, really close. I can smell his cologne, the woodsy touches, the twang of damp earth…his only luxury: an expensive cologne from Hermès, which makes everything he touches smell like Marín.

When he closes the curtain, I swear I'm about to fart from the nerves. We're here alone… As alone as we can be in an RV full of people, of course. But that fabric separating us from "the outside" suddenly creates a (probably false) atmosphere of privacy. I'm dying, suffocating myself on the cloud of cotton from my adolescent fantasies. I'm looking at him, but really I'm seeing stills from our wedding.

"What's going on?" he asks me again in a whisper.

"Dude, your feet are freezing!" Gus yells. "Stop touching me with your fucking feet!"

"They're going to kill each other," I joke.

"Don't change the subject," he whispers very softly. "What's going on? What the hell is up with Gus?"

"With Gus?" I'm baffled.

"What was up with that little walk?"

"It was just a walk." I turn onto my side and look at him with my brow furrowed.

Loren's whimpering drifts through the darkness of the RV when Gus starts up again like a broken record. Sensitive, sulky poet.

"Coco..." Marín gets my attention again with an almost inaudible murmur.

I focus my attention on him. Fuck. He's so hot; I don't understand how I didn't fall on my knees dying of love and lust when I met him that night four years ago. Marín's nose is so cute I want to kiss it. I want to bite it. I want to lick his forehead, like I'm baptizing him with my love. I want to kiss him so badly, so badly... I don't think I've ever been this close to him.

"What?" I answer, my voice trembling.

"Are you two getting back together again?"

"No," I assure him.

"You wouldn't lie to me, right?"

Jeez. Yes. Marín, I would lie to you. I lie to you every day. I don't know how to do it any other way because...I love you. To the tips of my toes. And if you knew it, I think you'd leave so you wouldn't hurt me.

"No. I'd never lie to you."

He stares at me. I get the feeling that he's studying my face through the shadows. My expression. My eyes. The rhythm of my eyelashes. This dude knows me better than my mother does.

"Coco...you... You're not still in love with Gus, right?"

"What?"

Boom, boom, boom, boom. My heart is beating so loudly it feels deafening. I'm giving myself a stroke. Or a heart attack. I'm not sure which.

"He doesn't believe you're in love with him."

"You talked about this with him?" I tense up.

"No. Well, in passing."

"But, Marín, for fuck's sake… Is it too much to ask you all not to stick your nose into my life?" At this point my secret is going to be a trending topic before we get back to Madrid.

"It's not like that. It's just tha—"

"What about you?" I counterattack.

"Lower your voice," he says in a whisper.

"What about you and Aroa? Dude…I'm your best friend and I've never pressured you to tell me why the fuck you broke up. She's crazy about you. She wants to get back together with you. What's going on there?"

"Nothing's going on there. It's a private thing between couples." He pauses and adds, "And ex-couples."

"It's just that I don't even know what phase of the breakup you're in," I complain. "But you're making a face because I went for a walk with my ex."

He turns onto his back and rubs his face.

"It's not like that."

"Your life is just for you. Mine is for everyone."

"No, Coco, really," he apologizes. "I've just had so much work…"

"No. You've been hiding out in your work. That's not the same thing."

"Maybe, but—"

"Every time you move, it feels like you're going to push the motor home's nose into the ground and we're going to sink, for fuck's sake," Gus grumbles.

"Oh my God! You're such a cunt!" Loren snipes at him.

At the perfect moment, the odd couple defuses the atmosphere. If Blanca were conscious, I bet she'd be recording it all on her phone. I get the giggles. Marín shifts and rolls back onto his side, looking at me. He jiggles me affectionately and puts his nose, his perfect nose, on my shoulder.

"Don't be mad at me, Coco. Sometimes I don't know the right way to say stuff."

"So what are you trying to say?"

"I mean, I dunno. Maybe I have nothing to say."

The hand that was jokingly shaking me is resting on my waist, like he's holding me. I can barely breathe.

"I'm falling out of bed," he whispers with a smile. "Hold me in somehow, Coco Puff."

"Don't call me 'Coco Puff.'" I push aside the sleeping bag because we're going to die of suffocation, and I thread one of my legs between his, making it into an anchor. "That's what Gus calls me."

"Well, then I'll call you by your name."

"Coco is fine, thanks."

"Coco is what everyone calls you."

"Fine then, Sardine."

"I love your name," he says suddenly. "Why doesn't anyone call you—"

I slap my hand over his mouth.

"What about you? Why doesn't anyone call you…?"

It's Marín's turn to cover my mouth. We're both laughing and we let our hands fall. God. God. God. Is this flirting? My right leg is between his! I'm wearing really tiny pajamas—just a tank top and underwear! This is less than three steps from being considered sex!

"You know what's happening here, Coco? I think I'm scared to say I'm ready to turn the page," he suddenly pipes up. And the idea of fucking suddenly self-destructs in a loud explosion in my head.

"Are you talking about Aroa?"

"Yeah." He nods. His hand tightens around my waist.

"Do you want…? I mean… Are you thinking about someone else? Is there someone else already—?"

"No, but…fuck. I want to keep living, meeting girls, going from flower to flower for a little while and then…falling in love. I want to feel how your bastard of an ex-boyfriend lives. I want my eyes to shine like yours do when you think about the person you're thinking about...who's definitely not Gus." I open my mouth to argue, but he shakes his head. "Don't say it, Coco. I don't want you to say it. If you lied to me about that, it's for a reason. I respect that, okay? I believe you, whatever you tell me. I see you shine, and I light up with you. I'm not going anywhere just because you don't want to tell me that. We can have secrets and that's fine."

"You're not mad?" I ask.

"At you?" He comes closer, kisses me on the forehead, looks at me, and smiles. I'm dying. "Never. I can't. I couldn't."

911? One crash cart to site 297, please.

17

MORE (AND BETTER) CLUSTERFUCKS

COCO

I wake up with a jolt. All the windows are open, and the breeze is slinking sensually across the inside of the RV. I'm not under any covers, but I'm not cold because next to me, Marín's body is giving off a heat that can only be described as delicious despite the fact that it's the middle of August. Judging by the light seeping through the skylights, it must be six in the morning. The sky has started to lighten, and you can make out a few shades of pink in it, slipping around the edges, almost dripping onto them, like oil and water. I try to change positions, but Marín won't let me. I don't know if he's awake, in some kind of twilight sleep, or completely out, but not even a molecule of oxygen would fit between us. His knees are nestled in behind mine. His breath is warming the back of my neck. He's using his arms as anchors, one under my neck and the other draped over my waist. By the way, the other thing lining up perfectly with my ass must be his cock. And...it's noticeable.

No. His cock isn't the first thing I think about. It's actually that this is a couple's position, two bodies that feel comfortable touching each other, rubbing each other. Two people with a shared intimacy.

After that...okay, fine. After that I think about his cock.

I clock my irregular breathing too. I've fantasized a hundred times about a situation like this, and the truth is I don't really know what to do because…I want to do something. In my imagination, all the mornings I've spent lounging in bed, listening to him start the day in our house, Marín would be holding me like he is now. And I feel even more nervous because I never thought I'd be in contact with his skin. I never believed this was going to happen.

His body. Mine. I move my hip gently. I know it's not right, but I need to see how he reacts…which doesn't take long. He breathes deeply, kind of huskily, and his hip moves too, rubbing a little. I can't feel the fabric of his shirt. He must have ditched it at some point in the night.

Is he asleep? Dreaming about Aroa? Is he awake? I could easily check by rolling over, but I don't want to shatter the moment. Something tells me this is the kind of thing that breaks and disappears if you think about it too much. I shift again, pushing my ass into his cock, and his right hand changes position, from my waist to my hip. He's asleep. He must be asleep. He's dreaming.

I want to touch him, but I don't dare. I content myself with rubbing again, up and down, and this time I draw out the movement. I hear a rough moan caught in his throat, and my sex tightens around itself. My body is begging for more. What the fuck is going on?

This time, his hand is the one moving my hip. Can he really be asleep? I move closer and then farther. Again and again. I can feel his hard cock behind me, against my butt. He's rubbing it, adjusting it, breathing faster and harder. For the love of God…maybe I'm the one who's asleep?

No, I'm not. His hand moves back to my waist, but only to slip under my pajama top and climb up in search of one of my breasts. His hand on my boob. I can't breathe. My nipple hardens, and I feel wet—so easy, so fast, so Marín. When his fingers tighten around my tit, I have to swallow a moan. God…Coco, move.

I do. He does too. His fingers grip me harder. One contained thrust, behind the bunk's curtain, which is making a muffled crunch. Another. I almost have to bite the pillow. I want to moan, and I want his other hand inside my underwear.

His mouth is half open. I know because his lips are pressed against my neck now, over my tangled hair. When I arch backward again and he arches forward, the heat of his breath condenses on a strand of hair on the nape of my neck.

Touch me. Undress me, for fuck's sake. I want your mouth between my legs while I grab your hair and pull. I want to tell him so many things. I want to say things I never even said to Gus. What would his response be if I did? What expression would I find on his face?

Marín, fuck me with your fingers, with your tongue, with your cock. Do what you want with me. I want you to come so deep inside me...

I'm losing my mind.

"Marín," I whisper.

He doesn't answer. He's asleep. I need to know if he's asleep. He rubs his cock against me again, and I put my hand between us. To hell with it. Under his underwear he's hot, hard. I grab him over the cotton and trace the contours of his erection with my fingers. He groans. I'm touching Marín's cock...and it's hard. This isn't happening. If this is a dream, I'll dive headfirst into a well as soon as I wake up.

He fondles my breast. I fondle his cock. I don't think I've ever been this horny in my life. But...what is this?

"Marín," I repeat.

I'm about to turn around, kiss him, put my half-asleep tongue in his mouth and lick his. Just the thought of it makes me even wetter. I'm going to do it. I can't take it anymore. I'm turning toward him, but...

The hand gripping me is losing strength. It feels further away. There's space between us. I can feel the cool dawn breeze on my skin. He's turning the opposite way.

He sighs. He settles down.

Fuck my fucking luck. This dude is asleep.

~

I can't get back to sleep. I'm still a little groggy for an hour, but I can't deepen it into real sleep. I'm too nervous, riled up, and a little disappointed to do it. All I want is for it to be daytime so I can check if there's anything different in the way he looks at me. Deep down, it's hard for me to believe a guy can do all that while he's in the deepest state of unconsciousness. If he was even slightly awake, I'll know as soon as he looks at me…right?

Still, I make the most of the opportunity. I'm so close to him, with one of my legs looped between his. My nose is in direct contact with his skin. It smells like him. He smells a little of me too. I wish we could always smell like this…

At nine, I get up, clambering awkwardly over his body. I'm not tired of the contact, but it's hurting me. My head has started spiraling. It's turned all this into a brutal mistake that will be the end of us. I've started thinking in absolutes, not taking anything else into account, without any perspective. If I don't find the strength to find out if Marín could feel something more for me, I have to move out of the apartment.

~

I go to the campsite bathroom, brush my teeth, wash my face, take a piss. I stand there for a few minutes, staring into space, remembering the feeling of Marín's muffled moan on my neck. I'm still horny. I should probably take a shower.

I put my pajamas back on after the shower, going commando. I go to the camper, crawl inside like a long-legged mouse, and grab the cash I left in the kitchen drawer yesterday, predicting this would happen. I'm going to go buy coffee for everyone. Yes, in my pajamas.

Deep down, I can't help being in a good mood; the shower washed away my fears, and now all I can think about is Marín and me, rubbing against each other. Hope. Hope swelling in my chest, zipping around my stomach, making it so I don't even need to breathe. I could live off it.

I work hard to set up a bougie breakfast layout. I fan out napkins, plates, a bottle of orange juice on the table. I light a candle to keep the bugs away and go inside to stealthily open the blinds to air it out in there. Blanca is the first to wake up, and she shows me by stroking my leg as I pass by her bunk.

"Jesus that scared me, Blanqui…"

"I want to die," she groans. It's like a scene from *World War Z* where she's patient zero.

I grab my first aid kit, strategically stashed on one of the shelves, and hand her an ibuprofen and a glass of water.

"God, Coco, thank you. I thought I was dead and this was my purgatory. Ibuprofen is my religion."

"Grab another one… Everything hurts." That was Marín, who's looking at me with eyes puffy from sleep from the top bunk. God. He's so hot. I'm oozing love.

"Hi," I say like an idiot.

"Hi, Sardine."

He gives me a beautiful smile and closes his eyes as he stretches. You know that feeling bordering on rage when you feel like you couldn't love anyone more? We should give it a name; there should already be one to label the feeling of wanting to rip out your heart and thrust it, dripping and bloody, into his hands as an expression of love. I love this dude. I love him so much I want to pass out.

"Hey!" Blanca exclaims from down below. "How does everything hurt you? Did you drink last night and I missed it?"

"No. Of course not. It's this bunk. I didn't want to move much 'cause I was scared I'd push Coco out of the camper and I'm stiff."

"Well then, come on, get up," I encourage him.

"I can't right now." He laughs.

"Why not?"

"Because I'm hard. And give me that ibuprofen. Even my balls hurt."

It'd be weird if they didn't hurt. Fuck my life. This dude was completely asleep and doesn't even have a clue that I grabbed his cock.

Gradually, the rest of the occupants are getting up. Aroa barely says a word. She folds up the living room bed, grabs her stuff, and heads to the bathroom. She's pissed off because I slept with Marín.

Loren pops up with hair like he was struck by a tornado, but he looks like a maharaja. He's sitting in a chair, grumbling about his terrible luck in the bed lottery, and clutching a coffee like it's Rose in that controversial scene in *Titanic*.

Gus is the last to emerge. He's still sleepy. As he comes out, he's scratching his leg with one hand and pushing his hair off his forehead with the other. All he's wearing is black boxer shorts, and he has a boner. He couldn't give less of a fuck about showing up on our "patio" like this, in front of everyone.

"For fuck's sake, Gus, we can all see your cock," Loren complains.

"I guess sleeping with you turned me into a total dog," he jokes. "Come on, man! It happens to everyone. It doesn't matter."

Blanca is sitting in front of the table, with her hair in a bun and looking pale. Her face doesn't look good. Gus climbs down and puts his hand on her hair.

"Blanqui...you look terrible."

"Thanks for the information."

"I still love you just the same."

"Kick rocks."

The exchange is much less tense than last night, but it's clear Blanca's not in a good place. I don't think she's happy he's here. I have to do something.

Aroa comes back and smiles so stiffly it evokes more dread than kindness. She puts her toiletries in the camper and climbs back out to curl up in the only empty seat.

"Did you sleep well?" Gus asks me with his eyebrows raised, bringing me back to the reality of the table.

Shit. Did he hear something?

"I mean, so-so. Marín is longer than a day without carbs. He was everywhere."

Everywhere. Including under my pajamas, pinching a nipple between two fingers. I glance subtly over at where Marín is sitting and he laughs.

"That's me. The chosen one: omnipresent."

"Coco, is there any chance I left my pack of cigarettes in the top bunk?" Blanca asks. "I need a cigarette before I die from this hangover."

"Yikes... Well, I think I did feel something at the bottom of the bunk," Marín says. "You'll probably have to root through everything."

"Were you two moving around a lot in the bunk or what?" Aroa says.

I stand up and go to look for Blanca's cigarettes, uncomfortable with the question. Marín was probably dreaming about some other woman and there I was, groping his handlebar.

I unzip my sleeping bag and shake it outside the bunk. A pack of cigarettes, some napkins crumpled into a ball, and a lighter. Man...this place is a pigsty.

I crouch to pick everything up, and when I go to throw the napkins away, I realize there's something written on them. It doesn't take long for me to recognize Gus's handwriting. It's a poem. In my sleeping bag...

Fuck my fucking life.

You talked to me about light,
and I believed in it.
We had no idea

why,
but suddenly,
we wanted the consequence.

Between your truths
and my lies
there's a chasm of possibilities.
But I don't know what to do with them.
I started to fall in love in words,
little one,
like fingers on a keyboard,
dancing a tango;
different names,
different places,
but the same dirty dance of my hand,
traveling upward,
under that white tablecloth.
I'll never forget.

And everything was fun.
And everything was new,
even if it was exactly the same
for everyone else.
Identical pieces pumping out on a conveyor belt.
The names change,
for just one scene.
A kiss in the bathroom,
a whisper in the ear,
message sent.
Cut. We keep rolling.

But I kept falling in love,
without realizing,
with the "what do I know,"
with the heat of cold nights,
with your topsy-turvy laughter,
with Tuesdays in Madrid
and Sundays over text.

It stopped being what it was,
it never became what it should have.
We fill and empty ourselves
on a narcissistic voyage to who we could never be.
There was hope, there was rage.
There were questions without answers
and we didn't care about the answers.
There were bruises,
intense nights full of silent footsteps,
expressions without a translator,
emotions about using each other and petty revenge.
There were situations, tricks, gimmicks and lies,
because I never understood how a half-truth
can be the worst kind of lie.

But now
we don't need words anymore.
I still stumble, even now
over the A's and the M's,
over the "come here" and the "go away."
Dying of pain,
I started to fall in love with

those little words.
What's left
is nameless,
I'm left with the relief of believing
you knew me.
You know me.
From my "a" to my "z."
You know me.

I don't know what to do with what I just read. I'm standing there with the crinkled napkins in my hand and my mouth hanging open. Blanca bursts in, and I shove them into the waistband of my pajamas.

"Were they there?"

"What?"

"My cigarettes. Did you find them?"

"Oh, yeah. Here you go: your cigarettes and your lighter."

"I got so shit-faced yesterday. It was so messy."

"Well, it's your bachelorette party..."

I go out of the camper without another word, like it's not a big deal, feeling so dizzy that I collapse into a chair staring into the void. I make eye contact with Gus, who raises his eyebrows at me with a smile.

"Coco Puff...did you see a ghost?"

Yours, sweetheart.

But this guy...what the hell does he want from me?

~

Aroa is barely speaking. She's biting her nails. She's beautiful in her tank top and yoga pants, but she looks like the lights are on but nobody's home. I'm in a huge fucking mess. I need to show her that poem. I need to share it with someone who will understand how confused it makes me, but Loren hates trying to glean something from a poem that might not actually hold up in reality. Aroa will understand. This is especially messy because, in spite of everything, I want my friend back, to be as close to her as I was before she started her relationship with Marín and he became the center of her universe. But still, there's so much stopping me: I feel like a cynic wanting to revive my friendship with someone who, in a way, I'm betraying by loving Marín. But now that he says he wants to turn the page, I don't know what to do. I should tell her because even though I'm in love with him, I still want to protect my friend and I don't want to let her keep building castles in the air… Fuck. I touched her ex-boyfriend's dick and I wanted to do a lot more with him. I still want to. Finger me on top of the camping table, Marín.

"Aroa, will you come with me to the bathroom?" I suddenly blurt.

"Are you okay?"

"I kind of feel like I'm gonna barf."

"Wait, what?" Marín looks at me with a furrowed brow.

"She's knocked up," Gus jokes.

"Yes, sweetie, you knocked her up yourself with the sight of your furry chest. Can you cover up?"

"Listen, Loren, am I making you a little twitchy?" Gus strokes his chest, half-joking, half-charmed by himself.

God. Get me out of here.

"Should I come?" Marín insists.

"No, no. I just want to walk a little and see if…it's just the hangover."

"And my testosterone. I know it's hard to get over."

"Shut up, Gus!" Blanca shrieks, cradling her head in her hands.

Aroa springs up and murmurs something about a nuthouse. She grabs her coffee cup and follows me over the gravelly site, dragging her feet a little. When we're farther away, she comes closer, stops, and asks me, "What's going on?"

I hand her the crumpled napkins without a word and give her time to read them. Fuck. It feels like an eternity. When she looks up at me, there's a face I can't decipher. She's no longer the Aroa full of hope who believes love will conquer all.

"What is this?"

"I found it in my sleeping bag."

"It's from Gus?"

"Of course."

She looks at the poem again, like she's checking it over, and then her eyes flit back to my face. "This doesn't seem weird to you?"

"Gus always seems weird to me."

"Besides that…" She looks at me and makes a face. "I was going to ask you to tell him to trim that chest hair, that blanket he's wearing is kinda douche-lordy, but I'd better stick with this."

"I liked it better when he trimmed it, but it's been a while now…"

"Is it some new trend?" Aroa furrows her brow. "Maybe he saw some Parisienne poet and now he wants to…? Bah, it doesn't matter. The thing is… Doesn't this poem seem weird to you?"

"I'm not really a big poetry reader, just his poems. Specifically."

"Coco…I don't know how to tell you this."

"Just spit it out."

"This… I don't know if this is for you."

I don't know why, but I feel like someone has pulled the rug out from under me. I'm baffled by the disappointment flooding my veins. "What?"

"This… It's not for you. Those Tuesdays in Madrid. Those Sundays over text. This 'it never became what it should' doesn't sound like your thing. This poem… It doesn't scream Coco to me."

"And who does it scream to you?"

"Gus. It reeks of Gus, but not you. Think about it. Maybe… Maybe you should've made a move. It's possible that…he's getting over it."

I snatch the napkins she's holding out and skim them again. Who is it? There's someone. There's someone else in his life. But…why the hell did I find this poem in my sleeping bag? "You're the one who said his latest poems are about me and he wants to get back together with me."

"And I did think that, but…" She takes the napkins again, like she needs to have them in her hand to drive home her message. "This is a side of Gus I don't see when he's with you."

"Right…" Why the hell does this bug me so much? I should feel relieved.

"I'm really sorry, Coco, but you're my friend. I love you… I can't lie to you. I'm sorry I'm not saying what you want to hear."

I look at her, biting her bottom lip, clutching the napkins and waiting for a reaction from me, maybe regretting being so blunt. She's doing what she should, and I'm a dirty dog because I know her hopes of getting back together with Marín aren't going to pan out. I should do the same as her and tell her a truth that will be painful but will also set her free as time passes.

"Aroa, I—"

"I'm sorry, Coco. I'm really sorry. But make a move if you want to get Gus back. Love doesn't last forever."

I close my eyes and grab her arm to make her stop apologizing. "That's not it. Let me talk… I know something that's going to hurt you, but I think you should know."

"God." She runs her hand through her blond hair, and I see her eyes immediately start shining. Brimming with tears. "Marín… What did Marín tell you?"

"I… I'm sorry, Aroa." I feel so bad. "Marín told me last night that he's ready to turn the page. He's given up on your thing. You're not going to get back together."

~

We take fifteen or twenty minutes before we go back because Loren gets worried and comes to find us. Aroa's not crying. Aroa is huddled in a ball on one of those markers with the street numbers and running her fingers over her scalp, like it soothes her.

"I knew it. It's my fault. It's all my fault."

She doesn't say anything else. And now I actually do feel like vomiting.

Loren stands in front of us awkwardly. He doesn't say anything. He just kneels down in front of Aroa, pulls her hands apart, and looks at her. For a few seconds he doesn't say anything, like he's expressing everything he needs to with that look. Finally, he has to add something.

"It's over. Aroa, it's over. Let it go. Start fresh. Don't stay here in a ball. We're going to destroy Blanca's bachelorette trip with all this shit. And she has her own shit. Forget it. Love yourself. Deep down, you already knew Marín was done."

I see Gus walking along a parallel street toward the bathrooms. He doesn't see us. Maybe I should go after him, ask him about the poem, but I'm scared. The last time I followed him to a bathroom to ask him for an explanation, he went down on me while I was standing up.

We decide to move. Aroa snuffles, takes a deep breath, says through clenched teeth that she'll do a good job, that Blanca won't notice a thing. When we get back to the site, she plasters on a happy, carefree expression… I don't know why she doesn't get more parts. She's a great actress. I'd have snot down to my ankles.

Blanca and Marín are talking quietly. I get the feeling Marín is trying to drag what's happening out of her. Good luck, dude. That girl doesn't give anything away. Something is going on with Blanca and her future husband, and after her blathering on about love last night, it couldn't be more obvious. It should bother me that she won't tell me, especially because I think Loren is up-to-date, but I've been so focused on my thing with Marín that…I think I forgot how friendship works.

"What's going on?" we ask as we walk up. "What are you talking about?"

"Nothing. He's giving me hangover cures." Blanca smiles. "This guy, the teetotaler."

Marín tips back in his chair and smiles. "Jesus Christ, Blanca, you're adamantium."

"Oh my God," she moans. "Stop worrying so much. We're on a bachelorette trip."

Marín doesn't seem satisfied with the answer, and Loren's flitting around anxiously. He looks at me, he looks at Aroa, and then he jerks his head. I don't think he wants Marín and Aroa to be too close right now.

"Aroita, can you help me clean up?" I say.

"Wait, I'll help," Marín offers.

"No, no. Don't worry. We'll do it. You figure out the food."

We leave them outside submerged in awkward silence, and Aroa and I concentrate on our task. Plastic plates and spoons in the trash bag. Some of the coffee cups are still half full. We put leftovers in the fridge and back in the cupboards. Diligently. In silence. We take our time, and it might even seem like everything is chill, but I feel like the weight of that silence could fall on top of me and suffocate me. Marín and I in a bunk at dawn. Gus's poem. Blanca's problems, which nobody seems to know anything about, except maybe Loren. Aroa's disappointment about Marín. Gus's bravado.

"Aroa, talk to me, please. I feel so shitty for telling you."

"Fuck, no, Coco." She smiles feebly. "You did the right thing. You were a good friend."

Yes. So good. Such a good friend that I've been dry-humping your ex, who I'm secretly madly in love with. Babe, I love the dude you're so upset about.

I'm the shittiest friend.

"Come on, Coco. It's Blanca's bachelorette party. Let's turn up."

~

When we come out, we don't see Loren, Blanca, or Marín. Gus must be taking a shower. We hear murmurs, and when we look around, we discover them on an empty site opposite. They don't see us. Loren and Blanca are talking. Something's going on here. Marín's running his hands through his hair, visibly flummoxed.

"Wait...what's going on? Is Marín telling everyone he doesn't love me anymore or what?" Aroa asks, her voice trembling.

"No, Aroa. He's not the one telling them something."

Blanca nods, looking at the ground. Loren is talking firmly. Marín seems to be in utter disbelief. What the heck is going on here? My head is about to explode.

When they see us standing outside the RV, they hurry over, fronting like everything's normal.

"What's going on?" I ask again, this time much more sullenly.

"Nothing," Marín answers. "I was telling them that we'd better find a motel for tonight."

"But...we're leaving here tomorrow," I say. "Is it worth the trouble?"

"The camper sleeps six," Aroa states flatly.

"No, no." Marín ruffles his hair, still obviously overwhelmed. He looks at me. I look at him.

My ass rubbing against his cock. The stifled moans. Marín's eyes trail down to my mouth and then my throat. It's possible they make a stop on my braless breasts under my pajama top.

"We're leaving. Tell Gus I'll meet him at the car." He runs his tongue over his lips and turns back to stare at me. "Last night's experience...was enough."

He was awake.

18

WHAT THE FUCK?

MARÍN

When Gus gets in the car, he's wearing one of his classic smiles. The ones that, when you don't know anything about him, could seem like he's charmed to meet you, for being born, to be living in his skin. There's a lot lurking underneath that, of course. We all have our own light and our shadows, I guess. He's pretty good at hiding his true self, but I'm starting to see through it.

"What's the big rush?" he says, apparently relaxed.

I bite back the urge to give him a slap on the wrist like my grandfather used to do when I was being an idiot. Instead, I grip the wheel and breathe. I don't know what the hell this dude is doing with his life. I don't know what came of the little stroll he took yesterday with Coco. I don't understand anything about his life. If we were close enough, I would ask him openly: *What the fuck are you actually up to?* But he's not my brother. I'm not in charge of him, and it's not my place to judge his decisions.

"Hey!" he says, snapping his fingers in my face.

I immediately grab his hand. The conscious part of my brain didn't capture the orders.

"Okay, buddy," I say, a little more gruffly than I'd like. "We need to find a motel."

"Why? I slept great."

Gus could sleep on a stage at a rock concert, but that's no excuse. Loren could too, and he spent all of breakfast complaining through clenched teeth about the night this one gave him.

"All six of us can't fit in there the whole rest of the week."

"Why?" He shrugs. "I'm pretty broke."

Why? Well...for him it must all be so much more comfortable because he's an enlightened being or maybe exactly opposite—an underdeveloped one—but I slept barely six feet from my ex-girlfriend, the one I don't know how to explain to that we can't get back together. If I had any doubts, they've dissipated. Our differences are still there, and they're not something that can be fixed by a few months of distance and a friendly conversation. If someone really loves you, they don't...

It doesn't matter.

"A motel is going to be pricey. It's the middle of peak season..."

"Whatever it costs." I cut him off.

I'm not exactly rolling in it, but I'm trying to be a good guy. And we can't stay in that camper for multiple reasons. For example, because Aroa is going to end up starting an Armageddon and I don't want Coco to be nearby when she explodes; she could get hurt. Or because the vibe is off in there. It reeks of things left unsaid. And because...I went five times too far last night, and I'm mortified right now.

I tried. I learned a few tricks from Aroa about faking certain stuff, and during breakfast I even convinced myself it was all going to be fine and dandy, but no. The conversation with Blanca and Loren did nothing but reaffirm it for me: This is weird. This whole thing is really weird. We're all fucking up our lives in a major way.

All this information is getting jumbled up in my head, and as I pull the car out, it's all crashing against the walls of my skull. I ask Gus to watch out for any signs that say VACANCY and I shut myself in my thoughts.

Aroa must know at this point that I've turned the page. I've tried to tell her so many times and in so many ways, but I guess until I saw her here yesterday, it wasn't even this clear to me. Now I know it can never happen. And she should know that too. If Coco hasn't talked to her, Loren probably has.

Coco…

What a mess.

I have the urge to let go of the wheel and cover my face or, even better, smack my head against it until the airbag springs out. Coco. If I confess what happened with Coco to Loren, he'll slap me across the face. Right now they'd be vacuuming up tiny pieces of me.

I don't know what happened to me. Months of not sleeping with anyone, I guess. Soft, warm skin pressed up against my body. The way she purred as she arched, pushing against my cock. I admit that at first I thought she was asleep, but in the end…no one can really do that stuff when they're completely out of it. What a mess. I rubbed up against Coco's ass like a dog. I nestled my hard cock against her butt, I fondled, I thrusted, I asked for more, pulling her closer to me. I wanted to bite her shoulder, to put my hand between her legs and two fingers inside her until I made her explode. Her. The most important her in my life, and now I've risked it all because of a morning wood moment. Two. Well, the former is my fault; the latter was pretty physiological. I wake up with a hard-on. What can I do about that? The difference is between dry-humping like a teenager or saying a concise "I can't get up right now because I'm hard."

God…I touched her tit under her shirt. She grabbed my dick. I want to die for a second and then be revived in time to jump out of the moving car.

"Motel," Gus says in a bored tone, playing with his phone.

"What?"

"Right there." He points to a three-story building. "There's a motel."

"I'm surprised you even saw it, you're so glued to your phone."

I peek out of the corner of my eye and see him close WhatsApp. I shouldn't get involved, but the whole thing this morning has blown my mind. "Listen, dude." I clear my throat. "Those poems you've been writing lately… Are they for someone?"

"You're all obsessed with looking for a name for something that just flows. There's no rhyme or reason. Past, present, future, other people, pure imagination, a song… Anything can be a catalyst."

I lick my lips. "They're really…good."

"Thanks." He sounds surprised. "I didn't know you liked poetry."

"I'm not an expert, but, well, I follow you, and…there's a been kind of a big leap from the old ones to this new stuff."

"Yeah…" He turns to the window and seems fascinated by the roundabout we're merging into. "I'm inspired, I guess."

"And there's no one special?"

"There are a lot."

"Okay, leave the bragging fuckboy outside the car. You know what I mean."

"No. I don't."

"Wow, suddenly you're an idiot."

Gus turns to me and shoots me a look somewhere between reproachful and surprised. "What the hell is up with you this morning?"

I don't answer. I splutter. "You went for a walk with Coco," I insist after a few seconds of silence. "Anything to report?"

"Are you her father? Or are you her boyfriend? I'm not clear on your role here."

"I'm her best friend. And her roommate."

"It doesn't matter where I went with Coco. Even if we had been fucking behind some bushes, we both know what the deal is."

"And what is the deal?"

"There's a spot there."

A few feet away, a car just left a free parking spot. I'll have to wait to give him the third degree some other time. I swear, normally Gus and I get along really well, but today he's driving me nuts. Not sleeping well makes me feel bad. Not eating well makes me feel bad. Fooling around with my best friend makes me feel bad.

The motel is terrifying. Seriously. Gus flashes sad puppy eyes at me a few times, but even though I'd rather go back to the RV of a thousand loves too, we can't. Neither of us can. If I'm in a hell of a mess, he's spent a year on a roundabout, going around and around endlessly.

"We can look and see if there's another motel in town. Or buy a tent. Let's go buy one of those pop-up tents that you just throw in the air and they open." Gus's tone is pleading, and even though we could go look for another motel, we don't, mostly because I'm pissed off and I don't want to admit that he's right.

"How can I help you?" The gentleman at reception is wearing a white tank top, a gold chain drooping over his chest, and a toothpick hanging out of the corner of his mouth.

Gus and I are both blown away when we see him. He reminds me of someone.

"One room please," I manage to say.

"One or two beds."

"Two," Gus hurries to say.

"Calm down," I say. "You can bet your ass that after the night you gave Loren I have no desire to try it out."

The man shoots us an apathetic look.

I slide my driver's license over the counter to hurry along the procedure. I want to take a shower, although judging by the lobby, I wouldn't be surprised if the kraken comes out of the drain.

The man makes crooked photocopies of our IDs on a mastodon photocopier roaring in the corner while we stare at each other.

"The thing is, he reminds me of someone."

As soon as he turns back to us, he smiles. My God. I have to contain myself so I don't let out a guffaw. Gus straightens up. I think we've both come to the same conclusion: This dude is the Ghost of Gus Yet to Come, an image of what this dandy next to me could turn into. With less hair on his head, more on his chest, shoulders, arms, and who knows where else, with a prominent gut and a tank top covered in sweat stains… The future Gus hands us a heavy wooden key chain with the room number engraved in red.

"Room six."

"Thank you."

"Don't get in too much trouble, okay?" he warns us as he creaks into an armchair that we didn't notice when we came in. "I was young once too, and I know this place is full of pretty girls, but…keep it down. You can do a lot in silence."

"Okay," we both say.

"I was like this too when I was young." He points in our direction. "The truth is, dude, I would've given you a run for your money."

I swear even the color of Gus's face changes.

"You didn't have a girlfriend in Madrid in the late eighties, did you?" I ask.

Gus's kick lands on my shin, but I swallow my yelp. I deserve it.

~

"Dude, that old guy looked like my grandfather," he says when we get to the room.

He's so freaked out he doesn't even notice the hovel we've just walked into. The sheets are faded; there's a worn armchair in the corner. The curtains are crocheted, and the bedspreads folded at the foot of each of the narrow beds are a blood maroon that exposes how much dust they've accumulated.

I peek into the bathroom nervously. Fine. It's clean. We've crashed in worse places.

"That really got under my skin. Maybe my grandfather has an evil twin."

"Or two. That guy looked like you."

"Me? Ha! You've got some balls!"

"Balls… Ask him to show them to you. It'll be like time traveling and seeing how your nether regions hold up after so much use."

The good thing about Gus is that he has a great sense of humor, so he answers with an echoing cackle. He stretches out on the bed, kicks off his shoes, and stares at the ceiling.

"I'm going to take a shower," I inform him.

"I'll go next. The whole putting-the-same-clothes-from-yesterday-on-after-I-took-a-shower-at-the-campsite thing didn't have the desired effect. I feel dirty. Did we make a plan to meet back up with them?"

"No." I shake my head. With all my cluttered thoughts, I hadn't even thought about it.

"Well, we should, right? I'm gonna message them. We'll bring a rotisserie chicken or something like that."

"Who are you going to text?" I'm curious.

"Well…Coco, for example."

For example? Ever since I found out what I know now, it's become very clear that Gus doesn't do things randomly. He doesn't miss a beat. If he's messaging Coco, it's because he's hoping to set off a domino effect. If I was at least okay with what he's doing and who he's doing it with… I'm not saying you shouldn't fight for what you want, but you should always be up-front about it. Honest. Although… Well, who am I to judge? I swallow. God, what a shit show. At least no one's inside my head right now, because they wouldn't understand a single thing and they could misinterpret what I feel.

"I'm going to take a shower," I repeat.

~

I undress in front of the mirror, which doesn't even fog up because I turn the knob until it comes out lukewarm, bordering on cold. I stare at myself in the reflection, and when I blink, I can almost see myself and the pleasure on my face when I felt Coco's fingers wrapping around my cock. I wince, and when I look down, I see that my blood flow is starting to head in a certain direction. It starts swelling like magic.

"No, for God's sake."

Jerking off now wouldn't exactly be a sin, let's be honest. The thing is... Thinking about...Coco? It's been a crazy few months, I've been under a lot of stress, and I guess deep down I'm still waiting for my boss to call to tell me I can come pick up the shit I left in my desk and return my employee card. It's stress; that's what's making me lose my head.

I look at myself in the mirror again. I have huge bags under my eyes. I need a haircut. I haven't even gotten a tiny bit of sun, and I still have that spring complexion: halfway between the paleness of winter and the toasted color of summer. Under the fluorescent light in this bathroom, I'm yellow. I'm halfway down every path... It's a good definition. Halfway to getting over my breakup with Aroa, halfway to accepting that I need to get laid without falling in love or even promising to call the next day, halfway to understanding what makes people keep secrets...or tell lies. I'm halfway to really understanding the foundation my relationship with the world is built on. Coco is half the world for me.

I look down. My dick is still swollen, but I've battened down the horniness with a barrage of dark thoughts.

The water is cascading over me pleasantly, cooling my skin, which immediately gets goose bumps; my nipples stiffen up, and when my hands pass over them as I lather up with soap...boom. I'm in the bunk, I'm feeling Coco's skin, I'm holding her round breast, and her nipple is between my fingers. I saw her in her bra once, accidentally, but I never thought touching her tits would feel like that. So…soft. Her tits are extreme, but not because of their size. They're soft, perfect in my hand, and crowned by nipples that I picture as dark, to go with her olive skin, and so hard.

I would have fucked her, to be honest. In that moment, if we had been alone, I wouldn't have pretended to be asleep. She was going to kiss me, I'm sure of it. Coco always says that sex without good kissing is like going to the movies without popcorn. She was going to put her tongue in my mouth, and I…was going to lose control. To yank off her pajama bottoms and panties, do the same with my boxers, and push into her wet pussy without thinking.

It would've been a mistake. It would've been the end. Just fucking like that, out of nowhere, with my best friend. A recurring mistake for others that I swore to myself I'd never make.

But first I need to accept the truth: I would have fucked her. Like crazy. With me on top. Thrusting and breathing in the scent of her neck and her sex. With me on top? Wait…

Gus told me once, drunk, that the thing he missed most about Coco was the way she would fuck him.

"She fucked me. She devoured me. She would get on top, and she liked pretending that I was the one in control. She wanted me to grab her hard, to shake her, but it was her, dude. She was the one fucking me, and I was the submissive one just pushing. It was a quite a show, having her on top."

I turn the shower a little colder.

At the time, I was uncomfortable having this information. Blanca would always tell me that Loren and I shared a defect: Something about our faces says, "Come and tell me all your shit." If we both started blabbing, I don't know where this group would end up. People's lies tend to create a tangled mess that brings them closer to their loved ones and tears them apart.

When my body has gotten used to the temperature, I turn the tap again, searching for a more intense shock. I want the blood to stop pumping into my penis. I want to make it so small that I have to lift it gingerly between my thumb and my finger. I don't want to even have a dick when I'm thinking about Coco.

It's...disgusting. Right?

Well, not disgusting. She's a woman. I'm a man. We're not blood related. I've always thought she was beautiful. I mean... She's cute, she has style, she's fun and chaotic. She's the kind of woman who's always on some wild-goose chase, who doesn't need to follow the rules to be good, who doesn't need to break them to be bad. She's... She's super tender. She rips through your life like a fucking hurricane and then never leaves. Any guy would want to be with someone like that. Even Gus should count his blessings.

"We broke up because I'm trash and she's a queen," he told me that day, drunk, in the midst of other confessions.

It's hard to know what Gus means when he talks like that. A week later, he posted a poem on Instagram titled "Queen without a crown." It was a farewell to Coco, and there was no doubt about it. It was a pretty bad poem, but it was the last. Somehow, for him, Coco was his anti-muse, I think because nothing he wrote could live up to her. She has too many nuances, and that frustrated Gus. Then he spent a few months writing like crazy about drinking and fucking because I think that's what he did once he "got over" that breakup that didn't seem to have affected either of them that much at first glance. Then he started writing about something else, and Coco started crying at night. I always thought one thing was a consequence of the other. Now I'm not clear on anything.

"Are you showering or doing some kind of tantric masturbation?" Gus bangs on the bathroom door, and I'm yanked out of my reverie. My hair is all foamed up with shampoo, but I don't even remember lathering up.

"I was touching myself thinking about you. And your sister."

"If we start talking about sisters, we'll end up beating the shit out of each other in the plaza."

I crack up. "I'll be right out, you jerk."

The towel feels like sandpaper, but it still dries me quickly. My dripping hair is creating a mosaic of tiny tiles of water on my shoulders. Gus hurtles into the bathroom as soon as I come out and spouts off one of his curse words that have nothing to do with poetry, more about physiological needs. His excuse that "I need to shit like a hoopoe" doesn't hold water. He's in a hurry. He wants to take another shower, douse himself in cologne up to his eyebrows, put on a flowery shirt, and get back to the campsite.

Now, finally, I'm starting to get it. I don't explain it to him. I think he'd just make everything more complicated. I have no idea what he's up to, what he's attempting, what he's doing, or why, but at least now I know that everyone, every single one of us, is keeping a secret on this trip. Unfortunately for Loren, his is knowing everyone else's. Mine… They're piling up, Blanca's is driving me crazy, and, somehow, they all have four letters in the middle of them: Coco.

19

FULL THROTTLE

COCO

Something's going on with Blanca. I'm dying to know what's plaguing her and why she hasn't told me.

Aroa is sad. She seems to be starting to accept that her hopes with Marín aren't based on anything real.

Marín is a little weird.

Gus is a dumbass. But he has a great ass, to be fair.

I rubbed against Marín like a cat in heat last night, and I think he was awake.

I'm somewhere between nine and ten on the scale of a girl-code-breaking, shitty friend and a terrible person.

I feel like Blanca is avoiding me, but I also feel like that assumption would be pretty egotistical and a little paranoid. She's not avoiding me; she's just trying to be Zen, and to do that, she's avoiding everyone. When Gus and Marín left, she changed into her bathing suit, gathered up her stuff, and settled in under one of the umbrellas next to the pool. She doesn't want to go down any of the slides. She says she's so hungover she'd probably just projectile vomit.

"Loren..." I whisper, taking advantage of Aroa going back to the motor home to grab more beer. "What's going on with Blanca?"

"She's hungover," he says through a loud yawn.

"What were you two talking to Marín about earlier? You were whispering. Something's going on."

"Don't worry about it."

"What were you talking about with Marín?"

Loren scoffs and leans against the edge of the pool, letting his legs float. "Blanca told Marín they should go to a motel, for Aroa's sake. It's obvious he doesn't want to get back together with her, and this isn't a good place for them to figure out their situation, with all six of us stuck under the same roof."

I stare at him, a little stunned. I'm a narcissistic and egotistical nutjob. I thought it was something else, like they were hiding something from me. Or maybe they are hiding something and they're just really good at lying?

"But everything's okay with Ruben?"

"Yeah." He nods confidently. "Look at her. She's probably talking to him on the phone right now."

On her sun chair, hidden behind her huge Saint Laurent sunglasses, Blanca's fidgeting with the tassels on her towel as she talks on the phone. I relax. She seems much less upset than she was this morning. When Aroa passes by and puts a beer on her chair, she responds with a smile. Relax, Coco. You're getting paranoid. Look at her… Blanca is the living image of success. She's a great lawyer who, I mean, yeah, she's super burned out at work, but she's fighting for her dream future career. She makes bank. She has a beautiful apartment. She's going to marry Ruben, who isn't the closest with our friends, but they make a great team. She has style. She's happy…

Is she happy?

Okay. I'm paranoid.

"You know what would help you?" Loren says, sinking into the pool all the way up to his neck.

"What?"

"Telling Blanca that you're not in love with Gus."

I widen my eyes. "Now?"

"Now. Why not? I don't get why you've been hiding it."

"Because I don't want to give her any more headaches." Loren looks at me with raised eyebrows and sucks his teeth. "Okay, fine. And because in the end she's going to ask me why I lied and then…I'll have to admit that I'm in love with Marín and…" I whip my head around to check no one's close by. Aroa is sitting on the edge of the pool, her feet on the sun chair where Blanca is slumped.

"So what? She's your best friend. Are you embarrassed?"

"Would you tell your best friend that you're actually a shitty friend?" I answer a little angrily. "Fuck, Loren. I want to steal Aroa's ex. It's not that easy."

"It's easier than you think."

I snort and lean my head against the side of the pool. "I have to tell you something." But I'm not looking at him as I say it.

"Please tell me you didn't fuck Gus in a bush last night?"

I sit up straight and shoot him a look. "Wait. You really think I fucked Gus in a bush?"

"It's Gus. You once fucked him in a closet."

"It wasn't a closet. It was…the storage room at work," I clarify glumly.

"Same diff."

"It doesn't matter. That's not it."

"I don't know if I wanna know," he grumbles.

"Well, I need to tell you."

Loren snorts and nods, but when I start to speak, he shoves a finger between us. "I'll listen, but in exchange, you have to tell Blanca that you're not in love with Gus."

"Why are you so obsessed with that?"

"Because she's your best friend, she thinks you're in love with your ex, and your ex is on the *Forbes* list for guys who have gotten their dicks wet the most this year. She's worried about you."

Ay, fuck. Different place, same shit. "Okay." I nod. "But I'll do it when I deem appropriate."

"Come on then… What do you wanna tell me?"

"This morning…Marín and I…rubbed each other."

Loren's expression looks like a hyperrealist painting of horror and destruction. "Excuse me?"

"Yeah, right. I know." A tiny smile plays at my lips. "Am I allowed to say it was pretty great?"

"Was it?"

"Totally. But brief." I let out a muffled scream. "Loreeeeen, I touched it."

"But, wait, hold up… You two woke up and suddenly decided that, after four years of living together, of treating each other like you're cousins, it was a good idea to touch each other's privates?"

"No. Not exactly."

"Explain yourself. And, please, try to make it fit in a tweet."

"But then you could tweet it."

"Who still has Twitter now that it's called X?" He gawks.

I'm not going to argue right now about what social media's cool these days, so I continue my narration. "I woke up, and we were holding each other. So…I moved my butt because…I don't know, I was probably still a little tipsy from the wine or something like that and it seemed like a good idea and…"

"Coco…cut to the chase, please. We look sketchy, whispering over here."

"Well, I jiggled my butt like a cat in heat, and he didn't hold back either. We were rubbing up against each other for a while." I pinch my thumb and finger together and add, "But when I turned around to kiss him, he turned the other way, pretending to be asleep."

"How do you know he wasn't asleep?"

"Because later, when they left, he said something and..."

"So witchcraft."

"A little." I nod. "Oh, God, Loren...am I going to fuck it all up? Or have I already fucked it all up?"

"You're both going to fuck it all up."

I don't want to smile, but it always makes me laugh when Loren suddenly seems like an eighty-year-old with superhuman knowledge of aphorisms. Then I have a jolt of conscience, and I whimper. "I'm a bad friend."

"Drop the bad friend shit. Is Aroa perfect? You're not doing this on a whim. You've been, fuck... How long have you been in love with Marín?" he whispers. "A year?"

"A little over."

"Did you try to break them up? No. Did you pressure them for your own benefit? No. Did you try to toe the line and just be his friend? Yes. Did you ever go too far? No. At this point, fuck, Coco, let every dog lick its own dick."

I grimace, and he apologizes for the expression while he tousles his hair with his damp hand.

"Look, Coco, I'm gonna be really honest. You're driving me nuts." I make a horrified face, but he hurries to explain. "Not you. Everyone. You have your lies, and everyone else has their secrets, and I don't know why you all end up telling me everything. And I understand what you're doing, you specifically, because you trust me and you're looking for advice, right?"

"Yes," I say, with my lips pursed.

"Well, here's my advice: If you're overwhelmed by the lie, start making it smaller. Don't feed it."

"Maybe you're right."

"Not maybe...I am. But come on. That's nothing new." A smile sneaks onto his mouth, and he elbows me. "Let's just have a good time, please."

And that plea came out of his mouth, but it easily could've come out of mine.

~

When Marín and Gus show up, the vibe is like a very tense steel wire, the kind that holds up bridges and makes a sinister noise when they snap in action movies.

Loren's right. I have to start doing whatever I can to make this better, and lying to my best friend because I'm embarrassed to tell her certain things is not it.

Gus is wearing a short-sleeve shirt that I'm not ready for, not because I'm into it but because it's going to trigger an epileptic attack. I never thought the textile industry would cram that many colors on one single garment.

"I come bearing chicken."

"Did you say chicken or cock?" Loren asks him very seriously as he dries himself off with his towel.

"There's chicken in the bag," he specifies, raising his eyebrows. "If you want to look for the other one..."

"Do I look interested?"

"I don't know. You tell me. I've never tried it with a guy; the time has probably come."

Gus is joking, but he's taking it too far, to be honest. Marín must feel the same way because his hand lands on Gus's shoulder a little heavier than you'd expect from a friendly pat.

"Let's end the comedy festival there and set the table. I want to call my boss and the artist formerly known as Noa. I'm worried her teeth might've been knocked out."

"Are you guys wearing bathing suits?" I ask from the water.

"Yup."

They answer in unison as they head back to our site. I look at Aroa, who's smiling politely. I look at Blanca, who lowered her sunglasses and waved. I look at Loren, who's beckoning me to tell me the time has come to get out of the pool.

"Aroa, will you go to the supermarket with me?" he says to her.

"Mmm?" she replies distractedly.

"Will you come to the store next to reception? We need to buy ice and more plastic cups."

"Plastic cups are bad for the environment," she points out. "But, sure. I'll make you all more conscientious little by little."

"Conscience, conscience…"

When we're left alone, I go over to Blanca and sit down, wrapped in my towel, on the chair next to her. "Blanqui…"

"What's up?" she asks.

"The water feels so good." I stroke her hair. "Don't you wanna take a dip?"

"No, no way. Plus the guys are here now and I'm hungry."

"Yeah. Me too." God, what a dumbass conversation. "Are you okay?"

"I have a headache…" She touches her temples. "Aroa brought me a beer, and I almost barfed just from looking at it. I swear I'm never gonna drink again in my life."

"Or until tonight."

"That's possible too." A smile unfurls across her face, and she pats my leg. "Coco…"

"What?"

"How are you?"

"Fine." I smile.

"No, seriously… How are you?"

I swallow. "This is your bachelorette party, Blanca, and here we are in the middle of a shit storm… We're ruining it for you, aren't we?"

"What? No!" She whips off her sunglasses and drops them. "The gang?"

"Yes. Aroa with her obsession with getting back together with Marín, me with my…shit."

"What are you talking about?" She laughs. "It's exactly what I needed to get my head out of work. I love our shit! This bachelorette trip couldn't be all alcohol and giggles. It wouldn't work without a little drama, you know that."

"Really?"

"I swear!" She holds up her right hand.

"Oh God, I'm so relieved! I thought you were avoiding me."

"I was avoiding everyone! I thought I was the one ruining it!"

"You? Why?"

"I mean, because…I'm kind of out of it. I dunno." She bites her lip. "And yesterday I got so ridiculously wasted…"

"What are you talking about, ridiculous? Ridiculous was when Aroa tried to look sexy downing a shot and she chipped a tooth."

Blanca laughs, but she suddenly looks away. Something's definitely bothering her.

"This trip is for you, so you can relax, have fun…" I insist.

"I don't want to seem ungrateful."

"You're just a little stressed. We're not exactly helping. In a few days, you'll be making us steal a supermarket cart again. Tell me, what's going on? Are you anxious about work or about the wedding?"

"I just don't want you to worry."

"I'm your best friend." A pang of remorse trickles down my side.

"Ruben and I haven't really been getting along lately."

I knew it! "How come?"

"I don't know." She rubs her eyes and then hugs her legs. "Too much work maybe. We see each other all the time, but we never see each other. Maybe I'm the problem, you know? When I'm with him…I feel bored. I feel…like I'm disappearing in my own life, like I don't have control over anything."

"If anyone knows what they're doing with their life, it's you, Blanca." I scoot next to her and put an arm around her shoulder.

"You know when you feel like you're not doing anything right? Mediocre at home, mediocre as a woman, mediocre as a friend…"

"Don't go there. That's not true."

"What if I'm not a good friend?" She looks at me gravely. "What if I'm not, Coco?"

Yeah, Coco. What if you aren't either?

"I have to tell you something," I blurt out. "But I'm scared you're gonna be mad at me."

"I'm not gonna be mad. I think I can guess. Loren says I'm paranoid, but…"

I raise one eyebrow. "What's your guess?" I ask.

"The Gus thing."

"You know?"

"Fuck, Coco… It's kinda obvious." Her expression changes, and she hardens again. "It's not like either of you is trying very hard to hide it. And by the way, I'm not going to give you any lectures. I told you a few days ago… If you want him, go for it. But just be aware that this could just be a relapse and he…well, Coco, you probably know this, but Gus has been in a lot more beds than—"

I smile and stop her. "Blanca," I say. "You're barking up the wrong tree."

"What do you mean, I'm barking up the wrong tree?"

"I lied. I've been lying for months. I'm not in love with Gus."

The reaction is immediate: Her shoulders relax, her eyes widen and shine, her lips fall open, she starts breathing faster. *I'm in deep shit.*

Her slap to my arm comes so fast I don't even see it coming. It stings, but she goes straight for another blow. "What?"

"Shh. I'm not in love with Gus, fuck's sake. But don't hit me. I thought you'd be happy."

"But...wait..." She shrinks a little more, rubs her face, pushes her hair away, takes another swipe at me, and puts her sunglasses on her head. "You couldn't be a bigger dumbass if you tried. You've been lying to me for a year!"

"Yes." I nod.

"Why? I've been so worried about you!"

"I mean, because...because...I'm in love with someone else and I didn't want anyone to find out."

"But Loren knows."

I sit on the next chair over again and nod. "Yes. Loren knows."

"Why?"

"Well, because...I don't know! It's that face he has. It makes you trust him. I've been so close to telling you so many times, but I always end up thinking that I'm going to influence you and that if the group breaks up it'll be all my fault, and...I'm ashamed to admit that I'm such a shitty friend. It was easier to agree when you asked me if I was upset about my breakup than to admit the truth."

"And what is the truth? And please don't tell me that you're actually in love with Loren because then I *will* have to climb the slide just so I can dive headfirst onto the concrete."

"Seriously?" I raise one eyebrow. "You seriously can't figure out who I'm actually hung up on?"

This time her expression changes slowly, in a silence that feels eternal. She doesn't take long to close her eyes and scoff. You don't have to be an expert in body language to know that she just said: *This is so fucking messy.*

"Marín," she whispers.

"Marín."

"Fuck." She reaches out toward me, and I flinch because I think she's going to hit me again, but she pulls me closer. She hugs me. She kisses me on the temple. Suddenly, she's squeezing really hard, and I have to pull away with a smile.

"Are you trying to strangle me with love or what?" I defend myself.

"Since when have you been in love with Marín?"

"Since…oof. He was still with Aroa. As soon as it ended with Gus, I realized that…I was head over heels in love. It's like…it was injected into me. When I tried to get it out of my head, it was already in my blood."

"And you had to live with him while he was still with Aroa…in love with him?"

"Yes." I nod.

"But you never said anything about the breakup, you were there for Aroa… You didn't try anything? You didn't talk to Marín? You didn't…?"

"No."

"But why not?"

"I always thought they'd get back together. I mean… I used to at least."

"Why don't you think so anymore?"

"Because Marín has turned the page."

She stares at me anxiously and nods. "Yeah. I guess so."

"Girl." I wave my hands apologetically. "I'm sorry. I'm sorry I hid it from you. It's just so messy."

"Yeah, Coco, but spending a year swearing you're hung up on Gus?"

"I know. I totally get it if you're mad. If you told me you had been lying to me for a year about something like this… Fuck, it'd be really hard to forgive. Lies should only be for…for not hurting other people, but they never end well. Someone always ends up hurt."

Blanca licks her lips and takes a deep breath.

"Look, Coco… We all lie. All of us. It makes sense you didn't want to gush about how you feel about Marín because, on top of everything else, you're probably scared. That's what happens when you fall in love, especially when you really fall in love. But…we all lie. We all keep secrets. We all shove skeletons into our closets and think they'll never be discovered."

"But they always are," I say.

"Not always. Sometimes they're found out, and other times, it rots you from the inside out. Does Gus know?"

"No. Well, yesterday Marín told me they had been talking and that Gus said he was sure I'm not in love with him. He also kinda snuck it in on the walk we took last night."

"And does Marín know?"

"Apparently everyone suddenly thinks it's obvious I'm lying, but no… He doesn't know I'm in love with him. And…last night, well, really this morning…something happened."

She looks grossed out. "Did you fool around?" She raises her eyebrows.

"No. It didn't get to that. It was just…like when you're crazy horny and you try to wake your boyfriend up by wiggling your ass…you know."

"Oh, God…and have you two talked about it?"

"No." I shake my head in a panic. "He made like he was sleeping, so…"

"So?"

"I don't want to ruin it. Maybe it's better if we act like it never happened."

"But it did happen, and on top of that, for you, it means something. Believe me…shutting up is never, ever the best option. It's like ignoring the pink elephant in the room: It's still sitting there."

"Marín, Aroa, Gus… It's such a mess, Blanca. Such a fucking mess."

“I don’t understand anything.” She shakes her head and pushes her hair out of her face.

I raise one eyebrow. “What do you mean?”

Blanca’s staring into space, but knowing her, she’s probably re-creating something in her mind’s eye… A memory, all the possibilities to take into account if you do or say something else, a fear…

Suddenly she discovers me there, like she wasn’t expecting me, but she smiles. “Coco…love is so complicated.”

20

DANCING IN THE MOONLIGHT

COCO

The good thing about this bachelorette party is that it's not a regular bachelorette party. First of all, because it's a mixed group, which sometimes causes a few problems. Second of all, because we have a lot more time and that gives us time to fit in a lot of fun, long, leisurely meals, quiet naps, self-absorption, ranting at each other, hours of sleep, the landscapes we'll drive through, the coffee and toast with olive oil and tomato for breakfast, time in the pool, posed photos, and a few candid photos. But like everything in this world, something as wonderful as finally having time to relax with your nearest and dearest has a dark side too: Carrying the weight of your secrets and lies for a couple hours at a time is totally different from lugging it on your shoulders for the entire trip. Many of us are starting to get tired arms.

Despite the impression Gus might give, with his smile that doesn't show his teeth and his air of a tortured poet, he has a special charm. When the sun is shining inside him, when he has a moment where everything clicks, he's charming. And that's what he's being right now: a charmer. And that helps ease the tension in the air: my rubbing with Marín, his irreversible breakup with Aroa, Gus's mistress-less poems, whatever's making Blanca seem so down, the information piling up inside Loren that, I'd bet my whole hand, he can't take anymore.

After lunch, Gus struck up a conversation with the middle-aged English couple in the next site over. They don't know much Spanish and Gus doesn't know much English, but they understand each other perfectly. They joke and tease each other about how there's a time difference even though Spain and England are so close together, and they chat about customs: paella, siesta, coffee... After a while, Gus shows up on the edge of their plot with two of the Styrofoam cups Loren and Aroa just bought so that the plastic ones wouldn't melt from the heat of the coffee (Aroa heard that's really toxic) and offers them to our English neighbors while we make the most of ours.

They ask us when we're leaving. "Tomorrow," we answer with sad faces. Our next destination depends a little on what we see when we get to where we're supposed to eat lunch. They're enthusiastic about our adventure, how we're all celebrating our friend's wedding and that we're not noisy at all... They love that too. Apparently, we're not brawling as loudly as we thought.

"Wow, look at this amazing hammock. This...is cool." Gus points at a rope hammock hanging between two trees on the other part of the neighboring site.

"We bought it in Mexico," they say excitedly.

"Maybe if I convince these losers...our next trip, nuestro viaje...más lejos, far away. To Mexico, tal vez, maybe."

"Have you...tried?" They nod at the hammock.

"No." He shakes his head. "But I'll have to bring one back when I go to put in my living room."

I don't think they understood that last part, but fifteen minutes later, the hammock is set up next to our motor home, next to the table where we're making lunch.

"Tomorrow you go...bye-bye. Enjoy it today."

We take turns trying it, but, of course, the one who ends up falling asleep in it is Gus, who suddenly looks like a communion boy. Blanca,

Marín, and I, sitting on the steps to the camper and some chairs, watch him with a smile, while Loren and Aroa take a siesta in their bunks.

Blanca is puffing slowly on a cigarette, and the smoke is making pretty white swirls, which disappear almost instantly.

"Look at him," Marín murmurs. "Seeing him all peaceful like this, anyone would think he was a good little boy and all that."

"He is a good boy," Blanca pipes up. "But…"

"But he doesn't know how to shut up," I add.

"I don't think that's the problem," she replies. "I think the problem is that he shuts up when he shouldn't and he talks when it's not his turn. And that gets him in a lot of trouble."

"That's a good description," Marín says. "The guy in the motel is his spitting image in forty years."

"Seriously?" We both smile at him.

"Yeah. But in a bad way. It's like the ghost of summers yet to come: If you keep going with a life of excess, you're going to turn out like me."

"This guy?" Blanca side-eyes him, raising her eyebrows. "He'll turn out better than anyone. He's very savvy. A survivor. When we least expect it, he'll announce his engagement to a duchess; he was born to be a kept man. To pamper himself, read, and drink good wine."

I glance over at him. Maybe. He lives hard, loves life, hates the world and sometimes himself, but Gus is at one of those points in his cycle when his poetry is speaking someone's name for him. I don't know if he's having trouble accepting it or if he doesn't want anyone to know, but there's something more than flirtation stuck in his head.

"He's into someone," I say softly.

"You think so?" Marín asks. "I asked him this morning, and he said—"

"That poetry is in the air and doesn't belong to anyone and blah, blah, blah…right? I was with him for almost a year. I know exactly when Gus is smitten because…he actually never has been. Does that make sense?"

“Not really,” Blanca teases.

“Neither Gus nor I was in love. I’ve never really seen him that excited about any of his dalliances. It’s the first time he’s been like this, and...he’s really feeling some type of way because he’s seeing life from the other side: melancholy, nostalgia, hostility... This Gus isn’t the regular bon vivant Gus. This is him in love. Look...”

I creep into the camper slowly so I don’t wake any of the others and rummage in one of the cupboards until I find the crumpled napkins. I creep out again and sit on the steps of the motor home after I hand them over.

“Aroa said some of his recent poems were for me, and I almost believed it. It’s an ego thing, I guess. The thing is... I found these crumpled up in my sleeping bag. I’ve been thinking about it, and he probably meant to toss them in the trash, but with the wine and the dark, he missed and they fell into the bunk. This poetry... It’s not for me. And we all know it.”

Marín and Blanca huddle over the pieces of paper as they read. Blanca has to wait for Marín to finish before she can turn each piece over and keep reading. When they’re done, they glance at each other and then at me.

“Um...wow,” Marín whispers, “I’d say Gus is in love.”

“He’s in deep,” I declare.

Deep. Like me with Marín. That’s why I recognize it—we’re both lovesick.

~

As with any nocturnal animal, you normally have to wait for night to fall before Gus perks up. When we were together, he didn’t usually stir from his lethargy until seven in the evening. But not today, of course. Today, after a catnap, he wakes up raring to go. And now he wants to go to the beach. And Blanca, Aroa, and I agree because we want to see the ocean, but Loren doesn’t feel like it.

Marín walks next to me with one of those half smiles that make a beautiful dimple in his cheeks, and I can't stop looking at it. I contemplate whether I should talk to him about this morning, but his expression puts me off. I don't want to face the moment of tension, especially not right now.

Aroa is trying to mask everything, but we're watching her. Well, in this case I think it's more like "we're watching it." My heart is split for Aroa. On one side, I understand that it can be horrible to see all your hopes of getting back together with the person you love crumble. And I feel bad because I'm barging into the rubble of what they had, trying to find out if the land is habitable, if I can scavenge something from here for myself. She's my friend, but he could be the love of my life. What am I doing? I was always one of those girls, teenagers, young women who looked down on anyone who would put bros before sisters. So what am I doing?

Well, it's not any man—it's Marín.

And, on the other hand, I have to admit that he's been pretty firm, especially for the past few months. The reason they broke up is still there, and for him it's important. What could it be? Gema… Maybe it's her.

"Have you talked to Gema?" I ask him, seizing her name popping into my head to break the silence.

"Yeah." He nods and smiles. "Although, apparently you have too."

"That was days ago. What did she tell you?"

"Not much. As soon as I get back to Madrid, I'm going to go pick her up. We're going on a sibling trip."

"Sounds like an awesome plan." I nod, looking forward again and meeting eyes with Aroa, who looks away instantly. "My brothers never took me on a trip."

"Never?"

"Does locking me in a closet with all the skis on a family trip count?"

"It's a point for them going to hell, that's for sure. Wanna come?"

"To hell? No, but there'll be an all-inclusive wristband waiting for me at the gate. Satan is filing his nails while he waits for me."

"Hell is reserved for people like Gus." He laughs, jerking his head toward him. "Writers, painters, models, DJs..."

"Sounds like a party, dude. I think I wanna go to hell now."

"I meant the trip, Sardine." He elbows me. "If you wanna come on our little escapade, I'm sure Gema would love having you with us."

An explosion in my stomach feels like a firework, and I could swear a spark escapes from my nose when I try to take a deep breath. Soooooooo we're not going to talk about how I touched his penis and he fondled my nipple, but from the looks of it, we can still be Sardine and Anchovy. And make plans. Intimate. Like...a couple?

"No," I answer more goofily than I'd like. "It's a sibling trip. I don't want to impose."

"Well...since yours are assholes, Gema and I can be your stand-in siblings. Anyway, we're practically like siblings already."

Being slapped by a six-foot grizzly bear would've hurt less than Marín letting me know I'm like a sister to him. My schoolgirl smile immediately transforms into a grin like a horse showing its teeth, and then I press my lips together, trying to look carefree.

"Why does your face look like an asshole?" Loren screams, dying laughing. "I've seen dog's asses that are cuter!"

I can't even answer him. I'm having a stroke. Siblings? I've touched his penis!

Blanca appears out of nowhere and grabs my arm, yanking me away from Marín. "Baaabe! Come here. I have a question about menstrual cups."

I follow her with my lips stuck together and wrinkled, pretty much like an asshole.

"What's going on with your face?" she whispers, trying to contain her laughter.

"He said...we're already basically like siblings. Like siblings. Like siblings," I mutter through clenched teeth.

"Oh, God…" She glances back, where Marín and Gus have paired up.

"Do you think you'll go to hell, Gus?" I hear him say.

"To hell? Let's see, let's see. Assuming I believe in hell, why would I be going there?"

"Because you're so slutty," Loren yells. "And because you take four hours to come. You make the rest of the men on earth look bad, so that condemns you to eternal flames."

I hear Gus give some foul retort, and I want to step in and tell him to stop being such a show-off, but I'm still in shock.

"Are you listening to me?" Blanca says, speeding up and steering me past everyone else.

"No. I was listening to my ex say that having the cock he has is a mortal sin."

"Well, listen to me because this is serious: That comment…sounds weird to say the least."

"I know. It's not even that big. It's got some girth, that's true, but you wouldn't exactly be saying: 'OMG, the Italian Stallion's descendant just showed up to pound me.'"

"Coco," she pleads. "We're not going to get anywhere if you keep deflecting. Marín told you that you're practically siblings."

"Yeah, I know. Don't beat a dead horse, please."

"Look, you're an idiot… You sound like you were born yesterday! When a guy says that after you grabbed his dick, it's because he's trying to check."

"Got it. You're still destroying my dreams, by the way, if you hadn't noticed."

"Read between the lines, Coco. You're so good at interpreting symbolic paintings, this should be easy. If he needs to check it's because…it's not clear to him!" she exclaims quietly.

I pull away from her a little and start to smile. "You're nuts, you know that?"

"Trust me. I'm a lawyer."

"And what does that have to do with the price of fish?"

"Well, there's definitely something fishy here. Lawyers are twisted, but we don't usually get stuff wrong, believe me. The thing this morning put him in the danger zone. He's insecure. This guy"—she glances back—"he's been touching his foreskin thinking about you."

A cackle bursts out of our mouths, and we squeeze our linked arms.

"God... Good thing I told you," I say. "I needed that."

"Loren wasn't doing that?"

"Loren?"

"Yeah, stupid question. I can already hear him: 'Coco'"—she puts on a serious voice to imitate him—"'forget it right now or you'll be responsible for everything bad that happens in the universe for the next five hundred years.'"

"What's with all the giggling?"

Loren and Aroa have caught up, and he grins at us. He knows we're making fun of him and that it's out of love.

"We were saying that you're always so understanding and no matter what happens you're on love's side."

"Love is so cringe. You'll understand some day. I'm trying to do you a favor, but you can't make a horse drink."

Love is cringe—it's probably true—but only when you're not one of the people involved.

~

I can't see us from the outside—mostly because it's physically impossible for me to do so unless I can figure out astral travel—but I think we're pretty close to being a summer beer ad.

We take a dip in a beautiful sea. It's clear, turquoise, and rough (the Mediterranean isn't always flat), and we goof around in the usual splashes and attempts at chicken fights. Gus ends up moaning because Aroa won thanks to the superhuman strength from the fairies she's descended from, but he gets all mixed up and says he was defeated by the elven power of her ancestors.

"You can't do it like that!" he says, grabbing his shoulder and explaining that it smashed into the sand on the bottom. "Like I was Captain America!"

The silliness takes hold of all of us, and soon we're all running around the sand, wrestling each other while we scream things like "with the power of Hitman" or "I'm Wonder Woman." Without a drop of alcohol, by the way. Forget spinning classes, Zumba, and the Chicago Marathon. We're panting, sweating, dunking each other, launching each other into the water, playing chicken fights. The only one who always comes out victorious is Marín because he's too tall for us to be able to tackle him and he always ends up charging me like a bull, hoisting me onto his shoulder, and then chucking me far out into the water. In the fraction of a second it takes for me to land in the sea, I say I love him a hundred times.

Sunset finds us sitting on the sand, our towels buried under the dunes we've been creating with all our frolicking. We're all lined up shoulder to shoulder. Blanca is to my right; Marín's to my left. Next to him, Loren grabs my bun and yanks me backward.

"This. This is the life," I murmur.

Marín looks at me out of the corner of his eye, and I flop backward and laughingly poke Loren so he'll leave me alone.

"This… Coco." I look back at Marín, and his eyes, fuck… His eyes are so clear, tinged with the orange of the receding day, the creeping night. I would dive in headfirst. To his mouth, to life, even to the ocean.

"This?" I ask because this silence, while we're both staring at each other, makes me uncomfortable when there's an audience.

"This and all of you. That's the life."

When he puts his hand on mine, on the sand, I have to work hard to rein in my emotions. *So you're saying...there's a chance?*

Maybe. And maybe this group can, finally, put down all the weights we're carrying.

21

THE PERFORMANCE

COCO

Once we've decided we don't want to make dinner and that we'll eat outside at the campsite's bar to celebrate our last night here, we realize the evening will include a show.

Our plastic tables are groaning under the weight of trays full of fries doused in ketchup and mayonnaise, and each of us is holding a burger dripping sauce everywhere. There aren't enough napkins in the world for us to feel clean, especially because of how hard we're laughing (kind-heartedly, don't get us wrong). When we see how seriously the kids from the campsite are taking their musical performance, it's impossible not to get the giggles.

Right now some girls who must have spent the last week rehearsing are giving it their all on the stage, dancing to a pop song. We're blown away. I'm twenty-eight, and I still haven't learned to move my hips like them.

"That's dancing, queens," Aroa says with a smile.

"When we dance, it looks more like that video of the dog doing the salsa," Blanca points out.

"I've seen you girls twerking, and it was pretty disturbing."

"Poetry," Loren spits, answering Gus. "Stick to poetry…and not the kind…"

"Go on, what kind? This erudite guy here," the accused teases. "The most poetry you've read is on the back of a sugar packet."

"You're an idiot. Neruda, Whitman, Baudelaire, Rimbaud..."

We all gape at Loren.

Suddenly, I jump up, throwing down my burger and clapping along to the music, like the retired ladies at the next table over.

"If the ladies at the next table start singing, tie Coco up because she'll be onstage next," Gus laughs.

"There's a better chance you'll start reciting poetry," I retort.

"Wowzer, the whole table's talking shit about poetry tonight. I mean... what's the prize? If you tempt me, maybe I will go up there and dedicate a few words to you guys."

"An ode to stupidity," Aroa adds with a half smile.

"I don't know what you'll win, but if you get up there, you'll definitely lose your dignity."

I take another bite of my burger and wipe my fingers and mouth on a used napkin. Disaster. Everyone looks at me and bursts out laughing.

"Better if Coco goes up there. We'd probably get some kind of compensation from the government for bringing her on this trip with us."

"Okay, come here..."

Marín grabs the clean napkin from under his plate and wipes my face. My eyes are about to roll back in my head from the sensory pleasure, but I glance at Aroa, who's openly watching us.

"Do you normally do this at home?" she asks. The good vibe from the beach must have been left back there in the sand. Her voice sounds friendly but tense.

"It's not usually necessary. We have bibs," Marín jokes. "God, you have so much mayonnaise everywhere, it's probably in your hair. You just need to get straight in a shower."

"Sounds like an indecent proposal," Gus points out.

Gus, dude, you're a dumbass.

"More like an older brother, right, Marín?" I feel like the look he gives me is filled with disgust, but that's just my perception.

He nods and smiles. "I'm going to have to apply for legal guardianship from the state on top of the compensation."

"The apartment would be way cheaper then."

"For the time you have left there, right?" Aroa asks.

I shoot Aroa a confused look. "What are you talking about?" I ask, casually.

"I dunno... Isn't your lease ending soon or something like that, Marín?" she questions.

Marín drops the napkin onto the table and shifts in his chair. "No. Our lease goes until the end of the year, but the landlord loves us and I'm sure he'd renew it. We pay religiously, we've never had any problems with the neighbors, we haven't broken anything... We're exemplary tenants. But, listen, is there a specific reason you're saying that?"

There's a challenge in the air, but Aroa doesn't bite. She doesn't even answer, but it's easy to see there's a little pebble of rage there. Marín is glaring at her, even though she turned her back to pretend she's watching the performance. She seems annoyed, even disappointed. I put my right hand, which is relatively clean, under the table and squeeze his knee. I'm trying to tell him that I've got his back, but he has to be calm. It's not the time to fight with his ex-girlfriend. It's becoming clear to me that part of the problem between these two sprang up because Aroa, who always seems so chill about everything, is kind of bothered that he lives with me and not with her.

"So...should we get a drink?"

It's the first time on this trip that everyone at the table looks appreciatively at Gus, who raises his eyebrows trying to break the tension that has robbed our little corner of oxygen.

"My treat."

"If it's your treat, then even I'll have one." Marín smiles at him.

"Are you calling me cheap?" Gus pretends to be offended, stabbing his chest with his finger, right between his pecs, over his shirt. But he quickly opens his hand and strokes his chest. "God, I'm so sexy."

We all cackle, and he stands up.

"Five beers?"

"Wow, you're such a cheapskate," Blanca moans. "I want a gin and tonic."

"And I want a rum and Coke," I say with a smile.

"Jesus…why not just get a candy liqueur. So sweet," Gus grumbles. "Anyone else?"

"I don't want anything." Aroa seems regretful and a little embarrassed.

I give her a little kick under the table, and when she looks at me, I try to send her a message telepathically: *Come on, cheer up.* I don't know, either I'm abnormal or it's just that I'm a fake and bad person. I probably have some kind of multiple personality disorder.

"I'll have a Larios Twelve with Coke Zero," Loren pipes up.

"Cool. Let's see," Gus puts his hand in his pocket and fishes out a twenty-euro bill.

"Will this be enough?"

If we lived in Paris in 1850, Gus would die of tuberculosis in a dingy garret, a scrawny alcoholic. And probably with syphilis.

~

It's two in the morning. We don't really know how that happened. We were planning to go to bed early because later today we have to pack everything up and get this show on the road, but after the musical numbers, we went nuts. The retired ladies did end up performing, and we were about to improvise something and go up there. Even Aroa cheered up a little…I think. She's such a good actress that you never know if she's put on a mask or if it's actually her. Now, after three rums, I wonder if that doubt could be applied to the rest of our lives together. I wonder if I really know her that well. We all keep secrets, that much I do know. We all lie.

We walk back to our site doubled over with laughter. We want to have a nightcap in the RV, but a quiet one because we don't want to bother our English neighbors now that we know how sweet they are. But halfway back, we come across the pool. And the temptation is strong.

It's surrounded by a tall fence that is locked at night, but from down here and with so many of us, it doesn't seem too challenging to hop the fence and go for a silent swim. Loren even tries it, but obviously just to prove it's not a piece of cake and get us to give up. When he climbs back down the wall supporting the fence and announces it's impossible, it only makes Marín more into the idea.

"Daddy longlegs," Loren warns him, cracking up. "If they throw us out of the campsite on our last night, I'll kill you."

"What's the big deal?" He laughs. "Either way, you have to sleep in a camper."

"RV," Blanca corrects him with a smile.

"Whatever."

"I get everyone else being stupid because alcohol is the worst, but you, you're always sober!"

"Sobriety isn't a synonym for boredom, cutie."

Marín looks around. Not a soul on the path. Everyone else went to bed with their dignity intact, while we begged them to serve us one last drink at the bar. The only noise is the summery sound of crickets and the ocean in the background. Far in the background.

"If you see someone coming, give me a warning. Sardine, help me."

"Of course, Sardine and Anchovy need to get in the water. They're Maríne creatures!" Gus laughs. "Should I write you two a poem?"

"Oh, Sardine, Sardine, hold my phone, for I'm going to jump," Marín recites pompously before he empties his pockets into my hands and gives me two phones: his work one (it doesn't matter that he's on vacation…it's part of his body now) and the personal one, his wallet, and the keys for the motel, which are heavier than a Castilian chair.

It's quite the disappearing act. He grabs the fence, climbs the wall, and, once he's there, puts one foot halfway and…boom. He's in. We're all looking at him like he did a magic trick.

"I wanna go too!"

"Shh," everyone else scolds me all at once.

I put Marín's stuff down and try to imitate him, but my legs are way shorter. I need someone to give me a leg up. Blanca takes one foot, Gus takes the other, and Loren pushes up. I feel like I'm flying, and for a fraction of a second, I think I'm going to die, impaled on the fence of a pool in La Marína, Alicante. But no, I'm over it, and the crash is imminent. An arm breaks my fall, and I land on Marín's chest, whacking my eyebrow pretty badly on his shoulder, but alive and well.

They all laugh, and the flash of a couple of cameras blinds me when I turn around triumphantly. They're taking pictures.

"Now the rest of you!" I say giddily.

"No fucking way." Blanca laughs.

"I'll meet you back at the camper." Aroa sounds surly.

"Aroa, you could jump this with the power of manifestation!" I egg her on.

"Your elven blood will protect you." Gus laughs.

"I'll wait for you back there."

We watch her walk away slowly, as if she's hoping Marín will insist, but he doesn't, and she turns the corner. We look at everyone else, who are all shaking their heads.

"Hurry up. We'll wait up for you," Loren declares, giving us his blessing.

Marín and I look at each other.

"What should we do? Go for a swim?"

"Don't chicken out now," we hear Blanca call as they move away. "Gus?"

"I'm trying to decide whether I wanna swim."

"You don't wanna swim," Loren declares warningly. "Trust me on that. If you get in the pool, within fifteen minutes we'll all be handcuffed in the back of a patrol car."

We hear him spluttering until we lose sight of them. When I look back at Marín, he's heading into the darkness, into the most cloistered part of the pool. When he gets there, he pulls off his shirt and focuses on unbuttoning his pants. Thank you, patron saint of idiots, for this gift.

I yank off my sweater, unbutton my jean shorts, and kick off my dirty white Converse so fast they almost fly into the water. Marín is looking at me, amused, with his pants hanging open, barefoot, shirtless.

That's right, life. That's right.

We drop our clothes onto the same chair, and as he slips into the water in his gray boxers, I wonder if Gus and Aroa are getting suspicious of us. Well, of me. Is my secret about to be vox populi?

"Come here, come on." Marín reaches out his hand with a smile. "You have no idea how good it feels."

I can guess how good you'd feel, eating you until your eyes roll back in your head. I'd suck your life out like a dementor.

"Come on!" He laughs. "When you drink, you turn into a dummy."

No. Not a dummy. It's just that when I drink a little, it gets harder to stifle the Coco who's dying to kiss you. Am I going to make my life even more messy? I mean, isn't it a disaster already anyway? This strange flirting, this strange "What's going on here?" has to go somewhere, and there are only two directions: Either we discover that it's mutual and love wins, or I have to find another apartment. So basically, I was already planning that. I have nothing to lose.

The water is the perfect temperature, and my skin soaks it up gratefully. I look at Marín, who flashes a dazzling smile back at me. He's happy to be doing this and doing it with me. I can tell. I go closer, and we both swim over to the side in silence, under the shadow of one of the slides.

"So now what?" I say with raised eyebrows.

"Should we go down the slide?"

"You're nuts! They'll hear us!"

"I know, Sardine. I was joking." He laughs. "It makes me laugh how gullible you are. Were you the same in school?"

"Exactly the same," I reply, mocking myself. "I really don't know how I didn't end up smoking or doing drugs or—"

"Having five kids."

I get the giggles and dunk under the water so no one hears me cackling. A bubble floats to the surface, and he yanks me up.

"Sardine, you don't have gills."

"That'd be cool though," I say stupidly.

"Cool? You wanna be even weirder?"

"Am I weird?"

"No offense," he says, stifling a smile. "But you are pretty weird."

"I'm not mad. What makes me weird according to your criteria, Mr. Marín?"

"All your favorite songs are at least twenty years old. Most of them are from before you were even born."

"I like the classics,"

"You dream about time traveling all the time, and you're convinced that if you were a university student in May of '68, you would've died."

"Of an acid overdose." I nod, teasingly. "I would've thought I could fly."

"You love your dirty Converse, but every day when you leave the house to go to work, you look like Anna Wintour…pure elegance. If you told me you had a duke's papers in that horrible bag you wear to go out, I'd believe it."

"My bag is horrible?"

"Horrible." He laughs.

"What else?" I want to change the subject because, it's true, my bag with the zippers is the ugliest bag any chic woman would be appalled by, but I'm attached to it and it's the perfect size.

"You open beer bottles with your teeth. That's weird. And you have the same fucking underwear in twelve different colors."

"Hey! You do too." I lift my chin toward his boxers, which are part of his uniform. "White, black and gray, gray and white,"

"I'm not finished. Respect your elders." He puts his finger in my face, demanding my attention. "You would eat soup eeeeevverrry day, even in the summer. Coco, that's weird. Plus, you're called Coco! Like a Muppet!"

"None of this seems that weird to me, babe. Maybe you're the weird one."

"You're weird. You don't have ticklish feet."

"Feet are my erogenous zone," I lie.

"I thought it was your ears." He raises one eyebrow.

Oy, oy, oy.

"Do you have any more irrefutable proof that I'm weird? Because the ear is an erogenous zone for everyone. If you said, I dunno, my elbow, then maybe."

"Having your elbow sucked turns you on?"

"I don't know. Should we try?"

Marín leans back against the edge and bursts out in laughter that ricochets off every night-cloaked surface. I launch myself onto him and cover his mouth with my dripping hand.

"Shh,"

"Shh," he imitates me, prying my hand off.

Okay. I'm really close. I'm sitting on his knees, which he's keeping flexed in the water.

"They're gonna kick us out," I say, trying not to focus on where I'm sitting. "Me, the weird one, I don't like getting kicked out, you know?"

He doesn't answer. He looks at me. He's looking at me with an indecipherable expression, like an unsettling smile, which is neither serious nor fun. It's like those ancient Greek sculptures, the kouros, where the hair was represented simply by a few almost geometrical lines with old-fashioned undulations and the smiles they wore were distant. Right now, Marín is in control of the situation. This is no longer a battle between equals, and I don't know when I lost control of my army.

"What?" I ask him, not moving, pretending this new dynamic isn't affecting me.

I don't think I know this Marín.

"Nothing." He shrugs. "What?"

Restrain yourself, Coco. Restrain yourself. Don't kiss him. It's important that you don't kiss him. You've only had three weak drinks. That much alcohol just turns you into a chatterbox. Yeah? Yeah. So let's talk.

"We're not gonna talk about it?" I say.

"About what?"

"About last night."

The crickets' chirping suddenly seems deafening. That and the way our bodies are making the water gently lap around us.

"Do you want to talk about it?" he asks. "I was avoiding it because—"

"Because you're mortified," I reply confidently.

"Because you didn't seem uncomfortable. If we can make like it was nothing, why talk about it, right?"

"To check whether you were asleep or not, for example."

"Ah." He raises his eyebrows. "Is that a complaint? Was I not participating enough?"

"Oh, oh."

I swing my arm out to swim away, but he grabs my wrist and pulls me back to where I was. *God. Don't touch me too much.*

"Are you mad?" I ask.

"No. But you brought it up, right? So talk."

"It was dawn… We… It's weird, right? I mean. That is weird. What we did and what… I dunno. Just completely out of the blue and everything. Just like, savage. We're not like that. We don't do things without thinking them through… At least, not that kind of stuff. You know what I'm talking about, right?"

"Yes. How you touched my cock."

He's staring at me as he says it. I wish he were drunk. Or tipsy at least.

"And you…" I splash out again, pushing myself away. There's no need to force it. I feel like I'm on very thin ice with shoes that are on fire. "You squeezed my boob."

"Own it. If we're talking about it, we're talking about it."

My God. Who is this guy? Because he turns me on even more than Marín…

"Well, look." I twist a little and my bra pops up over the water. "You put your hand under my pajama top. You grabbed this boob"—I point to it—"you put my nipple between your fingers and squeezed. Hard."

"Did I hurt you?"

I look at him with a smile on my lips that can be read as *Are we really gonna go there?* Jeez, Coco, considering you're so in love with him, you're being kind of a prude. No, that's not why. It's just that I don't want to go overboard.

"Come on, tell me. Did it hurt?"

"It made me pretty horny, to be honest. But you already know that."

"Yes." He nods. "Just like you know how hard it made me."

"Very. Right against my ass cheeks, by the way."

"Between the cheeks," he corrects me. "Up and down."

Jesus fucking Christ. What is this?

"Up and down and a little right in the middle," I repeat, sinking into the water up to my neck again.

"Sardine..." he scolds me, but like he wants it to be part of a game. I'm the naughty student. He's the professor who's trying to hold back in the face of temptation.

"Anchovy..."

"You're the one who wanted to talk about it, so...go for it." He leans back on the edge of the pool and looks at me. "I'll answer anything you wanna know."

"I don't have any questions, sir. I just want to make sure that..." *That you want to do it again. No. You can't say that, Coco.* "That it's not gonna be a problem for us. You know?"

"There's no problem. At least for me. What about you?"

"No," I lie again, but this time it's a lie by omission. *It's not a problem as long you keep doing it and make me finish. And I make you finish. Either with your mouth or...*

"So why does it feel like it is a problem for you?" he probes.

"Because I look at you and I think..." I start edging closer, gradually, but not too close, "that I've had your cock in my hand, you know? And we were there, rubbing against each other like dogs. You're my roommate..." I avoid saying best friend because I don't want to make him think about the friend zone.

"Well, good thing it's never gonna happen again," he points out. "Because I want to keep being that."

"Well, yeah, good thing," I add.

"It would be super awkward."

"Totally." *Give me an Oscar already, please.*

We fall silent. Both of us. An uncomfortable silence crosses both of our faces, and we look away. I kick away again.

"We should probably get out of the pool," I mutter.

His hand catches my wrist and slides me toward him.

I shoot him a surprised look as he keeps drawing me in until his mouth is level with my ear. We're both holding our breath. I want to put my hands behind his back and around his shoulders and stroke his neck and his hair, but I stay there, frozen, waiting for him to speak. When he does, I get goose bumps that are impossible to hide.

"I hate that I did something to make you feel awkward, but I hate silences full of things left unsaid even more. You brought it up, so let's at least set the record straight: It's a good thing it's not going to happen again, good thing it didn't go further, because I don't think I would've been able to stop it. I was dying to slip my hand into your panties, fuck you with two fingers, climb on top of you and ride you until the walls of the fucking camper fell down and your thighs were dripping. But good thing we were half asleep, and it was just hormones that made us a little crazy. That's the easiest solution, Coco. Otherwise, it would mean the end of 'you and me' as we know it."

He lets go of me, and I pull back a little so I can see his face. We were so close. I can smell the scent of his cologne mixing with the chlorine in the water.

"That's it. I've said everything I need to say," he adds. "Do you want to say anything?"

I nod slowly, looking at his lips, the drops of water beading on his perfect chin, his messy wet hair, his incredible nose.

"Good thing," I mumble. "Because I would've been the one wrecking the camper by fucking you so hard. And then…there's no coming back from that."

I'm already moving away, with my back to him, panting from the effort of restraining myself, when I hear Gus's whispering voice.

"Hey...kids...Marín. Let's go to the motel, dude. Everyone's gone to sleep already, and if I wait twenty more minutes, you'll find me asleep in the hammock being eaten alive by mosquitoes."

"Well, they usually go for the softest parts first," I trill.

I climb out of the pool edge closest to the part of the fence where he is. He looks me up and down and raises his eyebrows.

"Fuck, Coco. Here you are, straight out of my spank bank."

"Shut up." I pretend to laugh.

I avoid Marín's gaze as we gather up our clothes. He does his best to pull them on, still soaking wet. I put on my Converse. We jump the fence again, the other way this time. I'm dazed. Everything goes by in a flash. Every movement feels like the headlights of a car driving at night, in the opposite direction, blinding me and making me lose sight of the path.

"Did you catch my stuff?" Marín asks.

Our friend answers by holding up the wallet, the phones, and the room key.

Gus gives me a kiss on the cheek. I say goodbye by holding my fingers up to my forehead, in a kind of salute. I don't know why. I think I've escaped when Marín comes over, gives me a kiss on the temple, hugs me, even though I'm wet and in my underwear, and says into my ear, "If I lose you, I'll die."

~

I guess he wanted to clinch it, I think as I hear the gravel crunching under my feet, already almost back to the motor home. I guess it was his way of putting out a DO NOT ENTER sign for our own good. But...I think Blanca's right. And the only thing I can do is cling to that tiny glimpse of hope: He's not completely sure. He says no, but...

When I start heading up the steps to the RV, Blanca jumps out and blocks my path with her cigarettes in hand, almost scaring me to death.

"Fuck, you motherfucker," I pant.

She laughs. "Hey! What happened?"

"I thought you were already asleep."

"I was in bed, but I couldn't sleep. So I figured I'd sit out here and smoke a cigarette in case you came back. So spill. What happened?"

I have no idea where to start. I'm tired, a little frustrated, confused. I can't figure out which is rising to the top right now, which is the most important. I take a deep breath and let it out slowly. Blanca raises her eyebrows, but before I even start, she stops me. "You know what? I'll wait until tomorrow. Sleep on it. I'm sure we'll find a moment alone to talk about it. For now, just dry off a little before you get in bed or I'll kill you."

We're back to sharing a bed. I smile and hug her.

"Thanks, Blanqui."

"For what?"

"For being so good."

"Ay..." She kisses me on the temple, and her arms squeeze a little tighter. "Nobody's good, Coco. Or bad. Don't let life teach you that the hard way. Burn it into your brain. It helps a lot with the people you love."

My brain is a fucking tortilla, but once I'm (pretty much) dry and in pajamas, I grab my phone. I hear Blanca light her cigarette and move away, I'm guessing on the way to the bathroom to brush her teeth and piss.

I open Instagram, more out of habit than actual interest, and, of course, there it is. The first thing in my feed is a post from Gus. The photo is of the ocean. He must have taken it this afternoon. When I scroll down the app a little with my finger, I'm surprised to see it's not a poem. It's a block of text. That's not usually Gus's style...

> I was in a rush and I bumped into you. Now you're everywhere and there's no way to get rid of you. You talk in songs more than anyone could imagine and you don't always say what I want to hear.

You live curled up, maybe in your underwear drawer, between memories and urges, caressing my favorite ones, like you could still make me believe that you care what they are.

I find you in every inch of skin your hands caressed. And there are a lot. All of them. You didn't leave any territory unexplained and unconquered. Every kiss was you planting the flag of the free that was always us loving each other.

You're here, there, deeper inside and further away. You're there where my eyes go, there where you think, everywhere I imagine.

You live standing in some lyrics and kneeling in others, drawing a subtle dance of incoherence between wanting and fleeing every time you write your name. Or mine. Or a fistful of words that are saying the same thing.

You crouch in wait to nibble my neck, in case I forget you. You run through my head, lips, chest, and hands every time I think of you and I slip; every time I regret it and yearn for you at the same time.

The door to the camper closes, and I hear Blanca come in slowly, tiptoeing toward the bed. She climbs a couple of the rungs of the ladder, and her head pokes up into the bed; she smiles at me.

"Put your phone down and sleep."

"Did you see Gus's poem?" I ask.

"Oof." I see her roll her eyes as she lies down next to me, grabbing the unzipped sleeping bag we're using as a blanket, which she meticulously folds at our feet in case it gets chilly. "A poem at this hour?"

"It's actually more like prose."

Blanca turns and studies me. "What's bugging you about it?"

I think about it a little. What is bugging me? "Actually, nothing."

"Wanna know what I think?" she whispers. "It worries you that it doesn't worry you."

I think about it for a second and nod.

"Okay, good night," she says. "Tomorrow will be another day, and you'll see everything much more clearly. Tomorrow, we'll talk. Don't think about it. Sleep."

"Good night."

She settles down and closes her eyes right away, but I still lie there staring at the ceiling, trying to decipher who she is, the woman who managed to get Gus to say, "I miss you."

22

HANDS FULL OF PROBLEMS

MARÍN

"Is this the street?" I ask Gus, whose head is drooping against the window.

"No. It's the next one, I think."

I know exactly where I need to turn, but I was trying to break the silence somehow. Gus is very quiet. He's submerged in one of those thick silences, probably mentally swimming butt naked through big-lipped muses.

Maybe...and I'm just saying maybe...I feel the need to break this false calm because I feel weird too. I can even feel my damp boxers under my black jeans. Jeez. What am I doing with Coco? What was that? Why did I act like I would with a girl in a bar? A girl I want to sleep with, to be specific.

It's nuts.

I look over at Gus, who's still slumped against the glass, looking out at the street, which is oddly empty for the middle of summer.

"Are you tired?" I ask.

"No."

"Well, you're really quiet."

"You too." He side-eyes me, and for the first time since we got in the car, he shoots me a half smile.

"What's going on with you? Are you okay?"

"Dudes don't talk to each other like that." His smile widens.

"We're friends, right? It's normal for a friend to ask if something's happening with you."

"Are we gonna talk about feelings now?" he teases. "Make me a hot chocolate with marshmallows and I'll open up like a flower while we have pillow fights."

I snort. "That twisted idea of masculinity is pretty fucking annoying," I admit. "What are we trying to prove? How manly we are?"

"I don't know." He shrugs, as if he actually has no interest in finding out.

"Dude…you're a poet."

"Well, I guess I'm only capable of expressing feelings on paper."

"What a load of bullshit."

"Fine…you go first." He challenges me with his eyes.

I sail right past the motel, and Gus opens his mouth to protest, but he shuts up when he spots the neon sign at the end of the street: "Bar." From the look of it, I wouldn't be surprised if it was a front for a brothel, but I don't care. I don't want to go up to our room yet. I'll lie down in bed, and I'll start going around in circles in my head and…

I park and look at him. "Get out of the car. I'll buy you a drink."

"That's right, you dog. Get me drunk first."

The place is almost empty. Two locals who seems like regulars are sitting at the bar, but they're not talking to each other. They're both smoking, yes, inside the bar, and they're polishing off their drinks in rocks glasses, staring vacantly at the bottles collecting dust behind the bar.

A couple is making out in front of the foosball table. There's a dartboard on the wall and a slot machine in one corner. The sofas are made of pleather and covered in cigarette burns. It's the most desolate place on earth, but we stake out one of the corners for our own. Before I sit down,

I go to the bathroom and take off my damp boxers. I don't know what to do with them, so I just chuck them in the trash.

A waitress who reminds me bitterly of my mother (blank stare, undefined age but aging badly because of alcohol abuse; fried, bottle-blond hair with thick black roots speckled with gray) puts a glass ashtray on our table and takes our order. Gus orders a whiskey. I'm sticking to my sobriety more than ever, so I order a bottle of cold water. Gus gives me an incredulous look, but when I ignore it, he says, "You start."

Gus settles in his chair with one ankle propped on his knee and his arms stretched out over the back of the couch. He's wearing a kind of sleepy look of concern.

"You're not going to tell me what's going on?"

"Nothing's going on." He flashes a smile, the commercial one, the kind he gifts left and right when he's signing books.

"I don't believe you."

"Why don't you start? Because you'll have to excuse me, but it seems like you're the fucked one here."

"I'm not wearing underwear. How do you expect me to be?"

He raises one eyebrow and laughs. He takes advantage of the waitress arriving with our drinks to add, "Let me get this straight. You're not wearing boxers under those very tight jeans."

"You're an idiot." I laugh watching the woman heading back to the bar, not before taking a glance at my pants…right around my fly.

He smiles and takes a sip of his drink that, judging by his grimace afterward, isn't exactly fifteen-year-old scotch.

"Yum, hydrochloric acid," he concedes. "Come on, Marín."

"Come on, what?"

"Clear something up for me: Are you freaked out about telling me because I'm her ex or because she's your roommate?"

I raise one eyebrow. I can't stop my heart from pounding faster than I'd like. Did he see us? What could he have seen? Did we do something?

"I don't understand," I reply.

"You're cuckoo for Coco Puff." He points at me and leans back on the couch. "It's so obvious."

I lean forward, my elbows on my knees, and give him a confused look. "Excuse me?"

"You're cuckoo for Coco. Sorry, Marín, but it's pretty fucking obvious. It sticks out like a sore thumb. Does she know? Are you...you know, sleeping together? That's probably why you don't want to get back together with Aroa, I guess."

I can't believe it. I take a few seconds longer than normal to gather my thoughts and figure out a response that doesn't seem too freaked out.

"I'm not cuckoo for Coco, Gus. Coco and I are just friends. Best friends. She's...like my sister." A flash of apprehension makes my stomach clench, and I hurry to clarify that. "Not like my sister. It's...like she's a cousin."

"Kissing cousins. That's an expression, by the way."

"Seriously, Gus. That's not it."

"When I was with her, you were always giving me dirty looks."

"That's because you were a dick." I laugh.

"That's not true! It's just that we have different perspectives about relationships. Plus...have you seen the way you look at her?"

"She's my best friend. I look at her like that because I love her, for fuck's sake."

"You see!" he teases. "You love her!"

"Loving her doesn't mean I wanna marry her, Gus."

"Who said anything about marriage? What you wanna do is bang her."

I open my mouth, but then I freeze, like a dope, until a wave of anger takes over. "Are you fucking nuts? She's my roommate, my best friend, my fucking right hand!"

"Look, you're right-handed, aren't you? So that means Coco jerks you off?"

I grab a coaster and hurl it at him so hard it hits his forehead and bounces off. He gives a muffled complaint, and I grumble. I sound like a repetitive song from a nineties band, but all I can hear is myself saying, "No way, no way, no way..."

"These things go through phases," he says, rubbing between his eyebrows, where the coaster left a red mark. "You're in the denial phase."

"Gus, seriously. I don't like Coco. She's my best friend." He rolls his eyes and leans back again, glass in hand. He gestures for me to keep talking. "What's going on is... Exactly what's been making my head explode is that I've been acting like an idiot for two days and...I don't want to."

"An idiot with...Coco?"

"An idiot in general, and Coco just happens to be next to me. And I can't see. I swear I don't mean to, and then I go there, all riled up, like a dog in heat."

"Wait, wait, wait. Did you hook up?" And he starts to smile.

"No," I deny firmly. "But I'm getting stupid, dude. And you wanna know the worst part? You were right. This would never have happened if I had just gotten laid."

"I'm always right." He looks at his nails proudly. "I'm very wise, but you think I'm just a circus monkey."

"All right already!" I groan.

"So why didn't you just sleep with Aroa?"

I look at him like I don't understand. "With Aroa?"

"With Aroa," he repeats. "She's hot, she's up for it, and...she's your ex. Who hasn't slept with their ex just to...?"

"Just to nothing. Aroa and I are not 'Aroa and I' in any way anymore."

"But why?"

"Because our thing ended and..."

My phone starts to vibrate in my pocket, and since I'm not wearing underwear, the movement feels too risky to leave it there, doing its thing. Ten seconds more and I'd be hard all night.

When I take it out, I raise my eyebrows, surprised. It hadn't even occurred to me how late it is and who could be calling at this hour. I'm so caught up in my shit I didn't even think to worry if something had happened to Gema. But no. It's Aroa.

"You know, maybe she really is descended from elves and has powers," I ruminate. "It's Aroa. I'm gonna go outside for a sec."

Gus waves his glass of bad whiskey in the air and singsongs that I should fuck her. I wish life were that easy. I wish I could just get laid without having to worry about two hundred thousand implications I invent the second there's a chance that could happen. That fucking poet… He doesn't even like whiskey.

I pick up. "Is something wrong?"

"Were you asleep?"

"No. Gus and I stopped for one last drink."

"It's impossible to have a last drink when you never had a first."

"Did you call at this hour to correct my grammar?" I ask, a little annoyed without even really knowing why.

"No. Can you come here?"

"Is something wrong?"

"No, but can you come here?"

"It's two in the morning, Aroa. What do you want?"

"To talk."

"Can't we talk tomorrow? We're meeting at twelve thirty at the campsite gate."

"With everyone else. I want to talk to you…alone."

I suck my teeth and grip my hair with my right hand.

"It's important," she insists.

"Can't we talk on the phone?"

"Is it that hard for you to get in the fucking car and come?" she complains, taut, tyrannical, demanding that I bend to her will.

I really doubt anyone in the group, even Coco, who was her friend before we started dating, knows this side of her. She reserves this for the two of us. For the people who she lets see it.

"Look, Aroa, we've already talked about this." I stand my ground. "I'm not going to run every time you snap your fingers, like you're a princess. Do you understand? It pissed me off enough when you did it when we were together. So you can imagine how it makes me feel now, when the only thing binding us is politeness, more for everyone around us than for our own sake."

"I don't think you understand. I want to talk to you now, but if you'd prefer we can wait until tomorrow with everyone around. I'm sure that a lot of these things I want to say to you will be pretty interesting to Coco."

I shut up immediately.

"Don't be so sanctimonious, Marín. We've all fucked up majorly."

"I didn't fuck up." I say, defending myself. "Don't take it out of context..."

"In ten minutes at the gate." She cuts me off. "I'll wait for you on the bench next to the bar."

I go into the bar shaking my head. I hand Gus some cash and the room key.

"I have to go back to the campsite for a second."

"Did something happen?"

"My ex is a fucking tyrannical moron. That's what's happening. Do you think you'll be awake when I get back? We only have one key."

"I'm nocturnal, dude." He brings his glass to his lips and wets them. "I'll be reading."

"I'm going to pray a few Our Fathers that I don't end up sleeping in the hall." I turn around, but before I go, I look at him again. "Stop pretending you can stand that shit, Gus, please. You're drinking gasoline."

I must be right because he puts the glass down on the table without a word.

~

Aroa's wearing a short dress...or at least that's what I think before I realize she's wearing one of my old shirts, with the sleeves rolled up and cinched at the waist with a brown belt. Her hair is down, and her eyes look a little swollen, like they always do when she hasn't slept much. As soon as she sees me, she jumps up, walks toward me, and then breezes right past me. She's heading toward the car, which I click open with the key fob when I see her reach it.

I climb back inside and watch her toss her hair to one side.

"What's going on?" I ask tensely.

"I could ask you the same question."

I rub my face impatiently. *For the love of God.* "How many times are we going to talk about this, Aroa? We're never getting back together. It's broken."

"Broken things can be fixed. Say what you mean: You don't feel like fixing it."

"Well, no." I nod. "I don't feel like it. I don't want to. I don't want to do it. I don't love you anymore." I swallow so hard it feels like the whole campsite must have heard it.

"You don't even believe that yourself." She laughs bitterly. "Being such a hard-ass isn't helping you at all, you know?"

"Look, I'm going to be honest, okay? I loved you a lot. I loved you for three years, but it was destroyed. I don't even think it was that argument. It happened gradually. And of course I still love you. You don't stop loving someone overnight, but I don't want to love you, and I don't love you in the same way. It's over. I've turned the page."

"Right," she says sourly. "Well, fine. You've turned the page, okay. Listen to me: Either you stay away from Coco or—"

"What are you talking about?" I raise my voice. "Have you completely lost your mind?"

"Lost my mind? I'd have to lose my mind to not see it! You two are fooling around!"

"Paranoia. Great. Just what I needed."

"Look, smart-ass, Coco is in the middle of a fucking mess with all that Gus stuff..."

"A mess you've been sticking your nose in, by the way." I ignore the fact that Coco isn't really in love with him because if Aroa didn't say that, there must be a reason.

Aroa comes so close to me I'm practically breathing the air she's exhaling. I smell her. I almost feel her and taste her. She's panting, like she always does when she finally lets out the smoke billowing inside her the whole time she's faking being happy.

"If I see you all over Coco again, I'll tell her about Gema. That's the last thing I'm going to say."

She moves away and opens the door, but I catch her arm delicately. I want to say one more thing, not hurt her. She gives me a surprised look, and I get the feeling she almost believes I'm going to kiss her.

"Get one thing straight, Aroa. With Coco or without her, our thing is dead. Accept it. Let me live. Get over this obsession and be free. When I met you, you were incredible, and now...the only incredible thing about you is how obsessed you are and how toxic this has all become. Get out of the car."

"What the actual fuck is going on with you?" she screams at me. "It's Coco! What are you doing? What are you doing with her?"

"Now you're gonna try to make me believe you're doing this because you care about her and I might hurt her? It's Coco, for the love of God!

We're the same as always, and we're going to keep being like that because the only one who sees something bad here is you. Do you hear me? You!"

Aroa gapes at me, incredulous. "Marín…" she whispers, "I might be obsessed, but you're blind. Just the two of you taking midnight swims? Whispering in the bunk with the lights off? Since when has that been part of your relationship? If you want to lie to yourself about that, amazing, but you can't make me believe pigs can fly. I know exactly what was going on. I've known since the first time you looked at her differently. And you know what? This is not happening, especially not right in front of me."

"You're paranoid, you know that?"

"Look, Marín. I thought we were going to fix this. I thought we would do it right, that you'd be sweet, that we'd see how that argument and the reasons behind it were actually just a grain of sand for us. I really thought you'd realized how stupid it was to break up… But now it's so obvious you were just grasping at straws because this…"

"Wasn't working," I finish for her. "It wasn't working, Aroa."

"Of course not. Your head has been somewhere else for a long time."

The door slams so hard it makes the windows shake. I watch her storm away until she disappears into the darkness, turning into a white dot growing blurrier by the second.

I sit there for a while before I turn the engine on. This is unbelievable. Has everyone gone nuts? I don't have feelings for Coco. I'm not in love with Coco. Coco is…Coco. My Coco.

It takes ten minutes for Gus to open the door. He fell asleep. When he finally lets me in, he throws himself back onto his bed, face down, without a word. And I appreciate it. If anyone mentions the possibility that I'm cuckoo for Coco again…I'll scream.

23

THAT STUPID TENSION

COCO

Blanca and I agree: Marín's acting weird. Ever since he got here, since we met up at the campsite gate after we checked out, he's been weird. He's avoiding eye contact, and he's quieter than usual. He's avoiding me. I'm positive.

"Maybe he's spiraling about what happened last night," Blanca whispers, cigarette in hand, while we wait for everyone else to fill a cart at the supermarket we stopped at on the way to our next destination: a beach with parking for campers in Villaricos.

The idea is to eat there and then keep going.

"You think he's upset about last night?" I ask conspiratorially, in an almost inaudible whisper.

"He told his best friend he would've fucked her the other day. That's kinda hardcore. Let's give him a few hours to shake it off. He probably just woke up on the wrong side of the bed."

Just like Aroa. Aroa woke up weird too. Another one who's trying to avoid me. She grunted at me at breakfast when I asked her if she left the camper when we had all been in bed for a little while.

"Well, yeah," she said. "I didn't know I had to ask permission to go to the bathroom."

Okay then. This is fine.

We stick nine more bottles of white wine into the cart. We want enough to last until at least Saturday, so Gus goes back and grabs five more. Fourteen bottles total for five people and three nights. Maybe that's a little overboard. Maybe drinking doesn't make us feel that great. The last thing this group needs is to have fewer inhibitions, given what we've already seen.

But the whole time we're shopping, we're back to being a group of friends. We're peaceful, some of us are quiet, but that's no biggie, even if sometimes a silence settles over us that seems, in Marín's words, loaded with things left unsaid.

Once we've crammed all the groceries into the RV, Gus wants to ride with us.

"You don't wanna ride with me anymore?" Marín jokes.

"I've just never been in one of these monsters."

"You slept in this monster," Loren points out.

"Yeah, but it wasn't moving. I want…to try it out. Can I ride shotgun?"

"Are you going to be chill?"

"I swear."

"Ay, no," I grumble. "Don't make me go in the back," I beg. "I get so carsick it's like I'm on that ride: the paella one."

"Do you remember when we made you ride that?"

"When? When I vomited cotton candy all over the ticket booth?"

It was one of the worst experiences of my life. I can still feel the bitter aftertaste in my mouth.

"So you go in the car with Marín then," Blanca pipes up, as if it's nothing. That little *fucker*…

"No."

We all stare at Aroa, surprised.

"What?" Marín asks with a furrowed brow.

"Gus can go in the back. I'll ride with Marín."

It's not a big enough scene for anyone to complain about her rigging it. Not even Marín, who watches her walk past him on her way to the car like another head sprouted from her neck. These two are at a weird crossroads that could end in a passionate kiss on the beach or a fight they'll never come back from. I swallow. I wanted to go in the car with Marín. It would've been a good chance to find out if he really is freaked out about last night. But no. Fuck me. Aroa can go. They can fix whatever seems to have been making them so tense since dinner last night. It'll be better for the whole group.

~~~

Gus buckles in next to Blanca, all giddy with excitement. Well…saying he buckles in is pretty optimistic for his skills. His hands are so good at certain things, but they're pretty clumsy at others. Blanca ends up having to do it for him, and Loren and I get the giggles up-front because for a moment it looks like Blanca has a child with a beard and she's getting him all strapped into his car seat.

"Ready?" Loren says, taking off the hand brake.

"Dude, this is so cool!"

It's one of the things that make people love Gus. Sometimes, when he's relaxed, there's no audience, and he doesn't have to play a role and he's comfortable, he's himself, nothing else. And this Gus, the one he hides inside, is way better. Human beings normally do the opposite: We hide the darkest parts of our personality. We hide our obsessions, our insecurities, our visceral hates, and even those bad intentions that we try so hard to suppress, but they're still there. Gus flaunts all that proudly, but the hidden side is the excited little boy who asks for advice, who feels small, who finds the world enthralling. That passion is what drives him, but he'd rather make the rest of the world think he runs on disdain.
~~~

Blanca smiles at him. He returns the smile. I watch them in the rearview mirror, talking about something and laughing wickedly, and I breathe a little easier. Only a little because right now Aroa and Marín are in the car behind us, and I have no way of even getting a glimpse at what they're doing, seeing if they're talking or arguing or looking at each other the way I thought I caught them looking at each other the other night. Loren notices my sigh and glances over at me. He puts "Safe" by Daya on the stereo and raises his eyebrows, silently asking me what's going on.

"Marín and Aroa in a car," I whisper.

"Nothing's going to happen in there. They'll probably just clear up the situation a little. It'll be good for everyone."

"You think?"

"Of course." He smiles at me. "Coco, Marín isn't in love with her anymore. A man in love doesn't act like that with his ex."

"But the other day," I whisper, making sure Gus can't hear me.

When I look back, he's standing up. Fucking restless ass. He switches seats and concentrates on taking a picture out the window. Blanca is leaning on the table, with her seat belt on, looking at her phone, probably checking her work email.

"Blanquiiiiii." I get her attention.

She puts her hand up without looking at me, her chin resting on the other. "I'm stopping!"

"Disconnect!" I demand.

"It's August, Blanca, for God's sake," Loren insists.

"There's always stuff to do," she splutters. "Clients don't stop needing us just because it's summer. One more email and I'm stopping."

I look at Loren, and we both smile. This is her happy place. Her head is always full of work, but she couldn't live any other way. She likes having responsibility; she likes her nights working, her crazy mornings chugging coffee, whipping one blouse off for another in her office after a night of just catching a few winks on her sofa. She likes seeing the intense surge of her work ambitions coursing through her veins. I bet she even gets turned on by work.

"The other day, what?" Loren brings me back and winks.

"It's just that, the other night, didn't you see how Marín and Aroa were looking at each other? They looked like two little Disney characters in love."

Loren laughs softly and shakes his head. "I don't think so, Coco."

"You don't think so?"

"Haven't you ever wondered why they broke up?"

"Of course."

"Something so big they can't talk about it with the rest of the group and bad enough to break them up even though everything was going fine, or at least it seemed like it was… Don't you think it must be irreversible in some way?"

"What are you trying to say?"

"That it's possible that they love each other a lot, but you can't get the one who got away back."

Loren's words are still echoing in my head even when we get to Villaricos and park the camper. Marín and Aroa get out of the car just like they would have when they were a couple, except he doesn't sling his arm around her shoulders, like he always used to. They're just two people who drove together. There's no passion but no drama either. Maybe they did talk. Maybe everything will get better now. Maybe it'll be the same with us.

~

For a few minutes all we can talk about is how busy it is. There are at least twenty other RVs, campers, and vans parked next to us, but it's our fault for not arriving earlier, and we're still in the first row next to the beach. The parking lot is so close to it that some of the sand has started to conquer the tarmac. The sea feels so much like it's ours alone that it robs us of our ability to speak. It suddenly solves all our brainteasers; the white noise deafens the cries of all obstacles. The sea has always been there. It was there when we were born, and it will be there when we die; whatever we experience on its shores, I think as I gaze out, only feeds it. And it is beautiful.

I don't know when exactly my life became so connected to the ocean. The dreams, the desires, and even everything I haven't lived but want to. Everything is right there when my feet are buried in the sand, by the sea. Maybe it was the summer vacations with my family, always in an apartment with tons of bedrooms that we filled with noise. Maybe it's something that hasn't happened yet. I don't think I yearn for it just because I wasn't born near it. I carry the rocking water in my skin even though the first time I saw it I was old enough to have a vivid memory.

Someone grabs my arm, and when I turn to look, I'm not surprised to see Blanca. I smile at her, and she returns the gesture.

"Are you happy?" I ask her.

"I think tonight will be one of the most magical nights of my life."

~

It doesn't take us long to strike up a conversation with our "neighbors." They tell us there's some new rule saying we're not allowed to camp here, which means we can't open our awning or put chairs or a table under it, but we are allowed to "stay overnight."

"But laws are made to be broken," the father of the family says to us, his eyes glued to his kids, who are scampering around. "When we get here, we set up our campsite, and if the cops show up, you say you didn't know, you're really sorry, and you leave. They don't usually hand out fines. The important part for us is just to be clean and not light fires..."

We gather at the beach bar, Las Brisas, which is next door, to figure out what we're going to do. Some of us think it's risky to ignore municipal regulations so brazenly, but others think it's not that big a deal. We ask the owner of the beach bar. He tells us the police don't usually come around here, and as long as we're civilized, there's no problem if we spend the night here, put out our chairs, or unfold the awning.

"Anyway, it's summer, so it gets livelier around here when the sun goes down. You'll see."

We decide to stay for a while and see what happens. We drink a few beers and order some incredible calamari, which only makes us hungrier, so we order more, this time adding an order of fried fish and some shrimp fritters. By the time we order coffee, we're all stuffed, sleepy, and happy.

"I don't think I've ever been this relaxed," I say, stretching my legs out under the table.

I bump into Marín's legs. It happens all the time. We're the two "long legs" of the group, but normally he catches one of my legs and traps it between his knees or makes some joke about whether I'm half praying mantis. Today just:

"Sorry," I say.

"No problem."

I side-eye Blanca, but she didn't notice how cold Marín's response seemed to me. She's looking out at the sea with a cigarette in her fingers. It's so weird… I told my bestie that I've been lying to her for a year, and even though it made me feel better, I'm still lying, like it's a crutch my tongue has gotten used to. The place is great, the ocean is stunning, we're all together, the vibe is calm, but I'm not relaxed.

"I'm going to open a can of worms no one has mentioned," Loren says very seriously, "There's no bathroom here like there was at the campsite, and I'm still sticking to my suggestion that no one use the bathroom in the Imperial Boozer Cruiser. I really don't want to deal with any 'black water,' babes."

"Me either," Aroa spits.

"So we'll go to the bar." Gus shrugs.

"And where are you two sleeping?" Loren asks again.

"Well, in the Imperial Boozer Cruiser," Gus says swiftly.

"In the car," Marín corrects him, pretty gravely. "We'll put the seats all the way back, and it'll be fine. It won't be the first time."

"No," Blanca says kindly. "You're not going to sleep there the rest of the trip, Marín. It's a pain in the ass. It doesn't matter. Sleep in the RV. We'll take turns with the beds so Aroa doesn't always have to sleep on the one in the living room."

"I don't care," Aroa says. "Anyway, I'd rather sleep alone in the living room."

"And that, pals, is how we discover that elves and nymphs are also antisocial beings," Gus jokes.

"We'll take turns," Blanca insists. "It's my bachelorette party, and I make the rules."

Loren, Blanca, Gus, and I cackle. Aroa and Marín look down. Fine, maybe the conversation they had in the car didn't fix all the unfinished business between those two. What could the problem be?

~

"Aroa's jealous."

Blanca's declaration catches me by surprise. We're the first to spread our towels out on the beach and sit down on them. There aren't many people swimming right now, and while Gus and Loren are lingering over their coffee, Marín is talking on the phone with Noa's mother again and sending a few emails to his higher-ups. Aroa took a ridiculously long time getting ready for the beach just to end up saying, "You two go ahead. I'll be there in a minute."

I look at Blanca, surprised. "Jealous? Of what?"

"Of you." She raises her eyebrows.

"Of me? Why me? Because I live with Marín?"

"I guess we have a hotbed to choose from, but right now what's bugging her is seeing you two so close to each other."

"Come on… We're Siamese twins," I snort. "He's acting so weird."

"That's because she must have said something to him."

"What are you talking about?" It comes out sounding somewhere between incredulous and angry at the thought that it could be true.

"I heard her get out of the RV last night too, and she took too long to just be going to the bathroom. She called Marín and threw a shit fit."

"Aroa throwing a shit fit? I don't think so. She's a light being."

"Look, still waters…run deep."

"What does that mean?"

"I dunno." She shrugs and looks out at the ocean as she pulls another cigarette out of her beach bag. "Ever since yesterday I can't stop thinking about why they broke up. We've never pressured them to tell us. I didn't because… Well, I don't know. Maybe because I thought that what they were hiding made Marín look bad and I didn't want to know. You know how it is; we're different with our partners than we are with our friends. I didn't want something that happened between them to affect my relationship with Marín. So I let it go."

"So what about now?"

"Now I'm starting to think part of the reason they broke up is you."

I shoot her a curious look. "Me? The same 'me' who's been permanently friend-zoned by Marín?"

"That's changing. There's definitely a vibe… Something between you and Marín. I'm not just saying that because it's what you want to hear. I can see it. He seems tense. He's acting…all manly around you. Not like a friend."

"Come on, Blanca. Even if that's true, which I desperately want to believe"—I put my hand on my chest—"this is Aroa we're talking about. She does yoga at dawn, she's beautiful and…"

"And all of us, no matter who we are, beat ourselves up for what we're not."

"What do you mean?" I wrinkle my forehead.

"Look, you're gorgeous, tall, you have that kind of style you're born with that makes every outfit look like your signature, you're fun, brave, smart… You graduated with honors from your master's, and you went to a super-fancy bilingual high school, but you open beers with your teeth!"

"I'm starting to feel a little uncomfortable." I laugh.

"That's what I'm saying. When I look at you, I think you have so much going for you that I'm jealous of, but when you look in the mirror, you see something else. You think you're some slob, you feel intimidated by Aroa because she's blond and pretty and she seems like a fucking fairy doll, but she…doesn't see it like that. We all have insecurities, no matter what we're like. And mine, like how my thighs rub together when I walk and my stretch marks on my tummy, aren't any more important than yours. They're just…mine. And Aroa, babe, is jealous of you."

"Have I been getting too close? Is it obvious?" I start getting freaked out.

"No. That's not it. Although, I have to admit there's something different from how you two always are… Something's changed, but it doesn't have to be a bad thing. She's jealous about how close you've always been with Marín, how he only listens to you when we're all talking, how he uses you as an example for everything, how you make stupid plans and his sister adores you."

"Gema doesn't adore her"—it's a fact, not a secret—"but that's only because she hasn't really put much effort in. That's not a criticism, by the way. Some people just don't know how to talk to teenagers and they try…"

"Coco, Aroa is obsessed with Marín. Think about it for a second. She doesn't talk about anything else; she doesn't think about anything else. How long has it been since she's told us about an audition? Do you know what her brothers are up to? Because I haven't heard her talk about them in centuries. Not even any anecdotes about the foreigner she lives with. She doesn't call us to go out anymore, she doesn't ask us about our lives, or if you dare try to tell her something, she always just brings up Marín."

Blanca shuts up suddenly, and I realize Aroa must be coming over. She doesn't say anything. She drops her towel, smiles tightly at us, and heads to the sea, where she dives right in without asking if we feel like going swimming. Blanca and I give each other a significant look. It's true. It's been a long time since she's talked to us about anything besides Marín… and I get it, by the way. When you're hung up on someone, his name is always on the tip of your tongue. Everything is related to him.

~

It's a pretty chill afternoon. Swimming, sand, and a few beautiful photos Loren snaps when no one's looking. There are no cackles or races. We're not playing. Everyone seems to be in their own little world.

When we're lining up at the shower on the beach, I realize that despite how awkward it is soaping up here in a bathing suit, this will be one of those memories that we'll be nostalgic about later. That's how brains work; they make tiny details seem extraordinary, even if they weren't. But our minds condense the things that have become routine for a few days. A happy routine. This moment is not just an anecdote: a "We'd rather take a shower at the beach than get the bathroom in the RV all gross." It means that we're far away from Madrid, from our usual lives, from the rat race of waking up, getting ready, and going to work. It reminds me of the lyrics of an Izal song, "Bill Murray," and I don't know why. Maybe because that song played every Sunday in our living room for a while and it'll always sound like Marín to me. Songs or not, with music or without it, even the inconveniences turn this into something magical. We'll add poetry; we'll remember the color of the ocean, the sky, the sounds, the smells. And everything will take on a much dreamier quality than it has now because we'll no longer have it at our fingertips.

But here we are. We wait, clutching our towels so they don't get wet or sandy, while the others take turns to rinse off.

Aroa goes first, her back turned to us, contorting herself so we can't see her and leaving a burst of sweet smell in the air from her shower gel. And Loren asks us not to look while he shoves soap into his bathing suit and scrubs and we all crack up.

The smell of the ocean mixes with soap and the sun is setting, like a tired woman sick of her heels who starts saying goodbye at a party, promising to see everyone tomorrow.

"Your turn," Marín says to me, pointing to the shower.

"Don't you wanna go first?"

"I'm not in a rush." He looks at the ground and then at the beach bar.

"Okay. But…I'll wait for you while you finish yours, okay? So I can hold your towel for you."

He looks at me, nods, and smiles. He's so quiet. I'm dying to know whether it's our conversation yesterday in the pool or if Aroa gave him a wake-up call.

She and Loren head back to our parking spot, avoiding the sandy path so their feet stay clean and they don't drag more dirt into the camper, and Blanca and I take over in the showers, sudsing up while we talk about her shampoo, which smells really good and supposedly makes your hair stronger. Leaning against a short wall, Gus and Marín are watching us with half smiles.

"Can't you guys look at the ocean? It's beautiful." Blanca grins. "We want to"—she points at her belly button—"lather up."

Marín moves away immediately, and before Gus follows, he makes a few lewd gestures that, let's be real, he doesn't seem to have any desire to follow through with. We both smile, facing each other so that our bodies shield each other from outside eyes.

"If you need help, just say the word. I'm very clean," Gus insists behind us.

"You're getting out of hand, Gus, for the love of God," I tease.

"Now we can look at each other." And Blanca raises her eyebrows like a pervert before we both burst out laughing.

Gus is the one who holds a towel up around me, looking away, while I pull off my wet bikini. My friend is busy doing the same with hers, and I was too freaked to ask Marín to do it. Plus, it's nothing Gus hasn't seen before.

"Thanks, Gus. I would've showed my ass to the whole beach."

"At your service, Coco Puff."

I don't know why he talks so much shit. I think it's to hide that he's actually a good guy.

Blanca and I perch on the wall wrapped in fluffy towels, wringing out our bathing suits, with the excuse of holding their towels, which we put around our shoulders. And take in the views, like it's no big deal...and I'm not talking about the maritime scenery.

Soap is dripping down Marín's chest. He pushes his hair out of his face, cups his hands around his face, and then lets them slide down his chest. Fuck my life. I want to be those hands, I want to feel the surface of his hairy skin, I want to dig my nails into his pecs and ride him like a savage. I swallow.

"Girl..." Blanca whispers playfully, elbowing me.

"I swear my nipples are so hard the towel could hold itself up," I reply.

"Whoever taught you etiquette in high school would be so proud..."

Marín isn't a gym rat, but I think I like it better that way. He doesn't have washboard abs, but he has a perfect, flat belly with a cute little belly button and a line of hair that I'd love to follow with my fingertips until it disappears under the waistband of his black swimsuit. And those very masculine muscles that form a V down there, pointing to his…

I look at the ocean for a second, but I end up staring at him again, like my eyes have plans of their own and my brain can't control them.

"Do you think it would be out of line if I offer to dry him off myself with the towel?" I mutter.

Blanca snorts from trying so hard to hold in her laughter, and Gus and Marín look over at us. Gus has his hand inside his bathing suit and he's rubbing.

"Hey…don't overdo it," Blanca says to him with a smile.

"I like it really clean. Stop looking or you're going to have wet dreams, you pervs."

I don't know about wet dreams, but I'll definitely be dreaming about this…for months.

Marín comes over, sluicing water off with his hands. I hold out his towel and smile.

"Thanks."

"Should I dry you?" I offer.

He laughs and presses his finger between my eyebrows. "Silly goose."

Maybe Aroa really did say something to him because he's tense and seems uncomfortable…but it makes me feel better that we're still us underneath it all.

~

The bar owner was right. The vibe gets way more festive in the evening. The families filling one side of the parking lot trickle out, leaving behind the campers and vans that are going to spend the night here. We hear music coming from a few of them and chattering everywhere. Now that the family next door has left, our closest neighbors are a gang of friends who look like they're also on a bachelor party. They spent the afternoon fishing on the beach to our right and are now drinking a few beers under the glow of a lantern, sitting in their beach chairs, all wearing the same black T-shirt with red letters we can't make out.

We pull out a couple of bags of chips, but passing them around is a pain, so we end up getting out the table, the chairs, a bottle of wine, a few mussels, some pickles… We didn't realize we had bought so much stuff. Once we're settled in, looking out over the ocean, which is taking on an orange tinge from the sunset, we realize that Marín doesn't even have a soda to toast with and is holding a glass of water.

"Do you want a Coke?" I offer.

I sound pathetically helpful. That's what happens to me when someone's avoiding me—I try to get closer in any way, and I start being as friendly as possible.

"Ah…well…yeah. Tell me where they are. I'll grab it."

We both stand up.

"Coke? We don't have any." Blanca strokes my wrist, trying to get my attention. "Go to the beach bar and buy a few cans before it closes."

"I'll go." Marín pats the pockets of the worn jeans he put on after his shower, checking he has cash.

"I'll go with you," I say.

"No need. I think he can manage a few cans of Coke," Aroa declares. "Do you want some wine, Coco?"

"Yeah. Will you pour me a little while I go with Marín?"

I can't stand people telling me what I should do, sorry, especially if it stems from an internal tantrum. I spent so many years having to be a good little girl at the private school my brothers and I were enrolled in that when I started university, I promised myself I would always be myself and make my own decisions. My parents have always applauded this side of me, so I don't understand why a friend would try to boss me around.

"Does anyone else need anything?"

"Can you grab me a pack of cigarettes?" Loren asks.

"Me too!" Blanca adds.

"Of course."

"I have cash," I hear her say to Marín.

We walk along side by side. There's nothing unusual about finding us in silence. Sometimes at home we don't say a word for hours, while he's listening to music and I'm reading or we're both working on the couch with our laptops on our knees. But this isn't one of those comfortable silences between two close friends. This is the kind Marín hates, full of words left unsaid.

I buy two packs of cigarettes, and he orders the Cokes. Once we've secured the goods, instead of heading to the quickest path back, he tilts his head toward the beach, suggesting we take the wooden deck that forms a bridge to where we parked the RV.

"It's quicker the other way," I say because I'm an idiot.

"Are you in a rush?"

I shake my head and smile.

We stand next to the exit out to the beach. The sun is sinking into the distant edge of the sea, splitting the horizon in two. It would be beautiful no matter whom I was sharing this moment with, but it's not just anyone; it's him. That makes it even more magical. When he starts to head off, I stop him.

"Are you in a rush?" I ask him this time.

"No, but…"

"But Aroa will feel uncomfortable if we don't get back soon, right?"

He takes a deep breath and looks away.

"It's okay, Marín, but…let me ask you something. I don't want you to think I'm pressuring you. Just…do you care more about her stamping her feet than not being us when we're together?"

"No." He shakes his head. "Not at all. But I don't wanna make things worse."

"For her?"

"For the group." He makes a gesture, like he can't find the words. "For you. I don't know. This trip is pretty weird, Coco."

"No, not if you don't think about it."

"But you said it yourself yesterday: We're not the kind of people who do stuff without thinking about it. We're—"

"We're Marín and Coco. Coco and Marín. And if Coco and Marín want to stand like a couple of clowns gaping at the sunset, they do it."

"The advantage that Coco and Marín usually have is that there's no audience because they don't have to give explanations to anyone."

"We don't have to do that with an audience either. What's going on, Marín?"

"Nothing." He looks at me.

"I'm going to try again. What's going on with us, Marín?"

"Nothing." He smiles. "Nothing. Nothing bad. Maybe I'm the problem. Maybe... Maybe this is one of those moments of..."

"Marín." I go over and circle my arm around his waist. He doesn't move away, but he seems surprised by how close we are. "Are you okay? That's the only part I care about."

He takes the cigarette packs I'm holding and sticks them in the bag with the sodas before he puts it on the ground. Then he grabs my waist too and smiles. His dimples pop up around his mouth.

"I'm fine. I'm here. I'm with you. Even when I feel awful, that's a guarantee of something. I'm sorry if I'm being...stupid. And weird. But it makes me feel better that you'll never let me be distant."

"It's your choice. I can't force you not to be."

"That's not even a possibility with you. We're Anchovy and Sardine." A smile spreads across his face.

"And we're always salty," I tease.

He grabs my face and kisses my forehead. I take the chance to put my arms around him and press my cheek against his chest, over his black T-shirt, and take a deep breath.

"I don't want to piss Aroa off," I mumble in a thread of a voice, "but don't go away."

"No. I know. I'm sorry."

"She doesn't matter to you more than me." I'm suddenly emboldened.

"No. She never has."

I swallow and close my eyes, praying that he keeps talking. Faced with my silence, he does, and he puts his arms around me too.

"Maybe the problem was always that she knew that and I couldn't make her understand that loving you didn't stop me from loving her. But she never wanted to understand, and that's not my fault because you're in my life and you always will be. I've known that since the very first day."

"Because I can open bottles with my teeth?"

"It was because it was. You know that one poem of Gus's, 'Crushing Certainty?'"

"Yes." I press harder against his chest.

"Well, that's you and me, Coco. A crushing certainty."

"But—"

"But we're not sleeping together tonight, okay?"

He pulls away gingerly so he can look me in the eye and raises his eyebrows. I don't know if he can see my lips trembling. I don't know if he can feel my heart racing. But I nod. He does too.

"Certainties as crushing as ours have to accept that some people won't get it. She doesn't get it. Let's not make her suffer more."

I don't want to tell him that I don't understand what's happening to us either, what that certainty is. I vaguely remember the poem he's talking about, but only the feeling of comfort I was filled with when I heard it. It's one of the poems Gus included in his book and one of the ones I heard him read the first night we met. When I asked him whom he wrote it for, he told me that he never knew, that he thought he wrote it for the certainty that one day someone would be worthy of those words. It's a warm poem that feels like home…but is Marín saying it fits us because it's a sterile version of love?

My confusion slowly dissipates, replaced by the warmth of the safety of feeling like he's more mine than I did a few hours ago. I know love is silly like that. You're suffocated by doubts, and a single step is enough to feel like, well, maybe nothing has been solved but the wheel is still turning. Our thing, being the friend who's hiding how in love I am, but not completely losing faith because maybe… Maybe.

~

When we get back to the table, the whole vibe is different, warmer. They're all animated. Loren's cackling. Blanca's telling a story about the time when we had to convince Gus not to do a poetry reading naked. And, I'll be honest, I'm more pissed off than hurt at this point, and whatever's bothering Aroa seems like it's her problem. I'm going to enjoy the night. I'm going to live this vacation to the fullest. And tomorrow, now that the night is closing over our heads with a darkness I've never known, will be another day. But…

"Gus…" I take the chance when we're alone, while we're getting out the empanadas and a few other things for dinner.

"What's up, Coco Puff."

"Do you happen to have your poem here…the one about 'Crushing Certainty?'"

"The one from my book?"

"Yeah."

"I always have a copy with me. It's in the car. Wanna come, or should I grab it for you?"

"No, no. Tell me where it is and I'll go get it."

Gus raises an eyebrow, but he goes into the RV, opens a drawer where he saw Marín put the car keys, and hands them over.

"My bag is in the trunk. You know the one…it's the brown leather one I brought on our trip to Paris. The book's in there. If I'm not mistaken, it's on page twenty-five."

It's not page twenty-five, but he's not far off. Twenty-six. There it is.

Crushing certainty
yours and mine.
Your eyes on my mouth,
My mouth on your lyrics.

The creed on your lips,
the knowing of your doubts,
the Sunday of your week,
the hole I left in my life
not even knowing if you'd ever come.

Crushing certainty
of knowing you better than I know myself,
of accepting that you'll know how much I feel, think and hurt;
the understanding that I'll turn my chest into your house,
and my house into yours.

And loving you so much inside
never meant a problem,
because I didn't even understand
that crushing certainty.

When I put the book back where it was and before I go back to everyone else, I take a deep breath, control my breathing, and close my eyes. Gus can call it whatever he wants...but for me that poem is called "Hope."

24

THE HIPPIE NIGHT

COCO

We've flown through four bottles of wine. Gus is opening the fifth with skill I didn't think he had, standing beside the table. Next to him, Marín is cracking up because Gus is reminiscing about one of his readings in Madrid, where he got so nervous that he forgot to zip up his fly after he went to the bathroom. Even Aroa momentarily abandoned her moody silence to laugh with us. Loren can't stop giggling, and Blanca is covering her face with a napkin because tears are spilling down her cheeks.

"And I'm sitting there, reading my heart out with part of my boxers peeking out through my fly. You bastards!"

"Checkered! They were checkered boxers!" I pipe up, dying of laughter.

"We were trying to give you signs!" Marín defends us. "But you just kept going."

"Come on, man. That's because it was super confusing! Your friends come to see you at a reading, and every time you make eye contact with them, they're touching their nether regions like a bunch of lunatics. I thought you were all making fun of me!"

It wasn't that long ago, but suddenly it occurs to me how different we all are now. It was pouring rain that day, which had been pretty habitual that spring. It was Friday, and some of us met up beforehand to toast him and wish him luck. Blanca showed up soaked; she came straight from work, dressed in a suit and her heels splattered with dirty water, but she didn't seem to care.

Loren brought Damian. They had been in a silly spat about choosing the couch for their new apartment, and things were a little tense between them. We always thought their relationship would be plagued by explosive arguments until Judgment Day, but around Easter, not long after that reading, everything seemed to change: They decided to break up… for twelve hours. Now their relationship is completely different: Even Loren, who doesn't like cuddling (not even when he's the little spoon), is affectionate. You really don't know what you've got 'til it's gone.

Back then, Marín and Aroa were already broken up, but it wasn't this tense. She kept saying it was just a bump in the road, that they'd get back together when everyone least expects it. I suspected they were still sleeping together because it was easy to catch them in a wink or a complicit look. I figured they'd get back together too and be even more intense when they did. I remember I didn't even want to think about it. I avoided any reflection on the matter because I was scared that when they reconciled, I'd be out of my mind and our apartment and the family I've always considered us would break up. Now, a few glasses of wine deep, in the middle of this calm and velvet-dark night, I'm sure Aroa thought about it, but she didn't care. I wonder if Aroa has ever worried about my role in this story, if she's ever wondered what would happen to me when she got her wish and they went off to live together. Did she think we'd be three's company forever? She doesn't live in the clouds that much.

"What was that beautiful poem you read at the end?"

Blanca's question brings me back to the present. We've cleared the table of all the dinner detritus, leaving only the plastic cups full of wine, an empty soda can, another full one, and an ashtray full of butts that Blanca and Loren have filled to the brim without needing any help.

It's the blackest night we've ever seen. There's no moon, there are no streetlights, and since the beach bar closed, there hasn't been any light except the candles, flashlights, and dim pools of light spilling out from the campers. Marín is leaning back in his chair with his legs stretched out and his elbows perched on the back. He needs a haircut, and the jeans he's wearing have seen better days, but he looks amazing. I have to peel my eyes off him and force myself to look at Gus, who's pulling his phone out of his pocket.

"I think you're talking about 'Now That Everything Is Lost,'" he replies.

I furrow my brow because he suddenly sounds so tremendously sad.

A few looks are exchanged across the table. I try to catch Gus's, but it gets tangled in the look Marín and Loren are giving each other. Blanca's looking at Marín too. Something happened there.

I turn back to Gus, who's sitting on the steps of the RV. He rubs his mouth and starts to read:

Tonight is the last night I'll search for you inside me
frantically
only to find nothing.
Today the crumbs I tricked you with
are no longer enough.
Today, when everything has been said,
there's nowhere left to hide.

I've been weathering the grief like a champ,
using excuses, hopes, fear and bluster.
I've been reconstructing the city under your feet,
suspicion dawning that you destroy everything you step on,
and I didn't even realize I was the one breaking shit.

Memories
pile up in the room at the bottom of my chest,
they fall, they slip, they slide and they roll,
until there's no present that's worth anything,
until the past is the only thing that makes sense,
until I convince myself that I stole your future.

The worst part is the desire
that won't leave,
that says that one day I'll laugh about all of this,
but tell me, what am I supposed to do with all the desire?
The kind that makes me yearn for your perfume,
that makes me believe in you blindly,
makes me swell with pride for the woman you are,
fighting with you and for you,
begging, pleading, crying.
the desire for everything you told me,
you denied me,
that I wanted,
but didn't ask for,
and you won't give me.

Now that everything is lost,
now that even the dream is dead,
I think about the nights when I could sleep without thinking of you,
the day I'll see you and it won't hurt,
when I have no desire left,
and I don't hate the memories
that are left with you.

Silence hovers over the table. We listen to the waves breaking on the shore, some distant chatter, and a far-off song that sounds like "Turnedo" by Ivan Ferreiro. We're all staring at Gus, who's looking at his phone, silent, licking his lips, blinking slowly.

A tiny sound breaks the moment open. The whole scene could have been torn from a dramatic film. Everything is broken, not just the silence. It's Blanca's phone.

"Hi, Ruben," she answers, smoothing down one eyebrow. "Seriously? And I have to look at it right now? Fine…I'll check tomorrow." She pauses, stands up, and rolls her eyes. I guess she wasn't expecting a work call from her almost-husband at this hour. "I sent you all the documents in an email, but if you can't find it, I think I have it archived and…"

Her voice drifts away and melts into the blackness of the night.

When she comes back, everything seems to be the same as before the poem. Aroa's still silent but pretending she's fine, like she's not watching Marín like a hawk. Everyone else is talking happily, but…it's not one of those nights. It's not an all-nighter filled with nostalgia and laughter. Maybe it's the darkness, the quiet, the light drawing us inside like moths. Maybe it's because of something else, personal and nontransferable. I don't know. All I do know is that today is a day of retreat. It's pretty obvious at this point that we each have a rabid dog inside us, growling, chained up.

~

The boys have gone to the bathroom. It's midnight, and Aroa has started yawning. She wants us to do the bed lottery because she's going to bed soon, she says. Earlier she said she didn't mind sleeping alone in the bed in the living room, but I get the feeling she's changed her mind. Blanca faces the problem head-on.

"We don't need a lottery. Marín and Gus can sleep in the double bed,

Loren on one of the bunks, you take the other one, and Coco and I can share the one in the living room."

"You won't both fit there," she says tersely, but she doesn't offer to sleep there herself.

"What's going on?" Loren asks when he's the first to appear back under the lights of the RV.

"We're figuring out the bed sitch. I told Aroa you two could have the bunks, Coco and I in the living room, and Marín and Gus in the double bed."

"No need. I'll sleep in the car," Marín declares.

"We don't bite, you know?" Aroa snaps at him.

"Fine, then you come up with a solution."

Marín crosses his arms over his chest. He's radiating a slow-burning hostility. I know him; he's about to explode. He doesn't do it very often; he usually has enough patience to restrain himself. But we've all spent too many hours together with no chance for him to decompress by himself. Marín is super stressed. Even Gus, who's zipping up his fly as he walks up, winces a little when he sees him like this.

"What's going on?"

"Nothing. Aroa's choosing beds for everyone."

"Fine then." She doesn't hold back, and as she stands up calmly from her seat, she rattles off, "Loren and Marín in the bed up top. Blanca in the one in the living room. Coco in the top bunk, and Gus and me in the bottom one."

I was completely convinced that Gus wouldn't just be happy with his lot; he'd want to go to bed as soon as possible. But that's not the vibe I get from the face he just made. He stares at me and then at everyone else, his gaze slowly sweeping around the table before he shoves his hands in pockets and leans back glumly on the Imperial Boozer Cruiser.

"Those bunks are pretty tight, blondie. I don't know if we know each other well enough."

"I'm sure we do. Are they that narrow, Marín? Did you and Coco manage to get any sleep the other night?"

"I'm not going to answer anything you say in that passive aggressive tone."

"Let's all chill out a little," I try to mediate.

"Whoa!" She acts shocked, putting her hand over her chest. "I'm just trying to figure out the beds so nobody has to sleep in the car!"

What a mess…

"If he wants to sleep in the car, he can sleep in the car," Loren pipes up.

"But wait…what's the problem if I want to sleep with Gus?"

"Come on. I'll sleep in the car," the latter declares.

"Why? Did I suddenly turn into a leper without noticing?"

"Aroita, I never knew you were such a pain in the ass."

"Gus…" Blanca cuts in. "Let's not fight about this shit. Here's what we'll do, Aroa. Why don't you choose whatever bed you want, and when we go to bed, the rest of us can decide. This whole conversation is stupid."

"Done." Aroa pulls her hair back with a hair tie she had on her wrist. "The stupid one will go to bed. You can all figure it out."

"Wait, Aroa…" I try to say.

"Leave her." Marín sits down again looking pissed. "When she gets like this…"

She turns around when she was just about to climb in the camper. "When I get like this, what? Finish the sentence."

Marín takes a deep breath, refusing to look at her, and then gives an exhausted sigh that makes it clear he's more than used to this stuff. "Weren't you going to sleep?" he retorts, picking up his half-drunk can. "I wasn't talking to you."

If smoke could come out of a human's nose, Aroa would be an

industrial chimney. The door slams so hard it echoes across the whole beach, and we're all left in silence and with no clue what to do. But Marín jumps up. We all tense up, like he's going to follow her and we're ready to stop him, but he just brings his chair closer to the table calmly, with his Coke can in his hand, and looks at us with surprise.

"What?"

"Nothing," Gus manages to say, putting his hands up.

"Let's go the beach, right?"

And Marín's proposal is music to my ears.

~

Have you ever sat on the cold sand of a beach in the middle of the night? A beach where there's not a soul, where only the ocean reigns, no lights, no shelter from a boardwalk or the noises of everyone walking along it? There's no need for words; silence is enough because it whispers that you're right where you want to be. Nothing else is needed. But Marín still whispers to ask if he can put on music.

"Why not, you music junkie."

Marín flips through his Spotify playlists until he comes across the one he seems to be looking for. A kind of electric melody plays, and a woman's voice drifts over us, rough but sweet, like a wave filled with sand.

Loren is sitting a little farther forward with his hands buried in the sand, playing with it. I smile at his back; you know Loren loves you when he shares his silences with you.

To my left, Marín's arms are propped on his knees, and his gaze is fixed on the sea, which we're starting to see now that our eyes have adjusted to the dark. I scooch a little closer and rest my head on his shoulder. Unbothered, he puts his arm around my shoulders and kisses my hair.

To my right, Blanca hugs her knees to her chest, bundled in the skirt of her black floaty dress with bright colors embroidered on the bodice. She's barefoot, and her toes are buried in the sand. Gus suddenly materializes out of the dark and sits next to her, on her towel. They look at each other, they don't say anything, and he opens his fist, where he seems to have a collection of shells and tiny pebbles.

"Peace offerings." I lift my head up to look at Marín and see if he heard my whisper.

"Human beings relate to each other in very strange ways." He smiles down at me.

"I like this song."

I reach out and trail my fingertips over the hair on his left arm, which is still resting on his knees. Marín watches their journey without saying a word.

"It's Carla Morrison," he whispers.

"Is this okay?"

He looks at me with raised eyebrows. "Why wouldn't it be okay?"

"Sometimes I'm like Velcro," I say, making fun of myself.

Marín turns his head toward me again, and his smile is so sincere. "I like it when you stick to me."

"Even when it's hot?"

"Don't go overboard."

I crack up, and Marín's eyes stay glued to my mouth, my smile. His stretches into a smile and freezes there. I love him.

I don't even feel him move before he's pressed against me, so I give a little jump that makes his grin widen. His nose nuzzles into my forehead, sliding from one side to the other. My mouth is right there, in no-man's-land. If I just lifted my chin a little, our mouths would meet. I'm scared by the certainty that if no one else were here, I would. I'd do it. I can't take it anymore. I can't carry the weight of what I feel for him anymore. The heat of his lips lingers on my nose, and when he turns away, facing forward again, I curl up against his chest.

"Have you ever slept on the beach?" he asks.

"No. Never. Have you?"

"No. Should we do it?"

A little sand trickles onto my arm, and I turn around to see Gus and Blanca standing up.

"I'm fading." Gus excuses himself. "You get me drunk and you don't put on reggaeton or anything. I can't do it."

"Reggaeton, he says, the cool guy," Loren murmurs, lying back on his towel.

"I'm going to check on," Blanca adds, tilting her head toward the RV.

"Don't bother," Marín warns her. "It's not worth it. She won't listen to reason."

"Are you staying?" Gus asks.

"Yes," we say in unison.

"I'm not. I'm getting goose bumps from the breeze." Loren struggles to get up, rolling up like a croquette and making the rest of us laugh. "Assholes."

"Blanqui..." Marín and I are still snuggled up, and when he calls her, he barely moves. "Can you grab Coco's sleeping bag? So we don't have to go in and disturb everyone."

"Of course. What about you?"

"We'll share it."

My eyes must be shining bright enough to be a lighthouse for the whole Andalucian coast. I'm snuggling harder into his side, thrilled, when I hear myself ask:

"You sure?"

"I'm sure."

~

Gus is the one who comes over with the sleeping bag and a smile. I could swear I've seen that smile…a wolfish mixture of complicity and mockery.

"Don't freeze out here, lovebirds," he murmurs.

"It's not like it's winter," I retort, ignoring the "lovebirds" part. "The breeze feels so good."

"Remember when we knew what to expect from the seasons?" He laughs. "You're gonna freeze. Either that or you'll get crushed by the beach-cleaning machine."

"Write us a nice eulogy if we do get run over by that machine."

"Good night, couple."

That "couple"—did it have intention behind it?

We unzip the sleeping bag, spread the three towels out over the sand, and lie down on them, still fully dressed, and then throw the sleeping bag over us like a blanket. The breeze doesn't bother us, but it's nice to be under the covers for now.

"We'll have to shake it out well or you'll look like a breaded cutlet when you go to bed tomorrow."

"If my mother could see me. She claims I'm like the princess and the pea. And look at me."

"Without your feather pillow."

"That pillow is the shit. Don't make fun of it."

"Try this one out." He pats his chest.

Is that applause I hear? Ah, no, it's my crazy desires, chanting my name to cheer me on.

I rest my head on his chest, and he puts his arm around me again. I should restrain myself, but I take the chance to smell him when I take a deep breath. He smells like a mixture of Hermès, Terre, the shower gel Blanca lent him a few hours ago on the beach, and the scent coming from my hair: ocean, shampoo, conditioner…

"Are you sniffing me?" he asks, laughing.

"I'm supposed to be the spoiled one… Did you put on cologne?"

"No. It's just on my undershirt. If you're wondering if it's the second day I've worn it, it is."

"You smell really good."

"You too, Sardine."

I gingerly slide my right leg between his and tuck my foot below one of his. Far from complaining, he settles in, but he takes part of our blanket and pushes it off. Cuddled up so close like this…it's starting to get hot.

"The Perseids are on Saturday," he murmurs. "Gema sent me a message to tell me that a boy invited her to watch them in some field. I told her that sounded good but I was actually having a heart attack. I'm still recovering."

"That's why you're so grumpy, huh? The big brother…"

"Well, between Gema and Aroa."

"Give her time."

"Which one?"

"Aroa. Cut Gema some slack, Marín. She's the most responsible and mature kid I know."

"Yeah, being a teen mom is so cool," he murmurs.

"Marín!" I scold him, laughing. "Don't be like that. She's at the right age for first kisses. You did all that back in your day."

He turns and looks at me.

"What?" I ask.

"Back in my day? I don't have any more first kisses to give?"

"Don't twist my words. I didn't say that. You still have plenty…" *I hope just one, for me.* I sigh. "You still have plenty."

"Tell that to Aroa. See what she thinks."

"Well, you'll have to excuse me, but what Aroa thinks doesn't really matter."

"God…she's such a tyrant."

"That's not true," I say, trying to justify her behavior. "She's adjusting to a new situation."

"Ha."

"What does that 'ha' mean?"

"It means the obvious, Sardine. I spent three years with her. And I don't want to demonize her now. It's not like that. It's just that we…you and me, everyone else…we know each other as friends. As a couple… As a couple it's a whole other level."

"Well…" I rub my nose against his shirt. "Don't let it get you down. That's not what we're here for."

"So what are we here for?"

He turns his head toward me and smiles. I want to tell him that we're here to start, to get the truth out of all the lies we're telling, but I don't, of course. I just snuggle closer and whisper, "To have fun."

His phone is still playing music from under the blanket. I grab it and put it on his chest.

"What song is playing?"

"'Heavenly Day' by Patty Griffin."

"I like it."

"It's fitting."

The hand I let linger on top of the phone, on top of him, feels like it's tingling. I don't have to look to know his fingers are stroking mine. I'm scared he'll feel the echo of my heart pounding against his side, but he doesn't pull away. We interlace our fingers and play with them. He looks at our hands.

"We said we weren't going to sleep together," I murmur.

"You know something? We're definitely not here to keep promises for other people. We'll keep them for ourselves… We already have plenty."

I don't know what to add besides the silent promise that, whatever happens, tonight will lodge in my chest as the highlight of this trip.

25

GETTING TO HIM

COCO

It wasn't comfortable, to be honest, but the back pain is worth it when we wake up with the first rays of the sun and, without having to say a word, we both sit up on our improvised bed made of towels. The sleeping bag is thrown off to one side because we rolled around in it so much. A woman walking her dog on the shoreline looks at us, clearly touched. I know what we must look like. I wish we were what we look like, of course.

We shake off as much of the sand as we can and go looking for our shoes, which we find by the RV steps. I put on my sandals, he ties up his black Vans, and we head to the bathroom. It's six in the morning, and I want to keep sleeping, but the beach is not an option.

When we come out of the bathroom, we stare at each other, not really knowing what to do. I have sand in every crevice, and if I climb into a bunk with someone in this condition, I'd understand if they abandoned me to my fate at the next gas station we stop at. This can only be solved by a shower.

"Can you hold my clothes?" I say to Marín.

"What?"

His eyes are puffy, and he has terrible bedhead and a sleepy smile, the kind that makes you want to be with someone for the rest of your life.

"Shut up and hold this."

I pull off my red floral dress, which is wrinkled to infinity after last night, and hand it to him. I'm wearing a maroon triangle bra and ugly black culottes, but it was the first thing I found yesterday in my jumbled suitcase. Finding anything in that turmoil was a miracle. Marín looks at me with his eyebrows raised.

"Just like that, huh?" His lips form the words slowly before spreading into a smile.

"Well, yeah."

"No towel?"

"I'll air-dry, Marín, air-dry. Sometimes we have to get a little wacky."

I activate the sensor on the beach shower and stand under it, trying not to get my hair wet. My palms feel the water taking the rest of the sand with it.

"Is it cold?"

"Not really."

But my nipples are sticking out under my bra. I look at him over my shoulder… He has draped my dress over the wall we were leaning on yesterday and is pulling off his shirt.

"You're copying me now?"

His pants and shoes do a disappearing act, and he surprises me by jumping into the same shower I'm under. He grabs me around the waist when I yelp and stumble. My damp underwear. His black boxers. Water. It's way too early to be this turned on.

"There's another shower!"

"I'm not risking getting colder water than you."

He turns. His back is covered in sand, and I help him get it off, like it's a reflex. My hair is getting wet, but I don't care. When he's clean, I rest my head on his cool skin. I'm in heaven. I'm starting to think we actually were crushed by the beach-cleaning machine and Saint Peter has gifted me this beautiful loop for my own personal paradise.

I put my arms around his waist and bury my nose in his skin. I'm going too far.

"Coco..."

"What?" I murmur into his skin.

"I just woke up."

"And?" I don't get it.

"I can feel your tits against my back."

He turns back to me with a chunk of wet hair stuck to his forehead, embarrassed. I try to look down, but he hugs me to him, dying of laughter. Big fail, champ. I may not be able to see your erection, but I can feel it right where I want it.

"Much better, totally," I say drolly.

"It's a natural and uncontrollable reaction."

"No worries, no worries. You're in a safe space," I say ironically.

"It's your fault," he whispers, busying himself by wiping off the sand that's still stuck to my back.

"My fault?"

"All your fault, you little minx."

I cackle, and we hold each other. I think we're clean at this point, but when the water stops, I slap the button on again.

"This is turning into a vice," he says.

"We all have to die of something."

He pulls back enough that he can look at me. My hair is wet and plastered to my head. His too. He pushes it back. He does the same with mine. I press my belly button against his body to test his reaction: He holds his breath for a second and then lets it out in a pant. He's really hard.

"You're really hard," I murmur. In for a penny, in for a pound, right?

"Coco..." Her closes his eyes when I shimmy a little.

"Want me to stop?"

"You should, yeah." He swallows.

I put my arms around his neck and press my forehead against his clavicle.

"Fuck…" he moans.

"I stopped."

"Fuck…" he repeats.

"What?"

He hesitates. His right hand moves down from my waist to my ass. No, this isn't a hallucination… He's touching my ass. And he's touching it the right way, his hand wide open and clenching my flesh, digging his fingertips in with a groan and drawing me closer to him again. I think I moan. I think, because I'm in some kind of astral projection and I can't answer for what my body's doing.

We both start panting harder when his left hand slips between us and grabs my boob. He kneads it. I jut my chin down so I can watch his fingers sinking into my flesh and move my hips forward so I'm rubbing against his erection.

The water turns off again, and he takes three firm strides toward the wooden wall of the bathroom hut and pushes my back against it. His mouth is hanging open, and he's gasping for breath. I stroke his chest; he strokes mine, with both hands. I trail one down to his stomach. His eyes keep darting back and forth between my hand and my face. I don't say anything, but somehow I'm asking permission to keep going lower. He bites his lip and nods.

I snake my hand under the dripping waistband of his boxers and grab his cock hard. He groans, and I moan. I want more. More. I move my hand along his tight, hard flesh, and he puts his chin on my head, and he moans again, making me wet. I move my hand with my fingers wrapped around his cock, and we look at each other, mouths open, expressions of pure pleasure, fire.

"Touch me," I beg, nibbling his chest hair.

His right hand slips into my panties, and his index finger goes straight to my clit. I catch his skin between my teeth and moan, still pumping his cock. He slides one finger inside me. Two. He arches them inside me. He pulls them out. They glide back in. I'm panting hard, moaning, sucking my lips into my mouth.

"You're wet." And the words pour into my ear like hot liquid.

We keep moving our hands frantically, moans escaping from our mouths. With my free hand, I grab his wrist and follow his movements, pushing him deeper into me. I'm going crazy while he twists his fingers and caresses my clit with his thumb. Fuck. Fuck. Fuck. I want him to kiss me. I want his tongue in my mouth, and I want to know if he kisses slowly like I imagine, hard but lingering. Or if…

"Stop!"

I'm still pressed against the wall with my hand in the air when he pulls away from my body, panting, not understanding why I'm suddenly so empty, so cold. I stay frozen. I'm barely breathing.

"No." He shakes his head, not looking at me. "There's no coming back from this, Coco. There's no…"

I pull him toward me, tugging on his wrist. He relents. Our bodies find each other again, all by themselves.

"Coco…" he moans when his cock finds my heat, even with our wet underwear between us.

"We can come back," I moan too, rocking my hips.

"No." He puts a hand on my belly and propels his lower half back. "There's no going back, Coco. And if I have to choose, I'd rather have you forever, even if it's in another way."

I barely have time to accept what he just said. Before I know it, he's gathering up his clothes and striding toward the camper. At least five minutes pass before I can move. Taking three steps back to the shower feels like a voyage.

The water comes out much colder this time, but I appreciate it. I need to cool my skin, my ideas, my sex. I feel like bursting into tears when a mixture of disappointment and frustration hits me hard and makes me feel totally humiliated. But…what the actual fuck?

I drag my soaked self back toward our little corner of the parking lot. I don't see him anywhere, not in the car, although I was sure I'd find him there, with his head in his hands, wondering why he just did that with me, when I'm just Coco, his friend. I grab a towel and dry myself as best I can with it.

The darkness in the camper is violated by the beam of light that shoots in when I open the door. I kick off my wet sandals, drop them outside, and close it again. I left a long tank top in the bathroom when I took it off the other day to go to the pool, so I go in, peel off my wet underwear, and throw it on. I use a dry bikini bottom from yesterday as underwear.

When I close the door of the tiny bathroom again, I'm surprised to see Marín sitting on the bed in the living room. I make out Blanca and Loren asleep in the bottom bunk; Gus is on the top one. Aroa must be in the double bed. What an asshole… She went to sleep in the one that would be most disruptive. You've gotta be fucking kidding me.

I suck my teeth and cover my face because I'm mortified. I feel a lump in my throat, and I pray silently that I don't burst into tears right here in front of him. His hands pull me closer, guiding me by the hips until I'm between his legs and he can press his cheek against my belly.

"Coco—"

"Shut up," I whisper. "Please, don't say anything else."

"I'm sorry."

"No." I pull away.

He moves over to one side of the bed and beckons me over. I go because I'm an idiot. I sit on the edge, and he yanks me in until I'm next to him. He looks at me; he seems so apologetic.

"I'm sorry," he says again.

"It is what it is. Don't say it again."

"I'll say it a hundred times if that's what it takes, Coco. I'm sorry."

"Yeah, yeah, I know. I know that—"

"Shh…"

"I know you regret it and you think it's a mistake, and…"

"Coco…" He grabs my chin and forces me to look at him. "I got carried away, okay? I wasn't thinking. I don't know what… I don't know what's going on with me on this trip. I'm going crazy. I didn't want to disrespect you. I didn't mean to…"

"Disrespect?" A silent laugh comes out while I roll onto my back, staring at the ceiling. "This is unbelievable. I'm an adult, Marín, and responsible for my own desires! It wasn't like you were taking advantage of me. I wanted it, I wanted to do what we were doing, I wanted more and…"

I feel him sit up and lean over me, his brow furrowed. "I know," he cuts me off. "Me too. But you have someone in your head, and I'm just confused."

I raise my eyebrows. "You're confused?"

"So fucking confused," he admits. "And horny. No, don't look at me like that. I'm being really honest."

"And what percentage of responsibility do I have in that?"

"None. It's my fault."

"That's not what I'm asking… How much of that confusion, how much of that horniness, is about me?"

Marín bites his lip and looks at me. He looks at my mouth, my eyes, my mouth again.

"I can't even answer that, but honestly, a lot of it is about you. I'm not saying it's your fault or that you tried to or…"

"Marín." I put my hand over his mouth. "You need to learn, sometimes, when you try to clear things up all the time, you shit the bed. Some things just clear themselves up, okay?"

I pull my hand back when he nods, and suddenly he's stroking my wet hair.

"I don't know how to explain what I'm feeling because...because, fuck, I have no idea what I'm feeling."

"Okay."

"But I only stopped because...whatever you are, you'll never be a hand job to me, a right here, right now, up against the wall."

I smile—I don't know why, because I feel like shit.

"Forgive me," he says again.

"I mean, what exactly am I forgiving you for?"

"Well..." He flops down next to me. "For a lot of things. For not thinking, for prioritizing my cock over you... Think about it, Coco. I haven't even kissed you."

"You're asking me to forgive you for not kissing me?" He can't see me, but I must have an expression that could only be described as "baffled."

"For treating you like this. For not doing it right. For not... I don't know. I'm so confused." He covers his face with both hands. "Forgive me." I start to say he's like a broken record, but he suddenly adds, "For leaving you wanting more."

I look at him surprised. "That wasn't very nice, was it," I dare to say.

"No. It's not very nice."

He pulls his hands away and looks at me. A smile plays at both of our mouths. I can't stay mad at him even in the middle of this shit storm.

"You forgive me?"

"If you never leave me wanting more again, yeah."

"You're an idiot." He laughs. He rolls me toward him again and holds me. A few eternal moments of silence pass.

"I should hate you," I mutter finally.

"I know."

"But now, on top of everything, I feel bad for you."

"Because of my blue balls?"

"No, idiot. I'm sorry you're confused."

"Oh, yeah. It's a bummer," he agrees.

"Well, yeah."

"Total dog shit," he adds.

"A nuisance."

"A fucking twist of fate." And I can tell he's about to crack up, but I keep the game going.

"A real fuck-your-life moment."

He stifles his laughter, and so do I.

"You're so gross…always being the best. Fuck," I groan.

"What about you… You're pretty gross too."

"Me? After all that!"

"Well, yes." He smiles.

"Why?"

"I'll tell you, but you have to promise me not to say anything after. Just close your eyes and go to sleep."

"Sounds bad."

"Promise…"

"Promise." I try to sound revolted as I flip over in the bed, turning my back to him. "Why do I gross you out? Surprise me."

Marín comes closer, spooning me from behind, puts his arms around my waist, and brings his mouth to my ear. "How could you not? Stuck in my head, colonizing my life, making everything better. Coco, let's be honest: You've set the bar so high that no girl will ever, never ever be good enough. If I compare everyone to you, they'll always lose. And, jeez, I know I shouldn't, and it's bad that I do that all the time. Too much. How can I not be confused?"

I turn around. I look at him with my eyebrows raised so high I think they're going to meet the hairline on the back of my head. I start to say something, but the only thing I can do is let out a pathetic noise that makes my chin tremble.

"Marín..." I manage to articulate.

He presses his thumb over my lips and shakes his head. "You promised. And that promise is for us. Keep it, please. Help me."

For a few seconds, I don't know what to do. I should tell him. This is the moment. Fuck. This is the fucking moment I've been waiting for for the last year. *Marín, I feel the same way. Fuck, Marín, you've made the bar so high that no one else even exists. Let's do it, let's try it, let's turn our house into the fucking home we want and ourselves into the couple that we've been rehearsing for years.*

But he looks at me...and I know. I know this isn't the moment. I know he needs to chew on it, accept it, understand it. He needs to come to the conclusion that he's in love with me alone. But now I know. Marín is in love with me. He just needs to understand...because he will understand, right?

I give him a kiss on the nose, turn around, and close my eyes. I won't be able to sleep, but I'm going to do whatever I can to keep my promise.

26

WITH HER. ALONE WITH HER.

MARÍN

Okay. My head is such a fucking mess. I haven't even been able to swallow my coffee, I can't stop going in circles…with my spoon and my head, I should be mortified. I should be avoiding eye contact with Coco; I should be giving myself a hard time about this stupid shit I've gotten into. But I'm not. Because I can't stop thinking about her. In different circumstances, that would be nothing new. I think about Coco a lot. She's my best friend, we share an apartment, we…share everything. Fuck. The problem is that I'm not thinking about her the way I normally do. Now the only thing in my head is a succession of fantasies. Images I'm lingering on more than I should: her wet lips, my tongue on her hard nipples, my cock pushing into her, and the relief of her heat running down me like a fuse until it explodes down my spine. Coming. I want to come with Coco, on top of Coco, inside Coco. Whoa, I want to make Coco come.

Kill me.

We've exchanged a few smiles since we got up. I'm blushing like a little kid because…what the fuck do I have in my stomach? What I have in my stomach are butterflies. I'm about to fuck it all up, but in a big way. My life is a total disaster, I'm confused, and I'm not ready to start another relationship. I know I should give myself some time; I know I should meet girls, not take everything so seriously, just make having fun my goal for a few months. I can't dive headfirst into another relationship right now. With Coco it would never be a fling.

The problem with Coco is that it scares me. The problem with Coco is that she's not just any girl. She's the ultimate one.

For fuck's sake.

I would talk about it with Loren or with Blanca, but I don't want to embarrass her by talking to them about her when she'd probably be happier keeping quiet. I'd talk about it with Gus, but he's a motormouth, and he would take approximately three nanoseconds to make a loud joke about hand jobs in the shower.

Coco riding me. Coco under my body, with her legs spread open, taking my thrusts and my thumb in her mouth, sliding along her tongue, moaning, begging for more, getting really wild…

Fuck it all.

"What the fuck is going on with you?"

I glance at Gus, who's looking at me with a furrowed brow. We're in the car, following the RV on our way to our next destination, Mojacar. I've always loved the beach there. Coco's never been, and we found a spot at a campsite and a hotel next door.

Yes, a hotel. I'm not tempting fate anymore.

"Dude!"

"What?" I yell.

"I'm talking to you!"

"It must not be that interesting if nothing's getting through."

"Go fuck yourself." But he's laughing.

"What were you saying?"

"That I want a kebab right now."

I have to laugh. "Seriously?"

"Of course seriously. I'm so hungry I could eat a horse."

"I mean seriously, is that what was so important?"

"It's not like I interrupted your ascent to nirvana, bro."

"Feels like it."

Coco sucking me, looking at me, taking her tongue and…

"Tell me something!" I yell at him frantically.

Gus looks at me with an expression that's a mixture of confusion, surprise, and laughter. "You're fucking nuts. You must've woken up on the wrong side of the bed. Well…um, I dunno." He shrugs and looks out the window. "I don't want this trip to end. I'm having a great time."

"Well, we still have two nights to go."

"Everyone else wants to go out tonight. To that Mandala place. I don't know if it's gonna be my vibe."

"It's a place to go dancing. It doesn't have to be your vibe, and you don't have to be its. Not everything is about you. Does Blanca wanna go?"

"Yeah."

"Well, she's in charge. It's her bachelorette trip."

"Dude… Don't you think she's acting pretty weird with Ruben?"

"Weird with Ruben? I don't know. Why?" As if I weren't uncomfortable enough. Thanks, Gus.

"She's hella distant."

"Okay, explain it to me. And try not to sound like my sister talking."

"She's just weird; I dunno. I'm getting a bad vibe."

"In what sense?"

"I'm telling you I don't know," he says exasperatedly. "It's just a hunch. A gut feeling. Like the one that you're fooling around with Coco…exactly like that."

Well, I'd have to start paying attention to Blanca because this dude is pretty good at predictions. I pretend not to believe him, of course.

"She's probably just nervous about the wedding."

"It's pretty crazy, all this wedding shit. If I ever get married, I swear not even God will know. What the fuck? I'm not getting married. Why would I put myself through all that shit?"

"I mean…I guess there are people who believe in the institution of marriage."

"Do you believe in the institution of marriage?" he asks me, very formally.

"I guess. I've never really thought about it."

Evening time. The sun setting. Coco with her hair loose and one of those golden barrettes with a flower or a dragonfly that she wears sometimes. Lots of fairy lights twinkling over our heads. Friends. Only the real ones. *I promise to love you forever.*

I slam the brakes so hard it makes Gus and me fly forward. Thank God for seat belts.

"What the hell are you doing?" Gus yells at me, totally freaked out.

I could ask myself the same thing. What the hell are you doing, Marín?

~

The only room left at Hotel Marazul, which we booked in a rush through Booking.com before we left Villaricos, has a double bed. The look of horror on both of our faces makes it clear that no, we're not a couple.

"Oh God, this sucks," Gus complains, slumping over the counter. "Can't I get an extra cot sent up?"

The receptionist looks bemused. She has a customer-service smile plastered on, but she looks like she's been here a long time already, and we're a pain in the ass. Let's be honest.

~

The girls are rolling out the RV's awning when we find their site. The campsite, El cantal de Mojacar, has a special charm. It reminds me a lot of the summer camps I was sent off to as a little boy. I have good memories from those years, even though now that I think about it, it was the only calm month of the year: Not having my mother drunk as a skunk, sprawled out on the sofa or bringing that embarrassing boyfriend around, felt like the height of luxury. In one of those camps, I got my first kiss. A few years later, I got my first hand job at one of them too.

The gravel crunches under our feet, announcing our arrival. Aroa is yelling because she says they're putting all the awning's weight on her.

"For fuck's sake! I'm the smallest one here. Blanca should be on this side because she's the tallest. Her long arms will finally come in handy."

"Your ex has really turned into an impressive bitch," Gus murmurs, raising his eyebrows.

We're far enough away now that it'd be offensive if we run over to help them. I know Blanca and Coco. They'll shriek at me that they can do it themselves. They're extremely independent; they want to do everything themselves. And I love it.

Blanca drops what she's doing, shoves Aroa out of the way, and places herself under the awning to hold it up as they unfurl it. This is not going to end well.

"Aroa, come on. Don't get pissy. You can turn the crank," Coco suggests.

Coco's standing at the other end of the awning, putting up one of the poles. Her back is to me, but I can't take my eyes off her. She's wearing a loose white button-up with the sleeves rolled up and frayed denim shorts. On her feet, her white Converse. I want to lean over and whisper into her ear that I have a shirt in my closet I want to see her walking around the house in.

"Ladies." Gus greets Blanca and Coco by doffing his imaginary hat. "Hey, blondie, did you bring any Tums?"

"Tums?" Aroa asks, confused.

"Yeah, for the bad mood reflux you're having."

"Hey, let's just have a good time in peace," Coco jumps in grumpily, but she smiles when she sees me. "How's the hotel?"

"Good. Very romantic. You have to come see it." I don't know why the fuck I said that.

"We have a double bed," Gus adds. "We're gonna have a blast."

"This gentleman will probably show you the headboard up close tonight," Blanca quips, twisting and finally shoving the last leg of the awning in place. "Ah. Done. We're professional campers now."

~

We eat charred burgers and a disastrous salad that Gus and I, with all the best intentions, tried to make inside the Imperial Boozer Cruiser Coco scratches the blackened part of her meat with a smile, shaking her head with gentle disapproval.

"I swear at home he even makes bread," she says, trying to cleanse my image. "I expected this from Gus, but—"

"Hey! I used to make you those incredible breakfasts and bring them to you in bed," he grumbles.

A hit of jealousy surges all the way through me. Wait...what's going on here? I already knew these two spent their whole relationship fucking like they were possessed. Why does that make me uncomfortable now?

"You bought two baguettes and brought them to me in bed with a glass of water. One time."

"I brought you a baguette in bed a lot of mornings, Coco Puff."

The whole table cracks up, and Coco rolls her eyes. "Oh, sweetie," she complains.

"I brought you oatmeal in bed on your birthday." It pops out of my mouth before I can stop it. I'm startled.

Coco looks up from her plate and smiles at me. Her eyes are shining. Fuck. I touch my hair nervously and bite my lip. If she knows how to read me, and I think she does, she'll know exactly how nervous I am right now. What if the dude Coco is crazy about is me?

"You brought me oatmeal with cinnamon and coffee on that beautiful tray we brought in El Rastro, remember?"

"Look, now you know which of your boyfriends is better." Aroa's comment chokes all of us. It shatters the vibe, the look, the shine, the hope, and even my butterflies explode in a cloud that turns into rage. I look down at my plate and scratch my blackened burger.

"You're so sweet, Aroa," I grumble. "Always thinking about everyone else and making sure the whole gang has a good time."

"You seem to have a complaint."

"Should I make a list?"

"Yeaaaaaah," Gus exclaims.

"Let's just have a nice time."

"I can't take it anymore." Aroa throws her cutlery down on the table dramatically and heads into the building, which I guess must be the bathrooms. Nobody makes a move to follow her.

"Loren, you go," Blanca pleads.

"Can't I even eat in peace?"

"You're the only one who's not scared of her, apparently," Gus points out.

"Scared isn't the word. He's just the only one who doesn't want to abandon her at a gas station," Blanca replies.

"I thought about it, but it was enough drama just getting her to come out of the RV. She's impossible, that girl."

We all laugh, and Loren picks up his plastic plate and walks calmly over to the bathroom.

"Eating in the toilet is filthy!" I yell after him. "And not the good kind!"

Filthy. Like pulling Coco's hair with my cock in her throat.

Wait, what the actual fuck?

"Listen, after we eat I'm gonna head back to the hotel to take a nap," I murmur.

I need to relax, to be alone, have a little privacy…to touch myself. To touch myself a lot. That's the truth.

"Cool, I'll go with you," Gus says. "Then we'll be ready to turn up tonight. This whole not sleeping thing…"

"You slept for eleven hours," Blanca side-eyes him. She's always the first to get up in the morning.

"I'm like a model. I need a lot of water and a lot of sleep to look this good." He rubs his beard against the grain with a seductive look.

"Can't you take a nap here?" I ask him.

"Now you're sick of me?" He pretends to be offended.

"I can't remember the last time I spent ten minutes alone."

"Ahhh!" He smiles. "I know what's going on."

"What's going on?" Coco says with her mouth full.

"He needs love."

"What are you talking about?" I say tersely. "Shut up!"

"Love?" Coco asks, looking at Gus.

"Babe…Marín needs to jerk off. Probably in the shower."

The look between Coco and me last a few seconds longer than expected, and Gus and Blanca's eyes are glued to us.

"Jeez Louise," Blanca whispers slyly. "Goose bumps." She shows her arm to Gus, who sticks out his tongue and licks it.

The argument that kicks off makes everything chill out a little. There are no questions. There don't seem to be any suspicions. But yes, I need to go back to the hotel to touch myself, unwind, and see if all this is just the consequence of my overhyped imagination. Maybe there's still hope for me.

~

No. There's not.

I know when my head sinks back into the pillow, exhausted, with the third round of jizz in my hand and I feel that tingle. That one, the one that keeps coming back no matter how much I jerk off, no matter how much I imagine it, no matter how much I try... This isn't going to go away.

The first time, all it took was thinking about Coco and me in the shower. About finishing what we started. Right there, up against the wall, grinding, thrusting hard, her nails digging rhythmically into my ass. When I came, I bit my lip so hard it hurt, wishing with everything that I were doing it inside her. Aroa never wanted me to do that. She said she didn't like it, that it was kind of icky afterward. And I never really cared. Either I left everything in a condom or I pulled out at the last second and shot my load onto her stomach. Now with Coco I want to do it every way possible.

So, of course, I was still thinking about it, and I had no other choice but to do it again. My erection hasn't gone down, even after I walked over to the bathroom and stuck it under cold water. This time, my head created an image of her taking it in her mouth, wide open, staring up at me, like she's daring me to hold back while I come.

And I went from zero to a hundred.

The third time, I didn't even come...physically, I mean. I twisted with pleasure like a bastard, imagining coming all over her tits, her tan belly, ...

I hurl myself into the shower and turn the water so cold it feels like tiny razors hitting me. It doesn't calm me down. Well, it makes my erection go down and makes me stop wanting to masturbate like a monkey, but it doesn't calm me down. Because right in the middle of my empty mind, the question of what the hell is going on with Coco keeps popping up.

You don't fantasize about Coco. You carry Coco like a torch, with your head held high, with respect, like a prayer even the most fervent would believe in. Coco is...

Fuck my life. Am I in love with Coco?

~

My phone rings, and I jolt in bed. First of all, I'm startled because I must have been dozing off and then because I'm worried it's my work phone ringing, but no. It's my personal phone, and it's…Coco.

"Were you asleep?" she asks when I answer with a bleary voice.

"I didn't think so, but now it feels like I was. Did something happen?"

"No. I went to the bathroom to wash some stuff so I don't get the RV dirty, and when I came back, all the bunks were full. There are people passed out everywhere. All the soldiers have fallen, general. I await your orders."

"They're all sleeping?"

"Let's see…" I hear her footsteps on the gravel. "Aroa's probably awake, hating all of us. Now she's saying she doesn't wanna go out tonight."

"She wants us to insist."

"Should I?"

"No fucking way. We're not here to grant her wishes. That's what happens when you raise someone to believe she's a princess."

"I don't know, Marín. I never really thought she was like that."

"That's because you've never pissed her off before."

"I pissed her off now?"

"I don't think it's anything personal," I lie. "What about everyone else?"

"Loren and Blanca were talking in the double bed, but now the only noise is the deep breathing of a good siesta. There's someone in the other bed with the curtain drawn, and…unless some psychopath snuck in to take a nap, that must be Gus. And he snores. He snores like Loren, to be honest."

"Are you tired?"

"A little. But if I unfold the living room bed I'm gonna wake everyone up. Although, I dunno. If I push Gus to the back a little, we can both fit in there."

Crammed in that bunk with Gus? No fucking way.

"Wanna come here?"

"I thought you'd never ask."

~

She's wearing the same loose white shirt and jean shorts. She slips off her shoes as soon as she comes into the room and goes over to the window to look at the view, chattering on about the seaside decor.

"It's perfectly walking the line between cozy and tacky, don't you think?"

The only thing I think is that she's beautiful, that I love her bare neck when she pulls her hair up in a bun, and how tan she is.

"Do you want to sleep?" I ask awkwardly, almost interrupting her.

"I'd probably bug you in there."

"It won't be the first nap we've taken together," I say.

We've fallen asleep on the couch hundreds of time and even in my bed, watching a movie. We always joke that we're confirmation that "Netflix and chill" is always a lie: Others use it to disguise their sexual intentions, and for us…it means a two-hour nap. At least up until now.

Coco leans back on the dresser and raises one eyebrow with a smirk. "Well, excuse my hesitance…but you'll probably agree that certain things have changed since the last time we took a nap together."

"You mean because of"—*careful, Marín*—"our urges?"

A smudge of red pops up on her cheeks. God, I never noticed how incredibly beautiful she is when she blushes. I'm scared. I'll admit it. I have a flash of panic because I've never even kissed her and I have a fucking "I love you" on the tip of my tongue.

"Our urges, yes." She nods. "But this is just going to be a nap."

"But of course. Please, lie down, my lady."

She cackles and murmurs something about playing doctor. I'm going to make some retort when she unbuttons her shorts and drops them onto the same dresser she was leaning against a second ago. She's wearing transparent black panties with embroidered polka dots and lace around the edges…

I clear my throat. This is weird. Really weird. There's even something weird about the light streaming through the window.

"You coming?"

I'm wearing cotton shorts and nothing else. She's just in her shirt and panties. I can make out a white bra under the thin fabric, and she follows my gaze down to it.

"It's impossible to find matching underwear in that camper. My clothes are more jumbled than—"

"Than my urge to kiss you…"

She raises her eyebrows in surprise. No, I wasn't expecting to say that either. I lick my lips.

"We're fucking it up," I say, going over to the bed.

"Are you going to kiss me?"

"Do you want me to?"

I sit on the bed next to her and weave a couple of fingers into her hair, even though it's tied up. It's one of those messy buns women drive me wild with. She's looking at my mouth. And I'm looking at hers. She nods.

"Do you think I should?"

She arches, and it's enough of an answer even though its wordless. I lean toward her. I smell her. God. She smells like home. She is home. What the fuck is happening to me?

My hands don't ask permission to grab her waist and make her arch more. I slide one hand under her shirt and caress her stomach. She's panting. I think I am too, but I'm not sure because everything feels like a fucking astral projection.

I kneel on the bed and push in between her legs, which settle onto my thighs, spread so that I fit perfectly between them. I put my hands on her waist again and slide them down to her hips, pressing her into me.

"Now all that's missing is the kiss." She sounds like she's begging.

"All? We're missing a lot more than that."

"Like what?"

"Kissing. Biting each other. Licking the skin that…" I stop when I pull her hips up and down to rub against me a little and then I let her go and settle on top of her, holding her in my arms. "The skin that gets wet when we do this. We're still missing getting naked, fitting together, feeling how you moan when I'm inside you and exploding when…"

I push into her, grabbing the nape of her neck, and I'm barely two millimeters from her mouth.

"I can't believe this is happening," she says.

"I can't either. I want to stretch out the moment and…"

The pressure of her lips is perfect, and her saliva is sweet. I moan into her mouth and…

Knock, knock, knock…

"What is that?"

Knock, knock, knock…

It happens again.

Knock, knock, knock… Knock, knock, knock…

It's insistent, dragging on.

I open my eyes. The ceiling. I'm confused, foggy.

Knock, knock, knock…

It's the door. I must have fallen asleep. I was dreaming.

~

She's wearing the same loose white shirt and jean shorts. She slips off her shoes as soon as she comes into the room. She smiles at me. "You passed out."

"Totally." I scratch my neck.

"I can't have taken more than ten minutes to get here."

"Bah, shut up."

I grab her by the waist, hug her, bury my nose in her neck, and carry her over to the bed. This closeness is different from the one we had five days ago. Neither of us has changed, but everything between us has completely transformed. I never thought I would feel so full with my lips on the arch of her neck.

"Sleep," she whispers as a warning.

"Let's sleep."

I don't know why. I think it's because I want to stretch this game out, the first kiss, the desire. Or maybe because that dream was so weird. Even in my dreams, we're she and I. Coco and Marín. Sardine and Anchovy. This is the girl for me; that seems to be what this pounding in my chest is saying.

We settle on the bed, and she complains that her shorts are digging into her, but holding her from behind, I ask her not to take them off.

"Why?"

"Because I bet you're wearing those transparent black panties that are going to drive me crazy."

"I'm wearing gray ones with a picture of a duck on the back. They're the least sexy underwear in the world, I swear. My mother bought them for me." She laughs. "I don't even own black transparent panties."

"Well, if you see them in a store, don't buy them. I'm serious. My sanity is at risk here."

I press my lips into her neck and feel her shaking with laughter. I'm scared and happy. I feel full and simultaneously like I'm making room for everything I know she can give me, tossing everything else out the window, like a madman. I'm falling in love with Coco; it's starting to be pretty obvious.

Our legs intertwine; we hold each other tighter. I close my eyes peacefully. It's like we've always been two compatible pieces and we've been going around wondering why we don't fit with anyone else. But here we are. Do I believe in destiny? Is Coco my destiny? I met her in a bar one night when I wasn't even supposed to go out. I don't drink. What was I doing on La Via Láctea some random Wednesday night at two in the morning? What was she doing there? Coco doesn't go out in the middle of the week, not even when we were younger and had less responsibility. How did we hit it off so quickly? Why didn't I try to kiss her even though I thought she was incredible? I never looked at her that way. She seemed... Fuck, she seemed like fucking Wonder Woman to me. I can still see her going over to those strangers who were harassing two girls at the bar. She asked me to hold her beer and off she went. "Hey, lightweights, my friends have said no a dozen times. Even an ape would've gotten it by now. What's your problem?"

They called her every name under the sun, but she didn't care. Even when they threw her out of the bar for starting a fight. I remember saying goodbye to her thinking, *Some people have all the luck.*

Always, always, I just accepted that she wasn't for me. But...is she? What about that guy she's hung up on? The one she covered up by pretending she was still pining for Gus?

I squeeze her a little tighter and give in to being scared, nervous, jealous, overwhelmed before I ask her something that won't let me sleep if I don't. "Maybe this isn't the right moment, Coco, but I'm starting to wonder who the person is who makes your eyes shine and if—"

"You're so obtuse," she says, cutting me off, and I can tell she's smiling. "Who else would it be? It's always been you, you idiot."

27

A THOUSAND REASONS...

COCO

Marín wakes up before me. When I sit up in bed, I see him next to the window talking on the phone. I glance at my phone and find a message from my mother telling me to have a good time but be sensible enough at least for the last few days left, but not even maternal warnings can distract me from Marín. I can tell from his tone that it's work. He's serious but calm. He's still wearing the cotton shorts he sleeps in, and I know he's not wearing anything under them. His back has a perfect cleft in the middle and dimples below. It's a narrow but sexy back.

Does he want to kiss me? Does he want to as much as I do?

"Thanks so much. I feel better now. I didn't want to bother her, but I wanted to check how Pilar's recovery was going. Don't tell her I called because, well, she needs to rest now and not think about a tour or anything like that. She just needs to…to rest."

He turns and looks at me. He's smiling.

"Amazing. Hope she gets better really soon. If you need anything, you can call me on this number. It's my work phone, but I always have it with me." He pauses and nods as he comes over to the bed. "Take care."

He puts his phone down on the nightstand, sits, and pushes the hair off my forehead. That's always felt more special to me than most kisses;

it's almost involuntary. It's like reaching out to touch something shiny and you don't want to tarnish it but it calls to you.

"You were snoring," he says to me.

I cackle, and so does he. Only we know how to kill the tense vibe so thoroughly. "That's a lie."

"No way. You were snoring like a little piglet. It was pretty cute. In your own way."

"What time is it?"

"It's seven thirty. You should go get ready."

"Get ready?"

"Yeah. Aroa's gonna lose her shit when she finds out you took a nap here, and I'm sure she'll be looking for any excuse to try to stop us going out tonight. Go stick up for Blanca. You have to. If she wants to go out, we're going out."

"I don't think Aroa's going to make a scene, Marín."

"It's not her style? Well, I don't think anyone at your gallery would believe that the grimy sneakers you wore to the Izal concert are your most prized possession," he teases.

"That's because they don't know I went to that concert with you."

"And fifteen other people." He grins at me. "Seriously, I know it's a pain, but let's see if we can try not to ruin what's left of Blanca's night."

I'm about to disagree, but Marín covers my mouth with one hand and kisses it. Our first kiss, but a deferred one.

"Should we meet up at the site at nine? Tell Gus to come back here. If we leave him to his own devices, he'll keep napping until tomorrow. We'll take care of dinner."

"If I have to eat something cremated again, I can't be responsible for my actions."

"Woman of little faith… We'll make up for it."

"I've never had a four-hand massage," she chuckles. "That would be good payback. With a happy ending."

"Don't bust my balls." He smiles at me as he comes closer to my mouth again. "I'm not jealous, but I don't like sharing some things."

"You're going to have to clear up that confusion you say you have if you want that to mean anything to me. Oh! And…first of all, Anchovy, I'm not a thing. Second of all, shouldn't I be the one who decides…whether to share or not?"

He smiles. He smiles wide and nods as he looks into my eyes. I don't know a lot about love. I've never had a relationship longer than a year and a half. I get sick of them, I get overwhelmed, they get sick of me, I overwhelm them. I can't find the mold that fits my idea of a perfect couple, and maybe Marín is right and I'm much weirder than I think, but…I do know one thing: Stay with the one who loves your independence and knows how to see how important it is to you. Love someone who isn't afraid of the strong woman you are.

~

I'm floating as I walk back to the site. I confessed to Marín that he's the one I'm losing sleep over. I did it. And he didn't run in the other direction; he didn't give me a twenty-minute speech about how our friendship is so important, more important than anything else. He didn't throw himself into my arms and beg me to kiss him every day for the rest of my life either, but, come on, this isn't a romance novel. This is… What is it?

I run into Gus on the way out of the campsite. He has the sleepy face of someone emerging from the hours-long nap he must have taken. When he sees me, he puts his phone in his pocket, kisses my temple, and keeps walking before I even have the chance to say anything.

"Marín's waiting for you," I call after him.

"He can't live without me," he retorts without turning around, fishing his phone out again.

He seems glum but happy, like someone who knows his reason for smiling so much is about to vanish. I have to admit this is one of the most incredible trips of my life. I hope it is for Blanca too.

Aroa's sitting on the steps of the camper, and Blanca and Loren seem to be talking to her very seriously. All three are eating pumpkin seeds and drinking diet sodas. It might seem like nothing more than an everyday scene, but there's something intense in the air. It smells like a "little chat" from where I am, and when they see me, a strange silence spreads over our site.

"Hey..."

"How was your nap?" I ask them.

"Luxurious," Blanca says. "Although, I think I'm going to need a rigorous medical examination to confirm I'm not dead. I couldn't wake up."

"What were you talking about?" I sit in one of the chairs under the awning and grab a handful of seeds.

"We were wondering where you were," Aroa says.

I don't miss Loren's look, which doesn't seem too thrilled with her question.

"I was taking a walk on the beach." I show them my feet that I had the clever idea to go get all sandy on the beach before I headed back to the campsite.

I don't want to make Aroa feel worse, not because I'm scared of her reaction, like Marín thinks, but because she doesn't need to know the extent of everything that's happening between us. I'll have to tell her at some point, but...don't I have the right to experience this magic, like everyone else? Despite the fact that he's her ex. This isn't some crush—it's love.

I see Aroa relax, and I grab her soda, waving to ask permission to take a sip. She nods. She seems like she feels bad.

"Listen, Coco, I'm sorry I've been a little crazy the last few days. I've been coming face-to-face with the reality of where Marín and I are, and it's been kinda hard for me to accept it."

"Don't worry about it." I swallow my worry a little and fake a smile. "I'm sure you're actually turning the same page yourself, even if you don't believe it yet."

"Actually..." She wraps her arms around her knees and tucks her chin onto them. "Actually I think it's for the best. In a way, I feel like Marín never could have made me happy. He's never going to put anyone before his sister. Never. You know, Coco? No one."

I love her, but...she's a real asshole.

"Well, we should probably get ready for tonight, right?"

~

I end up being forced to drag my suitcase out onto the gravel and open it all the way just so I can find anything...like underwear and a bra that actually match, for example. Everything is wrinkled and balled up, but I manage to make the only "going out" outfit I packed look decent through persevering and using the blow dryer on full blast in the bathroom.

Aroa has already come out of the Imperial Boozer Cruiser wearing an oversized Smiths shirt like a dress and her shredded ankle booties because she can always be ready in the blink of an eye. That's what happens when you're beautiful, I guess. Although, the more I think about it, the more the conversation with Blanca keeps popping into my head, the one about her nuances. She must have some of her own too, I guess. In the end, I don't know how they managed to rot our brains so much that we all spend our whole lives wishing we were different.

I'm wearing a black, short-sleeved romper with a matching belt. On my feet are heeled sandals that Loren told me to pack "just in case." Blanca lends me her red lipstick and patiently draws my eyeliner on because when I try, I'm so jittery (and out of practice), I end up looking like an Egyptian pharaoh. And it's not a good look.

The humidity has made my hair go all frizzy, but nothing I can't fix with a flat iron and the hands of a friend, who has always been more coquettish than me and knows all the tricks. The result is stunning beachy waves, and I let her know by hugging her really hard.

Blanca's wearing a creamy kimono-style dress with a dark-green-and-dusty-pink pattern on it. Her hair is pulled back in a low pony, and she's wearing really soft makeup that flatters her big, brown eyes. She seems happy.

"You really feel like going out dancing, huh?"

"What reggaeton can't fix..." she jokes.

"Listen." I look around to check that, besides two English ladies and the gang of Germans who are sharing the counter in the communal bathroom with us, there's no one else around. "What were you talking to Aroa about?"

"Well, you can guess. It seems like she's seen a little reason."

"Yeah, besides the little dig that Marín will never prioritize anyone over his sister."

"In a way, that's kinda true, right?"

"Yeah, but I don't see anything wrong with it."

"Maybe it feels different when you're in a couple."

I suck my teeth. "Don't you be a Bitter Betty too."

"No, it's not like that. It's just that I think it's best..." She looks at her phone. "They say they're on the way. Come on, quick: What happened? Because only someone who doesn't know you would believe the whole beach thing, you liar."

I smile and give a little yelp that makes everyone in the bathroom look over at me. "Blanqui, it's all happening. He knows that he's the one in my head and this... It's moving forward, you know?"

She leans against the wall and smiles. "Ay, Coco...it's just a matter of time."

"A matter of time?"

"A matter of time, yeah. I've always thought Marín was in love with you even when he got together with Aroa, but"—she shrugs—"it was just easier."

"And you're telling me this now?" comes out in an unbearably high-pitched squeak.

"I don't think he knew, to be honest. Now, it's starting to sink in. But… go slow."

"Slow," I repeat.

"Yeah, slow. Dudes…get scared. They get scared"—she takes a breath—"easily and fast. And you have no idea how fast they are when they turn around to flee."

~

When we get back to the site, they've just showed up. Gus, dressed in a military-green T-shirt and black jeans, is brandishing a bottle of gin and chasing Loren around with it, shaking it like a maraca. Aroa is watching Marín from her chair with the disjointed look of a broken doll as he slides a few boxes of amazing-smelling pizza onto the table. And he's…so hot. A loose-fitting black shirt and matching skinny jeans. He must have combed his hair (just with his fingers, I know him), and his hair is slicked back from his face, although it still needs a good cut.

He turns toward me when I go over and checks me out pretty blatantly. He keeps his response measured and funnels it all into a smile that he hides by running his hand over his beard.

"Heels and everything, huh? You clean up nice." He points to the sandals in my hand.

"Button-up and everything, huh?"

Aroa shifts in her seat, scraping it noisily against the gravel. I turn toward her, uncomfortable. "Aroa, glass of wine?"

"Of course."

"Don't move or anything, huh?" Loren gives her shit, in his black T-shirt and favorite jeans, already pulling out a cold bottle of white wine.

"What does it matter? We're already standing. Do we need anything else?" Marín offers.

"Napkins and plastic plates."

Blanca comes out with the corkscrew and glasses, but just as she's about to turn to go back inside, Marín goes instead.

"Where are the napkins?" he asks.

"Wait, I'll go. You could go to the ocean and not find water."

Good excuse for us to look at each other without everyone else watching.

"Here they are." I crouch down to the cupboard where there's a stack of them.

He crouches down too. We look at each other, both kneeling.

"Your lips…" he murmurs.

"What?"

"Your lips." He nods toward them as he pulls a handful of napkins out of the open package. "Red. You haven't worn lipstick in forever."

"Yeah."

"Why today?"

"I don't know."

"You do know." He stands up and holds out his hand to pull me to my feet. "You're decking out our first kiss."

It's suddenly hard to swallow, but I smile. "Ah…am I going to give a first kiss tonight? I had no idea."

He looks outside and makes a playful face. "What I don't know is why we never said a word to each other."

"We were friends."

"Were?" He side-eyes me. "What are we now?"

"Marín and Coco."

He points to the door, but before he goes out, in a blind spot shielded from the outside, he corners me again. His mouth is so close to mine…

"With that lipstick everyone's gonna know," he whispers very softly.

"It's smudge proof." I smile at him.

"Not enough, I promise," he answers me with a smile. But before he lets me leave, he says, "Let's be discreet."

"You're making a lot of assumptions."

"Did you find the napkins or are you making them yourselves?" Gus asks from the doorway. "Oy, oy, oy…"

That last sound came when he saw how close we're standing, whispering to each other. I pull away from Marín, giving him a slap, and I laugh and yell at Loren to deflect, while Marín gestures for Gus not to say a word.

"You're a hemorrhoid! Didn't you say you wanted ice? I was taking it out of the tray!" I shove it into Gus's hand, and Marín and I look at each other gravely.

"Okay, okay, little couple…" he whispers. "Ay! Yes!" he yells exaggeratedly. "I always put ice in my wine!"

"Gus, shut up." We hear from outside.

That was, of course, Blanca.

~

If looks could be translated into words, transcribing that dinner would take a five-hundred-page novel. Marín looks at my mouth; I look at his. We both blush. The triangle of skin his collar leaves in view is making me nervous. I can't stop picturing myself smudging lipstick and spit all over him, and I don't know how to sit because something's telling me tonight will be the night. I don't think I've ever wanted to sleep with someone this much even though it tracks when you consider that we've had a whole week of foreplay. Doing it with Marín… Will we make love? Fuck like animals? How the hell does Marín fuck? I always tried not to pay attention to the details Aroa always proudly spouted off, but right now they'd come in pretty handy.

Blanca sometimes looks out into the black night and sometimes at her phone, where I get the feeling she's texting Ruben. Maybe these days apart are doing her some good in helping her figure stuff out, see everything more clearly. But, other times, Blanca is glancing at Loren. They seem to be locked in some kind of silent conversation that I want to be part of, but I can't understand it. It doesn't bother me. I assume they're just stressed about Aroa, who hasn't taken her eyes off Marín and me.

Gus, on the other hand, seems to be very focused on how many likes his latest post on Instagram is getting. To keep myself busy and make me stop looking over at Marín, I grab his phone and hold it up.

"Let me read it. I haven't been checking my phone much today."

"You must've been busy with other stuff," he says with a sly smile.

"Shut up, idiot."

He took a really pretty photo of the ocean, probably when I ran into him on the way back. On the photo, in typewriter font, he wrote "Silence" and the caption says:

I have a space in my chest for our embrace
One where I don't let anyone else in;
One where I don't even want the sun to come in.

I have a stomach full of the caresses of your skin,
A mouth wet with confused songs,
Eyes blind from going to sleep thinking
That I'll get over this story.

So, let's shut up,
Let's confess the impossible,

Without words that give shape,
Without anything that can break, be erased, stop existing.

Let's be,
Like that thing nobody has been able to explain,
Like the tingle that nobody could predict,
Like when we didn't say a word.

Can't we always be those people?
Those ones, little one,
Who make it hard or easy,
But in silence.

A WhatsApp pings on his phone right as I'm handing it back to him, and he tenses up. All I can glimpse is that it's from a "Malasaña." That little motherfucker. He probably didn't even remember her name so he saved her as the name of the place he met her.

"What the..."

He doesn't answer. He reads it as close to his chest as possible, where no one can see anything. Maybe Malasaña wasn't because he forgot—maybe it's a code between the two of them, a wink, a memory, the promise to tread on those cobblestoned streets again or traipse down Pez Street looking for a bar where they can grab a drink. It wouldn't be anything new; he's forever searching for that. Maybe Malasaña is *her*.

I seize the moment, since Loren is asking Aroa if she has any gigs lined up for the summer. It's weird; the blondie is one of those people who perk up a little, no matter how they're feeling, when the attention is on them. I've never noticed before. But that's not the important part; the important part is what I want to ask Gus. "Are you okay?"

"Me? Of course. Why?"

"I dunno." I smile. "You're not being obvious or anything, but I'm pretty sure there's someone special."

"No way. I'm talking to a girl, but that's it." He shrugs listlessly. "Nothing special."

"Well, it's kinda special that you're only talking to one, isn't it?"

He gives a half smile and slowly shakes his head.

"No way, Coco Puff. When you say it like that, it makes it sound like something it's not." He looks weirded out.

I pat his knee under the table and give him a complicit look.

"Gus, you're leaving a lot unsaid..."

"That's probably because I don't want to say it."

The reply sounds hard, but he says it with a wolfish smile, and I retort, "You will."

I grab another slice of pizza, and a hand slides me a napkin. My old one, completely grease-soaked, is balled up on my plastic plate. I follow the hand to its owner, who's smiling at me. It's Marín, of course.

"Take it, you filthy little piglet."

"The truth is I am a little filthy."

I see his Adam's apple bob up and down, and I can almost read his thoughts: *Don't do this to me right now.*

"Oh, yeah. It's true. I can vouch for it." Gus grabs another piece of pizza too and a napkin.

"I always get covered in stains," I add with a half smile.

"That's because you don't like cutlery. You like using your hands."

"And my mouth."

"What are you talking about?" asks Aroa, who must have caught a few words.

"How Coco is a total pig." Gus smiles.

I show her my greasy napkin and smile, but I can't hide the fact that it was a different tone.

"Maybe it's the copious amount of wine you've been drinking?" Marín asks slyly.

"Nuh-uh," Gus says. "It's just because you don't drink at all, so anything seems like a lot to you. Another little glass?"

"Thanks." I put my glass in his reach so Gus can pour more wine in. "Tonight I want to do it all."

Once I'm served, I glance discreetly at Marín over my cup, and I watch him smile as my foot snakes up onto his chair, between his legs. He raises his eyebrows, bites his lip.

I guess nobody except us understands where the hell that came from.

Mandala seems to be the hot place. We get there early, and there's already a line. And it's worth pointing out that it doesn't give a great first impression: It's one of those clubs where the women get two drink tickets for the price of entry and the guys one. I don't know which of the genders that's more discriminatory to. Of course, I can't keep my mouth shut.

"Quite the anachronism, bro."

"If you don't like it, go somewhere else."

"Relaaaaaax," I retort as Loren yanks me inside.

"Do you always have to fight with bouncers like that?"

"If they're idiots, then yeah."

Music is booming out of the speakers, and I'm surprised barely anyone is dancing. There are groups of people talking and flirting, and bartenders are slammed at the bars with so many people ordering.

We stake out a corner in the garden as our command center. There are a couple of members of the group who look like they want to abandon ship, but we didn't pay fifteen euros a head just to head straight back home. Loren and Blanca are both delighted by the music choices. Blanquita has many layers: She likes a night at some club just as much as one at a dingy patio where they only play Pachanga. I can get down to anything, and Marín says all music is respectable and has its place, so we have no problem either. But Aroa and Gus…

"If they play 'Despacito,' I swear I'll throw myself in that pool!" he screams.

"You just wanna see everyone get their tits out," Blanca mutters mischievously but loudly enough so he hears her.

"I didn't even notice them, you clown."

"You're the clown."

"Hey! I'm declaring a truce!" I yell. "Come on…let's divide and conquer. You"—I point to Blanca, Aroa, and Gus—"stay here and hold down the fort. We'll go get supplies."

"I don't drink," Marín says into my ear.

"Do you have two hands?" I turn to look at him with a smile.

"You know where I want to put them, right?" And he leans down to say it into my ear.

OMG, OMG, OMG. Marín wants to put his hands on you. Good thing I put on cute underwear tonight.

Loren pinches us discreetly and then drags us over to the bar.

"Reel it in a little," Loren says with a serious face. "Aroa's on the edge."

"We're not doing anything wrong."

"No, nothing wrong, but you're falling in love right under his ex's nose."

"What?" Marín yells, trying to hear over the blaring music.

"Do you want a bottle of water?" Loren yells back.

"No. Then it'll look like I'm on pills."

I can't help laughing as I lean against the bar.

"He's so cute…"

"Listen, how are we doing it tonight?"

"Doing what?" I see Marín trying to get the bartender's attention a little farther down from us, right at the end of the bar.

"Look…give Gus the car keys and twenty euros for his silence and you two go to the hotel. I'll make something up to tell Aroa."

I stare at him, surprised. It's like he knows more about what's going to happen than we do. "Blanca filled you in, I guess."

"No. But she didn't need to. I'm practically sprouting tits from all the hormones you two are giving off. If you can't wait until you get back to Madrid, fine, but don't touch each other right in Aroa's face anymore."

"I don't know why we need to be so scared of her," I whine.

"What are you two talking about?" Marín manages to squeeze into a gap next to us.

"Aroa." And Loren's look back at him is sharp and a little pointed. "I was telling Coco that if she explodes, we're all going to be in deep shit."

The look they exchange seems to be loaded with much more information than I have right now. Marín suddenly seems worried, and I get anxious for a second.

"What's going on?" I grab his arm.

"Nothing." He smiles at me suddenly. "But we don't want Aroa to vomit fire, right?"

"No. We don't want that. Or to explode so we're all in deep shit. Right, Marín?"

I'm in love, but I'm not stupid. I missed a chapter. I'm sure of it.

28

THE MISSING CHAPTER

COCO

I turn back to the bartender obstinately and order a round and a few shots.

"Everything okay?" Loren asks me.

My face must've changed when I saw the way they were looking at each other.

"Yeah. Phenomenal."

The wine, the looks I don't understand, the jealousy, the fear, the things left unfinished—all of it is thrumming relentlessly against my back. As soon as the shot glass hits the bar, I throw it down my throat. I hear both of them cracking up and telling me to take it easy, but I smile as much as I can and take the one I actually ordered for Loren. It makes me retch, but I chase it with a sip of my rum and Coke.

"Let's dance!" I say, faker than a wooden euro.

I don't wait to see their warning looks. If I'm missing something, if I'm lacking information about the story Marín and Aroa were the main characters in. Am I making a total fool of myself? Does that change my situation with him? Is it going to fuck up my night if I find out?

I'm carrying my drink and Blanca's, but when Gus suddenly pops up in front of me, I dump almost all of it over his head.

"Fuck, Coco!" he yells when he feels the liquid hit his chest. "A little ice play is one thing and this is…another."

"Sorry."

"No worries." He focuses on his shirt, brushing it with his hand like that'll dry it. He looks up, laughing and raising one eyebrow. "You're legless, Coco Puff!"

"What are you talking about!" I wave him off. "I just took two shots."

"Go puke them up. If this is how you are already, when they hit you, it's gonna be a pretty wild party." He grabs the drink I'm holding and hands it to Blanca. "Here, Blanqui. Gin and tonic. If you're wondering where the rest of it is, you can lick it off my shirt. Or my chest."

"If I lick your chest, I'll be coughing up hair balls like a cat."

"Don't mess with me or I'll say something outrageous and you'll get all mad."

I lean against the wall to follow the dialectical ping-pong match between them. I'm glad we're out in the open air and the music is a little quieter than inside. I was starting to get overstimulated.

"Did we take a long time or is it just me?" I ask Aroa.

"Forever," she replies. "And you smell like a minibar."

Great. Marín, who doesn't drink more than a beer at weddings, baptisms, and promotions, is gonna love my boozy breath.

"Do you have any gum?"

"Are you planning on kissing someone?" she asks as she rummages through her bag.

"I dunno. This place is full of cute guys, right?"

She hands me a piece of gum, and at the same moment, Marín hands me a bottle of water with the lid already cracked half open and winks at me.

"The trick is to hydrate yourself, Sardine," he says. "Drink a little. You're gonna be wasted if you keep drinking rum at that pace."

"Wasted sounds better than legless," I say.

"Who told you you're 'legless'? Aroa?" he asks, amused.

She shakes her head, unable to stifle a tiny smile. The power of Marín, I guess.

"It was Gus."

"Ah, of course. The poet."

All three of us burst out laughing.

"...a chick magnet," we hear Gus say.

"It's been so long since you bragged about your list of eternal conquests."

"Well, I'm the picture of discretion."

"Will you all shut up already? You're always the same," I say from where I'm standing.

"You're shit-faced!"

"You're a hairy beast!"

"You know what's not hairy? My balls. They're smooth, super smooth. Want one?"

"Yeah, on a stick like a Chupa Chup." I crack up. "Let's dance!" And I give him a pat like I'm his nanny.

"Do you think I'm your little dancing monkey?"

I take a sip of my drink and then chug the bottle of water Marín gave me. Then I pull Blanca to dance outside our little group.

I spin back to Marín, and we both start whooping as a song we love comes on. I tug on his wrist, and Loren wolf-whistles us as we start dancing.

"Ladies and gentlemen...Anchovy and Sardine!"

"Super salty!"

The alcohol has completely erased all my inhibitions and shame, so I'm moving like I would in my room, with no one watching. My arms are in the air, and one finger is looped around his, guiding me, drawing me closer, twirling me to the beat of the music.

He doesn't need to move much to be ridiculously sexy. His whole body sways to the rhythm, smoothly, nothing flashy, just elegant, sliding around me. For Marín, dancing is as easy as breathing. Like fucking.

I put my hands flat on his chest, and we smile at each other. I bite my lip in a kind of promise of who knows what…and I get the giggles because I don't know how to be sexy.

He hugs me as we cackle. "I'm going to have to eat you whole," he whispers into my ear.

"Sounds good to me."

"You prudes!" Blanca yells, waving her drink in the air. "Show us how a fucking sardine moves."

I move closer. My stomach is pressed against his. Marín laughs up into the sky, and I grab his waist and shimmy up and down a little.

"Like fish in water!" And then Gus starts whistling.

One of his hands is on my waist, and the other is on my neck. At first, I think he's trying to move me a little farther away from him, but before I can blink, he turns me around so my back is to him and bends me forward. It's not like I know how to twerk, honestly, but I know how to do something with my hips. Loren and Blanca join Gus, and they all whistle.

I grab one of Marín's wrists, and he twirls me back toward him. We always do this kind of stuff in the kitchen at home, when we put on music while we cook, although it doesn't feel like this.

The song ends, and we burst out laughing, clasping hands, bowing to our audience, which Aroa is not part of.

"Where's blondie?"

"She went to the bathroom." And Gus raises his eyebrows as he says it.

The vibe suddenly changes completely when Loren shoots Marín a loaded look. I grab my drink again and take a big gulp that goes down smooth, cooling the heat in my cheeks.

"We were just dancing," Marín says. "It's a fucking club, for God's sake."

"I didn't say a word!" Loren puts his hands up.

"You can't even sneeze when she's around, for fuck's sake," I complain, raging at the fun being cut short, from the sudden crash and, probably, because of the alcohol.

"I'm going to..."

"I'll go," Gus says, cutting Marín off. "I'm Switzerland. And I'm easy to break, like chocolate."

He downs half of his gin and tonic and winks at us before he puts his drink down and disappears into the crowd.

"What a buzzkill," I grumble.

"Come on. No way," Blanca says.

I look at her, and when she makes a silly face, I smile again. "I think I drank too fast."

"I'm going to buy cigarettes." She points at the machine I can see from where we're standing. "Let's do a lap when I get back? And get some air."

"Cool."

Loren and Marín are talking about Aroa. And the content of their conversation is pretty obvious. One is asking the other to calm down; the other says he's tired of this childish shit.

"I've always been clear, dude. Always," Marín defends himself.

"Yeah, but she's jealous, and...we can see her side too. She showed up all excited, thinking you were getting back together, and now..."

"Loren, I never gave her any indication that was going to happen."

"Yeah, I know, but—"

"Hey, I get it." Marín pushes his hair off his forehead. "But it's Blanca's bachelorette party. The only expectation any of us should've had is to help her have the best time ever, right?"

"Yeah, dude, but it's more complicated than that. We're humans. You are too and..."

I zone out from the conversation. I'm bored of talking about it. I grab my drink and down the last of it. I shouldn't drink any more. I look at my watch. It's super early to be winding down already.

Aroa suddenly appears. She's moving a little fast, but she doesn't seem mad.

"Hey," Marín says, grabbing her wrist.

"Huh? What?" she asks.

"Nothing. Um…all good?"

"Yeah, yeah. But I don't feel good. Does anyone mind if I go home?"

"You're leaving?" Loren asks, confused. "Wait, you don't feel good?"

Aroa grabs the bag she left in a corner, slings it across her chest, and rubs her face. "I don't like these places. I'm getting overstimulated by all the people and…"

"But it's Blanca's bachelorette party, Aroa," Marín says warmly.

"I know, I know. But I'm gonna be grumpy, she's going to notice, and that'll just make it worse. Where is she?"

"She went to buy cigarettes," I pipe up. "Have you seen Gus? He went to find you."

"Yes, yeah. We crossed paths. He's, he's still in the bathroom."

What's up with Aroa? Is this all about me dancing with Marín? She's being really weird. I go over. "Are you okay?"

"Huh? Yeah, yeah. I'm fine. I just wanna go to sleep. No one minds, right?"

"Wait." Marín pats his pockets. "I'll walk you there and then come back. I'll be worried if you leave alone."

"We're across the street, Marín," she whines. "It's two hundred meters away."

"It doesn't matter. There are a lot of drunk assholes around. Not like I don't think you can defend yourself, by the way. It's just to put my mind at ease."

I stare at them. Look how the tables have turned. Now I'm the one seething with jealousy.

"I'll be right back, okay?" Marín says to me, moving away from her a little. "Do you have your phone with you? In case I can't find you later."

"It's in my bag."

"Put it on vibrate, please." He leans down a little and smiles shyly. "I just want to talk to her for a minute, okay? I'll be back in ten minutes."

"Yeah, sure." I nod.

"Coco..." His hand finds mine, discreetly, down low, like it's not a big deal. We both look at our fingers as they brush against each other. "All I want to do is spend the night with you, you know that, right?"

I smile. "No, but I have the bad habit of always believing you."

He raises his eyebrows. "What...what makes you say that?"

"Nothing, nothing. I'm just...drunk."

"I'll bring you water when I come back. If you want?"

"Okay."

He turns away. Aroa is waiting for him on the edge of the terrace. I watch them wend their way through the crowd toward the exit, and soon they disappear into the other bodies, other faces. A bunch of strangers swallow them up.

"Fuck it." Loren doesn't answer. "Loren?"

Loren? Loren isn't here. I'm...alone.

I look around me. Blanca went to get smokes. Marín and Aroa left. Gus never came back from the bathroom. Where the fuck is Loren? I grab my bag and cross it over my chest, and stand on my tiptoes, trying to spot Loren's ridiculous hair in the crowd, but it's impossible. Loren's haircut must be in style—there are a lot of them floating around.

My logical side tells me to stay where I am, but the side being controlled by the shots I downed so fast at the bar is making me push through the crowd and I start getting overwhelmed. I rush in one direction and crash into a group of girls.

"Sorry, sorry."

I decide to go to the cigarette machine. I'll definitely find Blanca there, I tell myself.

I get the impression there are even more people here than when we arrived, and it's so hard to swim across the tide of people talking, laughing, dancing, and drinking in little groups. All I can see is the tops of heads, and none of them seem to belong to my friends.

It's really hot in here. I suddenly notice how my romper is sticking to my back. I have to get out of here. I don't want to be all soggy when Marín comes back. Because…he's gonna come back, right? What were he and Loren trying to hide from me? The reason Marín and Aroa broke up? What if Marín was always the guilty party? What if he cheated on her? What if he did something that's going to change the way I…?

I suddenly perk up when, to my left, on the other side of the bar in the middle of a jumble of people, I see Loren and Blanca. Blanca looks really upset. Loren's grabbing her hands, but she pulls them away, pushes her hair back, rubs her face… Is she crying?

I want to go over, but the crowd won't part. I'm suffocating. I'm really suffocating. What if I go back out again and then try to turn around from there?

The "excuse mes" I'm saying as I go aren't having any effect, so I elbow my way through. I can see the exit, and I can start to feel the air getting cooler. What's going on with Blanca? She just went to buy cigarettes. Did Ruben call her? Did they get in a fight?

I walk straight into a girl and stumble back a few steps. I grab the wall, which saves me from falling to the floor…in the nick of time.

In the nick of time.

In the nick of time.

In the nick of time.

It's the only thing playing in a loop in my head when I look up and I see them. My brain is stuck there, trapped, in the last thing I thought before

I saw them. Embracing. Clinging to each other. Looking at each other. She's touching his hair. He's resting his forehead on her chin. Intimacy. Complicity. If you're observant, it's easy to see when two people are keeping a secret. I've spent half the trip only seeing what I wanted to see, but not anymore. They're right there. Clinging to each other. Looking at each other. By themselves. Hidden. From who?

From me.

It's Marín and Aroa.

I sense a movement, and my head, which is still trapped in the loop of "in the nick of time," reacts, stopping me from seeing the kiss, if there is one. I'll be honest, I don't really care if there isn't. I've seen enough. I start to shove people out of the way, and I run out. I want to get out of here. I want to leave as soon as possible, to get some air, to forget all about it, to sober up, to be clear-eyed and realize that no, I didn't see anything intimate or complicit, that they haven't built a bridge together over so many years, that they don't share any secrets…that I'm the only secret Marín is keeping and that they were probably…

Someone suddenly grabs my arm and stops me. It's Gus. He's sweaty, and he looks nervous. Maybe dazed or drunk. When did that happen?

"I can't find anyone," he says.

"I want to get out of here," I blubber.

"Me too."

"Take me outside."

"Where?" he asks, confused.

"Gus…get me out of here."

29

CARDINAL SINS

COCO

The drunkenness is hitting me more and more the farther I get from the club. We haven't even gotten to the campsite when the image I saw of Marín and Aroa starts to warp into something else. Two people holding each other even more intimately…

"Wait here for a sec."

Gus leaves me perched on a stone planter on the sidewalk and runs across to the other side. He vanishes into another bar and then comes back, I have no idea how much later, with two beers. He smiles at me.

"There's no gathering worth going to without a nightcap."

"I don't want any," I say, slurring my words.

"I know. They're both for me. We have water in the room." He puts his arm around my waist and heaves me to my feet. I lean on his shoulder, and in that moment, I'm grateful for him. "Thanks, Gus."

"I don't deserve it."

"Of course you do. I'm dead weight."

"No. Your legs still work." He smiles. "You'll see that when you get in the shower still in your clothes, which always feels so good."

Through the haze of alcohol I realize that Gus is smiling sadly. "Where were you?"

"In the bathroom," he replies. "And then I couldn't find any of you."

"You didn't see anyone?"

"No. Why?"

"I saw Blanca and Loren. They were at the other end of the bar." And "bar" sounds really slurry on my tongue. I cringe. "Fuck. How did I get this drunk? This isn't me."

"No, it isn't you. Getting tipsy and giggling at everything is more your style. What happened to you?"

"What about you?"

We stare at each other as we walk into the hotel lobby. He sucks his teeth, like he's asking me to drop it and keep walking to his room. The walk seems to take forever, I'm not going to lie.

I know this room already. I took a nap here. With Marín, who almost kissed me, who was so sweet, who came closer, who seemed happy to be with me and…

Gus props me against the wall and stands in front of me, really close. At first I'm a little scared, but then I realize that he has one leg between mine to hold me up so I don't fall.

"I'm not that bad," I say with a half smile.

"I don't trust you," he teases. "Can you stand?"

"Yes, dummy."

He puts the beers down on the bedside table and then crouches down in front of me. I don't understand what he's doing until I feel immediate relief in my feet. He's taking off my heels.

"Enough of those, dude. They make you taller than me."

I giggle, walk past him, and flop onto the bed. He sits next to me and opens a beer.

"Water…" I plead.

"I put one next to you, you dope."

I fumble around next to me until my hand runs into a cold bottle of water. I sit up, grab it like it's the last one in a desert, and drink it. I'm lucky it all falls into my mouth, because I'm hammered.

"It's so dumb that I'm this drunk, for fuck's sake," I groan, hurling the empty bottle at the trash can opposite the bed and missing, of course.

"You drank really fast." He takes another sip of his beer, takes his phone out of his pocket, checks it, and then puts on a Spotify playlist featuring Marín's favorite song.

"What's going on with you, buddy?" I pat his thigh over his jeans.

"What about you?"

"Stop putting the ball back in my court. I know you, and something's going on with you."

"I was getting hella overwhelmed." He rubs his eyebrows with the thumb and forefinger of the hand not holding his beer. "I hate those places. You know that."

"I've seen you clubbing a thousand times."

"I have to be in the right mood."

"Did you talk to Aroa in the bathroom?"

"What?" He shoots me a confused look and then seems to catch on to what I'm saying. "No. I didn't even see her."

Huh...didn't she say...?

"What happened to you?" he insists. "Come on...if I'm remembering right, confessing our sins does us good."

"Are you getting nostalgic, Gus?"

"I am nostalgic. Don't change the subject. What happened?"

"I saw her with Marín."

"Aroa?" His brow furrows.

"Yeah. They were hugging. Like really hugging."

"They were probably...I dunno, talking about their relationship. Getting closure."

"They've been getting closure for...what? Nine months? Shit, Gus, I can't take it anymore."

"Or maybe you can, right? It's him."

"Was there really any doubt?"

"One or two. Sometimes I could swear you were still making eyes at me."

I cackle and slump back on the bed again. The ceiling is spinning a little. My stomach flips. "I'm probably going to barf up pizza in your bed."

"Our bed. I'm sleeping here with you, champ. Try to keep the pizza in your stomach, please."

I turn, and he's sitting, leaning back, staring straight ahead, propped up on his elbows in the bed. His expression... There's no mistaking it.

"You feel like shit."

"That's not true," he retorts.

"Of course it is. You never say it."

"When I feel like shit, I say it. But I don't right now."

"I don't think I've ever seen you down this bad."

"Thanks, Coco." He sighs and adds, "You're a huge help."

"Of course I am. Just like you. You're always..." I turn a little—God, I'm so dizzy—and I nuzzle my cheek on his arm. That makes him smile. "You're always there, Gus."

"I told you I'd always be here, right? I keep my promises."

"You're the only one."

"Don't fuck with me!" He laughs. "Not you, for God's sake. I treated you right. I think you're the only one who can say that. I was faithful. I just flirted in the DMs with a few girls and that's it... Don't look at me like that! I treated you like a queen!"

"And I treated you like a king."

"I wasn't complaining."

It's true. He never complained. We both treated each other well, we took care of each other, we worried about each other… It made sense. Even though we didn't love each other. Neither of us went out of our way for each other, it's worth pointing out, but that's just how we were.

I'm getting really dizzy. Lying down isn't a good idea. "You know your problem, Gus?" I say as I try to lurch up to sitting.

"Surprise me," he sighs.

"You swallow everything down, and in the end, that means you can't see past your own belly button and the tangled web of feelings you must have down there." I point at his chest. "Half of them must be rotten, fermenting."

"Fuck, Coco." He nods. "You don't sound that wasted."

"I'm all better! When you give me a shower, I'll be…fantastic!"

"You want me to give you a shower?"

It sounds like he's a little too into that idea. "If you tell me what happened, I'll let you give me a shower."

"That sounds suspiciously like prostituting yourself for information."

"Who said anything about sex?"

"Meh." He takes another sip of his beer. "Nothing really happened to me. I just got kinda bummed, you're right, but I was bummed for no reason."

"Right…"

"I mean… Look, listen, the thing with Marín… It's stupid. I'm sure he—"

"Wait, he was gonna call me when he came back," I suddenly remember.

"See?"

"No. You're not listening. He was going to call me when he came back from dropping Aroa off. It was supposed to be ten minutes."

"Why don't you call him?"

I don't answer. I curl up in a ball, staring at the wall, like he was a few minutes ago.

I turn back to Gus. "They're hiding something from me, you know? They're hiding something, and that's why they left together. He's playing me, Gus. What if he's playing me?"

"Marín isn't like me," he says in a thread of a voice.

"You didn't play me."

"Not you, no. You're the only one."

"He's playing with me, Gus. Maybe he doesn't know it yet, maybe he doesn't even realize, but..."

"All this just because you saw them hugging?" He sighs, "Come on, Coco..."

"It was a just a hug and a bad, sloppy, drunk reaction from me...until I saw the time." I look at my phone again. "It must have been an hour at this point, Gus."

"Not quite."

"What have they been doing all this time?"

"You think they're fucking?"

Gus's question catches me off guard, even though it's the most logical answer to mine. Thick saliva swirls in my throat. I need more water. I stand up, but he predicts what I want, puts a hand on my shoulder, pushes me back down, and goes over to the mini-fridge himself.

I'm looking right at him when he throws the mini-bottle my way, but it thuds into my lap without me even trying to catch it. It's not lack of coordination from the alcohol—I'm picturing them together. Exactly how I heard them a thousand times. *Right there, Marín, keep going... Right there, don't stop.* And Marín's moans couldn't be heard. They just made everything shake...the wall, the paintings, even my chest.

"Hey." Gus clicks his fingers in front of my face. "You okay?"

I struggle to my feet and stumble into him as he jumps to catch me. All I want to do is cry and sleep and be done with being this drunk and this whole trip. Gus doesn't understand. How could he?

"They're not fucking, Coco. Get a grip."

I grab my phone and show it to him. Gus looks at me with a furrowed brow.

"I'm gonna call him," I say.

"Sounds good to me."

"Are you sad, Gus?"

"You're being super weird, Coco," he moans. "Not like you haven't always been weird, but…"

"Gus." I grab his shoulders and hug him. I feel so empty, so alone. "Just answer me. Are you sad? Tell me."

He looks at me. He looks at me, and his brown eyes are shining. Is he sad? All you have to do is look at him. Sad, deserted, abandoned.

"You are," I say.

"Empty," he mutters.

The call starts ringing, with the phone on speaker. Gus looks at me.

"I hate that you feel empty. You're not," I say.

"I am because I force myself to be empty, Coco."

"Why?"

"How can I not? I'm terrified of actually living. I'm a bottomless well of disappointment for everyone around me."

"That's not true. Stop thinking like that." I'm suddenly angry. Marín's not answering, Gus doesn't love himself like he should, I'm an idiot. I'm pissed off, and I punch him in the arm. "You're worth more than all that shit you say. Tell me, what can I do to make you believe it? What can I do to make you feel better?"

"We used to know how to make each other feel good," he mutters. "Remember?"

"Yeah. We knew."

"It didn't cure it, but…"

Gus was hot. I remember the heat that came off his body after fucking. It was nice. When I would sit naked on top of him, my thighs still a little wet, and make him laugh as I stroked the hair on his chest. Gus always made me feel good. He never lied to me, never made me any promises he couldn't keep. *Marín, who are you? Where are you? Do you love me?*

"If he doesn't pick up, I'm going to do something stupid, Gus. So if you don't want to participate, you're gonna have to be very firm."

He knows me. He knows me well. Memories, kisses, poetry, sadness and feelings wash over his face, and it scares me knowing that I don't recognize all of them. These things he lived through, without me, have been the most intense emotions of his life.

The fifth ring hurts. The sixth feels like a slap. The seventh is straight-up pathetic. But I keep going. I want him to pick up and tell me he couldn't find me, he's coming to get me, to make something up, I don't know.

"Hang up," Gus says.

What happened after is both our faults, but more mine than his.

~

He's the one who takes off his shirt. I unbutton my romper as fast as I can, but it'd be easier if I work on his pants while he takes off my clothes. He's less drunk, and he was always more nimble.

My clothes fall to the floor in a black puddle, and I pull my feet out just in time as he lifts me up and balances me on his hips.

His unbuckled belt digs into my thigh, but I don't say anything. As soon as we're in bed, I push it away.

"Take those off." I pull his pants down, helping with my feet.

He sits up, takes them off, and then lies down next to me. I'm touching him. He's not fully hard, but he's reacting to my caresses. Meanwhile, he's kissing my neck—he knows I love that. I don't kiss his—I know he doesn't like it.

He unclasps my bra, and his teeth close over my nipple. I arch with a moan that's more pain than pleasure. He answers with little licks and his right hand inside my panties. He doesn't seem to be able to find the place he knew so well when we were together. Of course, there have been so many ports, and each one has its own lighthouse.

"There." I guide him to it. "It's right there."

"Do you have condoms?"

"No. Don't you?"

"I think I have one in my wallet."

The wallet is in his pants. There is a condom in there. Neither of us bothers checking the expiration date. Knowing him, it probably hasn't been there long.

"Coco..." he says before he opens it.

"Don't even think about asking me if I really wanna do this."

"I wasn't going to ask that. I was going to ask you to keep this between us. I... I'm screwing up too, okay?"

"But...do you really wanna do this?"

"Now you're the one asking?" He raises his eyebrows in surprise.

Gus yanks off his boxers unceremoniously, and standing next to the bed, lined up with my open legs, he focuses on opening the condom. I pull off my underwear. I don't think I've ever had more mechanical sex. My heart is racing, and I wonder if it's worth it, getting my friend involved in this, when he's nothing more than poorly digested anger.

"Gus, I don't want to give you any problems."

"Let's come, Coco. Then we'll see."

Gus licks his hand, touches himself with it, puts the condom on the tip, but...he grimaces as he unrolls it. He looks at it, frowning even deeper. It won't roll all the way down. He tries putting it back on the top. As I look down, the problem is obvious: He's not very hard.

I sit up and stroke it, wrapping my fingers around it, hard, how he likes it. I know he feels bad, his pride is wounded, but I keep going, looking at it, putting my mouth on his chest and biting it.

"Do you want me to suck it?"

"No. I don't like blow jobs with a condom on." He looks at it, makes another face. "This is the only one we have. Lie down..."

I do. He climbs on top of me. It's like someone ordered us to have sex. I don't think either of us really wants to do this.

"This is a fuckup," I moan when I feel him pushing into me.

"A big one. Ah..."

He tightens inside me, between my thighs. He's in, but it feels...weird. He pushes again. I moan. He does too. I feel pleasure but...

He pushes again and twists a little—he's still not hard. It seems like he's getting limper with each thrust. I grab his ass and dig my nails into it; he always liked that. I hold his gaze as his thrusts get even weaker. This isn't working.

"Fuck..." He pulls out. He touches himself violently. "Now this too?"

"Am I doing something...?"

"No, no. Coco...give me a second."

He tries again. He pushes in, gets the tip in, and then a few centimeters—the latex feels like its clinging to my walls tooth and nail. I'm not turned on, I'm not wet, and that doesn't help. The friction is anything but gentle. He penetrates me again. It's not going in right. I'm about to tell him to stop, but he gives a few more shoves. Nothing.

"Gus..."

"Fuck!"

He crumbles. I know him. And I know why. I know his defense mechanisms falling onto the bedside table alongside the wrinkled condom. This is his sex, it's his pride, it's the tool he's always used to make us believe he was a little bit of all of ours. He gets naked and he fucks us, but he doesn't give us anything. He was always cocky. But now he's not. Just because of a lost boner? No, of course not. The lost boner isn't the reason; it's the consequence. Gus let someone touch him how he never had before, and… that changed him.

I want to hug him, I want to hold him, I want him to tell me what happened, but I can't. I've never felt close enough to him to do that. It wasn't just him. It was me too. I was never interested in getting below the surface; that's the truth. Not like with Marín. Not like when it's love.

Gus doesn't put his boxers back on. He just flops back on the rumpled bed, which we didn't even pull the sheet back on, covers his eyes, and snorts.

"In the fucking bed I'm sharing with him, for fuck's sake."

"I know," I say. "It… It never happened, okay? Nobody has to know."

"Are we insane? What were we thinking?" He seems so angry. "God… Coco…fuck. What did we expect?"

I put my underwear on, he quickly puts on his own, and we embrace with real intimacy for the first time, an embrace that shows how ridiculous everything we did when we were a couple was: sex, caresses, confidences, all of it. This is the real intimacy we share. We're two friends, and the truth is we'll never be anything more.

"I'm sorry," he says, pushing himself away, suddenly uncomfortable with my naked breasts against his chest.

"It's fine. It's normal,…"

"No. That's not it, Coco." He sits on the edge of the bed, rubs his forehead, and lets his arms fall by his side, defeated. "I would've been able to do it."

"Yeah. I'm not saying you wouldn't. I just…"

"Coco," He looks at me, seriously. "It's a dick. It doesn't have that many secrets. I could've done it, I could've gotten it up. I know how to do it. But I didn't want to. I…didn't want to. All it would've taken was…was thinking about…"

"What?"

"Her."

"Her?"

"Her, Coco. Everything is about her."

I put on his shirt and go over. I slide my fingertips over his back.

"So there is a her," I confirm.

"Of course there is. You've always known that."

"Since when? I mean… Was it when you and I…?"

"No, no." He shakes his head vehemently. "I was faithful to you, Coco. She… It started something like…I dunno, nine months ago."

"But…"

"I'm not going to tell you her name, Coco. Don't ask. Don't make me name her now after…well…what I was about to do with you."

"Okay," I nod. "But were you two…?"

"No. We've never been… No. I don't know what we were doing. At first… At first it was just for fun. For both of us, seriously… I was honest. She was too. We just wanted to fool around, spend some time together, do something crazy. It wasn't premeditated—it just happened."

"But it turned into something else?"

"I don't know." He shrugs and rubs his forehead. "I have no idea what it is. But I'm… I'm bitter, Coco. I write too much about it. I carry it around everywhere with me. Some days I blame it all on her. Others I just miss her. There are nights when I want to hurt her with my poems, others I want to ask her forgiveness. Sometimes I just want to get under her skin, make her think about me, not forget me so fast."

"Gus," I say tenderly. "How do you know it's so fast? That girl's probably trying to get you out of her head and can't."

"I know. She told me."

"She…told you?"

"Yes. She told me everything. She told me we needed to end it, that she knew me too well and she couldn't do it anymore, that she felt awful, that she didn't know what she wanted but she wanted it to be with me. But I didn't."

"You didn't? But you just said you only write about her."

"I don't want it. I don't want her. I don't want to love her. I love her wrong."

"Fuck…"

I lean toward him and hug him. I wonder if he's okay, if I can do anything, if I know her, if… Thousands of words, hypotheses, ideas zipping through my head, and I'm stammering but he isn't. He doesn't want to talk anymore.

"Coco, I'm not trying to make you feel bad, but…can you leave me alone?"

I don't even answer. I'm sad.

I have a lump in my throat because I have a suspicion about who she is. It can't be, but…it would fit. Everything would fit. The problems, the long faces, how long he said they've been seeing each other, the complication, his fear…Aroa?

I have to go.

"I'm leaving, Gus, but…you can count on me. You know that, right?"

"I know. But you shouldn't say that. You're not going to be that happy with me either when you find out. I'm the master of fuckups. I spread my shit all over everyone."

If Aroa explodes, we're all going to be in deep shit. Isn't that what Loren said?

Yes. I have to go.

I don't hear any footsteps. There's no warning. I haven't even found my romper yet when the door to the room opens. Of course, it's a hotel. They have two keys. I didn't even think about it.

I'm holding my bra in my hand, and Gus is only wearing his boxers.

The bed is messed up. There's a condom that looks more used than it is on the bedside table. You'd have to be blind to think anything but that we did it and we really did it.

I could say that the look he gives us is worse than a scream, worse than an insult, a slap, but it's not true. Actually, it's like we just punched him. Marín takes a step back, not taking his eyes off us.

"Marín," I say in a tiny voice.

"It's not what it looks like, right?" He gives a dry laugh and rubs his forehead. "Motherfucker."

Nothing else. Motherfucker. Liquid rage pooling in his mouth. Hot ire in his throat. The sound of a door slamming. The silence of two people who have no fucking clue what they're doing with their lives.

Fear. Ah, it's true. This silence is fear. That's what it sounds like.

30

ALL BAD

MARÍN

I stumble back to the campsite, my eyes practically glued shut. It's the only way I can contain my rage. My heart is racing, I'm panting, I don't even notice I'm clenching my fists, and…I'm running. I'm walking so fast that within five strides I'm jumping the fence. I'm not thinking. If I thought a little, I would contain myself, I would walk it off, I would get lost, go get the car, and get out of here. But I'm going back to where everyone is… I need heat. A heat that isn't the result of rage.

I spot the camper's outside light, and I hurry over to it. Loren and Blanca are smoking in their camping chairs. Her cheeks are stained with dried rivers of mascara, her eyes are vacant, and the cigarette she's pinching between two fingers is eating itself without her even taking a drag. Perched next to her, Loren is rubbing her back. When they see me, she throws the cigarette away and buries her head in her hands.

"I think I'm gonna have to sleep here," I say.

I'm surprised by the defeated voice coming out of my mouth. This can't be happening. It's just…just a misunderstanding.

Blanca lets out a sob.

"Blanca, please, you can't let yourself get like this," Loren begs. "For better or worse, you were already used to this ugliness, this shit. What you have to do is—"

"Don't tell me what I have to do, please," she whimpers. "I'm doing the best I can. I can't force myself anymore."

"I know. I'm not trying to tell you what to do. It was just a turn of phrase. A bad one. But take care of yourself. Close your life to those who cause you pain."

"We're friends. We're all friends. What am I supposed to do? End up completely alone?"

I kneel in front of her and pull her hands apart to make her look at me. "You can't keep going like this, Blanca. This is toxic, and you know it."

She nods, holding back her tears.

"I don't want to know anything." She closes her eyes. "Not a single thing, please."

I slump into the seat across from them and rub my face. "Where's Aroa?"

"Sleeping," Loren replies. "Aroa doesn't give a shit about any of us."

I want to say that Aroa has never given a shit about anything besides her desires, but it took me three years to figure that out. What right do I have to act like a smart-ass now? And I don't want to get in any more shit.

In the distance, a few rapid footsteps coming closer break the silence enveloping us. I close my eyes. Shit. They hear it too; it's obvious who the person running over is, and I know what she'll say when she gets here. This conversation, in spite of everything, it's just for two. The two of us.

"Let's go inside," Blanca says, wiping tears and snot on the back of her arm.

"Classy," Loren quips.

"Go fuck yourself."

They both stand up.

"Good night," I say.

"Marín." Blanca lingers, clinging to the doorframe, hesitant.

"What?"

"Don't be too hard on her. She's going to feel awful when she finds out."

I hear her panting, both from exhaustion and fear. She's getting closer.

"Blanca…I'm not going to tell her anything. You're going to have to talk to her yourself," I say before she disappears inside the RV.

"Tomorrow."

I don't argue with her. Tomorrow will be another day. What I don't know is whether I'll be here tomorrow. Tomorrow…I promised my sister I'd watch the Perseids with Coco.

"And make a wish for me. And another for you two because you need it."

Right now my only wish is to disappear. I want to get out of here.

The door closes at the exact moment she appears, disheveled, her shoes in her hand and panting. She looks at me, somewhere between horrified and relieved to see me here. I stand up and walk toward her… but I go straight past her.

"Let's get away from the camper," I say gruffly. "Everyone's sleeping."

She throws her shoes down right there and follows me without a word. We sit on the wall that borders the more remote sites, next to an empty one. Above our heads, the pines (I think they're pine trees) are shaking, making music with their needles. It's like they're playing a song called summer. A dog barks in the distance. Some happy voices drift across the street, heading the other way.

I look at her. She looks at me. Coco always cries silently. I think she got used to having to do that in a house full of brothers who always found ways to laugh at her pain. I picture her as a proud child, the kind who doesn't cry in public when she falls down and gets hurt but finds a solitary spot to do it in. Like now, when fat, shiny tears are streaming down her face and she's not making a sound. It's not like I'm nobody, but we've always been at home, and at home, in your den where you feel protected, you're allowed to cry.

"Marín..."

"I don't understand any of this," I admit.

"Me either," she shoots back.

I furrow my brow.

"You said you would call me." She says through clenched teeth. "You told me it'd be ten minutes. And you left with her."

"Are you fucking kidding me, Coco?"

"Am I fucking kidding you? I saw you! I saw you holding each other, hiding away, and then you didn't call and—"

"You know the whole thing about the best defense being a good offense is bullshit? I have to ask you that before you end up fucking everything up so much there won't be any way back."

"You're hiding stuff from me," she says in a whisper. "This isn't an attack, Marín. I'm explaining myself to you. I'm explaining why I ended up with Gus in your room. I wish I could say something else, okay? But humans are like this sometimes."

"Like this? What does 'like this' mean?"

"Unfair and despicable."

"You said it."

"Don't play with me, Marín. If you're mad, show it. Don't put on some mask of indifference."

"*If* I'm mad?" I look at her, surprised. "How do you expect me to be? I'm angry, I'm enraged, I don't understand any of it, I feel like shit, and on top of it all, you're attacking me. What does that sound like to you?"

"It sounds like you're not understanding me, Marín. I was convinced that you and Aroa—"

"So you went and fucked Gus?" I ask, stunned.

"I didn't fuck Gus." She wipes her tears gracefully and leaves a smudge of mascara on her cheek. "We were going to, but we didn't. Not all the way. I'm not going to lie to you."

"Was he too drunk to get it up?"

She shoots me a disdainful look that I don't deserve, but I understand it. This isn't a fair fight. She's drunk, rattled, confused. Still, I don't feel much empathy for her right now, I have to admit. She should have thought about it before. I'm fed up. I've spent half my life excusing people for their handicaps, but not Coco. I've never been so disappointed.

"You left with her. I was all alone. I freaked out. I couldn't find anyone, and when I did, Blanca was crying, Loren was consoling her. You and Aroa looked like you were about to kiss and..."

I raise my eyebrows and swallow. "That didn't mean anything," I clarify.

She side-eyes me. "Ah, so, like, you did, right? You kissed?"

"She kissed me. She... I don't know... I just wanted to... It's just that..."

"Right," she says calmly. "The tables have turned, huh? What's the deal? You thought eyes can't see...?"

"That's not it," I answer. "But I thought you hadn't seen it so you weren't going to make a big deal out of something that meant nothing to me."

"Your ex, the one who desperately wants to get back together with you, kisses you in a corner and I see you hiding there, all...intimate. What do you expect me to think?"

"What did you think?"

"I called you," she says. "I thought you were playing me, you were just spending a little time with me while you decided whether you wanted to get back with Aroa, and that's what you were hiding from me. I felt like shit, and...I tried to convince myself that it was just typical drunken paranoia. That's why I called you. An hour after you told me you'd be back in ten minutes."

"I thought it was just gonna be ten minutes." I defend myself.

"I let it ring until I felt like a total loser. I was sure you two were together. What other explanation can you think of?"

"The reality."

"And what is the reality, Marín, and how would I possibly know it?"

I grabbed Aroa's hand so I wouldn't lose her in the crowd. Then I saw something. Something I didn't want her to see, so I pulled her into a corner.

Then she said to me, "You don't need to hide it from me. I saw it."

And she took advantage. She always does.

She hugged me. She asked me why we were hiding stuff. She confessed that she felt lonely, that she felt like we were all breaking up, that she didn't fit into the group anymore, that out of the two of us I was the one who mattered. I was trying to convince her that wasn't true when she kissed me.

Can I tell Coco all that without revealing secrets that aren't mine?

"There's no way you could know," I say finally. "You weren't there and I understand that what you saw led you to make a mistake, but…running off with Gus and sleeping with him… What kind of solution is that?"

"Not one at all. I wasn't looking for a solution. Is getting drunk when you feel shitty a solution? Eating a doughnut? Smoking a joint? Is 'going out and having fun' a solution when you get dumped? Or taking a bath? Or a vacation?"

"Okay," I cut in brusquely. "I get it. You just wanted—"

"To forget you."

I look at her. The words were filled with rage…a rage that I don't think I deserve.

"What have I done to make you want to forget me? Just console my ex and not answer your call!"

"I'm not saying it was logical, Marín. I'm just telling you what went through my head. We were both there, we were sad—it wasn't premeditated. It was just…a bad idea."

I put my thumbs under my eyebrows, pressing my tear ducts. My head is starting to hurt. This always happens when I get angry. I'm not good at this stuff.

"I'm sorry, Coco, but I wasn't expecting that. I wasn't expecting any of this from you. From Aroa..." I shrug and let my hands drop to my sides. "I would've expected it from Aroa."

"So what I'm hearing is that you would've tolerated it from Aroa, but not from me. Is that it?"

"No. That's not it. This isn't a competition. That's not even how I feel. All I wanted was to spend the night with you. I wanted to drop Aroa back here, make a few things clear to her, and then get back and kiss you. And I didn't care if anyone else saw us. I just needed to close that door completely, to make her understand."

"And did she understand?"

I look at her. "Of course she understood, Coco, but she doesn't want to close it."

"And that's my problem?"

"Is it my problem that you thought I was screwing my ex so you went and screwed yours?"

"I did not," she says, dragging out the syllables. She starts crying again. "I feel like a piece of shit, Marín. Don't talk to me like that."

"How should I? Honestly?"

"I feel like a piece of shit," she repeats slowly, holding in her sobs.

"That tracks." I stand up. "I'd love to say something else to you, Coco, but it tracks that you feel like a piece of shit because we were like excited little kids and you..."

"I what?"

"Ruined it. You ruined it."

I turn on my heel, but I can't walk away. Deep down, I regret everything I'm saying. I regret being so hard, I regret not being able to tell her that

I'll get over it, that I don't want to leave, that I'm not uncomfortable with her for the first time in my life. But lies don't work when it comes to Coco.

I push my hair off my forehead, feeling ridiculous. I can't stay. I can't leave.

"So that's it then?" she asks. "Everything's broken?"

"I don't know. I'm going to leave. I don't want… I don't want to be here."

Now I do turn around with the intention of leaving. One step farther, I start doing it. The little pebbles scattered over the sites crunch under my shoes, and the sound that up until now has always made me think of good things is driving me crazy. Memories.

Her fingers circle my wrist, and she tugs on me. I hear her whimper, but I want to leave.

"Let me go, Coco. We're not going to fix anything tonight."

She pulls on me harder, and I turn around. She hugs me. I can feel her hot tears seeping into my shirt, but I don't return the hug. I feel…betrayed. Not her. It's never like this with her.

"I don't want to hurt you, Coco. That's not it. I just feel wounded. It's just…"

She doesn't let me finish. Before I can react, her lips are on mine. And it's just… It's just a kiss. Some lips pressing against mine, just like it was with Aroa earlier tonight. When she did it, I didn't feel anything. I felt nothing when she told me that no one could compare to us when we were together, when she asked me to remember how good everything was before. In spite of remembering, it's like I wasn't capable of transforming that action into an emotion. Like these memories were someone else's.

What makes this act different from that one? Nothing. Physically it's the same. A woman's lips pressing against mine and trying not to let anything pull us apart. But then…why is everything different?

The tingles come back. I feel every inch of my skin, I feel the warm breeze caressing the hair on my arms, I feel my breath hitching in my chest. It's hot. It's a hot night, humid, but Coco is trembling. I can't help it. I wrap my arms around her and move in closer. I feel her sigh of relief and breathe it in when her lips part. No, I'm not in charge here.

I catch her mouth with mine, and my hands run up and down her back. Coco tastes like tears and alcohol, but I like it. I like it a lot. I close my eyes and let her tongue timidly caress mine.

It's her. It's her. It's her.

I put my left hand in her hair, at the nape of her neck, and my right clinches her waist. Coco clings on to me ferociously, and the kiss gets longer until our mouths can't take it anymore.

It's her, fuck. But not like this.

I pull away from her. Her eyes are still closed. My hands are still lingering in the same place, and I look at her. Black streaks of mascara down her face, her mouth, swollen from crying and kissing me, half open. Shaking. Begging through clenched teeth, "Please."

"Not like this," I say, letting her go slowly. "Not like this, Coco."

I take a step back. She opens her eyes, and I take another, looking at her. She hugs herself, and I go a bit farther.

"Marín…" she says.

"What?"

"It doesn't matter where you go… You and I will always, always be us."

And I know it. But tonight all I can do is get out of here. Far away… to somewhere I've never been with her, that doesn't smell like her, that doesn't remind me of her. A place where I can think and figure out why even though I'm so angry, I'd still keep kissing her until I forget my own fucking name.

31

CLARITY

COCO

When I curl up in a ball on the bottom bunk, I hate knowing Aroa's asleep right above me. Right now I wish I could start kicking until she wakes up and then drag her by the hair out of the RV and not let her come back in. I'm really pissed off...with her and with myself.

I'm numb. Exhausted. I don't understand a lot of things about what happened tonight. I'm confused, but the only thing I'm really worried about is Marín. What have I done?

I grab my phone and make a rookie mistake. I write him a WhatsApp. A super cringe one:

COCO:

Please...don't leave. Don't leave yet. Give us a chance to talk. Give us a chance to...I don't know. I can't justify my actions, but we need to talk about it, Marín. Don't leave before we can talk. Don't leave without me.

I stare at our chat for a long time, but the two ticks don't turn blue: They stay gray. He hasn't logged on. I don't think he will tonight. Finally, I put my phone down on the pillow and curl up tighter. If he were here, he would make me leave my phone outside the bunk. He hates that I sleep so close to it.

"That can't be good, Coco. One morning you're going to wake up with brain damage."

Look. He was right about that. It's already starting.

I close my eyes, but I can't sleep. I pick up my phone again. He still hasn't seen it. I open my chat with Gus and write him without thinking twice about it.

COCO:

I'm really sorry I pushed you to fuck up like that.

He instantly shows as Online. Typing.

GUS:

It was both of us.

Everyone knows at this point, I'm guessing.

COCO:

When I got back, Marín was the only one here.

GUS:

Tomorrow, just blame it all on me. I don't think anyone will have trouble believing you.

I scoff. He was a piece of shit and now we're two pieces of shit.

COCO:

Don't be a martyr. It'll all be okay.

GUS:

If this were my only fuckup, I'd agree, but I have a lot of yellow cards.

This is a red card. I'll give you a heads-up.

COCO:

Now you're using soccer metaphors.

GUS:

I do what I can. How are you?

COCO:

Awful. I cried, I attacked, I blamed, I begged and, finally…I kissed Marín.

GUS:

Totally your style.

COCO:

Is he there?

GUS:

Yeah, next to me, snuggled into my chest and babbling in his sleep about how much he appreciates me.
No way…he came in, grabbed the car keys, and when I tried to say sorry, he told me not to say anything.
Slammed the door on his way out. Fin.

Fuck.

GUS:

Listen, Coco. Stop spiraling.
Right now there's no solution and everything seems worse at night than it really is.

COCO:

Is that why you live more at night than in the day?

GUS:

Isn't that a song? Come on. Listen to me for once. Go to sleep. We have plenty of time to feel miserable. Good night.

I put my phone under my pillow again, but I don't sleep. I stare at the ceiling for at least an hour and a half. Marín never answers. He must be on his way home.

~~~

I feel uncomfortable as soon as I wake up. It's really hot in here. We've been really lucky up until now with mild days, but that seems to be changing. But on the other hand, we don't have much time left. A hard, shame-tinged nostalgia spreads through my chest. The heat woke me, but once I'm fully conscious, it's the memory of last night that torments me. It's time to get out of bed.

I find a handwritten note on the cute little countertop. It's from Aroa. It says she's going to the beach alone and she doesn't know when she'll be back and that we should make plans without her. I'm relieved but kind of think she's the fucking worst at the same time. A coward and a brat. Okay. The few hours of sleep have not calmed me down in the slightest.

I head out of the camper clenching the scrap of paper. The last time I checked the time on my phone, it was seven in the morning. Now it's noon and the sun is relentless. It's beating down, and there's not even a hint of breeze to soften this muggy, sticky heat.

By the way, Marín still hasn't answered. I don't know whether to feel annoyed or start calling hospitals.

Finding Blanca sitting on the terrace and holding a Styrofoam cup full of steaming coffee almost kills me. She's blowing on it, but I don't think that will be enough to cool it down much in this heat. I would kill for a coffee, but I'm already about to have a heart attack.

"I bought you a coffee," she says. "It's still boiling—be careful."

I sit across from her. She looks terrible: Her eyes are swollen and red, two huge purple bags under them, and she's pale. I take the coffee and two sugar packets and thank her.
~~~

"Are you okay? You don't look great."

"I had a bad night."

"It was really hot." I don't want to pressure her.

"Yeah, well." She smiles sadly. "And other stuff."

I pour the sugars into the coffee and sneak in for a second, looking for two cubes of ice. When I come out, I offer one to Blanca, which she puts in her coffee.

"Do you wanna talk about it?"

She flicks her finger at Aroa's note. She gives a half smile. "The princess is pouting," she says, changing the subject.

"Well, that makes two of us. I kissed Marín last night."

"And you slept with Gus."

Her reply isn't hard or malicious, but I can sense her disapproval. What did I expect? Friends aren't there to rub your back when you do something wrong.

"Not exactly." I spin the ice cube around in the coffee with my finger, careful not to submerge it. "That was my intention, yes, but it didn't happen."

"No?"

"No. Sometimes the universe works in our favor to stop us making things worse."

"You didn't sleep together?"

"No. I was ready to and we tried, but…Gus is in love with someone, even though he says he's not and he talks about it like it's a problem. He can't just do it with anyone anymore. I don't wanna get all TMI, but I think he's experienced what love really is and…"

"Seriously?" She raises her eyebrows. "Can Gus love someone?"

"You know what Gus's deal is?" I lean back in my chair and stretch my legs under the table. I'm starting to sweat. "He uses sex as a shield, Blanqui, but that boy has been touched for real this time, someone got under his skin, and he doesn't even have that safeguard anymore. He has nowhere to hide."

Blanca sighs, like she has no interest in getting into debates about Gus's love life.

"Blanca, do you think it's possible that Gus, that the girl Gus has been with…is Aroa?"

She's taking a sip of coffee when I ask the question, and at first, all I get as a response is raised eyebrows. "No. How would that make any sense?"

"It would fit. They hooked up nine months ago…more or less around the time Marín and Aroa broke up."

"That's just a coincidence, Coco." She puts her coffee on the table. She looks awful. "It's really hot, right?"

"Yeah. Listen, are you okay?"

"Yes. Yeah."

I take a sip of coffee, and I'm embarrassed to realize that my hypothesis that Aroa was the girl Gus is pining over only has one explanation. I find ways to make it about me. Suddenly everything I thought sounds so dumb.

"Blanca, why…? I mean, last night I saw you in Mandala before I left. You were crying."

"Yes," she sighs.

"Why were you crying?"

"There's something I haven't told you, Coco."

"I thought so."

"I know you're gonna be mad at me."

"I doubt it."

"Just wait." She rubs her face.

Loren pops out with eyes puffy from sleep. "Were you the ones jabbering like cockatoos for hours last night?"

"No, babe," I retort. "That must've been the site next door. Or in your dreams."

"Nightmares. I slept so badly. Is that coffee for me?"

Blanca doesn't answer. She's staring into nothing.

"Blanqui...are you okay?"

"I don't..." She moves her neck gently. "I don't feel good."

"What's wrong with you?"

"She didn't sleep well," Loren says, going over to her and putting his hand on her forehead. "Jesus, Blanca...you're drenched."

"It's really hot here," she groans.

"But you're drenched in cold sweat."

"Do you want me to go to the showers with you?" I offer anxiously.

"You'd be better off lying down."

"Eat something with sugar."

"There's a little orange juice left in the fridge."

Loren and I are talking over each other, but neither of us stops. I've never seen Blanca so pale. I guess we're all freaked out.

"Loren...get some water," I say when I see her trying to get up.

"No, no. I just need to wet my neck a little. It's... It's...this heat."

"Blanca, don't stand up," Loren says.

She ignores him. She looks at us.

"I'm just overwhelmed..."

The final "d" stretches out a little in her throat, and she takes a few steps. She's breathing fast, like she's just run a race. I'm about to tell her to take a deep breath slowly or she'll start hyperventilating, but when the chair falls and she doesn't even seem to hear it crash to the gravel floor, my warning feels a little late.

We don't have time to get around the table and chairs before she falls to the floor, even though it feels like it's happening in slow motion. Her eyes roll back in her head, her eyelids flutter closed, her knees give way, and her body falls, folding in on itself eerily. Loren manages to grab her wrist and soften the fall, but she probably didn't even feel it.

"Blanca! Blanca!" I scream, slapping her cheek. "Loren! Get some water!"

One of our site neighbors, a German as big as a car, comes over to us and asks in clumsy Spanish what happened.

"She fainted," Loren says, rushing in to grab a bottle of water while I hold her legs up.

We move fast, but we don't really know what we're doing.

People are starting to come over. Blanca's blinking rapidly, but she's not responding. Her chest is heaving because even though she's unconscious, she's still breathing fast and hard. A lot of people from the neighboring sites are starting to crowd around us, and everyone is giving advice with the best intentions.

"Sit her in a chair."

"No, keep holding her legs up."

"Call an ambulance."

"Wet her head."

"And her wrists."

Loren empties part of the bottle of water carefully, using his hand like a funnel, over Blanca's head and then on her hands. She seems to shudder a little. She's still blinking.

"Blanca... Blanca, please..."

My voice is barely coming out. I want to tell Loren to call an ambulance or a doctor or I don't know who, but I can't get the words out. There are a lot of people around. Too many.

Someone bursts through the onlookers, shoving their way through. He barrels toward us so fast I don't even see his face.

"But what happened? What happened?" he yells, kneeling next to Blanca. "Blanca, can you hear me? Get all these people out of here, for fuck's sake! Come on! Give her some space!"

It's Gus.

"Loren, grab her legs. Higher. About forty-five degrees. Blanca..."

He puts his mouth next to her ear, and then he pulls a towel off the strings we've been using as a clothesline and puts it under her neck and then tilts her head to the side.

He's moving really fast.

"Blanca," he whispers. "It's all right, okay? It's all right. Can you hear me? I'm here. I'm here. With you."

I stand up and move back a little. There's something in my body clenching my stomach into an imaginary fist, and it's not just fear. There's something that—

Blanca opens her eyes and splutters.

"It's okay. You fainted, okay?"

She tries to sit up, but he gently presses her shoulder back down.

"There's no rush. These people are leaving. Coco, get everyone out of here. Everything's okay."

"Gus..." Blanca stammers.

"I'm here, little one. I'm here. It's all over. You see? It's all over."

Blanca's shaking. She's shaking a lot, and I'm scared, but...I can't take my eyes off her, off Gus. The way they're looking at each other. Gus's voice, so used to performing in front of people, of trotting out words to make his fans tremble with desire, the ones who want to howl with pleasure under his body... That voice that's suddenly so tender, so sweet, it doesn't sound like his. Gus's fingers caress Blanca's temples, and he keeps whispering, "It's okay. I'm here, little one." Little one. Little one. Little one?

Her dazed smile only wakes up when she hears him. Their hands, fuck, their hands are clenched over her stomach. They're gripping each other so hard their knuckles are turning white.

"Coco, get them out of here, please," Gus says again.

I take a step back and turn to the crowd. "Everything's okay."

"Should we call a doctor?" someone offers, trying to help.

"No, no. We'll take care of it," I say, still in shock.

They all ask me to call them if we need anything, but all I can do is nod and thank them awkwardly. Their steps crunch away back to their own sites, and the noise of conversations drifts away.

Loren is still holding Blanca's legs up, but his arms are starting to shake. I drag over a chair and prop them up on that now that she's feeling a little better. She's dazed, but she's responsive.

"What day is it?" Gus asks her.

"Saturday."

"What's your name?"

"I'm fine," she says, trying to sit up.

"Don't get up yet."

"Honestly...I want to sit."

"What's the best song of all time?"

"'Que bien' by Izal."

"God, you're worse than I thought. I'm going to have to identify your body."

They share a laugh, but Blanca's is weak.

The laughter. The looks. Their hands still clenched. Everything around me goes blurry, and my stomach is churning, I'm stunned by the realization, but I'm noticing every tiny detail. The looks. All the looks. The ones they avoided speak loudly too. Like that afternoon, when we were having tapas, when they didn't even say a single word to each other. They were avoiding each other—they didn't hate each other. The sentences one would start and the other would finish in a kind of never-ending tennis match because they always seemed to have something to gripe about. And jokes, of course, jokes that nobody laughed at because we didn't understand them. "You two have the same weird sense of humor, for fuck's sake," I would complain sometimes. But they understood each other.

Their phones, always in their hands, carrying on a parallel conversation.

The crumpled napkins with handwritten stanzas…that weren't for me and weren't meant to be thrown in the trash—he probably hid them wherever he could think of, hoping none of us would catch him. Her. Malasaña. Nine months. "Ruben and I haven't really been getting along lately." The poems, all of them, about his "little one," him running around Madrid, his regret. The arguments. The tears last night, Gus stumbling around in a daze. It's her. It's her, fuck. My best friend is her.

No, Coco. They're not two people who didn't really get along. They were lovers. And you're the only one who didn't know.

32

NO MORE FANTASIES

COCO

Blanca refuses to go to the hospital. She won't even go to the Red Cross hut on the beach.

"It was just heatstroke. The sun was too much for me."

Yeah, it was hot. And…it was too much? Let me guess. Is it possible you were about to confess to your best friend that you've been sleeping with her ex for nine months? An ex you thought she was still in love with. But of course, that didn't stop you.

Fucking awesome.

When I was sure she was doing better, I went to take a shower. I needed to get away for a minute, to put on clean underwear, change into other pajamas that still smell like fabric softener. Little gestures to make me feel a little more clean.

When I get back, I find her sitting in the shade with a bottle of cold water in her hand.

"Are you feeling better?" I ask her, a little more dryly than I mean to.

"Much."

I look around, where Gus and Loren seem to be very busy going in and out of the RV. I, on the other hand, can't take my eyes off Blanca. Her, fucking my ex. Him, having an affair with an almost-married girl. Them, behind everyone's backs. Or just behind my back?

"Listen, Coco," she says awkwardly when she realizes I'm staring at her. "Uh… I… I want to finish the conversation we were having before I fainted like a damsel in distress. Maybe we can go buy something for lunch and…"

"Don't worry about it." I smile tensely. "Right now the last thing you need is a walk"—*with me*, I think—"in this heat."

And I smile stiffly.

"Coco…" Gus brushes my elbow gently from behind to get my attention. "We can trust each other, right?"

"Yeah. Why? Are you going to reveal some kind of state secret?"

Yesterday the look they exchanged would have flown right over my head. Not today, obviously.

"I was going to ask if you've heard anything from Marín," he specifies.

You know that feeling of immediate discomfort, like your feet melt through the floor and you're falling miles and miles into the magma core of the earth where you die? No? Well that's exactly how I feel right now.

"No." I swallow. "I haven't heard anything from him. He hasn't…" I take a breath. "He never answered the message I sent last night. He didn't come back to the hotel?"

"Not since last night."

"Fuck."

What if something happened to him?

I stand up and grab my phone. I have his number saved in my favorites, so the phone starts ringing almost immediately.

"What are you doing?" Loren asks.

"Swallowing my pride and calling Marín."

"I already tried," Gus says, looking over at Blanca, I guess to gauge her reaction.

If Marín is upset he found us in bed, Blanca…

Wait…Blanca? How could she have smiled at me when she saw me? Who buys coffee for the person she thinks fucked her lover?

"Fuck…" I blurt out loud.

"Did he pick up?" Blanca asks.

"He's not picking up."

"Should I try?" she offers.

"No." I take a few steps away when the voicemail picks up and I close my eyes as I listen to his message.

"Uh… Hi, leave your message. If you sing something, maybe I'll even call you back."

"Marín…it's me. I guess you're still mad at me, and you probably ran in the opposite direction as fast as you could, but I just need to know that you're okay. Even if you're crossing the French border. Please…just send proof of life. I'm worried." I hang up and go back to the table. Blanca looks at me with a furrowed brow.

"Nothing?"

"No, but…considering how angry he must be at me, he probably took off."

"Did you talk last night?"

"A little. But the conversation was pretty…heated."

"Do you want us to go look for him? And…talk."

"He's gone." I prop my elbows on the table and shove my fingers into my hair. "He left to run away from the problem and give himself time to cool off… Classic Marín."

"He's not running away. He doesn't like arguing."

"Maybe I should leave too," I mutter.

"If he's gone, I don't think he wants you to follow him," Gus pipes up, munching from a bowl of chips.

"Hey, don't you have anything better to do than give opinions on my love life?" I retort tersely.

"Marín is your love life?" He raises his eyebrows. "You two are moving pretty fast. You went straight from roommates to lovebirds. What happened to fuck buddies? Won't anyone think of the fuck buddies?"

"Gus…shut up."

I have to admit one thing: Blanca is the only one who can get him to shut up.

I'm still spinning my phone in my hands. He's gone. He went to Madrid, turned around, picked up his sister, and forgot all this. What a mess, Coco. What a fucking mess.

I look at Blanca, who shoots me a worried look. I don't even know how to feel—about Marín, about Blanca and Gus, about Gus. How can Gus be so calm? Did they talk? They must have talked. Are they still hooking up? Did they "break up"? What exactly did he tell me yesterday about "her"? God…my memories of yesterday are cushioned by an alcoholic cloud that won't dissipate.

I can't focus on that right now. Marín. Where is Marín?

I spring out of my seat. "Gus, will you give me your room key?"

"Huh?" he splutters through a mouth full of chips.

"Your room key. Give it to me?"

"Are you going to the hotel? What for?"

"I don't know. To see if he went there, if his stuff is there…I don't know."

"Girl, I left the room looking like a crack house."

"I don't give a shit. Give me the key."

"Want me to go with you?" Blanca offers.

"Uh…no. No. It's better if I go by myself."

Gus slides the card over the table, and I grab it and run off. I don't want to give myself time to think twice about it, to feel ridiculous or pathetic. Right here and right now, I need to make a move to at least try to fix it.

~

The four hundred meters between the campsite and the door of the hotel feel eternal to me, but I need to fix one thing at a time. First: Marín.

I'm planning on asking at reception if they've seen Marín, but just picturing myself trying to describe him (*He's the most handsome man you've ever seen, with these amazing eyes and a smile that could make the sun shine anywhere in the world, you know what I mean?*) freaks me out, so instead I head straight to the room.

When I open it, I'm surprised to be flooded by a feeling of calm. The bed is made, and someone, probably the cleaner, folded some of Gus's clothes into a neat pile on the desk. I know him… It definitely wasn't him. His brown leather bag is open on a chair, and I get a glimpse of majestic chaos inside with a copy of his book sticking out. The copy he signed to himself, need I say more. Seriously, what was I doing with someone like him? We weren't compatible at all.

A sound stops. It takes a few seconds for me to understand it was the sound of running water. My heart starts racing before I even have time to wonder if maybe the walls are so thin that the sound is seeping in from the room next door. But no. Someone's moving around in the bathroom.

I don't even think about it; I just head straight toward it like a nutjob and yank the door open. Marín's terrified reaction is like something out of a movie.

"Jesus fuck!" One hand flies to his chest and the other to grip the towel around his waist. "Fuck! What the fuck are you doing?"

I gasp.

He leans back against the sink, spluttering curses.

"You didn't leave," I manage to say.

"No." He shakes his head. "Fuck, my heart is in my throat. Give me a second."

"Should I leave?"

He doesn't answer. He's looking at the ceiling, and I can see his Adam's apple bobbing as he swallows.

"Shit, Coco, don't ever do that to me again for the rest of your life."

"The scaring part or...?"

"Let's take this one step at a time, okay?"

"I was... I was scared. I thought you had left."

"I did leave," he says, rubbing his cheeks, which are starting to get stubbly. "But here I am."

"So what made you come back?"

He licks his lips. He looks at me. "You really hurt me yesterday," he blurts out.

"I know."

"Explain why. I need to know. But, please, don't say you were drunk..."

"I was."

"It's not a good excuse. Try again."

"You make me feel insecure."

"Me?" He seems surprised. "I make you feel insecure? Coco, I'm your home. Find another excuse."

He's home. My home. I lean against the damp bathroom tiles and huff.

"Aroa is...perfect. She's incredible. At this point I know that...well, that she can get a little overbearing, but I saw you two and you seemed so good together and...suddenly you weren't together anymore. The most I could get out of you was that the breakup was for the best, that you weren't looking for the same thing. That was it. And yesterday I saw you two...together. You were giving off this energy of... I don't know. Intimacy."

"Intimacy?" He raises one eyebrow. "Intimacy, Aroa and me? Coco, that sounds like a lie."

"What if I don't know what intimacy is, Marín? What if I've never had it with anyone and that's why I confuse it with other stuff?"

"You've never had it with anyone? That's a crock of shit, Coco. Intimacy is what you and I have."

"You and I went from talking about farts at home to touching each other like we were on a conjugal visit. I don't know if that can be called intimacy or just a weird idea of friendship."

"Did I say anything about sex? I don't understand you." He takes a deep breath. "I swear I don't understand anything."

"And that… There's that too. You keep going on about how confused you are, how you don't understand anything, you don't know what you feel… I saw you with her, and then you didn't pick up the phone. I invented a monster, fine, but it's what I believed."

"And you decided sleeping with Gus was the best option."

"Sleeping with Gus was familiar, Marín, what I was used to doing when being with you hurt, but I didn't understand I was head over heels in love with you. It was like going back to my fucking comfort zone, the shitty one…the mediocre one. The one that wasn't you."

That seems to mollify him. He doesn't say anything.

"I'm not going to tell you I did the right thing, Marín. That's impossible. I didn't. I can't even promise you I did it for justifiable or understandable reasons. I did it because…I felt alone and abandoned and… because when I'm as in love with someone as I am with you, fuck, Marín, I turn into a shitty person. You know how long I've been hoping for this? Do you understand how much I like you, how difficult it's been to carry all that and try to fit it into the mold of what I'm supposed to feel for you?"

He looks down at the ground.

"You're disappointed"—I keep going—"and I get it. I am too because nothing is how I imagined and I imagined it so many times that I thought I had covered every single possibility. Everything was happening and—"

"Stop," he says.

"No, dammit. You know how many mornings I stayed in bed, listening to you padding around the house and thinking about all the things I wished I could say to you, do to you?" I'm going too far. "I've spent a year thinking about someone who was in love with someone else, someone else who, by the way, I introduced him to. All I could do was imagine, and I created my perfect story. Our first perfect secrets, our first moments of perfect magic, our first perfect kiss, our fucking perfect story that was never going to happen, but it was perfect."

Marín looks up at me again. "What else?"

"What else? For fuck's sake, Marín!" I yell.

"I mean it. What else? What else did you imagine?"

"Look, dude, I'm your best friend, and I'm head over heels in love with you, but if you take it too far, I'll have no problem kicking you in the nuts."

The indecipherable look on his face turns into a cautious smile. "Wedding? Kids?" he goes on.

"I swear I'll do it, Marín. I learned very early to get back at my brothers' humiliations with violent acts aimed at their genitals."

"I'm not humiliating you. I want facts. You're…"

"An idiot?"

"No." He shakes his head. "The other day I was driving and I suddenly thought to myself that if we got married one day you'd probably wear one of those golden clips you like so much, with dragonflies and… bugs."

"What are you saying?" My brow wrinkles, and my voice comes out all squeaky.

"What I'm saying, Coco, is that we all fantasize. We can imagine whatever we want, and of course everything will be perfect in our imaginations. But we're grown-ups, and we know life's not like that."

"Of course it's not. Life can be a fucking miserable whore."

"Hey, you can't take it too far either."

"I almost fucked Gus, Marín. I almost fucked my ex trying to forget that you were with Aroa."

"Don't remind me." His mouth flickers into a grimace. "Nothing is perfect."

"Well, that's fucked up because you don't know how beautiful our story is in my head." I snort and cover my face. "I never thought talking to you would feel this complicated," I declare.

"It isn't," he adds. "Look at me."

I let my hands drop and give him a weary look. "Did I fuck it up forever? I just need to know," I ask.

"You fucked it up, but not forever. I have a lot to learn here too."

"About how disappointing I am in reality?" I pout.

"No, about how trying to make everyone except yourself happy always ends badly."

"So now what? How do we fix all of this?"

"With an exercise of empathy, I guess."

"But I fucked it up."

"What did you tell them?"

"Who?"

"Them. Everyone else. What did you tell them? Where do they think you are?"

"Here. I told them I was coming to find you. I was worried. Except Aroa, she went off to the beach alone this morning and said we should make plans without her and…"

"Do you have your phone?" He cuts me off.

"Yeah."

"Well, send them a message. Tell them I'm here, that you're staying, and then…turn off your phone."

"Why…?"

"You asked how we fix this, right? Well, we're going to fix this. No more fantasizing."

Marín reaches his hand out toward me, his palm upturned in a silent invitation to come over.

Maybe it is… Maybe this is the end of fantasizing.

33

NOTHING IS PERFECT

COCO

His chest is damp when I lean into him. He smells like shower gel. A few drops of water are still clinging to his neck, and I want to scoop them all up with the tip of my tongue and drink them. Drink him.

"What else did you imagine?" He's not smiling, but there's something on his face that looks like warmth toward me again.

"You're not mad anymore?"

"I'm mad as shit," he murmurs. "But thinking about last night over and over isn't going to help me, and I've decided I want to forget about it. Tell me, how did you imagine our first kiss?"

"This is a punishment for yesterday, right? You're torturing me in your own weird way."

"No. The torture might come later."

I mean...how does he make torture sound so good?

"What was that kiss like?"

"It was a kiss..." I look at his mouth. God... Fuck me, he has the most beautiful mouth. "Almost by surprise. At home. Just some random day, a random moment, and suddenly...your eyes on my mouth, mine on yours, your hands on my waist and..."

"And I kissed you?"

"It's honestly pretty heteropatriarchal, but yeah. You kissed me."

"Did I say something to you first?" He puts his hands on my waist and looks at my mouth.

"That you'd been in love with me since you saw me in that bar, but what you feel is so intense that you never thought it was love... That to you, love always meant something else."

"And that's why I know it's true. Right?"

"Stop making fun of me. It's not funny. Either you're angry or you're not."

"Coco," he whispers as his hands wrap around my hips and squeeze me tighter to him, "I've been in love with you ever since I saw you in that bar, but it's always been so perfect, so intense that...I thought it wasn't love. For me, love was always something else...something disappointing. But... it was just with the wrong person. I know this is the real kind."

Okay, Saint Peter, it's not funny. If I died and this is the great beyond, I'd rather just know. I can barely even swallow.

"This isn't fair," I whimper.

"I had help, that's true. But now let me give you the perfect kiss in my own way, huh?"

His mouth falls open a little before it meets mine. His tongue rushes in voraciously looking for mine, and when they touch, I explode. Everything explodes, the tension, the desire, nerves, hope, and everything I ever imagined...and they transform into the movement of my hands climbing his shoulders and tangling in his damp hair.

Marín's kisses are deep, slow, bold, but short. One after the other, of course. And all wet, hot, with tongue, spit, and teeth. When he slides it softly along my bottom lip, I moan.

"Shh..." he says. "Send that message. And turn off your phone."

I pull my phone out of the pocket of my pajamas. Wait...I showed up here in pajamas? Fuck my life. I'm wearing fucking button-up pajamas in black. My phone is in the pocket.

"God, I must be off my rocker. I'm still in my pajamas."

"You're running around like a nutjob," he whispers.

"I think it's more correct to say that you drive me wild."

Marín turns me so my back is to him, and as I type into my phone, he kisses my neck. At first they're gentle strokes, his nose brushing against my earlobe and his breath on my skin, but little by little the space between our bodies disappears and his breathing gets faster. The change is almost imperceptible, but I'm paying close attention. My back pressed to his chest, my ass lined up perfectly with his cock, and his hands…which are starting to search for me. His mouth doesn't take long to kiss my neck… but a real kiss. None of those soft kisses that tickle. No. Mouth open, teeth that leave a mark on the skin, tongue that soothes the pain right away, and then lips that hurry to caress. Am I coming already? Is that what's happening?

"I'm still mad," he clarifies. "I'm just reminding you in case my behavior is confusing."

"It is a little, to be honest." I can't even open Blanca's WhatsApp to write to her.

"It kills me that you went to Gus to try… I don't even know what you were trying."

"To forget you," I finally say. "And to hurt you because I felt awful."

"Never do that to me again, please," he whispers seriously into my ear. "That's not you."

"I'm going to risk pissing you off again and ask you to never prioritize Aroa and her tantrums over me."

"The only thing that would piss me off is you not understanding that you've always been the priority, if it weren't for the fact that the prospect of sex puts me in a good mood."

"Prospect of sex? I don't know what you're talking about." I feel his cock nudge my ass. Hard. The fucking towel could disappear now, right?

"Hey, maybe you're not that mad? You're probably getting over it at this point."

"In your imagination, the first time we slept together... Is it like transcendental or do we fuck?"

"God," I moan. His hand grabs my tit, and his mouth is paying attention to the world of my neck again. "Both."

"It can't be both at the same time. You have to choose. Reality isn't that perfect."

"What would be more logical?"

"Type."

COCO:

Blanca, Marín was at the hotel. I'm staying here. We have to talk. You and I have to talk too, but first I have to fix this. I'm turning off my phone. Tell everyone not to worry.

I press send the same second his hand pushes down into my pajama pants.

"If you don't say, I'm going to choose for you."

"And you're going to choose to fuck," I say.

He immediately pulls his hands out of my pants and turns me back toward him. He's smiling in a way I've never seen. I wanted him to look at me the way he looked at Aroa, and I didn't realize that the way he looked at me was so much better. Now...he's shining more.

"No."

"What?" I officially lost the thread of the conversation when I said the word "fuck" out loud in the context of us.

"I'm not going to choose fucking. Do you know what pisses me off the most?"

"That I tried to hook up with my ex in the bed you were sleeping in?"

"For fuck's sake." He laughs and leans his forehead against my mouth. "No." He twists and looks at me. "What fucks with me the most is that I can't even be mad at you."

"You can be a little mad at me." I raise my eyebrows.

"Yeah, but…it just makes me think that if nothing is perfect, we don't have to be either. We'll learn from it. In fact…I think this can only be fixed by making beautiful love, Coco."

"Okay, but…I want candles and rose petals everywhere. And a string quartet playing Post Malone covers."

Marín raises his eyebrows. "Post Malone? God, you're the fucking woman of my life."

~

Kissing Marín is great. It's much better than I imagined. His lips are incredibly soft, and the way he slowly drags his teeth against my lips is like a lightning bolt that sends me out of my body. I'm not even fully aware that I've walked to the bed side of the room. I know I'm moaning in his mouth, that we're up against the wall opposite the bathroom and we linger there for a while, nibbling each other. God… Marín is one of those who like to take their time. At this point with other guys, I wouldn't even be wearing panties.

The towel falls before we get there, but I'm clinging so tightly to him I don't see anything…until I feel the edge of the bed behind my knees and I let myself fall back. And there he is. Naked. Holy shit.

Earlier, I wanted to marry his chin in a church wedding. Now I'm not so sure. I just fell in love with his cock, and I think it likes me too.

I stroke his chest and keep moving down, still staring at his face. He follows my hand with his eyes, not saying a word until I grab him hard. Then his lips fall open, and he lets out a gasp. His shoulders fall back when I slide my hand up and down on his cock. He writhes, gives a shudder, and the tip gets wet.

"Take off your clothes, Coco. I want to see you."

His face becomes charged with sex and desire, with his mouth open as his exhale catches and his eyes droop lazily.

I pull off my pajama top and then the shorts, throwing myself onto the same bed I was in yesterday with Gus. The thought surprises me because this room doesn't even feel like the same country anymore. With Marín, everything's different. I guess that must be it.

I'm wearing cotton panties that are nothing special, but he looks like he's bowing to them when he lies on top of me and works his way down toward them, kissing and nuzzling every inch of skin in his path. I open my legs and his lips nibble the fabric of my underwear… I feel his nose nudging into me gently, and I arch, begging for more. I'm embarrassed that he can feel how wet I am.

He slowly tugs them down as he ponders the perfect place to swoop down and slide his tongue between my lips. He doesn't toss the panties with the rest of the clothes; instead, he balls them up in his fist and keeps licking so slowly I think I'm going to lose my mind.

Marín. Marín is licking me. He's the one exploring the wet inside of my cunt with his tongue, slowly inching toward my clit, blowing softly… I twist his hair around my fingers and ask him to look at me. It's the first thing I've said since we started kissing, and my voice sounds strange, so pleading and needy. But he looks at me. He looks at me while he licks me, and I'm so excited it's making his mouth wet.

"I want you inside me," I moan.

"Already?"

"Yes," I beg.

"I want to keep doing this forever…" He clamps his mouth back onto me, and his tongue presses fully against my clit.

I tug his hair a little and moan. I twist.

"Yesterday…" he says, his thumb replacing his tongue and his hot breath making my sensitive skin tingle, "before you came here to take a nap, I jerked off three times thinking about you."

"About doing this?"

"No." He smiles sideways and buries himself between my legs again using his mouth, tongue, and fingers this time. I think my eyes are rolling back in my head.

I don't know how long passes before he stops. All I know is that it's long enough to break down every last inhibition and make my hips sway to the rhythm of his tongue. I'm about to come when he sits up and puts himself between my legs. He grabs his cock and starts slowly touching himself in a kind of sexual exhibitionism I wasn't expecting…and it's weird how he's the person I know best in the whole world, but we're in uncharted territory. He licks his lips and comes closer, rubbing the tip of his cock against my sex. We're wet, so close, on the brink—one thrust and he'd be inside me.

"What were you thinking about?" I insist as I watch him grab his cock again.

"Let's talk about that when we fuck like dogs. I'm dirtier than you were expecting, and right now I want to make love."

He lines his cock up with me and hovers over me, holding himself up with his arms. He moves his hips forward, and I feel pressure. It's thick, and my skin stretches to make room for him inside me. I close my eyes and moan, "More…"

He pushes in until I don't even have room to breathe, I'm so full. I can almost feel him pulsing. And he stays there, inside me, quiet, for a few seconds that feel eternal.

"Ah…" he moans when he moves a little.

"Keep going."

"God…ah…" He pulls out and pushes back in. "Coco, I don't know how slow I'm gonna be able to go…"

I climb up until my arms are around his shoulders and bring my mouth to his ear. I close my eyes and whisper, "I just want to feel you close… closer. Nothing else matters."

"Inside," he answers. "So close that I'm inside you."

The words, the ones we so often didn't need, occupy every emptiness that could be on our skin. They see us, they protect us, they're the pleasure that's growing between us. Because what's the difference between fucking and making love? Maybe it's the words, the ones that are said, the ones that float, the ones we slurp hungrily from each other's lips before they even emerge. The words embroidering the moment and making it special forever.

"It's you," I say to him. "It's always been you."

He doesn't answer. He presses his forehead against my lips, and his moans and gasps warm my throat, condensing on my skin. I can smell his hair. I caress him, tousle it, wrap my fingers around it.

He pushes in and pulls out…one, two, twenty, fifty times. I close my eyes. So deep. So hard. So wet we can hear it, the sudden emptiness, the pushing in.

His cock, fuck… His cock that finds a way of pushing even deeper in, making space, invading this intimate zone that feels like it belongs to him in a way that's never felt like this with anyone else.

We don't talk, the silence of our mouths supplanted by the sounds of our skin. The pounding, my hips, his moans, my whimpers of pleasure. I want all of him, all of it. So much. I'm so ravenous that I might have to concede that after all this desire, all this thinking about it, all this wanting, I haven't actually been focusing and I won't be able to come this time.

Ah. Umm. Spit mingling on our tongues. Tired moans into each other's neck. The sound of his fingers in my hair. The groan as he speeds up… His hips are rocking between my thighs faster and harder every time.

"Coco…I'm not wearing a condom." He looks at me finally, still moving. "Are you on…something?"

I nod. Blessed IUD. I stroke his hair; he smiles, closes his eyes, lets go. I stroke his back.

"Tell me you're close..." he whispers.

"I don't know if I'm going to be able to come."

He bites his lip. He's holding back. He raises his eyebrows. "Am I doing something wrong?"

"Yeah, making me like it too much. I'm really nervous."

"It's me..." He smiles. "It's me, Coco. And this was meant to be."

I have an "I love you" on the tip of my tongue, and I hold it and smother it with my tongue as much as I can. Finally, I pour it into his mouth in a kiss, wordlessly, as his movements get even faster.

"Please..." he moans. "I need to feel you do it with me. Touch yourself. Let me feel it."

I slide my right hand in between us and delicately rub myself with my finger. Marín watches me writhe and encourages me with his moans, which are getting higher all the time, clearer, wider, fuller. His moans are eating the oxygen, leaving us swimming in a bubble where we can't even feel the sheets.

"A little more. I need you to touch yourself a little more."

It's not happening, and I'm not even feeling a tingle. Should I fake it? *No. We're done with lying, Coco. After this, when he fills you up with semen, when you lie on his chest, when you feel like crying from how much you love him, tell him, tell him everything you think he still doesn't know. The pleasure... Pleasure will come. The orgasm will come; maybe not right now, maybe not like this, but it will come.*

Marín stops and pulls out of my body, panting. He looks at me.

"I'm coming, Coco."

"Do it. I want you to." I touch his hair and smile.

He teases me with a beautiful smile. "No, sweetheart, my orgasm doesn't matter more here. We either both get there or neither of us does."

He lies next to me and flips me around so I'm on top. He slips in so easily, so clean, so wet…that my nipples get hard.

"You do it. Do it your way," he begs.

My hair sways to the rhythm of my hips, even though a few strands are starting to stick to my neck and back from the sweat. I lean down, find my friction point, and let my hips move through animal intuition. I find the angle where he's deepest, that's right "there," that place he already knows. I melt, and then I touch myself. Marín caresses my thighs, grabs my hips, looks at me, smiles, says, "Yes, like that, yes." And I smile at him too.

Describing an orgasm is so hard that I wouldn't know how to put what I feel into words. A tingle, a threat of tumbling down into a dark place where everything is amazing and you don't know if you'll make it back whole. It's my skin, like a living organism, feeling like it's breathing, pulsing, spreading to every crevice, confirming that this is right. I know that a moan is clinging to my vocal chords, suspended in the air, halfway between an "ah" and an "mmm," an "I love you," "don't stop," "don't leave yet." And his answer is a hot torrent that fills me in two, three, four spasms. And while his orgasm and mine collide inside my body, Marín exhales a long, raucous moan, half groan, half plea that drips into my mouth as we kiss hungrily. Tongue, saliva, teeth, sighs. My sex is full of him, my mouth too, my hands are trying to trap something that doesn't exist except invisibly, and everything, everything is Marín in my body. And I'm everything in his.

Blanca once told me, in a confession that I now understand much better, that making love isn't exactly what they sell us. It's actually feeling vulnerable.

"We're used to fucking affectionately, Coco, but people only make love a handful of times in our lives. It has nothing to do with doing it slowly or kissing a lot—that's not what it's about. Making love is breaking. It's feeling vulnerable and letting the other in, with everything that means.

You let him in, he enters you, and in that moment, you both understand that you'll feel alone in your body for the rest of your life without him there. Making love is finding something worth dying for."

And maybe I'm a naive idiot, but suddenly I find myself thinking that, fuck, after this, dying, life being finite, is worth it because at least I know what making love is and everything else fades away. How would we feel if forever really meant forever?

No, I'll never lie to him again, I promise myself. So I have to tell him, even if it scares him, even if I shouldn't, even if it's clearly too soon or too late, but definitely not the right time.

"I love you. And I know, Marín… I know you're the one."

34

FEAR

MARÍN

I'm freaked out. Completely and totally freaked out. I don't know what I've done. I don't know what happened in this room. And I always thought I knew what I could do with my body. Is this what an out-of-body experience feels like?

My conviction that Coco is the ultimate girl for me is driven home when she snuggles into my chest. Normally, I feel the need to go straight to the bathroom after sex; everything smells like fucking, and after I come, that sensation makes me feel uncomfortable. But she curled up there, on my chest, and…we smell like sex, saliva, and semen…and I don't care.

I'm scared to death, and I think she knows it. We've spent too many minutes in silence, sharing slow kisses, which are tender but weird. I don't like silences that are heavy because they're full of things left unsaid, but sometimes you have to figure out how to soften those words.

"I know about Gus and Blanca," she suddenly blurts out, like she wants to clear the air.

"What's that?" I shift on my pillow, put one arm under my neck, and look at her. "You know? Since when?"

"This morning. Blanca fainted. Don't worry. She's fine. But, well, she fainted, and Gus showed up out of nowhere. All you had to do was look at them to see that they're in love."

"They're not," I correct her, fidgeting by twisting a lock of her hair around my finger. "They're not in love. Well…her, yes. She is. He's not."

"Believe me, he is."

"You know something, Coco? The feelings we carry in our hearts matter, but what we do with them matters even more. If that's Gus's way of loving…it'd be better if he didn't love her."

"What are you trying to say?"

"He's had a thousand opportunities to say, 'Listen, Blanca, I don't love you' or even just 'I made a fucking mess,' but he's always resorted to the same thing: He doesn't say yes, he doesn't say no, he blocks the door so it can't be opened all the way."

"But Blanca's getting married," she says.

"Coco…let's not judge people for how they decide to live their lives. It's all too complicated."

She presses her cheek into my chest and nimbly strokes the sparse hair there. "How long have you known?"

"Not long, a few days. They told me that morning at La Marína."

"Have you talked to Gus about it?"

"I tried, but no… He doesn't want to talk. And if he doesn't want to…"

Coco sinks into a heavy silence for so long that I start to think she fell asleep. I don't know what she's thinking about, and not even empathy can help me figure it out. I can't stop thinking, going in circles about what just happened between us. I just slept with my best friend—I'm more haunted by the knowledge that I've never done what we just did. And that makes me kind of nervous.

I feel weird because when I came inside her, the only thing I could think about is that my whole shitty life has had a purpose from the beginning and it was her. The painful childhood, the hard adolescence, having to watch other people raise my sister, not ever being either young enough to not care or adult enough to be able to do anything. Everything I've gone through, I went through so that the path would lead me to where I am now: on a bed wrapped in sheets drenched in sweat and love. With Coco.

How long ago did I break up with Aroa? Seven months? I don't know. I'm all mixed up. But even I know it's too soon to start branding things with forevers. I can't dive headfirst into this; I can't be reckless. We live together. That speeds everything up.

"Coco," I mumble, "how are we going to do this?"

"I don't understand how people love each other," she replies.

I look at her, and her eyes start bulging as she tries to explain herself.

"I don't understand it," she repeats. "Love…is that how it is?"

"Are you talking about Blanca and Gus?"

"Yes. Or Aroa and you. Or Gus and me. Is that how love works?"

"Is that how you love me?"

She raises her eyebrows and smiles ironically. "I thought you were pretending I didn't desperately confess my love."

"I'm not avoiding it. I just use my words differently. They have a different rhythm. Aroa would say, 'I love you' every time she hung up the phone, and it didn't mean anything. An 'I love you' now has nothing to do with what I really feel."

"And what do you feel?"

"Fear, excitement, skin… I've been feeling my skin a lot ever since… we finished."

"That's because I woke it up." Coco climbs on top of me, straddling me, with an excited smile on her lips, and I don't know how to tell her this without hurting her.

"I don't want to go too fast," I whisper.

"What do you mean?"

"We live together, I just broke up with Aroa, and this…has kinda caught me off guard. There are things that…I don't know, I have to think about how I want to do them."

"Okay." She nods. "And what do you propose?"

"The trip with my sister. That's a good chance for me to get my head straight. You don't mind, right?"

"No." She shakes her head with a half smile. "I'm just a little scared. I don't want that to mean that, well, I don't know. I'm sorry, but there's no going back. It either goes forward or it doesn't go."

That's exactly how I feel. I stroke her hair. "You've had a lot more time to prepare for all this. I'll admit that up until this trip, I had never even imagined or fantasized that you and I…"

"That you and I…what?"

"That…" I shimmy under her, playfully, relieved to be able to take the conversation in a less tense direction. "I'd lick you, come inside you, that I would lose my mind watching you come on top of me…"

"Stop." She smiles. "Don't make promises you can't keep."

"I'm not promising anything."

"I'm just saying I'm going to get all turned on again and you're not going to be able to right now. We don't want any disappointments…at least not in the first ten tries."

"Okay. Well, roughly calculating how much I want you and how much time we have…I think we can allow ourselves a bad one tomorrow. In the morning, if you want us to do it in the shower, I'll come up and ask you to do something that will horrify you and totally turn you off."

"You're an idiot." She kisses me, and her hair tickles me everywhere… even inside my chest. "I barely slept at all, I just tossed and turned… How about we put on the AC and we sleep?"

"I'm hungry," I say sheepishly.

"Well, you can order something to eat while I sleep. Turn on the air."

That. How no one can change her mind when she feels like she needs something. That's probably the first thing that drew me to Coco and the seed of all this. I should have known I was going to fall in love with her when I saw her come into the house with all her stuff and say, "Welcome to the first day of the rest of your life...with me."

~~~

She sleeps. She sleeps the way men supposedly do after sex—like a passed-out bunny. I get out of bed, fold her clothes, wash my face, and open an app to order food. When it arrives, I get an inkling that I was more excited for it to show up so I could wake her up than to eat.

I go over to the bed, in my boxers, and lie down behind her. I stroke her hair, her shoulders, her arm, and I look for a gap, a little corner of skin where I can kiss her. She smells like her, like me, like sex and happiness. I'm so fucking scared.

"Coco," I whisper.

She pulled the thin sheet over her naked body, but she didn't cover herself very meticulously, so I can see her left breast. I feel an irrepressible desire to put it in my mouth. Why the hell have I never sucked on her tits before? She has perfect tits, or at least that's how they seem to me because I like them so much. But no... Focus...

"Coco," I repeat. "The food is here."

"Mmm."

"I ordered you a chicken burger."

"Cool," she mumbles.

"And fries."

"Cucumber," she says, more there than here.

"Come on, get up."

"I'm tired," she moans.

Good. More excuses to do what I'm feeling the urge to.

I press my lips against her ear and say, "If you don't wake up, you won't
~~~

eat. And if you don't eat, you won't regain your strength. And if you don't regain your strength, I can't fuck you like a fucking dog in heat until you ask me to stop because you want to die."

She turns her head slowly toward me, with one eye closed. "Excuse me?"

"What?"

"I'll bet anything you want that you can't repeat that to my face."

I half smile, yank the sheet off her, and climb on top of her.

"I want to put my cock in your throat and have you suck me until your eyes roll back in your head. I want to fuck your cunt with my fingers. And then my cock. And I want to come in your mouth, on your tits. I want to fuck you hard with my hand around your throat, and I might slap you when you're about to come if you're into that."

"Okay…got it."

"Ah, no, no, no way. I'm just getting started."

"I get the idea, thanks."

"Thank you for coming. Now get up and eat."

I go to get out of bed, but she grabs my arm and tugs me back.

"What? Any other questions?" I ask.

"Yes. If you want to do all that to me after we eat, you have to remember that I'm the kind of girl who vomits if I do exercise without digesting first. I don't know if you're up for that."

"You're the worst." I smile. "What do you want? I'm not going to be able to wait two hours for you to digest."

"One, two, or whatever it takes." She returns my smile wickedly. "You might have a filthy mouth, but when it comes to fucking like a dog, I'm the queen. Gimme my burger."

~

She doesn't wait even half an hour after she eats to get naked again. She doesn't ask for permission. I'm lying on the bed, next to her, pretending like we're watching something on TV when she sits up, pulls off her clothes, takes off my pants, and climbs on top of me. She looks at me—she looks at me like she's daring me to say no. Like I could.

"Any requests?" she says, with one eyebrow raised.

"I want to see you get really slutty."

And she's in charge, but she grants my wishes with a dignity that blows me away. When I feel her tongue exploring my cock, I'm tempted to close my eyes, stroke her skin, and let go, but I have to look at her. God…she's fucking incredible. Her eyelashes flutter as she sucks, fills her mouth, moans, and the vibration gives me goose bumps. Her tongue runs over the tip, down the shaft… I have to twist the sheets in my fists when she licks my balls and jerks me off.

"Is this slutty enough to start off with?"

"Fuck, yes."

"Ready to take it up a notch?"

She asks me to choke her with my cock, to fuck her mouth, to be rough with her. And, her wish is my command. I was born to do whatever this girl with long legs, thick black eyelashes, and cherry lips asks, no matter how crazy it is. If she asked, I would get married, have six kids, quit music, and move to a fucking townhouse in the suburbs. If she wants, I'll reinvent myself entirely, for fuck's sake. And the most fucked-up part is that, even though I'm as horny as a dog, I know this isn't about the sex, as good as it is.

"Come on," she purrs. "Leave me breathless."

I push her head down when she puts it back in her mouth. I make her stay there, with my cock so deep in her throat that her chest swells, searching for air. Her spit slides down my skin; she uses it as a lubricant to pump faster, harder. I'm close to coming two hundred times. I have to multiply long numbers with decimals in my head to stop myself.

I push into her from behind, looking at her back. She says into my ear that I should do it, mount her "not carefully, affectionately—like animals," she purrs. And I grab her hair in my fist, wrap the ponytail around my wrist, and yank it gently as I push into her without asking for permission. I call her a slut and ask her if she likes it. She moans so thick and warm that I can't help it.

"I want you to show me what a whore you are. My little whore. Make me yours forever."

"You're not going to be able to think about anything else for the rest of your life," she promises.

We do it so hard that I'm scared reception will call to ask us to stop screaming and pushing furniture around. The bed has shifted at least half a foot from its original spot, and she's still asking for more.

"Harder. Harder, fuck."

The skin smacking against her every time I thrust is starting to sting, but I would rip it off if she asked. Right now, I belong more to her than myself.

Her on top. Me on top. On our sides. On all fours. Face down. We've raced through all these positions in twenty minutes.

She comes on my fingers for the first time. She comes wetter than I've ever seen a woman come, screaming, arching, and wild. If I like her being cuddly on Sundays, if I adore her trying to figure out how the hell to record a show, if I swell with pride when she tells me how she helped value a Juan Gristhen, I want her forever when she's wild.

I ask her if she still wants more. She nods, panting, and I slide the fingers I used to make her come into her mouth. When she licks them, I almost come on her leg.

I eat her again, but this time I keep going until she explodes. I know she's about to when her breath catches in her throat as she says she wants me to use her, to fuck her like I don't give a shit about her. She comes in my fucking mouth, and, fuck, I feel like I'll never get enough of this shit. What have I done falling in love with her? Have I condemned myself for life, or was I just wasting time by not doing it sooner?

I haven't fucked that many girls, but I've gotten around enough. I've spent a wild night in the bathroom of some club with a stranger whom I had no inhibitions with. Once a girl that I had just met in a concert hall whispered into my ear that she wanted me to put it in every hole before the night ended. And I did it. I had to ask her name as I was getting dressed because I wasn't sure we had even introduced ourselves. With Aroa I did everything we wanted to, but never—not with her or the stranger or any of the others—did I ever feel like this. I'm frantic. All the filthy things I want to do, say, promise are piling up on my tongue, but none come out. All I can whisper in her ear is that I want her really slutty.

I come like a beast. I don't understand how my body can keep creating so much semen. I cover her chest, and some even splatters into her mouth. And I'm never going to forget the way she wiped her mouth with the back of her hand and said, "We're going to break from all this sex, you know?"

And I do know.

~

When Gus opens the door to the room, the spectacle must be pretty mind-blowing. She's on top and she's riding me for the third time. I can't take anymore, but I'm not going to beg for mercy.

The first thing I think of is that I want Gus out of the room, the hotel, Andalusia, and maybe the whole country. I don't want him to look at her, to see her on top of me, moving her hips with her perfect tits in view. Then I remember he held these perfect tits a thousand times before I did.

"Fuck, Gus, get out of here!" she yelps, covering herself.

"The fuck!" he yells, horrified, shoving his face into the wall. "What the hell are you doing?!"

What are we doing? Please…

"Get out," I say.

"You're fucking!"

"Get out," I say, my tone steely.

His back is turned, and she winks at me, moving gently with me still inside her. I smile and shake my head. This fucking woman doesn't want to stop even when Gus is in the room.

"What do you want?" I cover a moan with a cough.

"The car keys."

"You don't know how to drive." Coco bites her lip and complains when I stop her and gently slide out from under her.

"Just for a second," I whisper.

I get up and find my pajama pants. I try to arrange them over my boner so it's not too uncomfortable, but…it's definitely not going down.

"If I take a deep breath, I'll get knocked up, you bastards. Do you have any idea what it smells like in here?"

"We've been fucking for three hours. What do you expect?" she pipes up, wrapped in a sheet.

"The keys, please. I don't want to know any more."

I stand in front of him, and he stares at me. "What the hell do you need car keys for when you don't have a license?"

"I need to go somewhere. Someone else is driving." He clears his throat.

"Someone else?"

"Give him the keys," Coco says. "Tell Blanca to drive safe."

Gus sighs. "It's not what it looks like, okay?"

"Of course. And we were doing yoga," she says disdainfully.

"I wanted to tell you a thousand times, but Blanca said…"

I go over to the dresser, grab the keys, and toss them to him. He's looking at her, and as much as I hate him seeing her like this, violating an intimacy that's so new and so ours, I'm more bothered by the bitterness emanating from Coco. She shouldn't be this hurt, right? She doesn't feel anything for him anymore. That's dead. Even though last night…

Stop, Marín. You're going to lose it.

"I'll be back tomorrow," he says very seriously.

"What do you mean, tomorrow?"

"We're going to... Well, we might be back tonight, but..."

"Okay, I don't wanna know, but try to clear this up today. You're going to kill Blanca, Gus. You're gonna kill her."

"I didn't know everyone knew," he grumbles.

"Yeah, because you two are so discreet."

"Just like you two, right?"

"Get out," I repeat.

"Simmer down," Gus says to me. "I'm still gonna punch you."

"Hey, hey, hey, where's all this coming from?" Coco complains.

This is a pang of jealousy that isn't really my thing. "Are you leaving?" I insist to Gus.

"Hey...you don't happen to have a...a condom?"

I can't stop myself. I open the door, grab him by the shirt, and toss him out. There's no time for him to even say a word before the door slamming echoes down the hallway.

"Come here..." She pats the bed she's sprawled across.

"I can't handle anymore," I admit. "Of all these twists and turns in the gang or physically."

"Well, it is what it is. But don't worry. I'm going to go slowly, my king."

~

There are a thousand songs running through my head right now. Songs I've been storing up in my memory because of a phrase, a melody, a word...pieces that make up the mosaic of what I understand about love.

They say that in the early years, kids learn through imitation. That's so dangerous...so much responsibility in the hands of people who sometimes don't deserve that trust. When I was little, my house wasn't exactly full of love. I don't remember my father, just like Gema doesn't remember hers. In both cases, Mama had the same "good" taste for choosing a mate. At least they said that mine left me the inheritance of my rare green eyes. Let's not mention mother-son love either. My mother is sick, and understanding that has saved me from hating her, but I needed it back then, and I needed outside help too. My aunt and uncle are an amazing couple who are raising Gema the way she deserves, but they were never around when I was young.

What I do know is that my obsession with music started back then, back when I discovered that people in songs loved each other the way I wanted to love my mama. The way I saw people on television loving each other. The normal way, judging by everyone around me, but not mine.

The folk song my grandmother was listening to on that old transistor radio when I complained quietly that my mother didn't have any food at home; the ballads my aunt loved and we would dance to, me up on her teenage bed and her standing next to it; the pop music I grew up with and dreamed I'd become a big star with; the classic records my mother's little brother gave me—all those songs and the ones I started getting into by myself have drawn the contours of the way I love. A sound investigation that every genre fits into because what controls it is the message.

Of all my relationships up until now, I thought Aroa was the one who came closest to those melodic promises of eternal love. I knew it wasn't going to be forever, but it worked and we could make it last. All that was missing there and lived in love songs was…well, just that, poetic license, glorification, unrealistic praise of an emotion that was more idealization than reality.

Or that's what I thought. Because all the love songs that come into my head are missing something to compare with what I'm feeling now. "Your Song" by Elton John, "Because the Night" by Patti Smith, "Stand by Me" (Tracy Chapman's incredible version), "I'm Yours" by Alessia Cara, "Wicked Game" by Chris Isaak, "La chispa adequada" by Héroes del Silencio, "Mi ninformana más bella" by El Chivi, "Lovesong" by The Cure—I don't know, they're all missing something. They're missing Coco. And I understand now that I have her sitting on my lap, on the hotel balcony, and we're clinging to each other, holding each other, with sheets wrapped around us, brushing against each other's skin. I understand now that night has fallen, now that we gifted each other this day of fucking and loving each other and we're drunk on the feeling and the surprise of being capable of feeling it.

Her feet are propped up on the porch railing, and neither of us is talking. I've been distracted for a while, caressing her neck with my lips, breathing her in. Thinking. My head is all over the place, jumping from the concept of love to the fear of losing it. And having it. What if we don't blossom into being the protagonists of a perfect love story? The kind that shakes the foundations of your life. I always thought I wanted a small love story. I thought that was just my way of experiencing love and that's why my relationships were…beautiful but small. I mean small as in the opposite of the sweeping love stories they make movies about. I wanted relationships that didn't cause me any problems, and coming to that conclusion while I caressed Coco—the one I know I'll love even if it hurts me that I didn't love her before—makes me feel kind of dismayed. It just dawned on me that I'm emotionally mediocre. And…I don't know if I'll be good enough.

"Are you sure the Perseids are today?"

"Yes." I kiss her shoulder. "They've been talking about it for days in the news and on social media."

"Well, I don't see anything." Coco turns to look at me and smiles. "Why are you so quiet? Is this about the thing with your sister?"

My heart jumps in my chest. "What?" I manage to ask.

"About your sister's date."

Ah, God, that scared the shit out of me. "No. Well…I'm worried they'll fool around. Actually, I'm worried they'll fool around, she won't like it, and she won't know how to stop it."

"Gema? You're nuts. She's totally clear that she doesn't have to do anything she doesn't want to."

"Like taking fucking iron vitamins," I mock myself.

"Exactly."

Coco swivels in my lap until her legs are dangling on either side of me. "Is everything really okay?"

"Yes," I nod. "I'm just getting used to the fact that I just spent the day fucking my best friend."

She smiles and nods. "In a little while we might even..."

"Oh, God." I pretend to roll my eyes. "You're gonna be the death of me."

"We have to make a wish for Gema," she reminds me, ignoring my complaints and stroking my face.

"I know. And another one for us."

"Yeah? Another one for us?" And her expression shows how happy that makes her.

"We deserve our own wishes, right? I don't wanna get fired and...if possible, I wish to get transferred to the international department."

"Ah." Her smile seems tinged with disappointment. "Well, I don't know what to ask for..."

She turns her gaze back to the sky, and I understand. She wanted a wish for us as a unit. Not a "you" and then on the other side a "me." One single us, one single wish. Coco is really in love with me, and I have no idea when that happened.

"Keep your eyes peeled. We need four shooting stars," I say, hugging her.

"Four? Do you want to wish for one for the landlord too?"

"One for Gema...like for her to grow into a very happy woman, for example. Another for you...like your boss retiring, just to throw anything out there."

"Or that I win the Euromillions jackpot. Some crazy amount of millions. That'd be cool. I'd spend the first million on a pool full of candy."

"Very mature."

"And the other two for you?" she asks me with her eyebrows raised.

"One for me and the other for us. For both of us…as one."

There it is. I hit the target.

"What should we wish for?" she asks.

"That this isn't too much for us."

I regret saying it as soon as it comes out, but I'm convinced that ignoring the possibility would be really irresponsible. Still, I kiss her. A kiss on the lips in the way that isn't chaste but isn't about sex either. The way a man who just turned the love of his life into his wife kisses.

"This is new. I wasn't expecting it," I clarify. "Just give me time to fit it into the life I had and give it the space it deserves."

"Of course. I had an advantage… I've loved you for a long time."

That's probably the most beautiful thing anyone has ever said to me, and I don't know if I deserve it.

"When did you realize you loved me?"

"When I stopped being jealous of Aroa because at least she made you happy. But it's all your fault, Marín…because you always treated me like I was the only woman on the face of the earth. That's what happens when you make someone feel really special—they want to be it at all costs."

Feeling loved is a two-sided coin: One of them smiles at us and makes sense of the need to find someone to cuddle with; the other bares its teeth because it makes us keenly aware of our own imperfections. Am I capable of loving her the way she deserves? Can I make her happy? Will my way of loving be enough for her? Am I really falling in love with her, or are we just destroying the best relationship of all time by trying to become lovers? Can she cure my broken way of thinking about love? Is it fair to put that responsibility on her?

"I love you," I say.

Fuck. What was that? I wasn't expecting it. I didn't even know I felt it as strongly as I said it, but she seems, as always, to know me better than I know myself and she smiles.

"I know. And I love you too."

I rest my cheek on her head, and when I look up at the sky…zasss. There it is. The first one.

"Did you see that?" we both say, giddy as kids.

"Quick, make a wish and don't tell me," she adds.

You, Coco. You always and me being good enough. You and not this fear. You with no space between us so I suffocate against your chest. You understanding, when you find out, why I didn't tell you before about Gema. Because you're finding out, you're going to find out, I'm sure of that. I just hope I'm the one who tells you.

35

NO MORE LIES

COCO

We don't know our people. It's better if we accept it. We don't know them like we believe we do, for better or worse.

I think this now, as Marín and I are tangled in the sheets, kissing. I woke up clinging to his arm, like I was afraid it would disappear in the night—what happened yesterday, the desire, him.

It's eight thirty in the morning, and we've both had our phones off since yesterday. The world has ceased to exist, and I'm sorry, but I don't care about anything, even if I do care a lot about the people who've been trapped in there in a switched-off phone. Maybe Gema got her first kiss. Blanca probably spent the worst night of her life saying goodbye to someone who I don't know if she loves. I don't understand anything. We've probably abandoned Loren like he's worse than a cigarette butt, each of us so wrapped up in our own shit. And then there's Aroa.

But who cares?

We haven't said anything since Marín opened his eyes and found me staring at him. I've never had the opportunity to see how he wakes up. The way his almost-golden eyelashes quiver and his pupils shrink, letting the sea of his unparalleled eyes pour over everything else. That sleepy smile. Those raised eyebrows, which seem to say, *Why are you looking at me and not kissing me?* The dimples. Shit. The dimples and his chin. Now the kisses are starting. On his chin. On his cheeks, which I'm sure he'll want to shave soon. On his puffy eyelids. On his mouth, which greets me with the best kiss of my life. Just woke up and he tastes good…better than good. It's too good to be real.

And we kiss, we kiss with no intention of it going further. We look at each other too, as if we're asking ourselves how this is possible. Four days ago, I was important to him, but it didn't involve sex. And now the big change isn't that we're having sex; it's that he's made me his.

And I'm thinking I don't know him as well as I thought I did. These kisses are mouthfuls of fear. He's trying to hide it, and I'm swallowing it and digesting it for him. I wish I could at least understand what's scaring him so much.

He strokes my cheek and smiles. A scared smile, even if he doesn't know it. I mimic him.

"That was the best day of my life, but"—my heart is pounding when I hear him whisper—"we have to get back to reality."

"And what does that mean?"

"We should turn on our phones and…go back to the campsite."

"What are we gonna tell Aroa?"

"Since when do we have to explain ourselves to anyone? If we don't even know what to tell ourselves, Coco, how can we give answers to anyone else?"

Him. He's the only one who doesn't know what to tell himself. I know exactly what I want, and it's him—he's for me and I'm for him.

"We have to say something."

"You slept here. That's it."

"I'm sick of lies," I say.

"That's not a lie." He flips onto his back, pushes his hair out of his face, and swallows. "Not saying anything until you're ready isn't lying, Coco. It's…making things easier for everyone."

I had always thought Marín loved fearlessly. He was never scared with me. He didn't care that his friends thought he was nuts when I moved in with him when we barely knew each other. "She could be a crazy cunt," "What if she robs you?," "Maybe she wants to kill you and make human sacrifices to Satan with your blood." He didn't listen to anyone. He gave me a set of keys to his house, a room where I could move in, and he made his life wide open to me. What's he afraid of now?

~

He invites me to have breakfast on the beach. The intimacy of the kisses when we woke up has died down, and now we're both quiet, circumspect. It's normal, I guess, after such a frenzied day. If I think about it, I'm a little embarrassed too: I practically devoured him yesterday. I asked him to shove his cock in so hard it would hurt. I begged him to pound me, and I came on the first thrust of our fourth fuck. He came inside me, on me, in my mouth. And he's Marín. It's weird.

"It's weird," I say to him, stirring my coffee so the sugar will dissolve.

"A little," he admits. "But it's a nice weird."

"You seem a little distant."

"I'm just going in circles in my head. We're going back to Madrid today, and…a lot of stuff has happened."

"I know."

"Blanca and Gus have been hooking up for almost a year." He grimaces at me. "How does that make you feel?"

"We weren't together when they started."

"Yeah, but he's your ex. And she's your best friend."

"Should I ask Aroa the same thing?"

"It's different. Aroa was never your best friend. She's always been…a free spirit."

"No." I shake my head. "It's actually not that different. I fell in love with you without meaning to. I guess the same thing happened to Blanca."

Marín doesn't seem to agree, but he doesn't say anything else. He just nods, his gaze lost out over the ocean. It's not that hot yet. And we still haven't turned our phones on.

"We should go," I say. "I want to talk to her. Last night, if they ended… whatever they are, she'll be destroyed."

"And you want to console her?"

"I want to understand it, and I'm sure she'll want to explain it to me too."

"Wait until you get back."

"Does Aroa know?"

He presses his lips together and swipes his hand under his nose. "I didn't think so, but the other night in Mandala…when we were leaving, I saw Blanca and Gus in a corner. I didn't know how to cover it up, but it definitely couldn't be explained by 'they're friends.' They were arguing, she was shaking him, and she seemed really upset, but when he tried to leave, she grabbed him, and she seemed… She seemed like she was begging him. I pulled Aroa into that corner where you found us so she wouldn't see, but she told me she already knew."

"Did Blanca tell her?"

"No. Blanca only told me. Loren knows because…he caught them."

"He caught them?"

"He caught them in the street…coming out of a hotel."

I blink. Fuck. Lovers—it sounds so sordid. I feel uncomfortable.

"Why did you and Aroa break up?" I decide to ask.

"Isn't that too much information after just a couple of days? Maybe we can relax and talk about that a little later." He rubs his forehead. "My head kinda hurts."

"You're being really weird."

"I'm sorry," he says. "I am."

"Is it because of me? Did I do something to…?"

"No." He furrows his brow and smiles at me. "Coco, what's happened these past few days is…incredible. I never… Well, I've never experienced this. And it's with you." He nods to himself. "I know it's you—you change everything you touch. And you know what is the worst lie that we can tell ourselves? That love doesn't change us. It does. Forever. Let me get to know this dude who almost vomited up his heart when I saw you this morning. That's all it is. And…pieces."

"Pieces?"

"Pieces. They have to fit together. And you have to…well, you don't have to do anything, but I'd appreciate it if you can understand that there were things without solutions even before all this…and I don't know if we're helping or making them even more difficult."

"I don't understand."

He grabs his coffee and takes a sip. He takes a few coins out of his pocket. "You will. Let's go?"

~

No. We don't know people like we think we do. Our parents, for example, were people who had nothing to do with us for years. They had their own dreams, lives, hopes, and obsessions, and we showed up and turned ourselves into the center of everything—and like gobbling monsters, devoured everything they had left to dream about. We were probably the best thing in their lives, but we accept that we're also the great nothing that consumed their pasts.

And if they, our parents, can keep one side completely separate from what we know of them, how could our friends be any different?

I'm surprised to see Aroa sitting on the patio as we approach. It's barely ten in the morning, and even though the campsite is cranking into motion, everything is quiet on our site. Except Aroa is giving off an energy that's pretty far from the peace she says she feels when she finishes doing yoga at dawn. I don't know if I ever really knew my friend or if she was selling us something she wasn't.

She doesn't get up when she sees us, but she seems grimly satisfied, like she gets pleasure from the pain of knowing she wasn't wrong. When we're close enough, we see that she has her bag and her sleeping bag next to her. She's already packed, and I can guess why. If there were any doubts, they're cleared up pretty quickly.

"You're a shitty friend."

I blink. I was expecting hostility and the need to defend myself, but not like this, mostly because Aroa's not like this. Or at least she's never shown it in front of me.

"First of all, calm down," Marín demands. "She's not used to your unhinged attacks."

"Unhinged attacks? Now you're both going to gaslight me into thinking I'm crazy, right? Where are you two coming from at this hour? Because you didn't sleep here."

"That's none of your business, in any way, shape, or form," he replies again.

"How about you let my friend," she spits, "speak for herself? Or did you fuck her so hard she swallowed her tongue?"

"This isn't what it looks like."

Could there be a worse phrase to start off with? Very good, Coco. Fucking great. There's no way to follow that up. I go over to her, I try to forge some kind of connection, to stop her from looking at me like I'm not her enemy, but she pushes me away. And she does it more violently than I pictured. I mean, I get it—I do because in a way I'm having to battle irrational jealousy about Blanca and Gus. I can imagine how she's feeling. I just have to treat her how I hope they'll treat me.

"Aroa, listen to me. Just listen to me for a second."

"Don't even think about touching me, you fake piece of shit. I don't know how I never put it together. You're both the worst, going around all holier than thou."

"I'm not holier than thou at all, Aroa. Let's all calm down and talk about it. I never wanted to hurt you."

"'I never wanted to hurt you,'" she mimics me. "Sure, but laying the groundwork so that my relationship with Marín went to shit, you had no problem doing that. How many times did you talk shit about your friend Aroa? How many times did you tell him—?"

"Never," we both say.

"Am I talking to you?" Aroa asks Marín.

"You're getting in my face," he mutters angrily.

"I told you, Marín. I told you that if you kept going with this shit, I was gonna get tired of keeping your secrets."

"Aroa, shut up."

"I don't feel like it!"

The door of the RV swings open, and Loren appears, disheveled and dumbfounded. "What's with all the yelling?"

"Come on. Is this a talk show? Anyway, that's your thing, isn't it?"

Loren furrows his brow. "Sorry, are you talking to me?"

"The referee's here now," she says through gritted teeth. "Coco, your friend Loren, your great confidant, Loren, knew everything from the start. Remember that when the shit starts hitting the fan."

"What does that mean?" I look at Marín and then at Loren. "What shit?"

"Coco, don't listen to her. She's going to take something out of context and make you believe it's a problem. But it's not," Loren promises.

"It will all make sense, Coco," Marín says. "I didn't tell you something, but only because... Well, at first I thought it was too soon to worry you, and everything was up in the air and…then it became the reason Aroa and I broke up."

"We broke up? That's a cop-out, Marín. You dumped me. You dumped me because nothing, nobody, is ever going to mean more to you than your sister."

"Well, no," he agrees. "Nothing, nobody, and especially not you. And you know why you don't understand that? Because you're a psychotic, egocentric narcissist."

"Wait, what's going on?" I turn back to Marín.

"Hey." Gus gets our attention from the door of the camper. He's wearing a wrinkled T-shirt and black boxers. "What's going on?"

"Come here, Gus," Aroa says, feigning enthusiasm. "Come here. Then everyone's here, and we can all go down together."

"Look, Aroa," Gus starts to say with a tone that I've never heard him use with her; it's his *I'm sick of this* tone.

"Aroa, you're making a mistake." Loren seems really pissed off. "It's not Marín you're going to expose. It's you."

"Me?"

"Yeah, you," he says very confidently.

"Hey, what's going on?" Blanca appears behind Gus in a nightgown, combing her hair with her fingers.

"What about you? Where are you coming from? Loren's bunk or Gus's?"

"Whichever one I fucking feel like. That's why it's my life, not yours."

Wow. I blink. Why do I get the feeling I'm the only one who has missed a bunch of chapters in this story?

"We're getting carried away," I mutter. "This isn't a war, Aroa. I fell in love with Marín. That's it. It doesn't mean that I wanted to hurt you. I never interfered in your relationship. I never tried anything."

"Now I see it. So what happened last night just fell from the sky?

Give it up already, okay? Give it up. The hypocrite thing is a bad look for you."

"He doesn't love you anymore," I say harshly. "What were you expecting? For him to spend his whole life waiting for you to get over your tantrums?"

"Tantrums? Look, Coco...you have no idea who the person you're living with is. You fell in love with him? You fell in love with the Marín you have in your head."

"That's not true, Aroa, but I definitely had no idea that my friend"—I point at her—"was like this."

"Marín is cold. He's incapable of commitment or of ever really trusting anyone. At the first sign of trouble, he runs and hides. Is that the Marín you fell in love with?"

"That's enough, Aroa. You're making yourself look ridiculous," Marín says brusquely.

"He wants Gema to move into your apartment. He wants her to live with him instead of with their aunt and uncle."

"And?" I ask. "What's the problem? He's her brother."

"You're a dumbass, Coco," she says exasperatedly. "Of course he's her brother, and of course you think that's perfect, a story with a happy ending...but have you ever thought about how you fit into that plan? Because, as far as I know, it's a two-bedroom apartment. What do you think, that he was planning on falling in love with you so you can move into his room together and Gema can move into yours?"

I side-eye Marín. "Marín?"

"Next year," he says. "All these plans were for next year. For when she starts high school. I thought I would figure out a solution before that."

"A solution?"

"How to kick you out of the apartment and still make you keep thinking Marín is God, basically."

"That's not true," he says to me. "A solution so you wouldn't have to move. And that's exactly what pissed you off, right, Aroa? That's why you told me I have to choose between you and Coco."

"You had already made that decision a long time before. Sorry not sorry."

"I made that decision the minute you made me choose because, look, I had no idea I even had feelings for her, but I knew that Coco never would've made me choose."

"You did that?" I ask her. "You told him he had to choose between us? But you and I were...friends."

"Such good friends that you wanted to fuck my boyfriend."

I look around at everyone, not really knowing what to say. It hurts that Marín left me out of his plans, but it's not that deep. I repeat that to myself a few times. My friend didn't have any problem telling Marín he had to choose between us, hoping that he would cut me out of his life—that does seem pretty deep.

"We'll move," I say to Marín. "Problem solved."

"Good luck. He's already filled in the paperwork for the school...the one right next to the house."

"That's bullshit," Marín says to me.

"We'll move," I say again. "It's not a problem."

"You're stupid, girl," Aroa snorts.

"I would have appreciated a heads-up, but it's not some big drama. We'll talk about it. And if you don't want"—I look at Marín—"to move, it's as easy as leaving my room..."

"We'll talk about it later." He cuts me off very somberly.

"Oh, big surprise," Aroa says. "Welcome to the real side of Marín."

"Talk about that when you two are alone," Blanca suggests. "It's nobody's business but yours, especially not Aroa's."

"Hey, where are you two at?" Aroa asks her and Gus. "Because it's been days since your last pathetic little poem."

"Jesus, Aroa, you're such an asshole." We all look at Gus in surprise. "Why don't you do us all a favor and get out of here already? You did your best to make us all argue, and it didn't work. That's it. Quit it already."

"I wouldn't talk so much if I were you," she tosses out there. "You're the one I have the most shit on."

Gus and Blanca side-eye each other.

"You're the one hiding the most shit here, Aroa. How long have you known about Blanca and Gus?" I ask her.

"I think you're the only one who didn't realize they've been fucking their way around Madrid, sweetie."

"So then...why did you tell me Gus's poems were for me?"

"If you have to steal someone's boyfriend, better for it to be the cheating one, right?"

"Are you hearing yourself?" Marín jumps in. "Don't you realize you sound like a crazy bitch?"

"Yeah, now you're playing the crazy ex card, of course. You and I were gonna get back together, Marín."

"What?" He looks at her, stunned. "What didn't you get, Aroa?"

"We were going to fix it."

"You waited outside my office, the gym, the soccer game on Saturdays, you followed my friends around, you showed up at my house...and every single time I told you the same thing: It's over."

"What about the last time we fucked?"

"That was months ago."

"Months, Marín?" She raises one eyebrow.

I look at them, and they look at me. He looks worried; she's smiling.

"I don't care," I say. "You're not getting anywhere with this, Aroa."

"You know what's going on with you?" Marín shoots back. "You're obsessed. That's why you're jealous of my sister, of Coco, of when I went out with my friends, my colleagues from the label, the people I had to hang out with for work. I had to go everywhere with you, the actress. Do you know how fucking embarrassing I found it that you would always introduce yourself as 'Aroa, his girlfriend, the actress?'"

"We can't all sell paintings," she snarls.

"The worst part is it didn't even have anything to do with me or what we had. You're obsessed with yourself, with your career, with who can introduce you to someone important, and now with someone who didn't choose you. You, Aroa, the perfect one, how dare I? The one who does everything right, who everyone envies and adores."

"Look who's talking, Marín the magnificent. Fucking coward piece of shit. Coco, start looking for a new apartment because—"

"Because what?" he challenges her. "Why can't you leave her out of this? You have a problem with me, not her."

"My problem is that this whole group is fake as shit."

"Well, straight back at you," Gus retorts.

"Go home, Aroa," Marín adds. "Do yourself a favor."

"There's no way for you to cover your ass and make your girlfriend understand that you're shitting yourself with fear, overwhelmed, and all you want to do is get out of here, run off with your sister, and find an excuse to get rid of her…but still keep looking like the good guy."

"You have no idea," I jump in.

"About what you feel, right? How beautiful…"

"I must be delirious," I mutter through my teeth.

"Stop sticking your nose in stuff that's none of your business," Marín repeats.

"Couple things, right?" she says with an ironic smile. "Coco, it's never gonna happen."

Marín shifts uncomfortably. He stares at her.

"What?" Aroa says, looking more like a stranger every minute. "Does she know what you said about her?"

"Don't do that," Loren pleads.

"You heard it too. I'm not going to lie. Or is it a lie that Marín thought Coco was pathetic around Gus? Like she had no dignity."

I look at him.

"It's not like that," he says.

"Of course. I'm sure you never said that you wish Coco would find a boyfriend because she's always bugging you, clinging to you all the time either."

"Shut up, Aroa."

"And that you're weird, Coco. He said you're weird," she repeats. "And he said that after fucking me in his bed. I'm sure you were in the next room dreaming about your children and your wedding, but he was naked and still inside me, telling me that you were weird when I asked if you heard us. 'She's a weirdo, Aroa. She probably likes hearing us.' And the thing about you being a spoiled little girl playing house in Malasaña? Did he ever say that to your face or just to me?"

I bite my lip. "You're a bad person, Aroa," I repeat.

Nobody adds anything else. She looks at all of us, maybe waiting for someone to say something, anything, that would make this better, to defend her or to… I don't know. Or to make it worse.

"You're both fucking cowards full of lies and guilt. Coco, you made a bad choice. Chicks over dicks. You're going to end up dropped like a cigarette butt, like he did with me and…who are you going to run and cry to? Her?" She points at Blanca. "The one who was fucking your ex without telling you even though she thought you were still in love with him? If you're going to excuse her saying you can't fight against love, get it straight. If these two have any real feelings, which I highly doubt, that was only after she sucked his dick all over Madrid like a fucking cat in heat."

"Shut up, Aroa," Loren says. "Shut up already."

"Didn't you put bros before hos when you made him choose?" I ask her.

"Jesus, bitch, you only hear what you want to. Fantastic. You two have that in common." She jumps up from her chair and grabs her stuff. "You're never going to look like me in your fucking life, Coco, as hard as you try. And he won't fulfill anyone. Deep down, he needs to have a woman by his side who makes him feel like someone. Is that you?"

"The best thing that ever happened to Marín was breaking up with you," Blanca spits, full of rage. "And you wanna know something? When we thought you were perfect at everything, we were right. You're really good at everything, even making everyone else feel like shit."

"Too bad, Blanca…and it's too bad that before I leave I'm gonna give you a little advice. I don't know what he's convinced you of this time." She points at Gus. "That this was the last time, that he won't do it anymore, that he's going to leave you alone, that this time he'll respect you and be your friend…but don't trust him. If he's capable of fucking a friend of yours while he was doing your thing…"

"You're such a shit-stirrer, blondie," she shoots back. "Coco and Gus didn't have sex."

"Who said anything about Coco? Go on, Gus, tell her. Marín, he didn't hold a candle to you, but I have no regrets. Now it's really all out there."

Silence spills over the site. Marín looks like a wax statue. He's not moving a muscle…just staring at Gus. Like Blanca, like Loren.

As if it were rehearsed choreography, all the movement kicks off when Aroa is out of our field of vision. And we have to move fast to separate them because in the blink of an eye, Marín has had enough time to knock Gus to the ground.

36

THE TRUTH IS NOT A SALVE

coco

“Son of a bitch!” he yells, pulling away from me. He doesn’t even see Blanca clutching at his arms or me trying to get him to look at anything that isn’t Gus. I’ve never seen him like this. Never.

“I’m a son of a bitch, Marín? Why? For hooking up with your ex when you were together or for hooking up with Coco when you weren’t together yet? Either I’m confused or you’re a hypocrite.”

“Hypocrite? Let go of me. Jesus!” he yells. “Let go of me! You fucked all three of them, like they’re not worth shit, you son of a bitch!”

“Marín. Marín.” I grab his face. “Look at me. At me. Look at me.”

“Blanca, I swear—” Gus starts to say.

“What are you going to swear to me now? What?”

Marín takes advantage of Blanca’s moment of weakness to break free. And this, ladies and gentlemen, really is a shit show. The blow leaves Gus so dazed he doesn’t even notice the blood streaming from his nose. Loren, who was holding Gus back, lets him go to shove Marín away.

“That’s enough, for fuck’s sake! What the hell is this performance for?”

“Hypocrite your fucking mother, you sicko. You’re sick. You just keep fucking, champ. Fill your time so you never have to look inside. You’re empty,” Marín spits. “You’re an empty son of a bitch.”

"Blanca," Gus splutters, letting himself slump back on the steps of the RV.

"Goodbye, Gus. Good luck," she sobs. "Good luck handling all this shit."

"I never wanted…this."

"Too bad your dick didn't get the memo."

Gus throws his head back. The blood from his nose is dripping onto his shirt. The sight would be funny if it weren't the end of who we were and who we could've been.

I yank Marín out of there. Blanca collapses into a heap of bitter tears. I hear her wailing that she fucked her whole life up for nothing, that she feels dirty.

"You used me," she cries. "You used me to make yourself feel good. You made me feel like I was special."

Gus doesn't even lift his head. Loren tells him he should leave.

"Get out of here!" Marín screams. "Get out of here already. Nobody wants you here! Fucking soulless brat! That's all you are! You're going to die alone!"

I tug on him hard again and manage to pull him in the opposite direction. I look back. Wreckage. Wreckage. Nothing else.

~

I'm sitting at the end of the bed, staring into nothing, waiting for Marín to get out of the shower. It gave me time to pack up all of Gus's stuff I could find, shove it into his bag, and send him a curt message telling him I'll leave it at reception.

COCO:

Find another way to get back to Madrid. You're definitely not going in Marín's car.

He answers me almost immediately:

GUS:

I need to talk to him, Coco. Let me talk to him for one minute.

My reply leaves no room for doubt:

COCO:

It's over, Gus. Some paths don't have a way back. I'll miss the person you are deep down, but you work too hard to hide it. Don't call. Don't write. Disappear from our lives, please.

If I ever got a message like that, it would kill me. That's why I hesitated before I sent it. But it is what it is.

When Marín comes back into the room, he still seems devastated. Apparently it wasn't a good idea to leave him alone in there, thinking about everything, but I needed a few minutes to get my head straight about what the most worrying part of all this is.

"Better?" I ask him.

"No."

He answers dryly, not even looking at me. He's looking at his right fist, which is swollen and turning purple.

"Marín, it's not a good idea to spiral about it. He's gone and he won't come back. Neither of them will."

"I can't believe it." He sits down wearing only his jeans, barefoot and with wet hair. "I can't believe it. With Gus..."

"There's no point thinking about it. We don't even know when it happened. It's water under the bridge."

He doesn't answer. He's staring hard at a fixed point, stroking his hair, miles away.

"Should I leave you alone?"

He looks at me, slowly returning to me, with his tongue on his molars. "Now what's that about?"

"I don't know. I feel like I'm annoying you."

"This is not the time, Coco." He rubs his eyes.

"Can I ask you something?"

"Well, it depends what that something is, to be honest."

"What is it that's bothering you? That Aroa cheated on you or all the lies that—"

"Drop it, Coco. It's too complicated."

I chew on my doubts and swallow them. If we keep going in that direction, we'll end up fighting, and I don't want to give Aroa that pleasure. "I'm going to leave, okay? I want… I want to talk to Blanca, and we have to pack everything up so we can leave."

"Okay." He nods.

I go over and touch his hair. He's still not looking at me. "We'll talk soon."

Marín lifts his head. "Yeah." He nods. "There's a lot to talk about."

"I'll see you at home?"

"Yes." When my hand lands on his shoulder, he rests his hand on it. "Sorry, it's just this is all so…"

"I know."

"You know?"

I have his expression stuck in my head when I get back to the campsite. All I know is that our goodbye kiss meant less than nothing. Marín wasn't there.

~~~
~~~

Blanca's not crying—she's howling. And the sound of her pain claws and gnashes its way into your chest. The closer I get, the heavier the air feels. All the lies we've told carry weight, and the one Aroa shared is still slithering along the gravel. I want to get out of here, soon and far. I want to go back to my house, where I never imagined Marín could…

Loren doesn't know what to say. He's just sitting next to her, inside the RV while she sobs. When I go in, Loren's look could be translated into a "hallelujah" in any language in the world.

"Coco…please."

"Okay…let me try."

When Blanca sees me, she clings to me. And she clings to me so desperately that it scares me. She curls up in the fetal position on my lap as soon as I sit down next to her. She blubbers "I'm sorry" so many times that the words stop having any meaning. I stroke her hair.

"Leave the apologies for later, Blanca. Right now I need you to tell me everything."

~

Blanca and Gus bumped into each other on the metro one day. They'd both had a shitty day. She was coming out of court frustrated and pissed off at the world and justice, which are not always… Well, they're not always just. He was bored. He was on the walk of shame from a girl's house where he had spent the night and the whole day too. And that might sound fun if it weren't for the fact that, even though hooking up with her was a win for him, he was bored. Everything was just repeating endlessly. Meaninglessly.

They didn't share their miseries with each other because they weren't that close…yet. He proposed getting off at Tribunal or Bilbao, grabbing a glass of wine in Malasaña, and toasting to routine. And she agreed, but it wasn't a glass, it was a bottle. And it ended up being fun. It had been a long time since they'd laughed that hard or felt so comfortable, and so they thought that sometimes the people you're destined to click with are disguised by indifference at first.

A few days later, he sent her a message. Something stupid, making fun of an ad. She responded politely. They started talking. "What are you doing?" "Here, working, bored." They started chatting as soon as they woke up. That was it. It was all very…natural, inoffensive.

Maybe I do actually like this guy. He's not so bad, Blanca thought.

A plan to see an exhibition. Nothing out of this world. But behind everyone's back because "they won't understand why we're going alone." Light flirtation. A slightly overheated conversation when they were drinking wine after.

"Sometimes I miss the passion of the beginning," she said.

"That's why I never go past it."

"Well, I'm jealous. You're saving yourself from a ton of bullshit."

"And a ton of good stuff."

"But you get to keep the best."

"You think?" Gus looked at her mouth. "If you think that, why don't you do something to fix it? Plenty of dudes would cut off their left nut to have an affair with a woman like you."

She didn't want to even consider it. Not the conversation or the lingering looks or the goodbye hug. They had drunk some wine. They felt alone. It was easy to picture it.

That was followed by a WhatsApp chat that Blanca could only describe as weird… Very intimate, kind of hot, right on the line between friendship and something dirty.

"We weren't talking about us," she says to me, wiping her tears. "We weren't talking about us yet. We were just…sharing our experiences. Even though it was bad. It was already bad. It was from the very beginning."

Gus went to see her at work one day. He told her he thought she should come out for lunch. "You spend too much time here." What a coincidence. It just so happened to be a day when Ruben wasn't there.

There was more flirting, more steamy looks... Fuck, they were steamy. Before she knew it, Blanca was up at dawn answering a message where he asked if her guy made her feel "full." An ambiguous question that led to the question "From one to ten...how much do you want to touch yourself with me, Blanca?" And at that point, it was already ten.

It stayed confined to the phone for the first few weeks. She knew it was just a crazy blip that she'd end up forgetting if it never went further than that, and she kept telling herself the only reason Gus was interested in her was that she was about to get married. "I'm a challenge." And he... What was he? A thrill.

But they saw each other. Any excuse was good enough. And the first kiss was brutal, all tongue, pulling hair, nibbling, and moans. On their first kiss, they nearly fucked.

"I know it was bad. To Ruben, to you because it didn't make sense, but...I felt alive... More alive than ever. I convinced myself that it would just be a fling that wouldn't hurt anyone because...because no one would ever know."

But when he made her come for the first time, with her back pressed against the bathroom door in that bar, one random Friday night when she said she was working late in the office, she let her guard down. And Gus got in.

When Blanca got into Gus's head and made everything even more complicated is something no one knows because if you know him even a little you'll know he'd never tell the truth.

"I think it was the first time we slept together," Blanca cries. "I felt bad, but I felt so good... I held him. I held him, kissed his chest, stroked his hair, and asked him if he thought I was a bad person. He looked me in the eyes and said no. And then he never looked at me the same way after that."

And then the poems started. They were no longer just voice notes with a few hot lines or songs that seemed to make it clear that his nature was sordid and volatile. Now they seemed…confused. The first poem she considered dangerous made her try to take a step back.

"I told him we should stop seeing each other. And I'll be honest, Coco. I decided that for my own good, so I wouldn't get in too deep. I wasn't thinking about him. Or you."

And that started the least beautiful part, of course. The part that wasn't exciting, just frustrating, toxic, manipulative, and malevolent: exactly what I think hooked them even more. Let's face it. The worst parts of ourselves are the hardest to rip out. When another person gets involved… there's nothing more addictive or more painful.

~

They still had a couple of months ahead of them, each playing their role in a competition to get away from each other, to make it clear how little they cared about each other, and to pretend those months hadn't brought them closer. In spite of everything they shared that had nothing to do with sex. And when they tried to stop, the pull was too strong and their thing was no longer anything but toxic.

"He doesn't love me," she swears, "but he doesn't want me out of his life. He wants me to get married, but he hates that I'm going to do it. He's with everyone besides me, but really he wasn't with anyone more than he was with me. I don't know…Coco. I don't know. This got out of hand a long time ago and…"

"Do you love him?" I ask her.

As an answer, a handful of sobs that are much more vehement than a declaration of love. You don't cry like that about someone who isn't so deep in your life it's tangled around your own guts. You don't cry like this for someone who hasn't gotten under your skin. You don't cry like that for someone you want to break up with.

"I'm so sorry, Coco. I never wanted to betray you. I don't know how I got involved in this. It had been so long since I had...lived...like this."

"We'll talk later about how I feel about all of this. It's not about me when I say that...it has to end."

"I know."

"But for real. It can't happen in any way. Not as a friend or a colleague or...anything. Gus has to get out of our lives because he doesn't know how not to hurt us."

"Was it me?" she asks me. "Am I the one who made him lose all his friends?"

"No. It was him."

~

Loren has packed up the patio. I help him with the rest in silence and leave Blanca in peace to clean the inside of the RV. I want to get out of here, and at the same time, I want this week to start again and to stay locked in a time-space loop before any of this happened. Before all the consequences of his actions hit Gus, before Aroa prioritized her obsession over us, before I found out what I found out about the side of Marín that I don't know...

As we pull out, Blanca's fidgeting with a fistful of little pebbles and shells. I realize they're the ones Gus gave her in Villaricos. Now I understand that smile that passed between them, and in my stomach I feel a pang of the warmth they must have felt, the moment of connection, the relief of feeling the weight of what they've been dragging disappear for a second, and I feel rage. I don't know if it's for her, for Marín, for Aroa, or for me. I don't even know how to feel, but at least I finally understand what lies can do for us: nothing good.

Marín and I are miles further apart than we were when this trip started in spite of what happened yesterday. Loren is fed up, and he doesn't need to say it out loud for me to know that all he wants to do is get out of this RV and get us out of his sight for a few days. Aroa is alone, like Gus. The difference between them is that she's leaving behind an insane obsession and he's leaving someone who could fill all those empty spaces he thinks he has inside him…if he wanted. And Blanca…what will she do?

"Are you okay?" I ask Blanca.

"Yeah. I will be."

I'm surprised to see her open the window of the RV and then let the wind mess up her hair with her eyes closed, smile at me timidly, and, with her cheeks still wet, throw, one by one, each of the pebbles and shells, which disappear on the highway behind us.

Yes. She will be.

37

IT'S OVER

coco

We drop Blanca as close as we can to her house, but instead of leaving right away, we sit there dazed, watching her walk off. I have a hollow feeling in my chest. As much as I'd like to suggest she come to my house instead of hers, that would just stretch out the waiting and the problem would follow her wherever she goes. Plus, I need to be alone…alone but with Marín. And I'm a little hurt by Blanca. It's impossible not to dwell on the fact that she did everything she did with Gus believing I was still in love with him. Falling in love with someone is one thing; embarking on a sordid sexual affair that gets out of hand is another.

The miles of silence were hard. Loren and I still exchanged a few words, but Blanca didn't say a single one. I saw her cry a bunch of times, silently, but after she explained her thing with Gus to me, I felt distant from her.

"It kills me seeing her like this," I say in a half voice.

"Me too. But she has to go through it. This wound will heal. It will now."

"How could she not tell me?"

"How could you not tell anyone about how you felt about Marín?"

"I told you." I smile at him timidly.

"That's too bad."

We laugh half-heartedly.

"You don't know how sorry I am."

"You're a cunt." He sighs. "But you're my cunt."

"We ruined your trip."

"Well, a little, but…I don't know how to explain this without sounding like a bad guy. It's just that…I feel kinda liberated. I was carrying so much information, and being with my friends had started feeling like strolling through a minefield."

"Did you know about Aroa and Gus?"

"No." He shakes his head. "If I had, I wouldn't have been able to keep quiet. I knew about Blanca because I caught them sucking each other's faces. It was really gross… I couldn't believe she would be that stupid… with the what, the how, and the who."

"And did you know about Marín?"

"He told me before he told Aroa. He said he wanted to consider his sister moving in with you two, but there was a space issue and he didn't want you to feel like he was kicking you out. I gave him my opinion that the problem was going to be Aroa, not you. He never mentioned it to me again and I swear, until she brought it up, I hadn't even thought about it."

"I still can't believe the thing about Aroa," I mutter. "She fucked up the whole group."

"Not really. We were already fucked, Coco. Just because you can't see the rotten part doesn't mean it's not there."

"But she was so…awful."

"I'm not going to justify her, Coco, but…trapped animals bare their teeth."

"You said it, not me—animals."

"What I don't get is how you never noticed how much she despised you." He smiles.

"Did Marín really say all that stuff about me? What Aroa said, is that true? I mean…is it…"

"Most of it was just exaggerations. There's nothing worse than a half-truth. Talk to Marín. Calmly. And don't rush it."

Loren starts up the engine, but instead of pulling out onto the road that would take us to the Camping K2 parking lot where we have to return the RV, he turns onto Plaza España.

"Where are you going?" I ask with a furrowed brow.

"She needed to walk a bit and think before she gets home. You need to get home as soon as possible and talk to Marín."

"Why as soon as possible?"

"You know Marín. He's going to put a little space between you, but remind him before he leaves why he got into this whole mess in the first place and why it's worth it."

I don't understand how, after the trip we just took him on, Loren can still have any wisdom left to share.

As soon as we get there, we heave my luggage out and execute a goodbye of few words. I hug him, and he groans as he hugs me back. He doesn't like cuddles, but he knows when we need his.

"Thanks," I say. "Even though you're a fucking double agent who knew everything."

"You have no idea how much it must've pissed Aroa off that you didn't give me shit about that."

"Give you shit? I feel bad for you."

We let go, and I take a few steps back. Loren promises he'll call me soon, but he needs a few days to decompress with Damian, and I get it. What he needs, and he doesn't want to say it because he thinks it'll hurt me, is a detox. We've gotten on his nerves, and he needs a vacation from this vacation. So the only thing left for me to do is promise that I'll wait for him to text or call me. I won't harass him.

"Call me if you need me," he says through the open window. "But, please…only if you really need me," he jokes. "Like: 'Loren, one thing, come bail me out of jail' or something like that."

"You betcha, jerk."

I turn my back to the RV with a smile that vanishes as soon as I move away. In spite of everything, I would do the whole trip over again. I feel… nostalgic.

~

When I get home, I'm drenched in sweat, and it's seven in the fucking evening. I'm tempted to dump my suitcase in the stairwell and sprint up the stairs, but I wait patiently for the little old lady who lives on the third floor to limp through the door. She's carrying a box of cookies, and it's so cute I want to die.

"Where are you going without your cane, Mrs. Maria?" I scold her.

"Gorgeous, don't tell my kids. I just can't get along with that cane."

"Let's hope you don't stumble."

"It was just a quick walk! All I wanted to do was buy some cookies." She smiles at me. "Hey, where are you two going up and down with so much stuff?"

"What do you mean?"

She points at my suitcase when I offer her my arm so she can lean on me on the way to the elevator.

"I'm just getting back from a trip," I clarify. "I went with my girlfriends."

My throat tastes bitter as I say it.

"Ah! I saw Marín come down carrying so many bags…"

"Come down? Don't you mean 'go up?'"

"No, no. We came down in the elevator together. He was in a hurry, he said. You've all given him such a strange name. What's his real name? He's so handsome, it must be something gallant. Rodolfo, for example. That's such a beautiful name, Rodolfo, like Valentino."

I don't want to believe her (not just about the Rodolfo part). I tell myself a hundred times that she must be confused, but inside our house the dwindling evening twilight greets me with a deathly silence. I call his name out loud, but nobody answers. Nobody's here. Only the empty carcass of what we were; after everything we went through these past few days, I don't know how to feel in here anymore.

I put my stuff in my room and look around the living room, the kitchen, his room, and even the bathroom in search of at least a note that explains why he left, without talking to me, in such a hurry. Nothing. Finally, I look at my phone, and there it is. I would have preferred a note, I'll admit it:

MARÍN:

If I'm not home right now, it's not because of you, it's because I feel a little overwhelmed and I need to see Gema. I'm not running to you this time, to your embrace, because...there are things that you can't heal for me anymore. We flipped the coin and on this side it doesn't really fit for me to take refuge in you. I love you, Coco, but I need to figure myself out. It's only a few days. We'll talk, okay?

Yes. I would've preferred a note. Holding a piece of paper before I read it twelve times and saved it under my pillow is more romantic than doing that with a fucking WhatsApp. I want to reply that this deserved at least a phone call, but I decide I'll write back tomorrow. And that today I'll die. At least for a little while.

The melodramatic soap opera playing in my head is quickly replaced by a very real heaviness in my chest. Once I've unpacked my suitcase, started a load of laundry, and put my stuff back where it belongs, I sit on the couch, and…I'm alone. But really alone. Marín's not here, and no matter how poetic his message was, he's not here because he ran away from me, from us, from what happened this morning…

I can't call Loren. I can't call Blanca. I can't call Gus. I can't call Aroa. Some of them need space, some time, and others will never come back. I've never felt so alone. Marín, this is not it.

I grab my phone out of habit, like we all do so many times a day: picking it up, unlocking it, and strolling through our social media like we're walking gloomily through a rainstorm. I forbid myself from posting anything bleak and depressing, but I quickly discover that someone hasn't followed the same rules today.

Gus's post smacks me in the forehead like a ball sack. Normally his photos don't actually say much for themselves; his followers know to go straight to the text, which is always the heart of the matter. I always told him he needed to be more present in his profile, but he justified it by saying he wasn't selling his face.

But today, the image accompanying the text says almost as much as or more than the poem, but only a few of us would know how to interpret it. It's the palm of his open hand, in black and white, holding a few pebbles and shells.

There are songs,
little one,
that crack open the chrysalis of who we were,
make us discover the desolate landscape
of what we didn't manage to be.
Here nobody has taken flight,
here we're all still caterpillars;

all that's left of the butterflies
is the bad joke of feeling them in the first place.

There are songs,
little one,
that are a hymn to falling out of love,
yours and mine,
which don't make any sense
if they're not being whispered into your ear
when we've lost.
Whispers of the beauty we knew how to make
for a minute
or two.
What a fuck up,
little one.
What a fuck up losing you so much and for forever.

There are songs,
little one,
detestable
chants of weeping and agony,
toxic lyrics we hide in
so I don't spit in your face,
with a love you don't deserve,
for not slapping me
with everything I lost.
Too bad,
a minute of silence
for those songs I adored

and now I can't stand,
because they'll always sound like you.

There are songs,
little one,
there are memories,
there are guts
and balls;
there's fear
and rejection.
There are stories
and ours,
because we never wove it.
We didn't weave
one line or another.
Or your name with mine.

Block me,
Little one.
I need to mourn you
and you shouldn't be forced to read it.

Any other time I would have scrolled on to the next post, but not this time. This time I'm carrying a heavy load on my shoulders, and I know that sincerity, truth, is not always valid in any format despite what I've learned about lies. Because if you want it, say it; if you're fed up, don't drag it out; and if you lie, do it so as not to cause pain. This post seems vulgar to me, dirty, an ill-timed confession disguised as something else—who knows what. This post is a justification to make himself feel better and try to hook Blanca into trawling the lines for something about her. And no, she doesn't deserve that.

For the first time in a long time, I write a comment under one of his posts, saying:

> If you want to cry for her and she shouldn't be forced to read it, do it in private, you fucking clown.

I regret it immediately. Of course. I'm not good at maintaining these bursts of dignity with my head held high. I'm not good at it, and on top of that, everything stings a lot today. The sound of the empty house, the corners full of color, the titles of the books Marín and I read together, and even the fucking cactus that we don't know how the hell is still alive. And when I start crying, I don't even know if it's because I feel disappointed or because I dreamed too much. You have to dream big and beautifully, my mother says, but not too much, so when reality arrives you don't lose hope and decide to just bury your head in your dreams. I've never agreed with her more, but maybe if I hadn't dreamed so much, I would understand Marín more and Gus, Blanca, and even Aroa. I don't even understand myself.

And this house… This house smells like always: The ancient parquet is still shining proudly since we re-sanded it; the paintings are still in the same place, and the same music would still be playing if I turned on the record player because Marín is obsessed with leaving a record ready. But…it's not the same house. It isn't. Maybe because we finally loved each other outside its four walls, maybe because it wasn't the scene of our first steps…but it could be for our last.

When I go back to Instagram to delete my comment, Gus has already liked it and responded "touché" and sent me a DM with one single word: "Sorry." All I can do is block and unfollow. That's the only thing I have courage for today. The only thing.

38

WEDNESDAY

COCO

Marín hasn't come back. He sent me a message yesterday. He said he and his sister had decided to borrow his grandfather's car and go on a getaway. He didn't tell me where or for how long. Apparently, when we flipped our relationship upside down, that became information I can no longer handle. Is he scared I'm gonna go hunt him down?

I wrote back as briefly as possible. Ever since Monday when I responded to his awkward goodbye message, I haven't heard from him, so, of course, I was disappointed and frustrated. I still am, but everything is so jumbled that sometimes I'm angry, the next minute I'm sad, and a few hours later I'm telling myself it's not worth the pain and that I'm worth more than this…only to then go back to the deep wallowing phase and hate every second since the group's whole flimsy equilibrium went down the drain. As a consequence of all that, he received a reply that was pretty sterile for us:

COCO:

Have fun. Give Gema a big hug for me and drive safe.

I deleted "you asshole piece of shit" at the end of the message before I sent it. Well…and "I love you." I deleted that too. If Aroa was right that

Marín thought I was pathetic about Gus, I have no desire to cross any lines. And for the record, I'm the last one who wants to feel pathetic. At this point, I'm starting to wonder if what anyone else thinks really matters.

I mean, it sucks that he disappeared, and it also sucks that I love him, but he's going to have to come back for me to say that to him. I'm clear about that at least.

It's Wednesday, and I'm bored. I spent Monday doing a deep clean, but it reminded me too much of him. We always did this stuff together: We'd wrap bandannas around our heads, take a photo for Insta announcing that we were tackling the house, put on a record, and clean. It wasn't a good idea. I ended up flipping through our old photos and thinking about the moment he said, "I love you" and I was all cocky responding, "Yeah, I already knew that."

Yesterday, Tuesday, I decided to go out for a walk, but strolling around Malasaña in August is hell, so I ended up grabbing a drink in one of my favorite bars. It was pretty disappointing. I don't know if it's because I went much earlier than usual or because I went alone, but the place seemed like a boring little dump. Just a dive bar with dirty walls, red lights, and mismatched tables where they serve bad wine and sometimes play decent music. I went home with my hands in my pockets and nothing good to say about myself.

Blanca disappointed me. I disappointed Aroa. Aroa let me down even more. Gus broke Blanca's heart. Loren has had it up to here with our problems. Marín fled. I'm left alone. He went to think. Did he go to think about how to tell me that he actually confused friendship for something more? Maybe it was all a mistake. He seemed really (too) hurt by finding out that Aroa cheated on him with Gus. When was he planning to tell me about wanting his sister to move in? Why was he so dry and curt when we said goodbye?

It's Wednesday. I'm bored, on vacation, and alone. These are the conditions that lead me to make the insane decision to take refuge at my parents' house.

~

Flor, who's helped out in the house for years, opens the door. "Helps out" is a euphemism in this case. Without that woman, my parents wouldn't even be able to find their underwear. Before Flor, a neighbor worked there, Doña Loles, who took care of me when I was little and who I love like she's my granny. I should actually say I love Doña Loles more than I love my real grandmother, who's a musty old snob who sleeps in formaldehyde.

Flor is always cooking something delicious, so I'm very happy when I see she hasn't gone on vacation, although I feel bad my family is being exploitative.

"Don't they give you vacation around here?"

"Hush, hush, I made them a deal. I wanted to go to on a cruise with my sisters in September because it's cheaper then."

"Oh, cool."

"I'm making ratatouille empanadas."

Look, now I have something good to say about myself: You're going to stuff yourself with homemade empanadas.

Mama's in her studio. She was an art professor at a private school for many years, and now that she's retired, she spends most of her time staining canvases as she experiments with avant-garde art. When I open the door to her studio, she's holding a paintbrush in her elegant hand, and I'm holding my third empanada. My brothers are probably right: I'm adopted.

"Coquito!" she greets me with a smile. "What are you eating?"

"Empanadas. Flor is cooking."

"If it weren't for Flor, we'd eat grilled chicken breast every night."

"And omelets." I smile.

"What are you doing here?"

"I got bored."

"Do you want a drink?"

Mama always offers you a drink. Well, not always. You have to fulfill a few prerequisites: You have to be older than sixteen, the age she thinks that even if you're not an adult yet, you should be; you must not have to drive in the next twenty-four hours, and you must be on her good side. Normally I always say no. Marín and I have joked for years now about what would happen if I said yes. Maybe that day has come.

"I'd love a glass of wine."

My mother drops her paintbrush and looks at me. "Go to the kitchen. I'm going to wash my hands."

She appears with a cigarette between her teeth and then she puts it between her lips and sits with me at the island in her immense kitchen.

"The drink, Mama," I remind her.

"Wait, I'm going to gauge the scale of the problem before I decide what kind of alcohol we need. What's going on?"

"Nothing's going on."

"If nothing's going on, I'll give you a sparkling water." She raises one eyebrow. "If you're sick, I'll make you a hot chocolate. If you're mad at a friend, we'll open a bottle of white wine. If it's a boy thing, I'll get out the cocktail shaker." She winks. "But if something happened with Marín, I think your father has some twenty-five-year-old scotch around here somewhere."

"Well, then I'd say I need an open bar..."

My mother is not my best friend, but I've always felt very free to talk to her. She gives good advice, she's never judged me, and she's always clear about what the problem is. When Gus and I broke up, she shrugged and said he looked like a guy who had "a lot of sex and not much affection," and I could only answer with a grimace. I'm not going to tell her about Marín and me breaking the bed in the Marazul hotel or the thing in the shower—not even the part about the bunk. What the hell do I want to tell her?

"The group is fucked," I say when she passes me a martini with an olive.

"You're exaggerating. It's not your fault. You got it from me."

"No, Mama, really. It's fucked. We were all keeping a bunch of secrets that blew up in our faces."

She takes a sip of her martini with a furrowed brow and gestures for me to keep going as she takes a drag of her cigarette, but I don't know what to say.

"What was yours?" she interrogates me.

"You already know all about it." I hazard a guess.

"Marín is the leader of a cult, and you've converted to his religion."

"If you swap leader of a cult for a fucking perfect dude and converting to his religion to being head over heels in love with him, then I guess we're on the same page."

"What about everyone else's?"

"Aroa and Marín broke up because she made him choose between her and me and he didn't want to. Marín didn't tell me that he wanted his sister to move into the apartment next year. Gus and Blanca have been having an affair. An affair, Mama! And on top of that, Gus slept with Aroa when she was still with Marín and he was fooling around with Blanca."

"And Loren knew all of it and the little scoundrel kept it all quiet."

"Yeah, but who could blame him? I would have done the same thing."

"You would have requested a transfer to Helsinki," she quips.

"Mama... I was living the dream, but now everything is terrible."

"Your generation is the best. Nobody understands any of you." She puts her glass down on the bar and looks at me. "If you came here looking for advice, you're going to have to explain a little more of the story."

I take a deep breath and start from the beginning. Mama laughs and tells me she misses being my age, that she envies how intensely we experience everything. "But keep going, keep going…"

Mama chews on her olive nervously as I tell her that I ran after Marín, our argument, how tough he was with me, and the kiss. "It was such a shitty night, Mami. I'm an idiot." And the morning, Blanca fainting, Gus scared to death and those looks they gave each other, and Marín and me, making peace.

"Just peace?" She raises one eyebrow. "Ay, Coco, God, please tell me you're being careful."

I skip telling her I wasn't careful with Marín, that I just took it for granted that I was safe. I just keep going with my story and how I ended up all alone. "I feel like I have no friends left."

My mother downs the last sip from her glass and sighs. "The Blanca thing will pass, and Loren's emotional indigestion will only last a few days. As far as Aroa… Coco, that girl is not right in the head."

"I know."

"And Gus… Gus makes me a little sad. I get the feeling that he needs to examine his conscience, but he's avoiding it because the day he does, the self-mythology he's built up using sex will crumble. Sex and…I don't know what. Misunderstood self-love. Ay, Coco, you were careful with him, right?"

"Mama!" I groan.

"Okay, okay." She holds her hands up and then lets them fall onto the counter.

I hear the annoying ticktock of my father's clock, which he winds religiously. I see my mother's shiny manicure, always perfect despite spending the morning dabbling in paints and thinners. My mouth tastes like martini and olives. The air-conditioning feels cool on my skin. Everything around me is lovely, but I'm being devoured by the absence that worries me most of all—that Aroa made her decisions, Gus won't come back,

Blanca and I will find our way, and Loren just needs space for a few days. But…what about Marín?

"What about Marín, Mama?"

She sighs. "My heart is split right now, and I don't know which advice to give, the mother's or the woman's."

"Can't you combine them?"

"I don't think so."

"Well, then give me both."

"I should know which to give you, Coco." She seems disappointed in herself. "But if you're ever a mother one day, you might feel, like I do, that the important thing in your life is that you make all your decisions with conviction. If you make a mistake, that's part of your path, but it's nobody else's fault. But I wish I could tell you what the correct option is."

"Mama, please…"

She shrugs and sighs again. "As your mother, I would tell you that life is too short to chase after cowards who don't value what it means to love and be loved. If he's scared, he should buckle up and get on with it because nothing worth it in this life comes for free."

"And as a woman?"

"As a woman, I would tell you to…try to put yourself in his shoes. If this works out, he'll be your companion for life, and you'll have to make an effort to understand him more than once, like he will for you. So do an exercise of empathy and…give him the time you would ask him to give you. Do what you would want him to do if the tables were turned. If that still doesn't work…Coco, my darling, there's no shame in retiring from a war when, battle after battle, you always tie. One emotion will always win out over the other. Balancing on the fine line between them is not living. Sometimes peace simply means throwing in the towel. It hurts, but you get over it."

I'm not gonna lie. Neither of those options sounds very good to me.

~~

I listen to my mother's womanly advice because it scares me less than the motherly advice. Once my father told me that if I can't decide between two paths, I should always choose the one that scares me the most because it will definitely be the one that will make me grow, but I think sometimes that doesn't apply to feelings. So I gird my loins, and when I get home, I put on a record that Marín is obsessed with, and I think. I draw a timeline between his needs and mine, and I do it with my heart open to both, putting my empathy for him over my ego. Then I pick up my phone and write:

COCO:

I know you need time and space to accept what happened between us. I know it changed what we were and the life we had, but at least for me, the excitement at discovering what's waiting for us outweighs the fear. If that's not true for you, don't wait until the end of August to tell me. We'll both need to start again.

When I press send, I feel like I've started some kind of inexorable countdown that won't stop until it reaches zero. The question is, what will the outcome be?

39

I'M LOSING HER

MARÍN

I don't know what to write back. I stare at my phone screen wondering if I even should have opened the message, but how can I not? It's Coco. It's Coco, fuck.

"What's going on with you?" Gema asks me, holding a piece of greasy pizza.

"I'm feeding you terribly," I say.

"Yeah, but that's not it. What's up with you? You looked at your phone, and then you made a face like you got your balls stuck in your zipper."

I smile and hold my phone without answering. "Nothing's up with me. Come on, keep telling me about how you want to study in Japan."

"Don't change the subject. Who texted you? Please tell me it wasn't Aroa."

"It wasn't Aroa."

"Aroa's, like, a little fucking unbalanced. We women can see it. We look at her face, and we can tell, big bro. And from woman to dumbass, I'm telling you, that girl is unhinged."

"You're a woman?" I waggle my eyebrows.

"Of course. Unhinged. But since she's blond, thin, and..."

"Hey, hey, hey," I stop her. "You're calling me superficial."

"Oh, no, you totally fell in love with her because of the speech she gave about gender equality at the UN."

"Where did you come from, you little freak?" I tease, throwing a napkin at her.

"Are you getting back together with Aroa? I don't like it, bro. I'm being honest. She looks at you like you're hers and no one else's."

"My relationship with Aroa is...not just dead, whatever's worse than that."

"Eviscerated and mummified."

"Yeah, that," I nod and pick up my slice of pizza. "But I have to admit I'm a little worried about what they're teaching you in school these days."

"So?"

"So what?" I chew slowly.

"Who texted you?"

"The bank. It was an overdraft alert," I lie easily.

"Hey, are you mad at Coco?"

"Me? What makes you say that?"

"I don't know." Her shrug makes her look like the little girl she is, as much as she talks like an old lady. "It seems weird you haven't called her."

"We've WhatsApped. I don't have to update you on every conversation I have with Coco. You know that, right?"

"Did something happen?"

I put my piece of pizza down on the plate and wipe my hands. "Listen, Gema...would you like to live with me?"

I know I shouldn't bring it up yet, that there's still a year before I could move her into my house and that my aunt thinks it would be better not to tell her anything before it's a done deal, but I need to distract her from the Coco conversation. I need to solve this, and...in a way I need her to help me do it.

"With you?" Her eyebrows knit into an expression somewhere

between yearning and fear. And I see myself there, in her, in her face, but the difference between Gema and me is that nobody offered and I sat there wishing until I was old enough to live alone.

"With me, yes." I take another bite of pizza, trying to sound relaxed.

"At your house?"

"Of course. You would have to move schools. But we could be together every day."

She looks at me, and I know she wants to. I know she feels like crying and she's not answering because she doesn't want a tear to slip out and make her all vulnerable. I know because the only reason I'm not breaking the silence is that I feel the same way. We stare at each other and swallow. When she finally talks, her answer is the last thing I expected to hear.

"What about Coco? All three of us can't fit in your apartment. It's only a two-bedroom."

"We could turn the living room into a bedroom," I say. "It would be huge, and it could be yours if you want it."

"What does she think about it?"

"Why is what Coco thinks so important?"

A garbled stream of sounds spills from her mouth before she stifles a whimper that makes my insides clench. I hurry to wipe my hands on a napkin because I know that what comes after that sound…is sobbing. She's my little sister, but I feel like her father. I know when she's going to cry.

"But, Gema…" There's a hint of scolding in my voice, and I really wish there weren't, but I can't help it. "Why are you crying now?"

She doesn't answer, just sobs and covers her face.

"Monster," I say, moving into the seat next to her. I'm glad this pizzeria is half-empty so she doesn't feel embarrassed. Teenage crying is common and weird, just like your own body, which is changing every day. "Why are you crying? Tell me. You don't want to come live with me? Is it about changing schools? If you don't want to leave your friends, I get it. I really do."

"You're an idiot!" She pulls away from me. "It's not about that."

"So?"

"It's Coco." She cries disconsolately.

"You don't want to live with Coco?" I'm super confused.

"It's you… Something happened to you. With her. And I don't want you to fight with Coco. Seriously. Not with her."

I hug her and swallow. Not with her. It's so true. Gema digs her elbow into my ribs, but I don't move away.

"Okay. Stop crying for a sec. Let's talk about this."

"No, because you're gonna treat me like a baby, and I understand stuff now, and I know you're hiding something from me…"

"Gema, crying isn't bad, but I'm not going to put up with tantrums," I say solemnly. "If you can express your emotions without exploding, I'll treat you like an adult and I'll tell you."

She wipes her tears and snot on my shirt, and…well, I deserve it. Then she looks at me, as if she's waiting for me to give her an appropriate explanation. She's a pretty demanding little monster, for fuck's sake.

"Something happened, you're right." I swallow. How can I talk about this without mentioning sex? "The last few days, we crossed some lines that you can't uncross and now I'm confused."

"I don't get it."

"Some stuff is just for grown-ups and I don't know how to explain it to you, Gema. But you have nothing to worry about."

"Of course I'm worried." She pouts. "Because you're half idiot, like all dudes, fuck. And I'm not some little girl, you know?"

"We're going to have to talk about your potty mouth."

"The pot calling the kettle black."

"Gema, don't be like that. It's normal for really close relationships to be strained sometimes."

"That's not what's happening here."

"Yes, that is what's happening. Look…Coco and I love each other a lot, but…" Why do I feel like I'm trying to tell my daughter that her mother and I are splitting up?

"Don't you get it?" And I realize how nervous she is when her voice shakes and a hiccup slips out. "What happened at the bachelorette trip? Did you kiss? Did you figure out that she loves you? Fuck, bro!"

Why she burst into tears again at this point is a mystery I have no answer for and I'm afraid I'll never figure out. "Gema, it's more complicated than that."

"Okay, so you did it." She assumes. "And now you're embarrassed or what? You're thirty years old! But it's Coco. It's Coco. You shouldn't have done it if you weren't sure."

"But the thing is I was sure, Gema," I admit. "At the time, I was sure."

"So?"

"So…I don't know if you're going to understand this, monster, but I don't know if I'm good enough to be what she deserves. I don't know if I'm ready for Coco because with her it's either forever or don't even try it, and I…fuck, Gema, I have broken pieces inside me that don't really have a solution to and I'm weird and she…loves me. She loves me more than…I don't know. I don't know how to explain it."

"Bro." Gema wipes her tears and looks at me, hiccuping. "You're going to regret this so much."

"You don't really regret it when it's the lesser of two evils, right?"

"But you love her." She sobs.

"Yes," I nod. "A lot. Really a lot. So much…so much that it scares the shit out of me."

"And is that how you want me to deal with stuff I'm scared of?"

Touché. "No. But I hope you're better than me." She covers her face with her hands, but I make her look at me. "Gema, I promise I'm going to try, okay?"

"Don't do it for me," she moans.

"No, for her."

"For her? No, you idiot! For you!"

~

That "for you!" is still echoing in my head when Gema's fallen asleep and I throw myself into bed with a book in hand. I've been carrying this book around since Sunday and haven't read a single word, even though I'm flipping the pages and staring at it, pretending like I am. This book is a symbolic space, and when I go into it, I can think, I can re-create, I can imagine, I can just be. But tonight, I don't even feel like opening it. I glance over at Gema, who's sleeping in the next bed over. She's going to leave smudges on the pillowcase from the makeup she swears she's not wearing, but who really cares?

Then I look at my phone. I grab it, reread the message.

Okay, Marín. You have to respond. Hiding doesn't make the fear disappear.

I start typing, not giving myself too much time to overthink it. I just need to let it come out, whatever it is. I wish when I'm done I'd just let myself send it, without editing it, without making the message more politically correct.

I type. I delete. I type more. And more. I change a word. I add two more. I reread it:

MARÍN:

I brought you with me in my suitcase, in my fingers, between my teeth. You're everywhere, whether you believe that or not. There are things that can't be changed, even if we're not ready. There are nights that transform who we are and the life we have, that's true, but I wish we were back in that hotel right now, Coco. I wish. I didn't think so much there, I just acted. But you know I'm not like that. I'm really not like that, and what I'm thinking now scares me. I need to think.

I send it. When I reread it, after it's already sent, I'm tempted to delete it, but Coco comes online, and it's too late. I bite back the urge to close the chat and wait for her response. Imagine my surprise when…it doesn't come. She just closes WhatsApp, and her "online" disappears.

I write again, suddenly filled with panic.

MARÍN:

Coco, please don't hate me.

It's probably a rookie mistake, but I can't help it. My heart is pounding so fast when I see the classic dots indicating that she's typing, but they have never made me this nervous before.

COCO:

I don't hate you, Marín. I hope these days of reflection lead us to the same place. They are giving me time to think too, and sometimes silence speaks louder than words. Good night. Send my love to Gema.

I say good night after she's already disconnected, and I hesitate over whether I should write an "I love you" to her too because I know, because I can tell that's the end of our conversation—at least for today. I suddenly remember one of Gus's poems from a while ago, one he wrote when they broke up and it seemed like a beautiful goodbye. It was the first time I recognized Coco, *my* Coco, in any of his poems.

It said:

I'll miss your skin,
the smell I'm drenched in when you sleep over.
My sheets will be dripping in pain;
the floor of my room,
bereft not catching your panties,
will go back to being frozen.
Coffee in the mornings
won't be warmed by your voice,
and I'll have to be the one to tell myself
that sleeping all day
means dying faster.

I'll miss
your skin under my fingers
and that way of telling each other
that we can eat in bed
if you're on the menu.
The races between your legs,
the kicks to my fear,
the Saturdays at readings,
the wine-drenched weeks,
your peals of laughter,
your velvet eyelashes,

everything you are,
which now only belongs to you.

I'll miss you,
but in the end,
we both know...
We didn't love each other that much.

I don't really know why that poem popped into my head right now, but when I turn off the light and try to make out the ceiling through the thick darkness, I wonder if I'm trying to prepare myself for the goodbye. I'm not a poet, and I don't even really know if those lines Gus dedicated to her when they broke up are that good, but I do know that last stanza wouldn't apply to us.

There's no ticking noise, and this time I don't need the flashing lights to know that I'm wasting time in a countdown...and I don't know if I'll react the right way when it goes off.

I'm losing her.

40

PUTTING THINGS BACK WHERE THEY BELONG

COCO

The colorful stones calm me. Sinking my hand in the plastic bins labeled with the names and properties of each one and toying with them, so shiny, polished, vibrant. I don't care that the woman in the store is looking at me funny or whether she thinks I'm going to steal something. I just want to keep touching them…a little more.

"Can I help you?"

I give her a slightly bewildered look, but before I can answer that I'm just browsing, my phone rings.

I know it's not him. That's why I smile at the shop assistant and answer reluctantly without even checking who it is.

"Hello?"

"You remember those vacation days you forced me to take when I started pulling out my eyelashes?"

It's Blanca.

"Yeah. We went to Zarautz."

"And it snowed on us on the beach."

"Yes," I sigh. "Although, we drank so much txakoli that I doubt it was real."

"It was real. It was, and there was a lot of it."

I stay silent and turn back to the inside of the store.

"How are you?" she asks.

"Fucking shitty," I reply. "You?"

"I concur with that assessment. Listen, Coco… I know I have no right to ask you this, but…do you have plans today?"

"Is feeling like fucking shit a plan?"

"More of a backdrop, I guess."

"Well, then, I have a backdrop."

"Do you mind if we feel fucking shitty together? I don't know what stage of your disappointment in me you're in, that's why I said I have no right to ask you this, but…I'm going to do something important tonight, and I'd like to be with you today. I promise I won't spiral."

I suck my teeth. I take a deep breath. "Shit, Blanca, it's all so shitty."

"I know," she squeaks.

"Half an hour at El Café de Alejandría, okay?"

"Thank you."

"Don't thank me. You're paying for lunch, and I'm hungry."

We say goodbye grumpily, but there's laughter in our voices. I think we're both pretty over all the drama.

"Hiya," I say to the shop assistant. "Could you please help me?"

"Of course. What were you looking for?"

"The truth. Do you have any crystals for that?"

~

El Café de Alejandría is full even though it's August. It never closes; Marín always calls it "the funeral home" because it's always open to soothe the soul. Behind the bar, Sofia, the bartender with lips painted red, is smiling at Hector, and I'm not surprised. He has always been one of our platonic loves.

Blanca is sitting at one of the tables in the back, peering out the picture window. She's wearing a red-and-white-striped dress and matching sandals. She looks pretty but a little gaunt. It's only been five days since we last saw each other, but I could swear she's lost weight.

"Hector gets cuter every day," I say to break the ice when I sit down.

"Who?" she asks absentmindedly.

"Hector."

"Oh, yeah, right." She nods. "Did you order?"

"What can I get you two?" Standing next to us, Sofia smiles with a little notepad in her hand.

"Two of those iced teas you make with lime," I order. I remember that Blanca loves them. "And to eat I'll have a sandwich, Sofi, with loads of stuff."

"Like bursting with stuff?"

"Exactly."

I look at Blanca, but she doesn't want anything else. Love sometimes opens the stomach, other times it closes it, and sometimes it even stabs it.

When Sofia goes back behind the bar, Blanca looks at me and asks about Marín.

"He's on a trip with his sister, avoiding me, slowly assassinating the person I thought he was and...chilling, I guess."

"He still hasn't wanted to talk about it?"

"Not about that or anything else. When I got home on Sunday, he was already gone. If that's not fleeing like a rat, you'll have to tell me what is."

"Marín always needs time and space to accept things, to make decisions."

"Yeah...you know what's happening? I've never really bought into the whole discourse that complicated love is the most romantic kind. I know not everything can work out right away, but if someone thinks loving me is a problem...I'm not into that."

"How can it be a problem, Coco, if you've loved each other for a long time?"

"Yeah, of course, but not like that. He fucked it up, Blanqui. He got overwhelmed, and I don't know if it's because of all the shit Aroa was throwing around, because we live together and he feels like getting into a relationship with me would move too fast, or because he regrets it. I don't know, but I wasn't expecting any of those options from him."

"Yeah…" Blanca smiles at me and clutches my wrist, fidgeting with a bracelet. "But he's not responsible for your expectations." I open my mouth to express my annoyance, but she hushes me and hurries to explain. "What I mean is, before you kill me, Aroa was kinda right when she said that you fell in love with an idealized version of Marín. He's human, Coco. Before you became a lover, you were his best friend."

"I hate the word 'lover.'" I squeeze the bridge of my nose.

"Well, you know what I mean. It's unforgivably spineless on his part."

"As unforgivable as…"

"Have you thought about what he would have to do to make you forgive him? What's your level of disappointment right now?"

"It goes up and down all the time, but it all depends on if he comes back, sits with me, and says what he has to say to my face. He hasn't even called me! We're only communicating through texts. Come on, dude!"

"That sounds logical, to tell the truth. Marín will come back. Of course he will. He can't just keep circling Spain forever with his sister as a copilot."

"I know that. All that really matters…is that he comes back. But the when… The when is starting to be pretty important to me. Every day that passes I'm getting further from wanting what his silence offers me."

She nods, and suddenly I feel completely and totally understood. Mama gives good advice, but Blanca, like Marín, has always been my safe space. I don't know why I didn't tell her I was in love with him sooner.

"I'm sorry I didn't tell you about Marín earlier."

"Don't say sorry for that, especially not twice. I was with your ex behind your back for ten months in a torrid, toxic, and sexual affair."

I grimace. I don't love hearing it, but I'll be honest—it doesn't really hurt. It bothers me, but it doesn't hurt; that's the best description.

"How are you?" I ask.

"I mean"—she smiles—"awful, to be honest. I can't sleep, my stomach is in knots, and ever since we got back, I can't even cry, so I have this ball of disgust and hatred in my stomach that's going to burst open and poison me."

"Sounds fun." I raise my eyebrows.

"I saw you unfollowed him," she says.

"Unfollowed and blocked."

"After the poem you commented on, right?"

"Yeah. You should do the same. It's freeing."

"I know. That's...my next challenge."

"What's he posting?"

"He's going through different phases." She sighs and looks out the window again. "One second he sounds melancholy, and in the next post his tone is raging. Then sad or fired up or vile... He's smashed all our memories into tiny pieces and turned them into things that aren't always pretty, but...I guess I should have seen that coming."

"You shouldn't read it."

"I know. And I tell myself that it's okay, that I can take things one step at a time, but the truth is its harder this way. It's a detox. If I'm serious this time, and I have to be serious, I have to stop following him. I'm waiting to get over the sad phase."

"What's the part that hurt you the most?"

"It's hard to explain." And in the pause created by Sofia bringing over our order, Blanca takes out her phone, unlocks it, opens Instagram, and searches for Gus's profile. Once it's on the screen, she turns the device and holds it out to me. "Maybe this is the best way to answer you. Go to December...in the middle. Every post is a chapter. A novella about who we were. He didn't leave anything out."

December. Surprise. Coincidence. Connection.

January. Thrilling, horny, forbidden. Poems about a woman, a real woman, who wonders what his skin tastes like. Passionate texts that get more explicit as they approach February.

February. There's a hint of farewell, followed by a touch of cockiness, a wisp of bragging, and suddenly…the promise of sex. Gus is talking, in a lot of these posts, to a woman who he promises feelings she's never felt before.

March is the month where everything changes forever. It's the first time he talks about skin… Skin as a link, skin as a portal, skin as a ticket for a journey that has to do with much more than bodies.

April gets confused again. It lurches around. He talks about a lot of women, about a life jumping from one bed to the next. He paints himself as an irresistible sleazebag and fuckboy but then talks about emptiness, disappointment.

May is devastating. Very toxic. Cuddles one day, a punch the next. He alternates between "I told you this is what it was" with "I have to accept that you're abandoning me." But every once in a while, it tastes like discovery, hope, the occasional argument, but makeup kisses too.

June and July are hard. They are for me because even though I've read all these poems before, they finally make sense now. I was missing something I needed to understand them…like a hieroglyphic I never identified that always meant Blanca. In June and July this story turns into a love story that's not beautiful or tortuous anymore—it's bad. Toxic. Unhealthy. Needy. Manipulative. Dry mouths locked in excruciating kisses. Cracked hands that hurt to caress. The rest I know.

I hand back her phone with a lump in my throat.

"I'm sorry, Blanca."

"Why?" she asks with a smile.

"Because all that love is good for nothing when it's the wrong kind of love. And I'm sorry. You don't deserve that."

"Well, we all deal with toxic love at some point in our lives. I'm lucky it's not how I love myself. At least I didn't lose respect for myself. I've learned to forgive myself, and I'm… Well, exactly that: I'm learning."

"So what are you gonna do?"

"First ask you if you think we can go back to being us and not feeling like our asses are clenched every time we hang out. I'm not hoping you'll forget it, but…"

"It will pass," I assure her. "But don't fall in love with Marín, please."

"He's adorable, but he's like my brother. He doesn't even have a penis, as far as I'm concerned."

"He does," I assure her. "And it's got way more girth than Gus's, even though right now that might seem like a lie."

Blanca picks up her iced tea and laughs.

"Seriously, what are you going to do?" I ask.

"Tonight I'm going to tell Ruben."

"Are you sure you want to tell him? You realize this might be the end?"

"Realize? That's more than understood, Coco. But I'm done with lies. We have to smash them, drag the truth out from inside, and then…shit on them. It's the only thing they're good for."

"So what are you going to do with Ruben? I mean, I thought everything was going fine and…"

"Obviously things weren't as fine as we all thought. Like I said, we have to pull the truth out of all the lies."

"Oh, speaking of truth and lies." I rummage in my bag until I find a super on-trend pink box. "I bought this for you."

"For me?" She opens the lid of the box, and the rose-quartz-and-silver ring makes a smile spread across her face. "You dumbass. I thought you were gonna get down on one knee to ask my hand."

"It's rose quartz." I point to the stone. "And the lady in the shop told me it's good for attracting balance and a loving energy."

She takes it out of the box and puts it on her finger and then stretches out her hand to look at it.

"I love it… Well, all said and done, I'm marrying myself."

"Okay. Well, let's wrap this up like it deserves. Gimme your phone for a sec."

I don't need to take the driver's seat. She's the one who opens Gus's profile on Instagram again, unfollows, and blocks. Then she blocks him on WhatsApp and deletes his number. She smiles at me after…and wipes her tears with the back of her hand.

"Don't ever let any guy make you think you need him to be happy, Coco. Choose someone to share your happiness. Guard it jealously. It's very expensive."

~

I stroll home after we talk for a few more hours. I've heard so many things about her non-relationship with Gus, and I can't stop thinking about how people are different depending on the context. With me Gus was always the poet. I never saw any other side of him. I didn't see him without his armor, to tell the truth, even though we trusted each other and we shared a few moments. Everybody chooses which face to show each person.

And I think, of course, about Marín…the Marín who was my roommate and best friend, and my only gripe was that he always forgot to turn the lights off. But there are so many people inside him: the self-sacrificing brother, the product manager square, the hurt son, the voracious lover, the understanding friend, the magnetic acquaintance, the sexy stranger who sits across from you on the subway, the good citizen, the perfect neighbor, the nightmare for the customer-service people at his cell phone company, and…the ex-boyfriend. And I have met most of them, yeah, but in passing. I have to admit that knowing the roommate and friend Marín like the back of my hand is nowhere near enough.

A lot of women might think that what I'm about to do is a bad idea, but as soon as I get home, I need to write him again. Actually, I'd kill to hear his voice, but one step at a time.

COCO:

I was with Blanca all afternoon. We're working it out. I know you're on, like, a spiritual retreat, but I thought you'd be happy to hear that.

He logs in right away, and my stomach flips like a teenager and makes me smile.

MARÍN:

Of course that makes me happy. Thanks for telling me. How's everything else going?

COCO:

Good. Chill. The house is too empty without you. I can't get used to it. It doesn't feel the same, seriously. I spend the whole day wandering around, moping.

MARÍN:

Well, it's a two-bedroom apartment. You don't have far to wander.

I don't know if he meant that as a joke, but…he sounds weird.

COCO:

You okay? You seem off.

MARÍN:

Yeah, I'm fine. I'm just about to pick up the car.

COCO:

Oh, I won't bother you then.
But...I'm going to take the chance to ask when you're coming back while I'm here.

MARÍN:

Ah, yeah. That. Um...

He's typing. He stops. Typing. Stops. Typing. Typing.

MARÍN:

I've been thinking that if I want to live with Gema next year, I have to start by spending vacations with her.

Uh-oh.

COCO:

All of them?

MARÍN:

Yeah. I was already away for a week with all of you and...I don't know.
My aunt thinks it's a good idea too.

COCO:

But...did you pack enough clothes?

MARÍN:

Yeah, don't worry.

I sit there with my phone in my hand and my eyes glued to the screen, waiting for him to add something else. Something like "Why don't you come see us for a few days?" or "I miss you." Something. But there's nothing more than a feeling of abandonment in the pit of my stomach. Another woman would say goodbye politely, pretending like she doesn't mind, but I can't. I close the chat and press the speed dial button to call him. He doesn't pick up until the third ring, even though I know he was holding his phone.

"Are you avoiding me?" I ask point-blank.

"No, Coco, I'm not avoiding you. I'm spending time with my sister."

"Yeah. Well...you're being really weird."

"I'm not being weird," he says defensively.

"Of course you are. You're being the weirdest. In a normal situation, we would've called each other every night and—"

"Well, this isn't a normal situation, Coco, and we also have to ask ourselves if what we were doing before was 'normal' as you call it."

"What makes you say that?" I ask, starting to get heated.

"I mean, because...we've been settling into certain routines, and I don't know if they really matched who we were."

"What are you trying to say, Marín? Because I'm not getting it."

He sighs. "You want the truth? I have no idea what I'm trying to say. I haven't been ballsy enough to call you, that's it."

"Well, that seems worrying to me."

"I guess it is."

"And when are you coming back?" I insist again.

"Um...the twenty-eighth or twenty-ninth."

I open my eyes wide, even though he can't see me. "It's not even the tenth yet!"

"You're always saying I never disconnect from work—it's a good opportunity."

I rub my face in silence while I think about how to respond. The battle was lost before it began because as soon as I open my mouth, something unmeditated pops out.

"It's a good opportunity to get away from the problem, to avoid talking to me, and to..."

"That's not it."

"Of course it is."

"Maybe a little, but that's not all of it," he clarifies.

"Marín, I never thought you were such a coward."

"I'm not a coward. It's just that before we have the conversation you want to have, I need to figure out what answers to give you, because right now none of them are obvious to me."

"You love me," I blurt out.

"I'm happy at least one of us is clear on that."

A slap in the face would've hurt less. "That was shitty."

"I'm sorry. There's nothing else I can say," he replies coldly.

"Wow, so this is the Marín Aroa was talking about."

"And that's a shitty thing for you to say too."

"At least tell me what's freaking you out so much," I counterattack, but all I hear is silence. "Marín...at least tell me what's freaking you out so much."

"Fuck, Coco... I don't know. I'm telling you it's not about being freaked out. It's just that...I want to get away a little, get some perspective. A week ago you were my best friend, and now that we fucked, we're considering living together and—"

"We already live together!" I yell.

"You know what I mean."

"No. I have no idea. This coward, scared Marín is a stranger to me. Sorry if I'm not used to him yet."

"I just need space to think," he says, sounding tense. "I'm not asking for that much."

"It's just that...Marín, we should be talking about this in person. You know that, right?"

"Yeah, but you can't force anyone to be ready when you want, Coco.

Everyone has their own process, and I'm scared to fuck it all up, hurt you, break you, or for this to end terribly and..."

"And so you'd rather not even try?"

"I just got out of a relationship. I just started getting to know you as a woman. It's too soon to even consider trying it. Please, Coco, you have to understand..."

"Of course." I perch on the arm of the couch and nod to myself. "But... do you understand me?"

"Of course I do."

"You make it seem like I'm trying to pressure you to take these huge steps. I just want us to talk, to figure it out! You say I can't force anyone to be ready, and you're right, but, Marín...it's just a fact that by the time that person is ready it might be too late."

"It's two weeks." And he sounds so tense it's like it's not even him. "Two weeks, Coco."

"Two weeks so you can get even weirder, so you can be colder, and so I can feel like I'm talking to a fucking Martian. You have to come back sooner."

"Okay. Now I am getting freaked out."

"Well, I'm really sorry, but I'm done having this hanging over us. We're you and me, Marín. With another guy, I wouldn't even bother, but it's you, and we can't get this so wrong. I need to know. Everything doesn't revolve around you. There's another person involved in this, and it's me."

"Okay, Coco." And he says it so condescendingly.

"I have to be honest. I don't even recognize you."

"I don't recognize you either. I thought you were the person who understood me the most in the whole world," he says. "But now I see that's only until it gets in the way of your own..."

"My own what?"

"Let's leave it there, Coco. I don't want to argue."

"No. You never want to argue. Probably better if we just hang up and wait for this shit show to magically solve itself."

"You're going too far," he declares.

"I'm going too far? I'm sharing my fears with you, Marín!"

"Respect the space I'm asking for. There's nothing else I can say," he says frostily.

"So what am I supposed to do while you think?"

"Think."

"I've already thought about it, for fuck's sake!"

"Well, just wait then, Coco. What do you want me to say?"

"I need you to come back before the twenty-ninth, Marín," I say. "I need you to have the balls to sit in front of me and tell me to my face that you're shitting yourself, that you're overwhelmed and you don't know what to do. I need it. If you love me…"

"Oh, for God's sake," he groans. "If you love me? Now we're making threats?"

"Threats? It's not a threat, but I think the cherry on top of this conversation is an ultimatum: If you're not back by the twentieth, I'll take that to mean you don't want the same thing as me."

"What does that mean? You'll ignore me when I come back? You won't even say hi? Or are you planning on acting like nothing happened? Suddenly we never fucked, we never said I love you, we never came like wild monkeys promising we'd be so happy…"

"It means that if you don't want the same thing I do, I can't keep hoping that one day you'll fall in love with me the way I deserve to be loved, so when you come back, my room will be empty and ready for Gema or whoever you want."

"Are you seriously threatening me?" he asks.

"It's not a threat. It's a promise, and I'm making it to myself, Marín. I want the person by my side to be proud of his feelings and not think loving me is a problem. I've already had enough shitty relationships. Think it over."

"Coco..."

"No, Marín. Think it over. The twentieth. If you're not here, I'm leaving. Good night. Tell Gema I love her. At least she'll know how to appreciate it."

When I hang up, I'm shaking like a leaf. I want to cry. I'm scared. I just played a huge bluff and...

My first relationship was with someone who never wanted to call it a relationship. Then I had ephemeral flings that vanished before they became anything, leaving a faint trail of shimmering, glittery hope in the air. My second relationship wasn't even that... It was just one more fling with someone who was trying to convince himself it was time to settle down a little. Gus and I were a couple because that's what we called ourselves, but...what was that relationship really about? Time and sex, I guess.

No. I don't want to feel like this anymore. I don't want to keep wondering when I'll be good enough for someone because I already am for me. So...wait, Coco, don't be so fast to freak out. No. You weren't bluffing. It was just...the voice you deserve.

I burst into tears when it becomes obvious he's not going to call back. And I cry for all the Maríns—the ones I know and the ones I haven't met yet—because it's honestly not looking good.

41

IT'S NOT GOOD FOR ME

COCO

The reflection looking back at me in the mirror is terrible. My lips are swollen; my eyes are red; my hair is tangled; my skin is gray. I'm the spitting image of a person in mourning. I spent the whole night crying.

I rub myself dry with a towel and put on the clothes I brought into the bathroom: ripped boyfriend jeans and a white T-shirt with a drawing on the back. I'm going to my parents' house for lunch. It's not even eleven yet, but given my dire mood today, I thought a visit to the bookstore near Opera would be good for me.

I'm coming out of the bedroom, with my shoes on, barely any makeup, and my bag in my hand when I hear the door close and the familiar sound of Marín jingling his keys. I turn to stone, right where I am. I can barely even blink. He's the one who takes two slow steps over to me. Serious, keys in hand, disheveled, in desperate need of a haircut, so handsome it makes me sick. I wasn't expecting him. When Marín says no, it means no. I don't know if the fact that he's here is good news or bad news for us.

He drops his keys onto the table in the entrance, which, by the way, we dumpster-dived when the kids of the widow downstairs emptied her apartment when they moved her in with them. Memories of better times, like the ones haunting every corner of this apartment.

He doesn't say anything—he just looks at me, rubs his chin and his mouth, and leans against the doorframe to the kitchen. He's wearing jeans and a white T-shirt. His eyes are glistening so much…

He puts his bag down with a sigh, and I stifle the urge to cry. This silence is much more powerful than words, but I don't know how to interpret it. The house is full of bleak energy. He takes a step. I take a step. We look at each other. I wonder for a few seconds if I want to kiss him first and then talk after or if the opposite would be better for us, but he seems to have decided already.

His right arm loops around my waist, and he pulls me to him. He closes his eyes, and I look at him… I look at his eyelids, the cover for those vibrant eyes… His straight, elegant nose, his lips. He presses his forehead into my shoulder, and I feel his chest swell as he takes a deep breath. I want to tell him so many things, but I don't understand anything. We both twist, silently searching for each other's eyes; we seem to be interrogating each other about what this means. But for now it can only be translated into a kiss.

We kiss.

It's a sweet kiss, innocent, mouth against mouth, almost childish. Kissing him still feels strange to me. It's an uncanny feeling, like when you step into a city for the first time but you've seen it a thousand times in the movies. I guess I've spent too long imagining it.

I stroke his cheeks, and he wraps his arms around me. We look at each other again and sigh, our lips still brushing. We poison ourselves with the carbon dioxide from each other's lungs, and we kiss again, this time a little more wet, nipping and tasting with timid tongues that still don't know whether this is out of place or welcome.

My back is up against the wall, and Marín presses into me. The memories of a house where we have been so happy, pushing us against each other, looking for corners that aren't full yet. We smell each other, we hug, our hands slide under each other's clothes, and suddenly we're kissing again. There's no more fear, no more barriers, and this kiss is so intense that it becomes an exercise in restraint.

"Wait..." He pulls back a little and brushes the tip of his nose across my cheeks. "I didn't come here to do this."

"I know. Let's stop."

"Okay."

But we kiss again, and we need more air. I can taste his spit, which is filling my mouth. I savor the air he's breathing. I want him to hold me tighter, and I press my thighs, my breasts, my belly button against him—I don't want any sliver of him to be untouched by my body.

"Fuck..." he pants against my open mouth.

"Stop..." I say.

He licks my lips and grabs my waist, and his hands climb up under my shirt, cupping my breasts. "Stop me, for God's sake," he begs.

But I don't have the strength when he kneads my tits and pants into my neck. Marín's hands digging their fingers into my flesh paralyze me. I've wanted him for too long.

"I didn't come here for this," he says again.

"I know."

"Let's go to my room."

"No," I say.

"Why?"

"Because I don't want breakup sex."

"Who said anything about a breakup?"

I smile in spite of myself. "You, even though you said it with your mouth closed."

"Coco...I need to say things to you, but please."

We stumble through the house devouring each other, open his bedroom door, and rush past his desk, next to the bed, full of music equipment, framed vinyl covers, and a poster from a seventies concert I bought for him in London. We tumble onto the mattress with me on top, and his striped sheets give us a cold embrace. He pulls off my T-shirt, and his mouth runs down my stomach, my sides… full of desire. We're avoiding even saying any words because they would all be lies. I unbutton his pants and do the same to my own, and he pulls my jeans and my underwear down. We don't take off anything else. I'm still wearing my bra, and he's completely dressed, but we maneuver through his boxers until suddenly he's inside me. I'm wet but not soaked. It's all moving so fast.

Marín thrusts between my thighs with his head buried in my neck; I hear him gasping and sucking in air. He whispers a word every once in a while, slowly and softly, in a low voice. And while his body is doing what it knows, what the animal inside him learned, my mind is traveling. I'm thinking how I'll miss it…him, the apartment, the memories. The obsolete music junk he collects so carefully, the songs we discovered together, the dinners sitting on the floor, he and I, like there's no one else in the world. I don't know why I'm thinking about that while we're doing this thing I don't know what to call because it's not fucking, but it's not making love either. I feel pleasure, but…what kind of sex is this? It's not sex, I guess; it's a physical way of trying to feel closer before we distance ourselves completely.

I weave my fingers through his tangled hair, and I feel relief, physical relief; there's something narcotic about that gesture that makes me feel connected to him because I know he loves when I do it.

"Where are you?" he asks me, still inside me, looking at me with raised eyebrows.

"Thinking about us," I mumble.

"About us…when?"

"Keep going…" I say.

He moves, and I settle my hips for one more charge. I'm going to come… I have to. So I touch myself, I stroke myself slowly while I look at him, and I hear him saying sorry he didn't even take his clothes off.

"I needed this." He sighs. "But I didn't know it."

"Keep going… Keep going…"

One of my hands is digging into his behind, under his unbuttoned pants and boxers, while the other speeds up, rubbing my finger against my clit. I'm not going to take long. I writhe, forget that this will be the last time we do it, and use my body to encourage him to let go too.

The orgasm is good, but it doesn't say anything about us. I get the feeling that he feels the same way when he finally lets go with a furrowed brow. I feel the heat of his semen filling me, and Marín opens his mouth to let out a soft moan that hitches in his throat. He pulls out and then pushes back in, like he's cold and seeking shelter. It's not pleasure—I'm more clear about that now. It's a matter of loneliness. Even with the person you love, sex can be mediocre sometimes.

We stay lying there in bed, staring at the ceiling. I don't want to move even to put my underwear back on, but I have to, so there's no moment of calm and postcoital affection, just a breath that is followed by the sound of clothes being put back in place.

"Should we go to the living room?" I ask.

"No." He shakes his head as he buttons up his pants. "Let's talk here."

He's standing up, leaning against the closed door. I'm sitting at his desk after a brief stop in the bathroom.

After a long silence, Marín clears his throat and starts talking:

"I feel like I won a prize," he says. "But I also feel like I cheated, like I was just handed it without actually competing. I've never done anything to, I don't know, seduce you…but I'm aware that I've always put you first in life ever since the beginning without really knowing why. I guess some things are too much, Coco, to understand and to hold." He pauses and looks at me, crossing his arms over his chest. "Interrupt me whenever you want."

"I will when I have something to say."

"You're my world, Coco. You have been since you moved into this apartment. Everything that matters to me is tangled up with you: my family, my house, my friends, my work. In a way everything leads me back to you. And that might sound really good, but it's not healthy."

"We're not healthy, Marín?"

"Yes, yes, we are, but throwing myself into this now wouldn't be. I… think it would be better if we can keep being friends, Coco, at least for now."

"Okay." I nod and look down at the ground. "I was expecting that."

"I love you. I wasn't lying when I said that, but…maybe our relationship has always been so intimate that we got confused. I know, I'm clear on you not being one of those girls that you can 'try out and see if it works.' With you it's either 'til death or not at all. You're the ultimate girl, Coco, and I don't know what to do with that."

"It scares you."

"Yes. I don't know if I can live up to it."

I lick my lips and take a deep breath before I look at my watch.

"This shouldn't have happened…" He closes his eyes, rubs his face with both hands, and then points at the bed. "It was a moment of weakness."

"For both of us."

"I…would rather have you forever, Coco. If I have to choose, I'd pick how we were, because any other way I don't know if I can be what you want me to be."

"Right. It's fine." I swallow.

His face transforms into a confused mask. "It's fine?"

"Of course."

"Are you saying that to be nice or because you came to the same conclusion?"

"No." I smile against my will. "Neither. It's because you didn't take me into account when you made your decision, so I should only think about myself when I make mine."

"What are you trying to say? If I don't want to risk our friendship, that's for you because I don't want to hurt you."

"No. It's for you," I assure him gravely. "If it were for me, you would have asked yourself how we can keep living under the same roof with everything you know I feel for you. You've made a decision, and, well, I can't do anything about it. But don't say it's for me. It's for you because you don't want to leave your comfort zone and I scare you."

He doesn't answer. He looks down at the ground.

"I don't know if you were expecting me to cry or beg, Marín. Maybe you thought I would be the one to drag this forward, so then, if it ended badly, it would be both of our faults because maybe you didn't know how to be my partner, but I insisted when you warned me. Whatever it is, I've learned that we idealize other people, and we tend to underestimate ourselves. I never thought you'd choose to be half in with me, just like I never thought I'd take care of myself the way I'm going to."

I take a few steps toward the door.

"Coco…" he begs. "I don't know how to do it any better."

"Of course you know, but you don't want to take the risk. You know taking a risk isn't the only way to lose? Somctimes just doing nothing is enough. Go back to your sister. When you get back, the room will be empty."

"Don't do that…"

"Of course I'm going to." I nod. "And if you love me, you'll understand." I take a deep breath. "I'd say goodbye now, I'd say thanks for all the years we've lived together, but I'm sure I'll break down, and I'd rather do that when I'm alone."

"I won't know how to live without you. Don't do this."

"You will know, even though we're going to miss each other a lot,

Marín. The good thing is that we're going to learn a lot. You'll learn that life doesn't always fit into your plans. This whole 'your way or the highway' thing...doesn't always work. I'll learn that, look, in the end I didn't love you more than I love myself. Good luck, Marín. Tell Gema I love her. And you—I love you too. But I love me more."

I grab my bag from the table and leave the house without looking back. I know. Deep down, I'm dying for him to run after me, to stop me, to tell me he was wrong, that he sees everything clearly now, that the future simply doesn't exist if we're not together, but...they're just wishes. Nobody's following me. Nobody's running. Nobody's saying anything.

And I keep walking.

~

I'm stoic for a little bit, seemingly calm, on the subway, but right before we get to Nuevos Ministerios, three stops from where I have to transfer, I burst into desperate, uncontrollable tears. And even though I try to cover them with my hands, the other passengers start looking. I'd be embarrassed if anything mattered to me right now. I just feel empty, a pain that feels like a sandcastle crumbling inside my chest, leaving me even emptier.

A stranger sits down next to me, hands me a tissue, and squeezes my shoulder.

"What doesn't kill you makes you stronger," she says.

Her eyes tell a story, her own, one I don't know, but I know it didn't kill her. I would smile, but all I can do is cry.

42

GOODBYE

Dear Marín,

Letter greetings are so weird, right? Or maybe we're the weird ones because we've gotten out of the habit of writing them. Whatever it is, "dear Marín" is much more than a formula because, well, you're Marín and you're dear to me. Very. Always. Although, I guess you already know that.

I realized that I was in love with you when I was standing next to a window in the apartment, drinking a Coke. You don't know how beautiful sunset makes you, Marín. I almost died of love and pain. You say that I'm the ultimate girl, and I'll say that you're the kind of guy that gets tattooed on your guts. Nobody will see it, but I'll always carry you inside me, even though I guess you're leaving a hole so that I can love someone in the future the way that I love you today. You're even great at that—you define what love means; you're the pinnacle, the landmark, the record of loving.

I'm going to stop writing this stuff. I don't want this goodbye to leave me feeling like a fucking nutjob.

As you'll see, I left the bedroom completely empty, except for the books on the nightstand. They're for Gema. She's always asking me for book recommendations, and since I don't plan on seeing her for a while, I left enough for her to have fun stuff to read for the next six months. Don't tell her that. You don't need to tell her everything. She's very mature, but she's still really young, and we don't want her to know that love is sometimes brutal, it hurts, and it can be very cowardly.

Thank you in spite of everything. Thank you for that night in November when we met, for being so open to the world, for being so receptive, for hooking me with one single look in Via Láctea bar. You fucked up my life a little because I love that place and now I'll never be able to go back there without thinking of you. Actually, you've drawn a whole map of Madrid where every corner is a memory. It's going to be hard to make this city my own again so it can stop being ours. Plaza España and that time I gave you a seashell I was carrying in my pocket. Atocha station, where for a while it seemed like our strolls always ended up. Every stupid cobblestone in Malasaña, which is a step, a jump, your boots, mine, a puddle full of our toasts, and my tears now that I have to say goodbye to all of that. Not see you later. Goodbye.

Thank you for this house. For the cactus, the "wall of fame," the peeled carrots you would leave in little baggies in the fridge so I would eat something with vitamins. Thank you for the Sundays when we didn't let the cold in, for the dusty-pink sunshine of summer evenings and the gray echoes of winter sunrises. Thank you for your bare feet padding across the hardwood floors and the promises that the noise of the water running in the shower brought to me in bed every morning. You probably won't understand me, but at this point I think it's pretty obvious that this note is more for me than for you.

I've said goodbye to the whole house already, so I won't need to come back. The pain will last a long time, I'm sure. I love this apartment, but as I walked around it a few minutes ago, I realized that I'd like any place where you were. The new couch didn't turn it into a home or the wallpaper in the hallway (which, by the way, didn't actually look that great in the light—I never told you because you seemed so excited), the cookbooks next to the stove, that wilted plant in the kitchen window, or those super-bright curtains you insisted would give the living room some personality. It wasn't the old furniture that time converted into being trendy, either, or the book or the lamps or that super-weird poster with the physiological diagram of a cat that you found at your grandparents' house and hung in the living room, you absolute freak. We made it a home, so this probably makes me a bad person, but I'm comforted by the thought that I'm not leaving my home here. My home, in part, is me. The same thing will happen to you. You'll still have part of your house, but half of the home is coming with me.

I'm happy, but it makes me feel really bad, I swear.

I'm going to miss you. I already miss you more than I ever thought I could. That's the truth. And I spend my days thinking about how difficult it is to define what hurts you when distance is what's causing the pain. The hollow feeling in your chest, the heaviness in your stomach, the rough skin that doesn't even get touched anymore, how hard it is to keep breathing when I can't smell you. What the fuck am I doing? Trying to forget you. With the knowledge that I can't because I don't want to. I don't want to yet, but I will.

I'm leaving, Marín. I'm not going to ask you not to come find me or make you swear you won't write to me, but I will ask you not to do it in vain. If you miss me but everything is still the same, don't do it, because it will be egotistical and unfair and you're not like that. Come if you decide that this is the dumbest mistake we've ever made in our lives, if the "let's just be friends" was just the "boo" in a stupid prank that isn't funny anymore and, what the fuck, if I'm the ultimate girl, I'll be the only one in your life. Come only if the reasons I'm leaving no longer exist because you have to understand that as a friend you really hurt me and it was even worse because I felt like you were mine. Mine isn't the word. I'm not talking about ownership or belonging. It's about skin. And you and I understood each other's skin before we even touched each other.

Don't come back for your friend Coco because she doesn't exist anymore, but come if your life stops making sense the way you always wanted it to because I'm not there. Come with a purpose or don't come, but if you come, don't take too long because life is what I'm living with you now.

I love you,
Coco

PS I watered the cacti. Don't water them again for at least a month or they'll drown.

PPS Don't stop calling Blanca and Loren. We'll know not to overlap. This doesn't have to leave either of us with no friends.

43

IN WHITE

COCO

September in white.
I have nothing to say.
There is no chapter.
There are no words.
Silence.
White noise.

44

BLANCA'S WEDDING

COCO

It's strange the way autumn has fallen over the city in a matter of days. Last week I went to work in short sleeves and a light jacket just in case, but today I had to get out all my scarves. I love it. I'm not a summer girl and especially not after all this. I think the cool has arrived to cool our skin down from what the heat brought us.

The street is beautiful. I've always thought that Madrid is especially pretty in the fall. It looks like a girl with reddish hair, dressed in warm tones, with her lips painted a red that you only get a glimpse of at sunset.

The sun is shining today. Blanca was always scared that today, October 20, her wedding day, it would rain, but no—a warm sun swept the shadows from the pavement, chasing the cars and crowning every person who came out onto the streets this Saturday.

It's a beautiful scene. The colors, the warmth of the sun already yawning beyond the road, the people milling around excitedly outside the church. Green, red, blue, pink dresses. Shiny shoes. Dazzling smiles. Today is a wedding day, and only happy songs will be played until the women stumble barefoot down the hall and the bride and groom stare at each other, spellbound, sharing one last dance. Today is a wedding day.

Loren looks amazing. He tamed his hair with some styling gel and is wearing a beautiful shirt. Next to me, Blanca smiles and looks down at her shoes, happy. She says she found them this week in a window display and they whistled insinuatingly at her before they seduced her completely with their evil ways. In the midst of so much color and laughter, I feel a little gray. A little more than usual, I mean. Lately, it's always gray inside my chest.

"So the whole moving-back-in-with-your-parents thing… It's not that terrible?"

"No. You know my mother. She does her own thing. I have no idea how all five of us survived."

"It made you strong," Blanca jokes. "She's a dragon mother."

"Dragon mother?"

"It's a super-tough parenting style that a lot of mothers in China use. I won't try to explain it any more than that because I'm sure I'll fuck up some part of it, but google it," she insists. "It's fascinating."

"Thanks." I pat her knee through her dress. "You look really beautiful today, Blanca."

"Stunning," Loren agrees.

"Thank you so much. The day deserves it."

We look out. People seem eager to start heading to the reception. They're either really hungry or really ready to make some toasts. Maybe both.

"I'm scared to ask this," Loren says, still looking forward. "But I guess today is the day. Have you heard anything from Gus?"

"No." Blanca looks at both of us with a sad smile. "I stopped following him on social media, but…I've done a little stalking. Apparently, right after I blocked him, he decided he was going to take a break from Instagram and Facebook. He's writing a new book, he said. He needed to detox."

"Yeah, from himself," I mutter.

"You know something? In a way I would have preferred it if he had kept doing the same stuff as always: the poems, the messages, the calls with some flimsy excuse…"

"Girl, of course. You don't just get over your vices cold turkey." Loren sighs. "Look at me with cigarettes. I'd smoke ten thousand cigarettes right now."

"That's not why. It's because…in some twisted way I think this was the first time he proved that he loves me and that I really matter to him. And it's still hard for me to accept that it all ended so badly."

"Let's not think about this today," I ask.

We turn back to look at the people. One woman is going around with a wicker basket, handing out little bags of birdseed to toss to all the guests.

"Should we go out there?"

"Not yet." Blanca laughs. "Let me take a breath."

"Aroa is still MIA, right? We haven't gotten any proof of life?" Loren asks.

"The other day I got a Facebook invite for a party where she's on the decks, but I think she sent it to all her contacts and didn't even realize I was still in there," Blanca says.

"Well, she unfriended me," I point out with a smile. "And blocked me."

"That girl," Loren cackles. "I swear when she dropped that bomb that she had slept with Gus, I thought I was dying. I thought: *That's it. Tomorrow, we're gonna be in the news.*"

"Yeah." Blanca nods. "I swear I pictured myself killing her. Deep down, if I hadn't been holding Marín back, I think I would have taken advantage of the chaos and impaled her with a beach chair."

"She was so fake… She totally played us."

"Hey, since we're putting it all out there…have either of you seen Marín?"

It's like I mentioned a dead person. Both of them glance at each other and then sigh.

"I saw him yesterday," Blanca announces. "He told me that… Well, that he wasn't going to come today because…he didn't want to create tension. Plus, he doesn't really understand any of this, even though he wished me the best."

"How is he?"

"Skinny. And with big bags under his eyes." Loren grimaces. "Subdued."

"Looks like shit." Blanca looks at me. "I think that's the best description."

"Yeah, well. Another one who's doing what was asked of him." I take a deep breath and let it slowly escape through my lips.

A silence falls over us.

"What did we expect?" Blanca asks in a thread of a voice. "Because after 'surviving'"—she makes little air quotes—"the most unique bachelorette party in history, I think the next logical step would be being recruited by the CIA to become secret agents and give us ridiculous code names like 'dish towel,' 'spoon,' and 'urinal.'"

"It'd be better if we win the lottery." I smile.

"Now, seriously… Now what?"

"Now?" I look at her. "We fight to be happy, kids. It doesn't come for free."

"Aren't we already?" Loren replies. "Being happy is just a handful of moments, and every once in a while we have brushes with glory."

All three of us smile. I guess he's right. Even if things are still so weird between us, even if we talk a little less than before and it's hard for us to get back into our old routines and it's taking a little effort to follow the new, unbreakable rule of never lying again, we're still lucky. Not everyone comes out of something like that trip in the camper even stronger.

And me? Am I lucky? Roughly speaking, of course. I'm free. I'm healthy. My life isn't in danger. I can chase my dreams without anybody holding me back. I was born in the bosom of a family that may be a little eccentric but nothing serious. I have a job. I have friends. So, yes, every day, when I wake up, I have piles of reasons to appreciate the life I have, even if I forget them—because even though our little dramas are nothing more than first-world problems, they're still our dramas. That's what happens when your basic needs are covered: Problems just change out of their shirts and put on a flamboyant costume, full of feathers and sequins. Mine waits for me every day, dressed up like a ridiculous carnival queen, with way too much makeup and heels she can't stand, sitting at the foot of my bed.

I find myself dangerously close to thirty, and I just moved back into my parents' house, to my teenage bedroom. In the wardrobe, I still have a Jonas Brothers poster from back when the littlest one wasn't even hot yet. I could afford an apartment for myself, but right now I don't feel ready to live alone, and going back to having roommates is something I never even considered. Not to mention the worst part: I miss Marín. Fuck, I miss him. Every day. Every hour. He's still the first person I think of when something happens to me, the first thing I think about when I wake up, my first wish when an eyelash falls out, and...the first image that floats into my head when I close my eyes and try to sleep. They say it'll get better with time and that one day I'll smile when I think of all this... It's not that I don't believe them; it's just that I'm still so far from that point.

If he hasn't come back, it's because nothing has changed. Because he doesn't love me enough to have swallowed his fears. And that's not something that is going to make me happy.

So am I lucky? Yes. But my life is still under construction because I knocked down a load-bearing wall—a wall I had built part of my dreams and aspirations on. But, look, I've learned something very valuable: Never build anything of your own on a third party because, one way or another, they always leave.

"Come on..." Blanca says. "I think now is the moment."

All three of us stand up from the pew where we were sitting and head to the door of the church. Someone hands each of us a bag of birdseed, and we smile conspiratorially.

An explosion of cheers and shouts of joy greets the newlyweds as they come through the church door. All three of us, dying of laughter, infiltrate the guests, throwing fistfuls of birdseed so the couple will never lack anything in the journey they're starting today. No, we have no idea who they are, but we still wish them the best. These people, the happy couple who made the most of the date Blanca's wedding cancellation opened up, are a symbol for us, something that shows that, maybe through poetic justice, maybe through karma, one person's pain can end up being someone else's happiness. And you never know which side you'll be on.

We scamper off before any of the guests notice that we're crashers. Anyway, there are always so many people at weddings that you never know who invited them, but we don't want to take any risks. As we dash down the sidewalk, we laugh and make plans for the night. A few glasses of wine in Lavapiés and then grab dinner wherever. We'll see. The important part is that there's much more to Madrid than Malasaña, which holds so many memories.

"Hey," Loren says, furrowing his brow. "Haven't you wondered how these two had time to organize a whole wedding in so little time? It was barely two months ago when you canceled yours."

Blanca laughs. "A good wedding planner."

"Don't be like that," I grumble. "It's a love story, and thanks to the universe, some things don't have an explanation."

Right?

45

ECHO

MARÍN

I have an echo inside me. Every sound in my body ends up producing it, and I feel it all the time, everywhere, reverberating inside me, constantly reminding me how empty I am. Because…there's only an echo in empty places, and ever since she's been gone, that's what I am. I'm an empty space. Nothing more.

A few days ago I met up with Blanca; she invited me to go see the couple who booked her original wedding day, but I know she was just being polite. She knew I would decline the invitation. Coco and I are not ready to see each other, of course. It's only been a month.

"You look like shit, you know?" she asked me.

"What were you expecting? I was trying not to lose my best friend, and I ended up alone."

"It wasn't about not losing your best friend, Marín. Don't be like him—you're not Gus. You're perfectly aware that you fucked it all up and you seized the first excuse that sounded convincing."

"I wasn't ready. I'm still not." I'm aware that she's right and that my answer is an excuse that exonerates my guilt.

I know, from Blanca and Loren, that she's doing well. She must be climbing the walls at her parents' house, but Coco is one of those people who find a comfort zone wherever they are. Like my chest—my chest was her comfort zone for one night. If I think about it, my hands unconsciously start patting myself, as if to make sure I still have organs, bones, muscles, and skin. She took all the nerve endings.

The house is so empty that I've decided I'll only spend time between its four walls when it's absolutely necessary: to sleep and shower. The rest of the time I live at work. I asked for more projects, making up an excuse that Noa, her accident, left a bad taste in my mouth. I don't want to have even a minute to think about how buried deep in my desk there's a mug with Coco's face on it cropped from a picture we took with Gema. We were a fucking family. What was I thinking? Am I an idiot? Yes.

I can't stop thinking about what could have been.

The other day I met up with a girl. It grosses me out just thinking about it, but I did it. I downloaded one of those hookup apps, and I jumped on the first match to meet up with someone. It was Saturday, the office was closed, everyone had plans, my sister's not talking to me, and if she does, she just answers in monosyllabic grunts or with a speech about the twenty thousand reasons she thinks I'm useless and I fucked up her life. Hers. Blessed adolescence, where we only see our own belly buttons.

The girl was very pretty. I liked her when I saw her come into the bar where we planned to meet. She greeted me with two kisses on the cheek, and when I asked her, without beating around the bush, if she liked what she saw or she'd rather pass, she ordered a glass of wine and sat down next to me. We had made a pact not to waste time if we didn't like each other and also…that it wasn't a date. It was a meeting between two people who didn't have plans and felt like spending a little time together with no pretensions of getting to know each other any better than that.

She gave me a blow job in my doorway. A good blow job, I have to admit. I brought her up to my house, and I couldn't even let her into my bedroom. We fucked on a chair. On a fucking chair. With her on top. I didn't go down on her, and I didn't even come. I told her this happens to me a lot with strangers, but it was the first time it ever happened to me—and the last because I swear I'm never going to fuck anyone again in my goddamn life. I'm so disgusted with myself. I don't even know what my intention was.

Of course I've thought about calling her. About waiting at the door of her parents' house if she doesn't pick up. Even about sending her flowers, for the love of God—flowers that I know would end up in the kitchen because her mother would rescue them from the trash. There's not enough fauna or flora in the world to make up for it. Well, maybe if I sent her an otter—she always thought they were adorable.

Okay, I'm driving myself crazy. So why don't I face it head-on, call her, say to her, I don't know, that she needs to come show me how to use the hair dryer or how she folds fitted sheets? Any excuse, for fuck's sake. Well, I don't because I have her request branded in my brain. To tell the truth, I've read the letter so many times, I have it memorized.

Come only if the reasons I'm leaving no longer exist, because you have to understand that as a friend you really hurt me and it was even worse because I felt like you were mine.

I'm still scared. I still doubt whether I can give her what she wants. I still don't know if she's the only woman I'll ever love in my fucking life or just the best friend I'll ever have. Why doesn't anyone teach us how to discern between emotions? Why doesn't anyone educate us from the outside in?

Come on, Marín… If she was just your best friend, if you felt nothing…why would sleeping with someone else make you feel so disgusted with yourself?

The weather app on my phone says it's going to be cooler today, so before I leave the house, I grab my black denim jacket and I throw on my black sweater, which could fit two of me in it. *Head-to-toe black*, Coco would say if I hadn't been an idiot and she was coming out of her room right now and heading into the bathroom. I've never felt more like dressing all in black. I want to disappear. From everything.

I go down the stairs carefully; the wooden steps are so polished by time and use that they can turn into a slide, and judging by the drops on the landings, it's starting to rain. Great. I don't even know where we keep the umbrellas at home because Coco was the one who made me use them. Without Coco but with pneumonia—cool, good prognosis.

On the other side of the door, someone is sitting on the stoop. Their hood is pulled all the way up, and at this hour, I'd guess it's some drunk person who passed out there. I'll have to be the one to wake him up and gently tell him that more than two octogenarians live in this building and if they see him, they'll have to double up on today's dose of Warfarin.

I open the door. "Hey, buddy…it's seven thirty. Time to go to bed."

"I'd like that if I could actually sleep." He stands up nimbly and pulls off his hood as he turns toward me.

"Fuck… No fucking way." It's the first thing that comes out of my mouth, but if I had time to think, the result wouldn't be much better.

"I'm not in the mood, Gus," I say. "Go home and to hell."

"Is this all about Aroa or because I'm the ghost of Christmas Yet to Come?"

"What are you talking about?"

"Let me buy you a cup of coffee."

"I don't want to have coffee with you," I point out. "Not now or tomorrow or the next day or in 2035."

"Well, that's too bad because I'm not here to ask for forgiveness, like you're probably thinking. I came to talk about you and Coco. That's it. It's free advice, and I'm giving it to you even after you punched me."

I lean against the wall and look him up and down. He's a fucking mess. "You look pretty scary, you know that?"

"I'm not in a great place." He zips up his sweatshirt and pulls the hood back on. "I've been better."

"What's that about?"

"What's that about? Look, dude, if you don't want to talk to me I'll go back where I came from, but you don't have to start laughing your ass off because I have no friends, no girl, and no shame."

"You never had any shame."

"Okay." He turns around and starts walking. I whistle at him.

"What?" he says gruffly without turning around.

"The only place that's open at this hour is Starbucks. Does that work for you?"

"I wasn't planning on spending five bucks on coffee, but I'm not going to argue about that right now."

The Starbucks next to what used to be the Fuencarral Market doesn't have tables and it's tiny, but we didn't come to have some hours-long catch-up. I still want to bash his nose in with my fist. So, with cardboard cups in hand, we sit on a wall, in silence. He seems to be waiting for me to finish typing on my phone to tell my boss that something unexpected came up and I'll be getting in a little late today.

"Talk," I say, putting my phone in my pocket and taking a sip of coffee.

"How is she?"

"Who?"

"Who else? Her."

"Your her or mine?"

"You have a her, Marín?" he asks ironically.

"Look, this wasn't the deal. You said you were going to tell me something about Coco."

"No shit." He laughs mirthlessly. "And you're going to deny me even knowing if—?"

"She's fine. What do you want me to tell you? She's been fucking great without you. I swear she's actually even prettier since you disappeared."

"Did she…get married?"

"No," I reply, like it's obvious. "But that was as easy as…"

"As going to the door of a church to find out? Of course, but what if I had seen her there in a white dress? What would I do with the vomit? Swallow it back down?"

"If you loved her, you wouldn't have done any of what you did."

"The thing is I don't love her. Well, not like she loved me. It's..." He rubs his few-days-old stubble. "It's complicated, and I don't expect you to understand."

"Of course," I say self-deprecatingly. "Jeez, dude, you have nothing to lose at this point. You're still saying you don't love her?"

"It was special," he says. "It always was. It wasn't just another fling; I never treated her like all the rest. With her it was...different. It was intimate. But it wasn't love."

"Just like I said, you're going to keep denying it to yourself."

"Look, Marín, that's my problem, okay? Who cares what name I want to give it, what I want to call it? It's over. I fucked it up, and I didn't know how to tell her or ask for help, and we went to shit."

"You went to shit because you have a totally toxic way of looking at relationships, Gus." And I swear I'm not saying it to hurt him. I just...want him to know so he can do something about it. "Love yourself a little more, dude. Don't look for reassurance where you are now because most of the time, you're going to end up alone. In the worst-case scenario, alone and with some venereal disease that'll kill you."

"Yeah?" He raises his eyebrows. "What about you, Marín? What about your relationship with Coco?"

"What about yours?" I counterattack.

"Ah, now that I recognize. I do that a lot, Marín, the whole dodging-the-issue thing, blaming everyone else, defending myself with an attack. You wanna be like me? Is that it? Because you're going down a great path. In two days, you'll have dethroned me as idiot of the year."

"Now you're the one who doesn't get it, Gus. I don't know if you ever will."

"Explain it to me." He crosses his arms over his chest. "At least try."

"I violated the intimacy and trust we had, and...I'm mortified because I did it the wrong way, there's no way to fix it, and...you know her. She's forever, dude. She's forever, and she deserves someone who loves her like hell. Can I do that?"

"Look, Marín, I went out with her for a year. I know her pretty well. I've seen her laugh up a lung, cry out of rage, dream out loud, suffer, come—"

"Okay," I cut him off. "I get it."

"I know her intimately too, but...I never thought she was forever or that she was the ultimate girl. She deserves someone who loves her like hell, you're right, but I never felt like I had this heavy responsibility you've imposed on yourself."

"Because you're an irresponsible dick," I retort.

"Cool. So what are you? Because the only thing that makes sense to me is that you think she's forever because for you she is. It has nothing to do with her. Coco doesn't have any labels on her; she wasn't born marked to be 'the kind that's forever or not at all.' And, like...she never has been for any other guy. Don't you get it? That idea is all about you, about how you see yourself, not her nature and her... I dunno, her fucking DNA. You're out of your mind in love, you bastard, and you're losing her."

"So what do you care?"

"Let me do at least one good thing this year, okay?"

"You just wanna win points with Blanca, don't you? You want it to slip out in front of her how sweet you were to come help me—"

"No." Gus gets very serious. He actually seems nervous. "You have to swear, Marín, on your sister. She's never going to know we saw each other or talked or anything... Do you understand me? She's never going to hear you talking about me."

I furrow my brow. That does throw me off. "Why?"

"Because she'll forget." He smiles sadly. "What I did, how much it hurt… She'll forget if she never hears my name, if she doesn't hear from me, if she doesn't see me. And I want to give her that. I owe it to her."

"You fucked Aroa when you were with her," I say. "And while Aroa was with me."

"Yes, and I'm sorry, but Blanca and I weren't together. We weren't… Not in the strictest sense, okay? The thing with Aroa was a mistake, and I knew it even as I was doing it, but if it helps, I think we both needed to show ourselves that we could do it. Aroa always…" He pinches the bridge of his nose. "She was always really jealous of Coco. You know that better than anyone. It's sad, dude, but it wasn't even about you or me. Her struggle was always about being better than Coco, having everything she wanted or had ever had."

"What's your excuse then? You hooked up with your friend's girlfriend."

"My excuse is that I'm a jerk. I don't know if that's good enough for you."

"Yeah." I nod and take a deep breath. "It's good enough."

"Marín, here's the deal: We're a fucking walking moral of the story. Life showed us with a bang how fear can destroy anything we love, but…there are two endings here. On one side, there's yours, and on the other, there's mine. I got stuck on how romantic the pain we were causing ourselves was, and I broke it. It can't be fixed, and even I'm aware that it's over. But… you haven't completely fucked it up yet."

"It's too late," I say harshly.

"Well, you'll never know if you don't try."

"I can't see her, just like you can't even say Blanca's name."

"Because it lingers on my lips, Marín. If I say it, it lingers…"

Fuck. I put my hands in my hair.

"Tell her you're an idiot, Marín. Accept it: You are, like we all are sometimes."

"That won't fix it."

"You know something weird about you, Marín? You're like a fucking movie screen where everything you want is projected, everything you're really hungry for, but your back is to it and all you can see is the light bouncing off the screen. Turn around, soak up the film, and tell her about it. Coco's not gonna be able to say no to that."

"To what?"

"To family," he says very confidently, almost petulantly. "You're dying to have a family. You've been building one for years. You just never called it that, projecting your desires onto that house. That's all you have to say—that that was what you wanted all along and you want it with her."

I don't say anything. I'm pretty shocked, but I don't want to admit it out loud. I just want him to leave, to be honest.

"Is that everything?" I shoot him an evasive look.

"No. Last thing: Let her tell you that's what she imagined too and she'll find some space for you. Her life doesn't revolve around you."

"Don't fuck around," I mutter. "You're the last person I need to mansplain it."

"What are you talking about?" he says.

"I'm saying I'm not like you, dude. I'm not like you. What I wanted, desired, or imagined doesn't mean shit to me. All I'm worried about is not being good enough for what she wants from me."

"Okay, then that's it." He straightens up, takes a sip of his latte, and wipes his lip. "God, this stuff is gross. I'm out of here."

"Great."

"You'll probably never see me again in your life."

"Somehow I doubt that." I sigh.

"Remember…if she asks, this never happened. And if…if you can somehow stop her from buying my next book, I'd appreciate it."

"Another chapbook full of arrows?"

"When is poetry not full of arrows?" He smiles jauntily. "By the way... you say you're not like me, right? Well, prove it."

As I watch him heading off, he pulls his hood back over his head. The last thing I glimpse before he disappears into the crowd is him tossing his coffee in the trash. I don't know why I feel bad. Deep down, I loved that bastard. I appreciated him. I admired him. But there's no going back.

I feel like I just had an extraterrestrial experience, a UFO sighting, a vision, a spectral visitation. Son of a fucking bitch... He's right. It was like talking to the ghost of a Marín who never lifts a finger to avoid this fucking nothingness, which, like in *The NeverEnding Story*, is eating everything that lives inside my chest.

And no...I'm not like Gus.

46

NO

COCO

My heels clack across the gallery's elegant marble floors. I have an important appointment with a client interested in making a six-figure investment in a good painting, and I've set aside a few pieces I think might interest her. It's not the typical done deal; this woman knows what she wants, what she doesn't, and what she should read and investigate before she buys anything. Young, beautiful, successful...a mirror you want to look in, of course, but above all a client who it's in my best interest to keep satisfied.

I glance at my reflection in the glass covering an especially valuable piece that's part of an exhibition right now. My hair is styled in loose waves with a middle part, and I'm wearing a dress with a tailored blazer over it and some black Jimmy Choos I borrowed from Mama. I'm not wearing tights, but I did get a little chilly today for the first time as I walked to the metro on the way to the gallery.

"You look really nice today," a colleague says.

I turn toward him, weirded out. "Excuse me?"

"Sorry," he says. He's old enough to be my father, and he's near retirement, but right now he looks like a bashful little boy. "I didn't mean to make you uncomfortable. I didn't mean to be offensive. It's just...you came back from vacation seeming very stressed and now—"

"Antonio." I cut him off. I don't want to talk about my personal life with him, and I don't need his compliments. "I have an appointment with an important client, and I want to impress her. Do you think lipstick projects a more confident image?"

"Yes." He nods. "Without a doubt."

"If you don't mind…I'm going to run to my office for a sec."

The sound of my heels accompanies me to where I've stored my bag. Inside I find a red lipstick, powerful, strong; I get a twinge in my stomach when I realize it's the one I was wearing this summer when Marín and I…

"Coco." My boss pokes her head into my office.

"Is it time already?"

"I didn't know you were expecting a visit," she says. "But yes. It's time. Were you in the middle of something?"

"Just putting on lipstick." I smile. "I want to seem like a strong woman who's secure in myself to encourage her to buy something with a lot of zeros."

"A lot of zeros?" She grimaces. "I'm not sure if there are a lot of zeros in that bank account."

I don't ask anything else. I just run my tongue over my teeth and stride out.

At first I don't see anyone. The gallery seems as calm and silent as always. I notice it started raining really hard outside and that the security guards are huddling inside, watching it rage.

A few wet footprints on a previously impeccable floor lead me to one of the corners, where we have a reproduction of a work by Juan Gris that I valued myself and bought from one private collector to sell to another. In front of it, wearing a frown, is someone I wasn't expecting to find admiring avant-garde art at nine thirty on a Wednesday morning.

I don't know whether to run forward or backward, so I just freeze. The sound of my shoes makes him turn around. That's enough for me, just like the first time we met in that bar in Malasaña; a single glance gets me hooked. It's his eyes, I tell myself, which have something special about them that I've never found in any other gaze. I don't know if it's a handful of truth or a constellation of possible unlived lives. I swallow. He does too, and he turns all the way toward me, putting his hands in his pockets.

"Guitar, fruit bowl, and carafe," I say, feeling my heart pounding in my throat and my stomach.

"What's that?"

"The painting." I point to it. "It's called *Guitar, Fruit Bowl, and Carafe*. It's by Juan Gris, one of the most important figures in cubism. He was from Madrid."

A small smile plays at his lips. "Yeah, Sardine?"

"Yeah. He has a portrait of"—I take two steps toward him and add—"of Pablo Picasso that is exhibited in a museum in Chicago, and it's one of the first cubist works painted by anyone besides Picasso or Braque."

"Do you like cubism?"

"No." I smile. "I appreciate it as avant-garde, but if you ask me if I'd like a cubist painting hanging in the living room, I'd say no."

"No. You like symbolism."

"What am I gonna do? I love George Lacombe."

"Plus…what was the name of the one that gave me the creeps?"

"Morea. I always thought you went into a kind of fugue state when I told you this stuff."

"If I dig deep, I'll probably remember something else."

"No need. It's not a test."

"No…you're wrong. This is my final." He sighs. "When do you have time to talk?"

I look at my watch. "I have a meeting in half an hour, and I wanted to prepare a few things."

"Can we have lunch together?"

"Um…" My voice won't even come out. "I don't know, Marín."

"What don't you know?"

"If this visit fulfills the prerequisites of the terms that were…established between us."

"I need to talk to you," he says.

"Yeah, okay, but—"

"Look, I'll wait for you on the terrace of Ramsés, okay? I'll order a glass of wine for you…at around two?"

"One thirty would be better," I say. "My day is a little…"

"Of course. So one thirty. See you there?"

I nod and bite my cheek. "You're not working today?" I ask before he heads toward the door.

"No. I took the day off."

When he opens the door and disappears under a curtain of rain, I try not to think about his clothes getting plastered to his skin even though I don't know who I'm trying to fool.

"What did that guy want?" asks my boss, who just materialized next to me like a ghost.

"Fuck, Nati, one of these days you're going to scare me to death." I put my hand on my chest.

"I don't like him for you." She wrinkles her lip. "He looks like a…I don't know, late-night rocker."

"No. He's not a late-night rocker. He's a rising star of the music industry, but only I know that for now," I say, half in a trance.

~

It's stopped raining, but the Plaza de la Independencia is covered in a thin glistening layer of water that makes it look like a huge whale made of cement and asphalt. I'd be lying if I said I wasn't nervous. I have two opposing forces in my chest: the one that says the time has come and the other that's screaming there's too much pain. I seem to have an inner drive inside me that fights for my pride tooth and nail. How else would I have found the strength to make the decision to distance myself from Marín?

I'm tempted to call Loren or Blanca and tell them everything, but I don't know why. I have reservations. I don't think I want to get them involved until I know whether this is fixed. So…I dial my mother's phone number.

"Did you sell it?" she asks me as soon as she picks up.

"Yes," I assure her. "She was very happy. She told me that it's going to brighten up her penthouse in the Castellana. Mama…this girl must be my age, and she has a penthouse in the Castellana."

"Well, you have a Jonathan Brothers poster in your closet."

"You're an idiot." I laugh. "It's the Jonas Brothers, and I ripped that poster down. Do you have a sec to talk?"

"Yes. Of course. I'm just drinking a Tom Collins."

I can't do anything but laugh. "He came back," I hear myself say, suddenly much more serious.

"He came back? Marín?"

"Yeah. He showed up at the gallery this morning. He's waiting for me at a restaurant. I'm on the way now."

"And? Did he say anything?"

"No, but…I guess he came for…"

"Coco—your expectations. Control them. They're like runaway horses. He probably just wants to tell you, I don't know, something about his sister."

"He would have called, right?"

"Well, let's stop speculating. What do you want? What is it that you want from him? What do you need from him to be able to share your happiness?"

"My happiness right now is a lettuce leaf that someone accidentally put in the microwave. Am I making myself clear?"

"Am I making *myself* clear? Think about yourself, Coco! Your needs are the ones you should be worrying about. Nothing else. If you don't take care of them, you won't be the only one who suffers. Do you know what I'm talking about?"

"Ay, Mama." I let out a kind of whimper.

"Okay, go. Talk to him. But if he wants to start a cult and he wants you to join and be his right hand...say no."

Anyway.

~

Just like he promised, there's a glass of white wine waiting on the table for me, next to his plain glass of water. I see him, but he doesn't see me. He's engrossed in reading an old, worn, earmarked book whose pages started yellowing decades ago. And I'm hit so hard by something it stops me in my tracks. It's a memory—a false memory, something that never happened, something that maybe never will happen. It's us, the two of us, next to the ocean. He's wearing a white shirt and has sunglasses on, and he's reading an old book, like this one, like those books he buys in that old bookstore on Arenal Street. He's stroking the pristine white tablecloth covering the table in this "memory," and it makes me laugh to think he always had such long fingers that even when he wasn't touching me, I could feel it.

He looks up, and the superimposed image of this false memory bursts. He spots me. He smiles and stands up as he puts the book aside. There's no kiss or hug before I sit across from him at the table.

We look at each other. Neither of us says anything. Just a silent hello sitting on our lips. I grab the glass of wine and take a timid sip, just to have something to do. We must look like two strangers on a bad date, but inside the bubble that always springs up around us, it feels different, even pleasant. I just have to look at him to know what he came to say, but I need to know what words he'll use to say it. I'm almost expecting him to do it with a song, to slide his headphones across the table and ask me to listen to something, but we both know that wouldn't be enough. Months ago that would have done it for me. Not now.

"Coco," he whispers.

"It's hard, huh?" I smile at him.

"Fuck." He runs his hand through his hair. "I'm realizing that, out of the two of us, you're the brave one."

"But you're the hot one."

He lets out a chortle and whispers that I'm an idiot.

"I know what you came to say," I murmur, looking away. "But I still need you to say it."

"Don't think I'm trying to get out of it. I need to say it too. I came this close to choosing a few songs to say it for me, but..." I laugh, and it makes him smile. "What are you laughing at?"

"How well I know you."

"Coco..."

"What?"

"I'm sorry. Forgive me."

"What are you asking me to forgive you for, Marín?"

"For the time, for what we missed, for getting stuck on the border of what we were and what we wanted to be. For not knowing how to do things in a better way."

"I've always thought we put too much responsibility on words. They can be pretty, but...look at Gus's poems. What are they besides pretty? Nothing."

"No, they are something, but in his case they weren't enough. He has too many words, and I don't have enough. I don't know how to say this to you."

"Just say it."

He leans forward on the table and takes a deep breath. "Ever since you left, I've lost my home. Everything echoes. I echo. I want to disappear."

"Missing is human," I reply stubbornly.

"I know, but that's not it. It's just that… I mean, Coco…"

"I mean, Marín."

He runs his fingers through his hair again, leaving it disheveled. I want to smooth it with my hands, but right now I can't touch him. He has to keep going.

"You know those stories we read when we're little? The ones Disney turned into a whole empire? I think we try to make love match that image and then we dismantle the myth, sometimes making it more sordid and other times more practical through experience and desire. Through age. Well, I went too far. I stripped away everything about what should have been love, I just left a bare skeleton that could barely stand up. That's why my relationships have always been…mediocre. They didn't have any magic. Or poetry. I was looking for someone to be comfortable with, who I wanted to kiss, who I was into sleeping with and didn't bug me…and, don't get me wrong, who wouldn't get in the way of my career."

"Sounds awful," I mumble.

"What I'm trying to say, Coco, is that I built a way of understanding love that couldn't hurt me. The more you feel, the more you risk yourself, the more you open up, the more you give, and then when that ends… nobody gives you yourself back. I didn't want anyone to be able to disappoint me. That's why I didn't understand."

"What didn't you understand?"

"That I fell in love." He shrugs. "Head over heels, like an idiot, at first sight, a fucking arrow that almost split me in half when you looked at me in that bar. I could describe, thread by thread, what you were wearing that night, how your hair was wavy, and I think I even counted the lines on your lips, Coco…"

I raise my eyebrows, but I let him continue, even though my heart is clenched like a fist.

"'Crystals' by Of Monsters and Men was playing, and I've never been able to listen to it since because the red light of the bar melded with the lipstick that had started smudging on every glass you sipped from. And you were laughing and saying that everyone was an asshole sometimes, that it was a human right, and I wanted to be an asshole so you would say it to me. I didn't identify it as love, I'm sorry, but I can't help but wonder what would have happened if I had said to you right then that you were the love of my life and that if it wasn't with you I didn't think I'd be able to do it with anyone. You would've thought I was nuts, I'm sure. You definitely wouldn't have moved into my empty room a week later, and we never would have gone on that trip to London. How did I not realize it was love, Coco? I told myself you were the luckiest thing in my life, for fuck's sake! A beautiful, fun best friend, who sleeps in wool socks in the winter and naked in the summer, who gave me advice about my life, about women, about my sister. What could go wrong?" He raises his eyebrows, desperate, like he can't find the words. "Everything! Everything went wrong, always, even though we disguised it as something else! You have no idea how much I suffered through your whole relationship with Gus, who seemed to make you shine and dance and fly, and I was sitting there, holding the hand of a girl all my friends thought was perfect and feeling nothing. I thought I was envious of you for knowing how to live life that way, but I was actually jealous that I wasn't the one making you feel those things. We have to admit that we never worked as friends, Coco…"

"Of course we worked," I retort.

"No!" The middle-aged couple at the next table look over at us, and he lowers his head and his tone. "No, Coco. We spent four years being the happiest fucking couple in the world without kisses, without sex, but with everything else. Was I scared to put a label on it, close the house to everything else, and just be you and me? Yes. Of course it scares me. But… you know what? Even without putting a label on it, this distance is almost eating me alive, and I don't want to live like that. I want to live with you, always, for the rest of my life, until I die." Marín looks at the table, not at me, and takes another deep breath. "I want to live in you, I want you to live in me. I want you to be my family; I want to be buried at your feet… Fuck, Coco, there's no way I could love you more, but if you let me, I can love you better."

I swallow. Jesus fucking Christ. I can't say anything. Nothing except yes, but I feel ridiculous selling out so fast, so I decide on something that might be stupid: I stand up. He stands up at the same time, scared, and his expression grows somber. "Coco…"

"It's not that… I…" I don't manage to say anything. All I can say is yes, yes, yes, yes, yes, but I resist. "I want to leave."

"Okay…I came on too strong. I get it. Uh…think about it. Just think about it."

I grab my bag, buckle up the belt of my jacket, and in a daze try, mostly successfully, to swerve around the rest of the tables on this terrace.

"Coco," he calls out, standing next to our table. "I'll wait for you at home, okay?"

At home. There's a lot in those two words. At home, without a possessive pronoun to clarify whose house it is, which implies it is a home, that we are a we—but in my mind, the we he's proposing no longer exists. He's talking about a past that was happy because I learned to chew up love and swallow it instead of sharing it through kisses, nibbles, and cackles, as it should be. Loving in silence is so awful, fuck. Loving in silence traps it in time, in space, turns it into the mummy of a love with all its organs ripped out. I want to tell him to wait wherever he wants, but that home is no longer ours; it doesn't represent anything more to me than conjugating in the past tense. I left that apartment; I moved back in with my parents. If it had really been our home, that never would have happened.

"Coco—"

"No," I blurt out all of a sudden.

"No?"

"No!" All the yeses piled up so high they turned into a no. "That's not my house anymore."

"Well, then we'll choose another one."

"But you're obsessed with that house."

"But I'm more obsessed with you." He lifts his hands and then lets them fall back to his sides. "We'll do whatever you want, Coco, your conditions, it's your life. Just…let's try to make them fit with mine together. Please…"

I'm vaguely aware that all the diners on the terrace at Ramsés are watching us intently, but I don't care. I'm standing on the sidewalk, the rain has started again, and I'm getting wet. He's still standing there, and when we look at each other, there are no waiters or tables or restaurant or Madrid that looks like a big, beached whale in the middle of nowhere. And finally I stop turning it over in my head, and I spit out two single words that I remember from that song I heard for the first time with him.

"Say it," I demand.

"I love you."

"No. Say my name. I don't want to be Coco to you anymore. Coco was your best friend, your roommate. Coco introduced you to your ex. Coco would die for you and you didn't see her. I don't want to be Coco ever again, Marín, at least for you."

He smiles. "Okay, but come here."

"No." I shake my head. For the record, I feel ridiculous, childish, crazy, but I need a resounding yes. I need my conditions, my needs covered, my promises, my words, my Marín. "Say it."

"You're getting wet."

"So come out here. Then you'll get wet too."

He smiles, scratches his nose, and walks without bumping into any tables. When he's in front of me, a few fat, cold drops quickly soak his hair. "We're going to catch pneumonia." He smiles.

"I don't want that house. I don't want to be Coco. I don't want..."

His arms suddenly circle me, and his face is close to mine. Water is streaming down our noses and cheeks. "Maria, just tell me what you want and we'll do it. We'll do it."

"It's a long list." I smile.

"We have time."

His lips brush against mine, but I pull back for a second to really look at him. This person is no longer Marín. He's not even the guy I was so in love with because that was a one-dimensional character, the good guy in a film where the main character manages to defeat the bad guys and save the girl and... I want to be honest, I don't need anyone to save me. What I want is a partner to start again with, and he and his shadows, he and his emptiness, he and his fears, his cowardice, his clumsiness...fit perfectly with my own humanity. I don't want a perfect man, like Marín was in my head, but I want the guy behind all that.

"No more Coco and Marín, Carlos..."

"Never again, Maria..."

When we kiss, just like in the movies, we don't notice the rain, the cold breeze, how uncomfortable our drenched clothes are starting to get—just each other's lips and tongues, but...we're startled out of our reverie by the applause from four tables that have been avidly following our argument, and since this isn't a movie, we're mortified.

"Fuck," he splutters, cracking up, pressing his forehead into my shoulder. "Give me ten bucks so we can pay quickly and get out of here. All I have is a card."

And this, this man capable of fucking up the most romantic scene in the world to ask me for ten bucks, is the love of my life, and there's nothing left to say no to.

47

US

MARIA

On Castelar Street, right where it meets Cardenal Belluga, there's a very odd two-story building. On the corner, it's topped by a kind of round turret that starts at the front door and goes all the way to the top, on the terrace, with a crumbling, old-fashioned railing. And it's beautiful, even though it's not made of any kind of precious material. Blanca says it's inspired by neo-Mozarabic architecture, and I say that we've finally found a house we'll want to live in forever. Finally, after two years of "trying out" apartments that were always missing something. It was expensive but perfect.

The building was originally a single dwelling, now converted into four roomy apartments: two slightly dark first floors and two penthouses with access to a nice terrace. We live in one of those, the one on the left.

We had to apply for a mortgage that made Carlos lose sleep for a while. It wasn't unusual to wake up in the night and find him sitting in the bed, with his headphones on and iPad in his hand, pretending to work while he did calculations. Up until last year, before they transferred him to the international department at his label, his salary wasn't enough to make any miracles happen, but luckily I'm doing pretty well for myself.

So a few months ago we redid the kitchen, trying to preserve as much as we could. We kept the original floor, tiled and beautiful. On it, Carlos's bare feet sound different from Marín's on the hardwood in our first apartment, but I like it even better.

Our bedroom is my favorite room in the house, where I would spend a hundred percent of the time I'm here, but I can't, of course. I fell in love with the ornate fireplace, which is still beautiful even if it doesn't work. We covered part of the floor with a pretty rug, sanded the walls, and painted them white. The bed has an antique wrought-iron headboard that reminds me of the one in *Bedknobs and Broomsticks*. In one corner, we have a dresser that always has at least one book on it and a bottle of perfume and a cactus. On the other side, my dressing table: a wooden table with a couple of drawers topped with a round mirror. On the wall opposite the bed, another big mirror, this time rectangular, which used to belong to my grandparents. We just have it propped against the wall, telling everyone it was easier that way...and we're not lying: It's easier to move it when we feel like playing around to see how we look when we make love.

This room is where everything we really are was born: We talk, we decide, we share, we have sex, and we laugh...but all in whispers because Gema's room and ours are only separated by a bathroom.

Living with a teenager isn't easy, especially with her because she's smart as a whip and she has us wrapped around her little finger. We had to learn quickly to take turns being bad cop so we can throw her off the scent and win a battle every once in a while. In general, there usually aren't problems, especially now that she knows what she wants to study, she feels at home, and her head has settled down a little. But sixteen-year-olds are intense...

The living room has beautiful light that spills onto the bookshelves that take up the whole wall next to the big window. Rugs, leather poufs, the couch, the coffee table, the round dining table we use for lunch on weekends—the room is full of surfaces where we can flop down and spend time together. That's one of the rules of the house: One night a week, we have a movie night while we eat dinner, and Sunday lunch is sacred, whether you stayed up all night or not. It's a custom that all three of us find comfort in. We have a family. Of our own.

This house is our home, Carlos and Maria's, where Coco and Marín are forbidden, even when Loren and Blanca come over for dinner or to hang out. We're Maria and Carlos here.

~

Carlos comes into the kitchen, where I'm drinking tea and reading *The Flowers of Evil* by Baudelaire for the millionth time, wrapped in a gray chunky-knit sweater with a cowl neck and skinny jeans. I love Friday afternoons, when we both finish work early and have the whole weekend ahead of us. The sun isn't shining today—it was cloudy when we woke up—but the house looks so pretty in this gray light.

He has a folder tucked under his arm, his iPad and the backpack from Loewe that I bought him to celebrate his promotion hanging from one shoulder. His thick hair is a disaster because he needs a haircut, but I love when he buries his fingers in it until they disappear. He's also wearing a thick sweater, but his is crew neck and black, combined with his classic matching skinny jeans. The worn brown ankle boots are the cherry on top… *Ay, Mama.*

"So hot."

"Right back atcha." He leans forward and gives me a kiss on the forehead. "Is Gema back yet?"

"No. She sent me a message saying she was going to the library for a bit."

That's a lie. She texted me saying she was going to be at her boyfriend's house, but Carlos doesn't know Gema has a boyfriend. A few weeks ago

I caught them in their underwear in her bed, fooling around. I almost had a heart attack, but it was my fault for barging in without knocking. Since then, we've decided it'll be our little secret, at least until she works up the nerve to tell her brother she's going out with someone. To repay my silence, she promised not to go all the way yet…and to be very responsible if one day she decides she's ready. Carlos is going to want to die when he first finds out, but, well…he has to accept that his little sister is growing up and she's about to be a beguiling woman.

"But she'll be home for dinner, right?" he asks with a furrowed brow.

"Yeah, yeah. Around nine, she said. Do you have to work?"

"No." He pulls a chair out from the table and sits down next to me. "You look a little green?"

"I feel awful, to be honest."

He nods and bites his bottom lip. "Should we do it?" he asks me.

"Now?"

"She's not home. She can't catch us."

"I don't want to."

"Well, I do."

"But I don't want to," I repeat.

"Don't be like that. Come on."

I drum my fingers on the table as we look at each other. He nods, like he's saying the moment has come and stands up; he has to tug me along to get me to follow him.

~

Our bathroom is not even close to modern, but we like it like this. It has character, like the dried flowers that are always on the sink, which is right where our eyes are glued, sitting on the edge of the claw-foot tub I'm obsessed with.

"Now?" he asks.

"No. Wait a little. I'm not ready."

He doesn't say anything. He bites his cheek and looks at the watch my father gave him when we got married. Yes. We're married. I think Blanca and Loren still don't believe it really happened, like we drugged them or it was some kind of joke ceremony. But no. We got married, for real, with a wedding dress, hair clips shaped like dragonflies, a bouquet of lilacs and mini daisies and other wildflowers. It wasn't on the beach, like everyone was expecting, but instead at the house my parents have in a village in Leon. It was insanely cold, and our noses were red in all the photos, but we're so happy it makes us laugh. Me, all flowers and draped chiffon, and him, all black suit and white shirt.

Why did we get married? For the party, let's be honest. And it was worth all the money and stress just for that moment, when everyone had gone home to sleep and dawn was starting to break and the two of us, bundled up and alone, drunk with happiness, took turns on the wooden swing my father hung from the red-leafed beech tree at the back of the garden, which was covered in fairy lights for the wedding.

"Maria…now." He says very seriously, like he does when he's so nervous he's about to vomit.

"What if…?"

"What if nothing. Give it to me. I'll look at it."

He stands up from the edge of the tub, and I do at the same time. There's a scuffle in front of the ancient sink that leaves us giggling.

"Give it to me."

"No, Carlos! You give it to me!"

"You're gonna throw it out the window. I know you."

"How am I gonna throw it out the window? Come on, please, give it to me!"

I have to dig my nails into his hand a little to make him let go so I can grab it. Then I actually do open the window as fast as I can and hurl it out.

He crosses his arms and looks at me, not knowing whether to laugh or scold me.

"Okay, now what?" he mutters.

"We already know what it says."

"I still think we'll need confirmation at some point," he retorts.

"When it turns eighteen."

My comment tips the scale toward laughter.

"Maria..." he begs. "We've been doing this for a week."

"I know! But it's just that...I'm not ready."

He sucks his teeth and nods. "Okay. Come on, go sit down in the living room. I'm going to turn up the heat and I'll bring you a blanket."

"Thank you. You're so good to me. So wonderful. You're the best," I rattle off quickly.

"Yeah, yeah. And you're a pain."

I settle in on the couch, in my favorite corner, and turn on the TV. Maybe we can watch a movie to distract us a little while we wait for Gema, but the first thing that comes up on Netflix is the new releases, and one of them is Aroa's movie...which won her the Silver Shell at the San Sebastian film festival and turned her into the new face of Spanish cinema. Well, she was definitely a good actress.

I hear Carlos coming over, and I start babbling:

"They're advertising that damn movie again. We're gonna have to watch it at some point. But you know she gets her tits out, right? And I don't want you to see your ex's tits again, even on screen."

He sits down next to me, in that graceful way of his. Fuck, where the hell did he get it from? I'm a little enthralled by the way he looks at me, with a half smile.

"My love," he whispers. "Let's make this decision together. It scares me too but..."

"I don't wanna know."

"But we already know." He smiles. "You're throwing up every morning, you've missed two periods, and your bras are starting to get too small. We've been doing it like crazy people for three months, and four months ago you took out your IUD."

"Yeah." I swallow. "But you… Just give me a few days to get in the right mindset."

"Does it scare you?"

"So fucking much. What if I'm a shitty mother? I wasn't expecting it to happen this fast," I moan. "What do you have in there? Anti-aircraft missiles or what?"

He smiles, and his dimples knock me out. "What about me?" He thumbs his chest. "I don't even have an example to follow. What if I'm a shitty father? What if I forget the kid in a cart at the supermarket? What if I don't know how to teach them good values? What if it's born with my nose?"

"If it's born with your nose, that's fine, but for the love of God, don't let it inherit your ears. I don't like the shape of your lobes."

"You're an idiot." He nuzzles my neck and kisses me. "We'll do the best we can, just like this. This house, this family, Gema. We'll do it, Maria. I have no doubt, even though I'm freaked out. This time I'm ready to be the one who pretends not to be scared, okay? So I can comfort you."

I suck my teeth and whimper.

"I went out and found it in the alley," he whispers.

"I figured."

"Do you wanna know?"

"Can I say no?" I smile.

"We're expecting." His hand slips under my sweater. It's warm, and I feel butterflies, the fucking butterflies, fluttering even harder.

"We have more than enough love, my darling," he says, looking at me. "We need to share it."

We snuggle into the sofa, with the TV still on, on standby, emitting a cold, blue light to rival the dim, warm glow of the floor lamps dotted around the living room. No, we don't need a movie on the screen because we already have the next premiere in our heads. Family. The plan. The promise. The music. Bare feet padding around the house. Laughter. Tears. Sleepless nights. Pain. Worry. The happiness of someone sneaking into our bed every morning. Absurd conversations. Diapers. Looks. Excitement. Life. Isn't that the meaning of all this? Life. The one we live, the one we create if we want to, the one we dream of.

At least we can make ourselves feel better by knowing we're trying... We'll always try, every day, whether it works or not, because we can't give the fear any more strength.

We don't say anything for a while. We just hold each other and inhale each other. I guess we're also thinking about how and when we'll tell the family, which includes Blanca and Loren.

But we don't say anything, maybe because the truth hiding behind lies is this: Usually the thing we keep quiet is the one that matters the most. At least...that's all the truth in my lies.

EPILOGUE

I hear Carlos before I see him. I could pick the sound of that stroller rattling out of ten thousand…although the singing that usually comes along with it helps. Today they're singing "All You Need Is Love," if you can believe it. They barely know how to say "mama" yet, but they're already singing in English.

"Look! Mama!"

"My little bacon bits!"

They both turn around happily in their double stroller. The little jerks—aren't multiples supposed to be smaller babies? These two are going to eat us out of house and home.

I kiss Lucas on the cheek and Emma on the forehead. Carlos, on the mouth.

"She's hasn't come out yet?" he asks.

"No. You got here early."

"I didn't have to drug them to finish getting them dressed today."

"Shut up, you animal. Someone's gonna hear you and think we drug our children."

Carlos puts his arm around my shoulder and kisses me on the temple, telling me I have to relax and not take life so seriously.

"Hey!" Blanca rushes out, as always, trotting along, her jacket half on, her bag dangling and looking stressed. "Sorry, sorry, sorry. It went a little over."

"No worries. We just got here. Actually"—Carlos checks his watch—"you're early, I think."

We came to pick up Blanca at the women's association she volunteers at on Friday afternoons, providing pro bono legal advice. And we came all this way because it's next to a tapas bar with a Michelin star we all love. Loren and Damian should already be there, but we're coming from different directions: I from the gallery, Carlos from the subway.

Blanca is kneeling, giving the kids kisses and speaking to them one at a time. Way too fast as always; she's gonna blow a fuse one of these days.

"I had to rush today. The women have a literary talk now. Someone's coming to read them an excerpt from something that… Look, girl, I wasn't actually listening. The point is they had to get the room ready and…"

I don't know how she notices him. We didn't make a single peep, although both Carlos and I saw him coming. He saw us too. He looks different. His beard is trimmed, his hair's combed, and he's dressed differently, more formal. Blanca had her back to him, talking, distracted… How did she notice, for fuck's sake? There's something, let's be honest, there's something ineffable about love, something invisible, like a fishing wire that tugs on the intangible part of our breath and cuts it off when it's close. That must be it.

She doesn't say anything, just trails off with the sentence half-finished and stands up. She turns around gingerly. He's almost next to her, and we… We don't exist anymore.

"This is impossible," he whispers with a timid smile. "Impossible."

Blanca doesn't answer. She swallows. She smiles shyly, and I know what she must be saying to herself. Gus and she have been avoiding each other with no problem for three years. Three. Why now?

"What's up?"

"Not much. What's up with you?"

"Oh, God..." Carlos looks down at his boots awkwardly. It's the stupidest, most tense conversation in the world. I wish we could just run off, pushing the stroller in the opposite direction.

"You're not helping," I scold him.

"What's up, Gus?" he says, sticking his hand out to Gus. "Congrats on the prize."

"Thanks, Marín. You too, on the kids." He bends down a little, toward the stroller. "They're amazing. What are they now, twenty months? What are their names?"

"Eighteen months yesterday," I say, surprised—he has a good eye. "They're called Bacon and Bacon Bit."

"Don't fuck around, Coco."

"Maria..." Carlos elbows me. "They're called Emma and Lucas."

"Jeez Louise, Marín...they have your ears," he says with a smile.

"See? Divine punishment," I murmur, but Carlos ignores me.

"You... Do you have kids?"

Blanca is about to faint, I think.

"Me. No, no. Not yet. Well, I mean..." He side-eyes Blanqui. "I don't even have a girlfriend, so... But I love them. So...what are you all doing here?"

"Blanca"—I point at her, and she raises her hand, as if to say "present"—"volunteers with an association, and we came here to pick her up and grab a bite to eat."

"Here? What a coincidence! I'm here to read a few poems."

It's been almost four years since we last talked to Gus, and every day has built a wall, but I don't know how long it will stay standing because I'm realizing a lot of things never change, and I know. I still recognize Gus's lying voice perfectly. And it's a lie. This is no coincidence. He engineered this meeting.

"Listen, folks, I have to get in there. But I'd love…I dunno, to catch up sometime."

All three of us look at each other. Blanca takes a deep breath and recovers her ability to speak.

"We're meeting up with Loren at La Orilla. It's right next door, and we'll probably still be there when you finish. Why don't you drop by?"

"Oh, well…yeah? Is that okay with all of you?" He looks around at all of us, even though I know the only opinion he cares about is Blanca's. "Well, great. See you after."

"Great. See you soon."

"Wait 'til you see how happy this makes Loren," I joke through gritted teeth.

We wave goodbye dopily and keep walking down the sidewalk. The kids are still singing "All You Need Is Love" when we finally hear the reaction slip out of Blanca's lips.

"Shit."

Shit. Nothing else is needed. Love, darling, is much more complicated than it seems, and sometimes, time only proves it right.

READ ON FOR MORE ROMANCE FROM ELÍSABET BENAVENT IN *A PERFECT STORY*.

1

ONCE UPON A TIME...

MARGOT

So your boyfriend dumped you. You might even hate your job. You probably spend your days yearning for things you'll never be able to afford. Have those extra summer pounds teamed up with the ones from Christmas? Don't worry. And don't worry if you don't fill out your bra. Or if the chairs at restaurants squeeze your thighs. If your mother never approves of anything you do...and anything you don't do, of course. If you gave your heart to that idiot. If you feel like you're married to your mortgage. If your boss is a fucking psychopath. If you suspect you've been cheated on, that you're going to get fired, that you've put your foot in it.

It doesn't matter! Seriously. I promise you, it doesn't matter. And one more thing. If you get frustrated or even bitter watching TV or looking at magazines or social media and seeing how wonderful and easy other people's lives are, I'll tell you a secret: They're not. The thing is, everything is always more complicated when you see it up close. For example, I had everything, and I lost it all just by putting on sneakers and going for a run... I didn't have everything, and I didn't lose it. Pay attention. I'm telling you this from the bottom of my heart. Nothing is that serious, and your life isn't going to end. Just...new possibilities will open up.

Look, let me tell you a perfect story, okay? One that will seem perfect too, in the beginning. Once upon a time, there was a modern princess. She didn't have a castle or sit sighing on a balcony where she could look out over her entire kingdom. She didn't comb her ridiculously long locks with a brush made from enamel, gold, and horsehair. She wasn't waiting for Prince Charming to save her from the wicked witch.

Although…I'm pretty sure my mother counts as a witch.

What I mean is, somehow, those princess stories still clutter up the corners of our minds. Sometimes they're microscopic, and other times they loom large. There are no more princes on horseback or little birds helping us get dressed for a date that will lead to love and happiness. (I mean, really…sometimes it's hard to believe they made us think some nerd was capable of sweeping us off our feet.) But we still believe in stories. In fairy tales. And they've convinced us we want to be princesses.

Take a look at Instagram. You don't have it? Well, don't download it just to see if this is true. But…I'm sure you'll know what I'm talking about. Perfect lives. Lives of luxury. Photos where you can almost touch that hazy fantasy of a dream existence. Shiny, glittering, every hair in place. Yes, most of the time, social media is trying to sell us unrealistic perfection that pushes us to find something that doesn't actually exist. Now little girls want to be version 3.0 of the princess in the story, with a designer bag, clutching a mysteriously pink coffee on the edge of an infinity pool in Tahiti. It doesn't sound bad, it's true. I want it too…but the difference is knowing that there's no perfect life behind that photo. Just…a life.

I say that from personal experience. No, I'm not an influencer or a YouTuber or a model, but, in a way, I've been observed, examined, judged. How? Well, I lived (was trapped, more like) in a fairy tale, the old-fashioned kind that isn't always as shiny as it looks. I was born into an upper-class family. I was born with a string of aristocratic names and a hotel empire attached to them. When I was born, members of the royal family even went to my baptism. I was born condemned to be a princess in a story I didn't believe, but nobody ever thought to ask what I, Margot, believed in.

I know I had a million privileges at my fingertips that other people don't have, but...just let me tell this story my way.

Once upon a time, there was a woman who had everything and a boy who had nothing.

Once upon a time, there was a love story trapped somewhere between success and hesitation.

Once upon a time, there was a perfect story.

And only you can decide how it ends.

2

SUCCESS. APPROPRIATE AND ANODYNE.

"Where are you vacationing?"

That was Mama's favorite question. She asked it at Christmas, when the family was all gathered around a table creaking under the weight of glasses, cutlery, and silver crap as useless as it is old. She asked it during Holy Week too, when we're obligated to go to her house to eat *torrijas* made by a rotating cast of cooks, each one inevitably fired.

On the anniversary of Papa's death, when we traveled to our grandparents' country house to lay down flowers and hear mass, she would ask us too.

"Where are you going on vacation, girls?"

And the reason she always asked exactly the same thing was mostly because she's an old-fashioned snob who worried too much about what would happen if high society didn't see her daughters skiing in Switzerland, lazing on a boat in the Mediterranean, or sunbathing in French Polynesia. That and being skinny enough to see your hip bones through your clothes were the only things that mattered to her. Oh, and "marrying well," of course. Marrying successfully.

No shit, Sherlock.

The first time I heard her talk about success, I was too little to understand or question the characteristics she valued. The idea calcified in my mind, like the word *caterpillar*, which I always pronounced "capertillar" until one day I finally understood what it meant, but not quite like that. Success for my family was the baby in a baptism, the bride in a wedding, and the corpse in a grave. The only respectable aspiration, the very purpose of human existence. A pain in the ass. And this concept felt like a school bully: Either you were with him or you were a victim of his whims. And that's where that same tired question came from too.

"Where are you going on vacation, Patricia?"

My sisters and I shot each other looks and smiled stealthily, our eyes glued to our bowls of vichyssoise light, which was more like dirty leek water that smelled like a pond. It was the first sentence my mother had uttered to us since we started the dinner to celebrate my sister Candela coming back to Spain for my wedding.

Yes. My wedding. Welcome to this story that starts where others end happily ever after.

"I'm not asking you. I already know you're going on your dream honeymoon." My mother lifted her gaze to mine, seized her glass, and smiled at me.

"Your dream," I heard Candela whisper, forcing an imitation of my mother's old-fashioned, aristocratic accent.

"Alberto wants us to spend the first two weeks of August traveling, but with the children..." Patricia, the oldest, shot a warning glance at Candela, trying to stifle a smile.

"I want to go to Greece," my brother-in-law explained as he glanced at my terrorist nephews, who had already eaten and were playing suspiciously quietly in the drawing room next to the dining room.

"Traveling with them is exhausting," my sister insisted. "I think we'll rent a house in Formentera for the month."

"Formentera?" Mama looked worriedly at Lord Mushroom, as we called her second husband, and then at Patricia and Alberto. "Isn't that full of—"

"People?" I tried to cut her off before she said something offensive.

"Well, people, yes, but I'm referring to...people...you know..."

She waved her hand vaguely. This often happened to her, not being able to find the words. She would often...leave things unsaid. Mama is... Well, she's lazy in a way someone can only be when they've never understood that "work gives dignity." She's the closest anyone in this century has been to those ladies Kate Winslet hung out with in *Titanic*. Ladies whose only job was regular cosmetic surgeries resulting in majestic, stretched cat faces. As always, she'd just gotten some little "nip," so she was pumped full of her customary pills, ones that take away her pain and, if she swallowed them with alcohol (which she usually did), even eliminated that pesky sensation of human existence.

"Why not Saint-Tropez?" she asked after a sip of wine.

"Because..." Patricia looked to us for support. "Isn't Saint-Tropez pretty passé?"

"Ah, you're right." She nodded. "But Menorca sounds better than Formentera, don't you think, darling?"

Her husband, Lord Mushroom, nodded. He had a noble title, but the truth was, he was like a fungus, very regal but with zero pulse. Sometimes we weren't sure that he had even a hint of life in him, but other people insisted he could form complete sentences. We also suspected he'd been getting lip fillers lately. Every once in a while he had the weirdest pout.

"And you, Candela? Where are you vacationing? You'll have to find somewhere warm to make up for your life in Iceland—"

"I live in Stockholm, Mother, which is the capital of Sweden, and...I had to take off quite a few days to come here." She made a face. "So I'm going on vacation in your guest room."

"Working all day." My mother sniffed disdainfully. "People will think you don't have a penny to your name."

"Well, if I took a few selfies in the room you put me in, I could convince some of my friends I've been to Versailles. Rococo is also pretty passé, Mother. So eighteenth century."

Patricia and I dabbed our mouths with our napkins so they wouldn't see our smiles. The staff cleared our plates and were serving the second course in less than a minute. A steaming filet mignon was placed in front of each dinner guest. In front of me, a cup of kale.

I looked at my sisters. I looked at my brother-in-law. I looked at my mother.

"Oh, darling." She smiled at me. "Sautéed kale. Really good. Really healthy. Very low calorie."

"But..." Candela started to say.

"Just wait until you see how great you look in your dress."

I took a deep breath, plastered on a fake smile, and cut off my sister.

"Thank you, Mother. Cande, don't worry about it."

"With all the beautiful names you all have, I don't know why you insist on calling each other these ridiculous nicknames. Like you. *Margot.* Margot? What kind of name is that? Margarita. Ana Margarita Ortega Ortiz de Zarate."

Present.

ABOUT THE AUTHOR

Elísabet Benavent is a graduate in audiovisual communication from the Universidad Cardenal Herrera CEU in Valencia, and she has a master's degree in communication and art from the Universidad Complutense de Madrid. She worked in the communication department of a multinational company until she became a full-time writer. She is an international best-selling author of twenty novels, and she lives in Valencia, Spain.

Website: betacoqueta.com
Instagram: @betacoqueta